MAJOR KARNAGE

GORD ZAJAC

ChiZine Publications

FIRST EDITION

Major Karnage © 2010 by Gord Zajac
Cover artwork © 2010 Erik Mohr
Cover design © 2010 Corey Lewis
All Rights Reserved.

LIBRARY AND ARCHIVES CANADA CATALOGUING IN PUBLICATION

Library and Archives Canada Cataloguing in Publication

Zajac, Gord, 1973-
          Major Karnage / Gord Zajac.

ISBN 978-0-9813746-6-6

          I. Title.

PS8649.A39M35 2010   C813'.6   C2010-902883-X

CHIZINE PUBLICATIONS
Toronto, Canada
www.chizinepub.com
info@chizinepub.com

Edited by Helen Marshall
Copyedited and proofread by Brett Alexander Savory

MK numbers 1-4 originally published by Kelp Queen Press

MAJOR KARNAGE

For Alicia

MK#1: MAJOR KARNAGE

CHAPTER ONE

Karnage woke strapped to his bed. It was a welcome change from the straitjacket and the Hole, but the catheter still stung like a bitch and he had to scratch his nose something fierce. The sickly pink glow from the overhead fluorescents was giving him a headache. He shut his eyes. The smell of rotting piss and shit from dirty bed pans filled his nostrils.

So, Karnage thought, *this is retirement.*

He could hear Heckler's hysterical laughter coming from elsewhere in the ward. One of the nurses—probably Fridge—barked at Heckler to shut the fuck up. There came a shout of "fuck you" from Velasquez, followed by a much more colourful stream of invectives in Spanish—the kind only Velasquez could conjure with that magic vocab of hers. Fridge—it was definitely Fridge—shouted at Velasquez. Velasquez shouted back. Karnage did his best to shut it all out. He knew where it was all going to end: sooner or later, out would come the stun gun, and after a long series of screams, Heckler and Velasquez would be electrocuted into silence.

Karnage felt movement near the foot of his bed. He ignored it. Whatever Fridge wanted, it could fucking well wait until he was good and ready. Even if it meant getting electrocuted.

"Major?" a voice whispered. It was Cookie. What was he doing out of bed? Karnage squinted one eye open. Cookie stood over Karnage's bed, leaning on his IV drip, his head wrapped in bandages.

"Major," Cookie whispered, "are you awake?"

Karnage half-opened his eyes. "Sit down next to me. Try not to be noticed. I don't feel like dealing with these assholes yet."

Cookie gave a half-nod and sat on the bed near Karnage's head, turning his body away from Fridge.

"What's on your mind, Corporal?"

"I finally got it figured out, sir." Cookie looked around, making sure Fridge was well out of hearing range. He leaned in closer and in a low voice said, "I'm not crazy."

"That a fact?"

"Yes, sir."

"What about them voices you been hearing in your head?" Karnage said.

"That's what I figured out. They ain't voices. They're communications." Cookie tapped his bandages. "Figure it's got something to do with these electronics in my head."

"I thought the doc said those things'd clear up them voices?"

"Nah," Cookie grinned. "They just clarified 'em. Cut out all the background noise."

"That a fact?"

"Yes, sir, it is."

"Hmm," Karnage said. "What sort of communications you been getting, Corporal?"

Cookie leaned in close to Karnage's ear and whispered. "They're from outer space."

"Outer space, eh?"

Cookie's face fell. "You don't believe me."

Karnage looked Cookie straight in the eye. "Cookie, you ain't never lied to me yet. No matter how crazy they say you are, and no matter how much they muck with your brain, I reckon you ain't never gonna be able to tell a lie with a straight face. But I'd be lyin' if I said I weren't sceptical. Keep going. Communications from outer space. You been interceptin' communiques from enemy spy satellites?"

"No, sir. See, this is where it gets interestin'. These communications? I think they're comin' from . . . aliens."

"Aliens, eh?"

"I mean the extraterrestrial kind, sir."

"I had a feelin' that's what you meant," Karnage said. "What makes you think these communications are extraterrestrial in nature?"

"Well, sir, I done cracked every code known to man—from *Navajojibwe* to *SuperSanskrit*—and this ain't like nothing I ever seen before."

"Now that's sayin' something," Karnage nodded. "Wait a minute. What do you mean 'seen'? You been writing this stuff down, Corporal?"

Cookie took one last look around before rolling up his sleeve. Lines of jagged squiggles ran up and down his arm. "I been transcribin' these here messages, Major."

"They look like squiggles," Karnage said.

Cookie nodded. "That's exactly what they sound like, sir."

"They sound like squiggles?"

"Yes, sir!"

"I don't know, Cookie. They all look the same to me."

Cookie grinned. "That's what I thought, too, at first. Just random squiggly noises. But there's a pattern to 'em. Took me forever to start noticing 'em, but that's what I been trained to do. There's all sortsa variations. You gotta listen carefully to pick 'em up."

Karnage took another look at the markings on Cookie's arm. They were red around the edges, like Cookie had been pressing too hard when he was writing it down. *Probably scribbling like a madman to get it all down*, Karnage thought. He still couldn't see any differences. Karnage looked at Cookie's earnest face.

"Cookie," he said. "If anybody's got the ears to pick up on that sort of stuff, it's you. Go on, Corporal."

Cookie beamed. He wriggled closer to Karnage's head and pointed at the first squiggle on his wrist. "You see this here? This is how all the messages begin. It's like a greetin' or something. And this one right next to it? That always comes next. I think it's a kinda confirmation code. Lets the sender know the transmission's bein' received."

"They look the same to me," Karnage said.

Cookie's head bobbed up and down like a parakeet. "That's what I thought, too. At first. But the second is tilted just three degrees to the left. See?

Karnage looked again. "Yeah, now that you mention it—wait a minute. This is all in your own handwritin'. How do you know it ain't just yer scrawl that's gone and tilted three degrees?"

Cookie stiffened. His voice was clipped. "Sir, I transcribed it exactly as I heard it, sir."

"You mean to say you can hear a three degree tilt?"

Cookie nodded. "Yes, sir."

Karnage looked Cookie up and down. "Cookie, you are impressin' me all over again."

Cookied relaxed. A smile pulled at the corners of his mouth. He warmed to the subject. "I can't make much sense outta the rest of it yet. Just seems like a lot o' gobbledy-gook. But there's certain patterns that keep popping up. I think it's a numbering system."

"Numbers, eh? Numbers for what?"

"Well, if I had to guess, I'd say they're co-ordinates."

Karnage's pulse quickened. "What kind of co-ordinates?"

Cookie shrugged. "I don't right know, Major."

Karnage strained against his bonds. He desperately wanted to grab Cookie by the shoulders. "Could it be military targets? Some kind of tactical strike?"

Cookie hesitated. "I-I don't really want to guess here, Major—"

"Guess, Corporal! Guess!"

"Now you gotta realize I'm just conjecturin' here. . . ."

"Cookie!"

Cookie leaned in within inches of Karnage's ear. "Well, if I had to guess . . . I'm thinking these are plans for some kind of . . ." Cookie's voice became the barest of whispers. ". . . invasion."

Invasion!

The word set off fireworks in Karnage's brain. His ears burned. His blood pumped hot and fast through his body.

He always knew this would happen. There would always be another battle. Always had been. Always would be. It had just been a matter of time. And now, after all these years, that time had finally come.

GORD ZAJAC

Karnage strained against his bonds. His voiced boomed with his best drill sergeant bark. "Corporal! We've got to act fast! Call the general! Mobilize the infantry! Get me my rifle! Get me outta this bed! Uncle Stanley won't get the drop on us this time. There's a battle needs fightin' and we're the grunts to do it. Don't just stand there, Corporal! Do something! Velasquez! Heckler! Koch! On your feet, soldiers!"

"Major, please," Cookie frantically jerked his sleeve back down over his forearm. "Fridge'll hear you!"

"What the hell's going on over there?" Fridge unholstered his stun gun. Blue sparks danced across the metal tines. "You boys need a little lesson in discipline?"

"No, Fridge," squeaked Cookie.

"We don't have time for this!" Karnage wriggled and struggled so hard the bed's casters bounced on the floor. He jerked his head at Fridge. "Cookie! Crack him across the neck like you did those Uncle Stanley *skerks* back in Kabul! You can take him!" Karnage turned to the other patients. "Come on, troops! Mobilize! He can't take us all. On your feet, soldiers!"

"Nobody do nothing stupid," Fridge pointed at Velasquez and Koch who were in the middle of rising up off their beds. They halted. They looked from Fridge to Karnage and back again.

The doors to the ward burst open. Doctor Flaherty walked into the room. His balding bespectacled face wore a wide grin. A pair of nurses flanked him on either side. They were the spitting image of Fridge though they went by the names Mammoth and Skyscraper. Straggling behind them was a less portly and slightly hairier doctor they'd never seen before. His ID tag read "Johnson." He looked furtively from side to side as he scribbled notes on a clipboard. Flaherty was in mid-sentence, gesturing grandly into the room.

"And in here we have—Stevens, what's going on here?"

Fridge slapped the stun gun back down to his side. "The ol' major is having a freakout. Nothing I can't handle, Doctor."

Flaherty eyed the stun gun. "Indeed. Let's see if I can't get through to him first, hmm?"

MAJOR KARNAGE

"Doctor!" Karnage barked. "Get me outta this bed. This is an emergency!"

Flaherty turned to Johnson. "You're in for a real treat here. The major isn't usually this talkative. Normally all we can get out of him is his name, rank, and serial number."

Karnage struggled against his bonds. "Doctor! We have a situation here! Time is of the essence!"

"Major," Flaherty's tone was soft and cordial. "I'd like to introduce you to Dr. Johnson. He'll be replacing Dr. Kubota, who opted to resign after that little incident last week. Dr. Johnson, may I introduce you to Major John Karneski."

"Karneski?" Johnson's jaw dropped. "Do you mean . . . is this Major Karnage?"

"We prefer to refer to our patients by their given names here. Isn't that right, John?"

"That's Major to you, asshole," Velasquez shouted from her bed.

Johnson reached a hand out towards Karnage. "It's an honour to meet you, sir."

Flaherty grabbed Johnson's arm. "I'd advise against that, Johnson. It's always a good idea to give the major a wide berth."

"But he's strapped to the bed," Johnson said.

"Still, one can never be too careful around the major. Isn't that right, John?"

"Doctor, you are wearin' my patience down to a bloody stump! I don't have time for this rigamarole. You gotta let me outta this bed on the double before the enemy gets the drop on us!"

"What enemy, John?" Flaherty asked.

Karnage sneered. "That's the big question mark, isn't it? Who is the enemy? Who can you trust? I thought I knew who the enemy was. But then some civilian assmonkey is stickin' medals on my chest with one hand while shovin' my sorry ass into this hellhole with the other!"

"John, I can understand your frustration, but you're going to have to learn to let go."

"Doctor, you are interferin' with a military operation! That is in direct violation of military ordinance number—"

"John," Flaherty's tone grew firm. "There are no more military ordinances. There is no military. Your continued persistence in believing in this delusion—"

"Delusion, my ass! You can take your world peace and your Nagasaki treaties and shove 'em down your piehole! You know what your problem is? You got the wrong guys locked up, that's what. There are enemies out there just waitin' to pounce on you when your guard is down. Like a lion stalkin' a herd o' gazelle. You get me? And when guys like me get locked up while guys like you run the asylum, you gotta wonder just what the hell went wrong with the world. But the enemy doesn't care about the why. They're just waitin' out there with their seventeen inch bayonets . . . waiting for the right time to shove those blades right up your ass! That time is lookin' to be now, Doc. So you best unfuck yourself and lemme outta this bed!"

Flaherty turned to the other patients. "Who did this? Who riled him up like this?"

Fridge jerked a thumb at Cookie. "The old major was fine until Chucky there started hovering over his bed."

Cookie squeaked.

"Charles?" Flaherty turned to Cookie. "Was it you?"

Cookie stared at the ground. He nodded.

"What did you tell him, Charles?" Flaherty said.

"You don't have to tell him shit, Corporal," Karnage said.

Cookie looked at Karnage, then Flaherty. He quickly darted his head back down again. He gripped his forearm tightly.

"What do you have there, Charles?" Flaherty asked patiently.

"Nothin'," Karnage said. "He's got nothin'!"

"Let me see your forearm," Flaherty said.

Cookie made another squeak and slowly pulled up his shirt sleeve, revealing the squiggles. Flaherty looked at the mass of writing, then at Cookie. "Are you hearing voices again, Charles?"

"They're not voices!" Karnage shouted. "They're alien communications!"

"Aliens?" Flaherty's eyebrows rose so high they nearly met his receding hairline.

"That's right! Aliens! Extra-*tee*-restrials! Unidentified Flying Objects of Death! You get me?!"

"I'm afraid I do." Flaherty sighed. He turned to Cookie. "I'm very disappointed in you, Charles. You should have come to me. I'm here to help."

Cookie fingered his bandages and whimpered.

Flaherty turned to Fridge. "Take Charles to the showers and clean him up."

"No!" Cookie yelped. "I haven't cracked the code yet! You can't take 'em off until I've cracked the code!"

"Charles." Flaherty's voice was stern. He looked at Cookie over the rims of his glasses.

Cookie instantly deflated. Fridge grabbed Cookie under his arm and dragged him away. Karnage squirmed and wriggled as he shouted.

"No! Don't let 'em do it! You're a trained soldier! You can take 'em! Bite off his ear! Knee him in the crotch! Tear out his guts! Snap him—"

Karnage winced as jolts of electricity shot down his spine. An alarm softly pinged. An angelic female voice emanated from the base of Karnage's skull. "Warning. Sanity Level upgraded to Lemon Breeze. Please refrain from violent behaviour. Thank you."

"What was that?" Johnson said.

Flaherty's eyes lit up. *Just like Cookie's*, Karnage thought.

"Oh, it's an ingenious little device! Major, would you mind if I showed him?"

"Go to hell."

Flaherty shook his head. "You really need to learn to be more co-operative." Flaherty flipped a switch beside Karnage's bed. The bed flipped onto its side. Flaherty pulled a long-handled pointer with a U-shaped end covered in rubber from his labcoat. He slipped the U around the back of Karnage's neck and pushed his head forward. There was a tiny LED display at the base of Karnage's skull. The screen pulsed a soft pale yellow.

Flaherty turned to Johnson. "I call it the Sanity Patch. This is just the prototype. I designed it myself. Think of it as a sort of sanity fail-safe, if you like. It's tied directly into the central nervous system. It scans the major's brainwaves for indications of violent tendencies. There's a tiered system with a number of different warning thresholds. Currently the major is rated at Lemon Breeze. That's pretty good for John, actually. The thresholds move all the way up the colour spectrum to indicate his state of mind. The scale runs from Snow White to Tricycle Red. Fortunately, John has never hit Tricycle Red. The furthest he has ever hit was Frosty Pink. And that was plenty close enough for our liking. Wasn't it, John?"

"Eat donkey dick," Karnage growled.

"What happens if he hits Tricycle Red?" Johnson asked.

"Tricycle Red activates the fail-safe. The subject is terminated before he can cause further harm to himself or others."

"Terminated?"

"He means if I hit Tricycle Red, my fuckin' head blows off," Karnage said.

"Is that true?" Johnson asked.

"I wouldn't put it quite like that, but yes. The subject's spinal cord is severed from his brain. It's not as barbaric as it sounds, really. It's a worst case scenario, something we work diligently to prevent. Don't we, John?"

"You're nuts," Karnage said.

"I'll be the judge of that." Flaherty winked at Johnson.

"I ain't the guy implantin' explosives into people's brains!"

"I wish you'd stop looking at it that way, John. I'm trying to reintegrate you back into society. You have some extremely violent tendencies that simply must be addressed before anything of the sort can happen." Flaherty turned to Johnson. "Come along, Johnson. Let me show you the O.R."

Flaherty headed to the door, expecting Johnson to follow. Johnson didn't. He took a few steps towards Karnage and put a hand on his shoulder. "I just want to say how much I appreciate the sacrifices you made for us in The War."

The War!

Karnage's eyes bulged. His heart hammered in his chest.

The War!

The entire room dissolved. Karnage's vision filled with flames, crumbling buildings, and death.

The War!

Rage pulsed through his limbs. The straps binding him to the bed bulged. There was the faint sound of tearing.

"Johnson! Get away!"

Karnage's bed straps exploded in all directions. His right hand whipped up and grabbed Johnson by the throat. The Sanity Patch sent electric jolts shooting up his spine. He didn't flinch. The Patch's cheery voice informed everyone that Karnage's sanity level was now at "Peachy Keen."

Karnage slowly sat up, lifting Johnson into the air. His voice hissed through his teeth as the remaining straps gave way one by one with a loud snap.

"Don't . . ."

Snap!

". . . talk to me . . ."

Snap-snap!

". . . about *The War!*"

With a final snap, Karnage erupted from the bed. He lifted Johnson high into the air. Johnson grabbed futilely at Karnage's wrist. Johnson's face was beet red. The Sanity Patch crooned "Tangy Orange" as Skyscraper and Mammoth charged towards Karnage. Karnage turned to meet them, smiling crazily.

Battle! This was what he knew. He kicked the bed with his foot towards the charging nurses. Skyscraper dodged out of the way as the bed slammed into Mammoth, knocking him down. Skyscraper whipped out his stun gun and stabbed it at Karnage. Karnage deftly sidestepped Skyscraper, tripped him and pulled the stun gun from his fingers. He slammed his knee into Skyscraper's back, and slammed the stun gun into the base of his skull. Karnage gave him full blast until Skyscraper's screaming and flailing subsided into silent fish flops.

The major rose up just in time to catch Mammoth full in the gut with the stun gun. He juiced him hard, all the while keeping a firm grip on Johnson's throat, whipping him around like a rag doll. Once Mammoth stopped moving, Karnage threw Johnson up into the wall, pinning him by his neck. In the back of his mind somewhere, he was conscious of alarms blaring and Flaherty screaming for security. A voice at the back of his neck whispered that he had just hit "Sharp Cheddar." Karnage didn't care. They could ring their alarms and call their security and blow his head off. None of that mattered. Karnage's entire world had shrunk down to just him and Johnson.

"You want to talk to me about The War? I'll tell you about The War. New Baghdad. 1-1-5-2-5. Urban warfare on a grand scale. You ever been at ground zero while a whole city block is crumbling around you? I have. I lost thirty men that day. Benneli. Kahr. Mossberg. Weatherby. I'll never forget their names. The only reason any of us survived was we were holed up against a column in that underground parking lot when it came down on top of us. I had thirty thousand tons of steel and concrete pressing down on my chest. You know what that's like? You know how that feels? It feels a lot like having your throat crushed." The pressure increased on Johnson's throat. "Like that. Real slowly. Millimetre by millimetre. The life slowly sucked outta your body. Every few minutes, you hear a fresh snap—like that one. Your veins bulge out—just like that. You want to breathe so bad, but you can't. You know why? Cuz Uncle Stanley's gone and dropped seventy-five megatons of radioactive shit on your head. And all you got is one pinky you can use to dig you and your buddies out. You want to talk to me about The War? I'LL TELL YOU ABOUT THE WAR!"

A pair of taser barbs lodged into Karnage's neck, and 40,000 volts of electricity coursed through his body. He spasmed and gritted his teeth. His fist refused to let go of Johnson's neck. Johnson's body quivered and flailed from the charge. A second set of barbs lodged into Karnage's thigh. Another 40,000 volts joined the chorus of the first. Karnage let out a yell as he fell to one knee. His grip on Johnson's throat loosened, and the other man fell to the ground, gasping. Something wet and broken rattled in the back of his throat.

Karnage looked up. Four nurses stood over him, each armed with a taser. His mouth was full of the taste of blood. He grinned. "Is that the best you got?"

Two more sets of barbs shot out and caught Karnage in the chest and bicep. Karnage laughed like the madman he was as 160,000 volts of electricity plunged his body into the peaceful depths of unconsciousness.

CHAPTER TWO

Karnage lay in a pit of darkness. A single shaft of pale light shone on his head. He felt the familiar pull of the straitjacket on his arms and crotch. He was back in the Hole. *Home sweet home.*

The Hole had been specially constructed just for Karnage. The walls were soft and yielding, yet slick and smooth enough to prevent any kind of solid grip. The room was just wide enough to prevent him from bracing himself against opposing walls and climbing up. The height of the walls was somewhere around two or three stories. They'd done their best to make it escape-proof.

But Karnage knew better. Nothing was escape-proof. It was all a matter of time. He'd escaped from worse places than this during—

The War!

Sand and heat and bullets and flames. Crumbling bombed out buildings givin' Uncle Stanley the perfect cover. Snipers snipin' your platoon, one wide-eyed recruit at a time. Blood flowin' like cheap whiskey at Happy Hour. Privates screamin' for mothers and fathers, wives and sisters and lovers and brothers. None of 'em listenin'. None of 'em there. Nobody but your dying buddies and the bloodthirsty enemy hidin' around every corner. Death from above, below, and everywhere in between. Tanks versus pistols. Choppers versus bayonets. Machine guns versus fists. Everybody's dying around you, but you keep your head down and you do the job. Kill or be killed. Kill or be killed. Faster, soldier! Kill-kill-kill!

Karnage slammed his head against his knee. The soft tones of his Sanity Patch pinged their gentle warning in his ear.

He couldn't think about . . . *it*. No point in thinking about . . . *that*. Nothing but pain and hurt lay that way. His troopers were counting on him. He had to be strong. Uncle Stanley wouldn't get anything out of—

No. Uncle Stanley was done. Ancient history. It was over. They had won . . . hadn't they? They'd been given medals. He remembered that. Somewhere in some lockbox in the asylum lay seventeen medals, seven citations for bravery, and a set of major's stripes.

Karnage lay his head against the wall. He thought about his squad up in Ward Three. Velasquez. Heckler. Cookie. Koch. The finest troopers he'd ever served with. Who cared if they were sane? *No one alive could outsoldier 'em.* Karnage smiled. *No dead ones, either.*

Karnage heard a door open in the distance. Echoing footsteps moved towards him. He looked up. A man's silhouette appeared in the shaft of light above. It was Flaherty.

"Ah, I see you're finally awake," Flaherty said. "How are you feeling? Would you like any painkillers?"

"I'm gonna kill you when I get outta here." A sharp jolt shot down Karnage's spine.

"Warning. Sanity Level upgraded to Citrus Blast. Please refrain from violent behaviour. Thank you."

Flaherty tsked. "Temper, John. We wouldn't want you to lose your head."

"Where's Cookie?" Karnage said.

"Cookie's showing signs of relapse. I was hoping those implants would improve his condition. I've scheduled him for exploratory surgery in the morning."

"Quit carving up his brain, you eggheaded bastard!" Karnage threw his body into the wall. He bounced off harmlessly. Another jolt of electricity ran through his spine. Karnage shrugged it off. He glared menacingly at Flaherty as the Sanity Patch crooned "Tangy Orange."

"It seems these mild warnings aren't working. You're obviously not taking your Sanity Levels seriously enough. I think I'm going to have to turn up the voltage," Flaherty said.

"Sure," Karnage said. "If you can't get me to blow my own head off, you'll just fry my brain right inside my own skull."

"That's not true."

"Sure it is! Jackin' up my Sanity Patch. Carvin' up Cookie's brain. Don't think I don't see what's goin' on here. Me and Cookie stumbled onto your little invasion plan, and now you want us out of the way."

Flaherty blinked. "My invasion plan?"

"I don't know how you factor into all this yet, but I'll figure it out. I ain't gonna stop until I get to the bottom of the whole thing."

Flaherty shook his head. "I've clearly underestimated the depth of your psychosis. You are, quite possibly, far more insane than I had originally imagined. I'm starting to think the Sanity Patch is nowhere near enough. If you continue to believe in this delusion, I may have to resort to more drastic treatments."

"Sure. You'd like that, wouldn't you? Carve my brain right outta my skull and stick it in a mason jar! Turn me into a walkin' vegetable. Don't think for one second you and your alien pals can intimidate me. I seen more shit in one day than you could see in a hundred lifetimes!"

Flaherty removed his glasses and rubbed the bridge of his nose. "John, I sincerely hope this turns out to be a temporary delusion. Otherwise . . . well, I won't speculate. Nevertheless, I will state this: there is no conspiracy. There is no alien invasion. No one is out to get you or your comrades. We really are doing everything we can to help you. Please believe that."

"That's just what I'd expect you to say."

"Good night, John." Flaherty stepped away from the light. Karnage heard his footsteps echo back towards the door.

"You can't hide the truth, Flaherty! *You can't hide the truth!*"

The only reply was the slammed door echoing in the darkness.

CHAPTER THREE

Flaherty descended the steps of the Veteran's Home. He fished his car keys out of his pocket and let out a long breath. What a trying day. Sometimes he wondered why he even bothered. He knew his methods were a bit . . . well, unorthodox, but that's why he'd accepted this position. If he could cure these soldiers, he might finally win some acclaim from his colleagues.

The sun was just disappearing over the horizon. It cast violent purple and orange hues across the night sky. The mountains were a dark silhouette in the distance. Flaherty stopped a few feet from his car and soaked in the view. The desert could be harsh, but the heat was already cooling and the sky was clear. It was going to be a beautiful night. He took a long deep breath.

Swirling winds kicked up around him. Flaherty coughed and choked. He covered his face from the fierce attack of the sand-laden winds. Darkness enveloped him, descending like fabric dropped from the sky. Flaherty looked up. Something round and oblong had blocked out the sun. It floated high above him; its span was impossibly huge. Flashes of light danced across its surface, illuminating panels and hatches.

Unidentified Flying Objects of Death!

"No," Flaherty whispered.

A panel slowly opened directly above him. Something long, phallic, and menacing lowered towards him. Deep greenish hues curled and swirled around its bulbous end. Flaherty's hairs stood on end as the air charged with static electricity.

Flaherty ran towards his car just as his world filled with an intense painful green. Every atom in his body was ripped apart in a single nanosecond.

He didn't even get a chance to scream.

MK#2: KARNAGE UNLEASHED

CHAPTER ONE

Karnage woke with the fierce rays of the desert sun beating down on him. The smell of burning plastic hung heavy in the air. He looked around.

He was lying in the middle of a giant smoking crater. The walls of the Hole were about two feet high, their ends melted and blackened.

The asylum was gone.

Karnage leaped to his feet. *Where's my platoon?!*

"Cookie! Velasquez! Heckler! Koch!" Karnage's voice echoed across the desert. Somewhere in the distance, a vulture screeched. *Dead. They're all dead. Just like in—*

The War!

Karnage's mind filled with violent images. The Sanity Patch throbbed. Warning interrupted warning as the sanity levels shot by: Daffodil, Citrus Blast, Peachy Keen, Tangy Orange, Sharp Cheddar, Coral Essence, Frosty Pink—

Karnage slammed his head into the glassy surface of the crater. The visions shattered. The Sanity Patch crooned "Strawberry Shortcake," then went silent.

"Pull yourself together, soldier!" Karnage barked in his best drill sergeant voice. "You're made of sterner stuff than this. On your feet, mister!"

Karnage jumped to his feet. He struggled up the walls of the crater, hindered by the straitjacket, yelling at himself all the while:

"Come on, mister! Double time! Move it! Hustle-hustle-hustle!"

Karnage struggled over the edge of the crater onto a melted chunk of asphalt.

"All right, you maggot," Karnage panted. "I don't wanna hear no more talk about anybody bein' dead. I got no bodies and I got no dog tags! Now nobody's declarin' anybody dead until we got dog tags or bodies to prove it! Do you hear me, soldier?!"

"Sir, yes, sir!" Karnage moved to salute himself, but the straitjacket kept his arms tight to his body.

"Oh, right." Karnage dislocated both shoulders and pulled his arms over his head. He lowered his tied sleeves until they rested on the ground. He stomped on them, stood upright, and pulled hard. There was a satisfying rip, and the strap holding the sleeves together gave way. The ends were still sewn shut. Karnage looked around for something to cut them with.

There was nothing left of the asylum. It looked as if it had been scooped out of the ground, leaving a perfectly spherical hole. All that was left was a single car in the parking lot, shimmering and floating in the desert heat, and three quarters of a sign welcoming people to *Steve Dabney Veteran's Home: Support Our Troo—*.

Karnage took a closer look at the edge of the crater. Its edge was sharp and clean. There were no blast marks. No signs of thrown debris anywhere. He'd never seen anything like it. *Nothing leaves a blast radius that clean.* A tingle ran down Karnage's spine. *Nothing human, anyway.*

The aliens! It must have been. It was the only explanation that made sense. Karnage looked up to the sky. A pair of vultures circled over a backdrop of wispy clouds. There had to be a way to find those aliens. Had to be a way to stop them. If only there was some way to detect them—

Of course! Camp Bailey! Camp Bailey was home to the Godmaster Array, the world's largest radio communications array. If anything could help him find those aliens, it would be that array.

Karnage's foot kicked something solid in the sand. It was an arm. The shoulder had been charred to blackness. The hand still held a set of keys in its soft, manicured fingers. Karnage grinned. He knew that hand. *Flaherty.*

"Looks like you got yours, didn't you, you bastard?" Karnage bent down and pulled the car keys out of the fingers with his teeth.

As he approached the car, he realized that it wasn't just shimmering and floating in the heat. The car was actually hovering a few inches above the ground. Giant silver spheres glimmered in the wheel wells. Karnage gave the car a gentle poke with his boot. It pushed to one side for a second before drifting lazily back into place. *The miracles of modern science.*

Karnage suddenly felt old. The world had changed a lot in the years he'd been in the asylum. How much had he missed out on? What else had changed?

There was only one way to find out.

He bit down on the key fob in his mouth. The trunk popped open. Inside, Karnage found a first aid kit and a bag of golf clubs. He fumbled open the first aid kit with his teeth and found a small pair of scissors. He kicked off his slippers and sat on the edge of the trunk. He looped his baby toes into the scissors handle, and with much fumbling and cursing, he was finally able to snip open the ends of the straitjacket's sleeves. His fingers free, Karnage trimmed the sleeves of the straitjacket down to wrist length and cut off the excess restraining straps. He put the straitjacket on backwards, so the straps ran up the front of his chest.

Next, he fished through Flaherty's golf bag for a weapon. He settled for a wedge with a head the size of a medicine ball. DB-SANDSTORM 5000 had been engraved into its face. Karnage gave it a practice swing. The golf club beeped, and a cheery voice said, "Slice! Relax those wrists." He swung it back the other way. "Hook! Check your stance." The club may not have been happy with how Karnage was handling it, but it felt good and heavy, and the shaft was short enough to be effective in close quarters. He slung the club over his shoulder like a rifle and looked at himself in the side-view mirror.

The buckles up the front of his straitjacket and the high-necked collar had the look of a uniform. He saluted his reflection, tossed the golf club onto the rear seat, and hopped into Flaherty's car.

The dashboard was a smooth contour of white. There was no steering wheel. No pedals. No instrument panel. Just a single blank screen in the middle of the dashboard. A tinkly melody oozed from the car's surround sound speakers, and a series of hieroglyphs appeared on the screen. They depicted a cartoon cat showing various emotions: Happy, Sad, Angry, Embarrassed, and Petulant. A female voice wafted from the speakers: "Please enter your password now."

Karnage scowled. "Shit."

A question mark appeared on the screen. "Have you forgotten your password?"

"Yes," Karnage said.

A hand print appeared on the screen. "Please place your palm on the scanner for biometric identification."

"One sec." Karnage got out of the car, and scooped up Flaherty's severed arm. He hopped back into the car and mashed the palm of the severed arm against the screen. The car sang a happy chime. "Thank you, Dr. Flaherty. Please enter your new password now."

Karnage punched in a new password—*Angry-Angry-Happy-Happy*—and the engine whined to life. There was another chime, and the screen showed a cartoon cat in a bright red convertible driving off into the sunset. "Password reset. Thank you, Dr. Flaherty. Welcome to the Dabney Motors X-500. Where would you like to go today?"

"Can't I drive this thing myself?"

"Please re-state your destination."

"Take me to Camp Bailey."

"Checking . . . your search for Camp Bailey did not match any locations. Did you mean Campbell Dabney Hospital? Dabby Tabby Summer Camp?"

"How can you not know where Camp Bailey is? It's the largest military base on the continent!"

"Your search for Camp Bailey did not match—"

"Is there some kinda manual override on this thing?"

"Please restate your destination."

"Goddammit!" Karnage punched the dashboard. His neck buzzed.

"Warning. Sanity Level upgraded to—"

"Shut up!" Karnage banged on the screen. "You know Globesat coordinates?"

"Please enter Globesat coordinates now."

"3-2-5-3-8-2-7. You think you can find that you lousy piece of . . ."

"Destination set. Globesat coordinates 3-2-5-3-8-2-7. Current charge level is adequate for this trip. Would you like to relieve yourself before—"

"No!"

"Please fasten your seat belt, and thank you for choosing Dabney Motors."

The car wound its way along bends and twists in the road, slowly descending from the asylum's rocky plateau to the main highway. Flaherty's car rode like a dream. Karnage hated it. He liked to feel the terrain he travelled over. Every bump. Every pothole. Every bend and dip in the road. But Flaherty's car would have none of that. It sailed across the pock-marked road like it was a sea of freshly churned butter. The smooth ride made Karnage want to puke. As if to urge his churning stomach onward, the centre console assaulted Karnage's eyes and ears with an endless stream of commercials.

"Nothing beats the smooth cool taste of a Dabney Cola. . . ."

". . . tonight on DABNEYCOPS, law enforcement officers crack a dangerous piracy ring. . . ."

"Hey." Karnage knocked on the console. "Do you do anything else in there besides play commercials?"

A question mark appeared on the screen. "Would you like to watch a film?"

"No."

"Would you like to hear some music?"

"No!"

"Would you like to play a game?"

"How 'bout I start askin' the questions around here?"

A giant *DiN* logo filled the screen.

"The Dabney Information Network provides access to all the latest sports and entertainment news, celebrity gossip—"

"You can start by tellin' me why everything's called Dabney."

The monitor cleared itself, and a giant *DC* logo appeared on the screen. "The Dabney Corporation, an advanced technology company, was started in the basement of its founder, Galt Dabney, where he created the first Dabby Tabby video game, *Dabby Stays Home*. We've come a long way since Dabby first bopped across Galt's computer screen. Hard work, imagination, and a commitment to bringing happiness and cheer to the world have helped us grow into a company that touches more than ten billion people across the globe. Headquartered in Dabneyville, the Dabney Corporation employs 1.3 billion employees in its various sectors and—"

"All right, I get it. You're big. What do you use for cash around here? Never know when you can use some local currency."

The screen changed, showing Dabby Tabby leaning against a money bag and giving a thumbs up gesture. "Welcome to Dabney Financial Services. Please place your palm on the scanner for biometric identification."

Karnage placed Flaherty's hand on the screen.

"Thank you, Dr. Flaherty. Would you like to pay debt, refinance debt, borrow funds, or check balances?"

"Borrow funds?"

"Please enter the amount you wish to withdraw."

"I can do that in here?"

"Please enter the amount you wish to withdraw."

"Well, if you insist." Karnage punched in what he considered a reasonable yet significant sum. The console whirred. A number of thin purple bills emerged from the base of the screen. Karnage grabbed them. The bills felt hot, like they'd been freshly printed. They featured Dabby Tabby prominently on their faces. His arm was wrapped around the shoulder of a man with a long face and pencil-thin moustache. The words "In Galt We Trust" ran in a semi-circle underneath them. Karnage rubbed the bills between his fingers. "Is this legal tender?"

"Each Dabneybill is one hundred per cent backed by the Dabney Corporation's guarantee of—"

The console beeped. A surprised Dabby Tabby appeared on the flashing screen. "I'm sorry. Apparently this vehicle has been reported stolen. Please remain seated until an authorized representative can verify your ownership. Thank you." The car pulled over to the side of the road and the engine turned off.

"Guess I'm hoofin' it the rest of the way." Karnage pulled on the door handle. It wouldn't budge. The console beeped again. "Please remain seated until an authorized representative can verify your ownership. Thank you."

"Like hell." Karnage reached into the backseat for the golf club. The seatbelt tightened against his chest, pulling him out of reach.

"Please remain seated until an authorized representative can verify your ownership. Thank you."

Karnage sucked in his chest and stretched his arm into the backseat. The belt tightened further, digging into his neck. Karnage fought to suck air into his lungs. His fingers touched the cold metal of the golf club's head. He dragged it forward, then wrapped his fist around the handle.

"Please remain seated—"

Karnage smashed the club through the driver's side window. The club shouted "Hook!" as the Sanity Patch crooned "Peachy Keen." An alarm blared over the car's speakers, drowning out both the Sanity Patch and the club. The monitor filled with a picture of Dabby Tabby covering his mouth in an oops-like action.

"I'm sorry. Apparently the anti-theft device on this vehicle has been activated." The car hummed. Karnage felt the hair on his head stand on end. "The chassis has been electrified with 200,000 volts of electricity. Please stay clear of the vehicle until an authorized representative can—"

"I dunno which of you is pissin' me off more." Karnage snagged a shard of broken glass from the window and started sawing through the seatbelt's shoulder strap. "The one who wants to fry me alive or the one who wants to blow my goddamn head off!" The shoulder strap gave way. It whipped up into the harness. Karnage pulled the limp waist belt off his lap.

"Please remain seated—"

"Fuck you!"

Karnage tossed the golf club through the window.

"Slice!"

He pulled himself into a squat on the car seat, and launched himself through the broken window. He landed in a tuck-and-roll on the pavement.

Flaherty's car spasmed and rocked. Sparks flew across its hood. Karnage watched from the shoulder on the far side of the road. He rubbed his stubble-covered chin as the vehicle pleaded with its non-existent passengers to please remain seated. He imagined Flaherty's arm flopping around on the passenger seat.

"This is where we part company, Doc." Karnage saluted. "See you in hell."

CHAPTER TWO

Karnage stuck to the road. The slippers he wore were fine for shuffling through hospital wards, but they'd be torn to shreds on the desert terrain.

The pyjamas were fairly well suited for the desert, though. The thin, loose-fitting fabric would promote air circulation and keep him cool. The golf club made a fine walking stick.

The straitjacket was draped over his head to provide him some protection from the desert sun. The heavy fabric would be a burden, but it would help keep him warm during the cool nights.

The sun was still low on the horizon, but pretty soon the temperature would go up and he'd start sweating. Sweat was the enemy. He currently had no water nor means of getting any. He'd have to do everything he could to keep his body temperature below thirty two degrees. He couldn't travel for long by day. The heat would kill him. He needed to put a couple of klicks between himself and Flaherty's car, then find a well-camouflaged spot away from the road to dig a shelter and rest until dusk. After that, he'd get back on the highway and follow it until dawn, keeping an eye out for water and any sign of Camp Bailey. He wished he had a compass or knew what his current Globesat coordinates were. For now he'd follow the highway and navigate by the stars.

His first night in the desert was easy.

The moon was full and bright, lighting up the desert landscape in cool shades of grey and blue. If anyone drove by, he'd spot them from miles away. But no one did. Karnage's only company was his Sanity Patch, cheerfully singing out notifications as his Sanity Level dropped from Peachy Keen down to Frothy Cream. Occasionally he'd swing the golf club over his head, just to hear its friendly voice yell "Slice" or "Hook." Once in a while he managed to get it to cry out a triumphant "Bunker Busting Backswing!" But not often. Apparently his sand trap skills still needed a lot of work.

MAJOR KARNAGE

Towards the end of the first night, Karnage found an empty plastic water bottle lying in the gravel beside a half-eaten sandwich still clinging to its plastic wrap. Karnage chucked the sandwich (digestion wasted too much water) and added the bottle and plastic wrap to his inventory.

He found a lush patch of desert brush near a dry creek bed. He dug down with the golf club until he hit damp soil. Water filled the base of the hole. He filled the plastic bottle with his hands, filtering the water through the thin fabric of his pyjama top stretched over the opening. *What I wouldn't give for some potassium permanganate.* He chugged it down. The grit in the water caught in his teeth. He hoped it wouldn't give him the shits.

The shits never came, but by the end of the second night, he hadn't found another source of water. So he drank his own piss. Just as dawn was about to break, he dug a hole in the ground and used the plastic wrap and water bottle to create a makeshift solar still.

The still worked about as well as he expected, which was not well at all. By the beginning of the third night, the water bottle was barely a quarter full. He gulped it down, then filled the bottle with his piss, and chugged it again. His piss was thick and orange, more like a syrup than a liquid. He imagined the blood in his veins going the same way, slowly turning to mud as the water drained from his body. Muddying up his body. Muddying up his brain.

He couldn't let that happen. He had to keep his faculties. If he lost his mind, he'd lose everything. *Focus, soldier. Stay the course.*

The cold desert wind whipped at Karnage's face. His lips were chapped. His eyelids felt like sandpaper against his eyes. His joints were stiff. Every movement was sluggish. He felt as if he was slowly drying up, like a ball of clay left out in the sun. He wanted to lie down and curl up and sleep. Let the winds pull the last of the moisture from his body, and let the rest of him crumble and blow away.

No. He had to keep going. He couldn't give up. He forced his screaming feet onward. Willed his stiffening joints to creak forward. He squinted his eyes shut, relishing the discomfort. He *would* make it out of here alive. He *would* find those squiggly alien bastards that kidnapped his troops, and he *would* rescue them.

Failure is not an option!

Karnage hugged the straitjacket to his chest, trying to warm his shivering hands. *Heckler. Velasquez. Cookie. Koch.* Karnage repeated his comrades's names as he marched on. *Heckler. Velasquez. Cookie. Koch.* It became his mantra, his reason for being. *Heckler. Velasquez. Cookie. Koch.* He could hear their voices cheering him on with each agonizing step.

"You can do it, Major!"

"Damn right, Cookie."

"You got the cojones, sir!"

"You got that right, Velasquez."

"You've got it in you, sir!"

"Amen to that, Koch."

"I've got faith in you, Major."

"Is that you, Heckler?"

"You bet your ass it is, John."

Karnage grinned. Now he knew he was hearing things. Old Heckler hadn't spoken a word in years. Not since that day in Kandahar, the worst day of—

The War!

Battle and bullets and flames! Bombers buzzing as they fly overhead. Their payloads whining as they hurtle towards the scorched earth. The night sky strobin' and flashin' and pulsin' like a goddamn disco inferno. Debris and dirt and mud and pain and screams flyin' in all directions. Forward march, soldiers! Forward! Take 'em all! Shoot and fire and kill and die-die-die—

Karnage slapped himself. The Sanity Patch crooned "Citrus Blast" as the visions of battle faded, returning to the black expanse of starry night.

A single flickering light refused to clear from the sky. Karnage stared at it, trying to will it out of existence. It disappeared. Then, a second later, it flashed back. It didn't look anything like an explosion or muzzle flash. In fact, it looked more like—

Letters! Pink and green neon letters winking in and out of

MAJOR KARNAGE

existence. Were they real? Or was he finally losing his mind? Karnage squinted, trying to see them better. The flickering letters coalesced into words. "Upchuck Charlie's. Good Eats!"

Slowly, ever so slowly, the road curved towards the sign. If he'd had the energy, Karnage would have cheered. Step after agonizing step, the sign grew larger before him. His body ached more than ever. On some primal level it believed it was already there. That the mere sight of this sign was salvation enough. He could stop fighting now. Lie down, close his eyes, and—

Karnage let out a short grunt as he jerked himself forward. *Keep moving, mister! You ain't saved yet! You got a ways to go! Don't give up on me now! Lift those knees!*

Karnage's feet stepped off the road and onto the smooth pavement of the parking lot. The diner was a dark shadow of chrome and mirrored glass beneath the flickering sign. A smaller neon sign hung in the double glass doors of the entrance: OPEN.

A feeling of relief washed over Karnage. Just a few more steps, and he'd be back in the welcoming glow of civilization. His eyes caught a second sign hung beneath the OPEN sign. "No shirt, no shoes, no service!"

Karnage checked his reflection in the glass. His eyes were sunken. His cheeks hollow. The stubble on his face was thick. Karnage buckled up the straitjacket and tucked it into his pyjama pants. He ran his fingers through his hair a couple of times, trying to work out the knots. There wasn't much he could do about the slippers. He hoped there was enough of them left to constitute shoes. He braced the golf club against his shoulder, thrust out his chest, mustered what he could of his military brace, and marched into the diner.

Inside, the diner was bright and gleaming. All chrome and glass shining off a polished floor of black and white checkerboard linoleum. A blue-haired waitress—whose name tag proclaimed her to be Darla—was sitting at a booth, stuffing napkins into dispensers. A grime-covered short order cook mopped behind the counter. The bell above the door tinkled as Karnage walked in. They looked up and stared. Feeling conspicuous, Karnage gave his straitjacket one last smoothing down before mustering enough saliva to speak.

"Evening," Karnage said.

"Evening," Darla said.

"Mind if I sit down?" Karnage asked.

The short order cook loudly cleared his throat. Darla looked at him. He shook his head madly. Darla shook her head back, as if to ask if she wanted him to say no. The cook nodded. Darla nodded back, as if to ask if she should say yes. The cook shook his head. While they shook and nodded their heads, Karnage fished the crumpled wad of Dabneybills from his waistband and held them out. "I can pay," he said.

Darla looked at the money, then back at the short order cook. He shook his head again.

Darla broke the silence. "We can't afford to be picky, Charlie."

The cook thrust a dirty hand towards Karnage. "For gawdsake, look what he's wearing!"

"The sign says no shirt, no shoes, no service," Darla said. "Doesn't say nothing about no straitjackets."

Charlie scowled. Darla scowled back. They traded facial expressions back and forth, a silent argument raging through the air. Finally, Darla launched a particularly vicious raised eyebrow, and Charlie crumpled.

"He pays up front." The cook scowled and retreated to the kitchen.

Karnage slid into the nearest booth. Darla gave him a menu. "You want something to drink, sweetheart?"

"Pitcher of water," Karnage pulled a couple bills free of his wad and placed them on the table. "Orange juice. Salt. Sugar. Baking powder."

Darla looked up from her notepad. "Baking powder?"

Karnage nodded.

"Okay." Darla picked up the bills and disappeared into the kitchen. Karnage looked over the menu. Everything on it was branded with Dabby Tabby. Dabby Burgers. Dabby Fries. Dabby Pizza. Dabby Ice Cream. Karnage shut his eyes. This cat was making his head throb.

Darla returned with his drinks and a small saucer full of baking powder. She nodded to the condiments on the table. "Salt and sugar are right there, sweetheart."

Karnage dumped the orange juice and baking powder into the pitcher. He poured in a handful of sugar and a sprinkling of salt after it. He mixed it up and drank straight from the pitcher. He fought the urge to gulp and took slow sips. He didn't want to puke it back up again.

"That drink got a name?" Darla asked.

Karnage wiped his mouth with his sleeve. "No."

"You decide what you want yet?"

"You got anything on this menu that don't got a cat on it?"

Darla pointed to a peeling sticker at the base of the menu. "Well, there's the zardburger. I don't recommend it, though. It's what puts the upchuck in Upchuck Charlie's."

"Gimme two of 'em."

"Don't say I didn't warn you." Darla took the menu and disappeared into the back.

Karnage took another swig from his pitcher and closed his eyes. He'd done it. The desert had tried to kill him, and he'd given it the finger. He'd made it this far, he could make it the rest of the way. He'd find out what kind of supplies they had here before he headed out again. Get himself a proper canteen and some desert survival gear. Even a plastic knife was better than none at all. He had money. He could resupply this time and do it right. Now all he had to do was find Camp Bailey, and he was—

An eerie static burst into Karnage's ears. There was something about it that caused the hairs on his neck to stand on end. Something not quite right about it. Something downright . . .

. . . *squiggly.*

"INCOMING!" Karnage dove under the table, covering his head with his hands, waiting for the first wave of the alien attack.

It didn't come.

"Are . . . are you all right, sweetheart?"

Karnage looked out from under the table. Darla stood beside the radio, her finger on the knob. She turned it off. The static went with it.

Karnage picked himself up from under the table. "Did that sound . . . squiggly to you?"

"Squiggly how?"

"Never mind." Karnage sat back down. Darla gave a half smile and quickly disappeared back into the kitchen. She came out just long enough to serve Karnage his food, made a great display of looking very busy, then disappeared back into the kitchen.

Karnage tore off a chunk of zardburger and did his best to chew. *She thinks you're crazy, you damn fool. And maybe she's got a point. Jumpin' at the damn static from the radio. What the hell kinda soldier are you?*

But the static *had* sounded squiggly. At least to Karnage's ears. But had it been the right kind of squiggle? And what angle had it come in on?

Cookie would have known. But Cookie couldn't help him now. Nor could Koch. Or Heckler. Or Velasquez. He was all that was left of his once mighty platoon.

Karnage worried a gristly bit of zardburger between his teeth. *A one-man army, huh? Sounds like a goddamn hero. You don't fancy yourself a hero, do you, soldier? We both know that heroes don't do nothing but get folks killed.*

Karnage's ears picked up a new bit of white noise. There was nothing squiggly about it. It was the high-pitched buzz of an engine. He looked out the window. A pair of lights crested the horizon. They floated down the long strip of highway, weaving back and forth. There was something in the way they moved that put the hairs on the back of his neck on end. They weaved across the road like they owned it, and were hoping like hell somebody would try and challenge them on it. A pair of smaller red lights flashed to life below the larger white ones.

Karnage scowled. "Cops." He pulled the golf club up against his thigh.

The flashing lights pulled into the parking lot. They were attached to bikes hovering inches above the ground on spheres like those on Flaherty's car. The cops floated to a stop right outside Karnage's window, their beams shining in his face. Two helmeted silhouettes were just visible beyond the glare of the lights. The lights flicked off, and the silhouettes dismounted. They stood at the window, looking in at Karnage. Karnage ignored them. He took a bite of his zardburger and pretended to enjoy it. The figures moved from the window and headed for the door.

The bell above the double doors chimed.

Karnage kept a discreet eye on the cops through the reflection in the window. They had kept their helmets on. The mirrored visors masked their faces. The helmets were stylized Dabby Tabby heads. Stubby ears jutted from the top. A nose and a pair of eyes were sculpted into the helmet just above the mirrored visor. Their boots made a sharp *clack-stomp* against the linoleum. The badges on their chests were sculpted out of Dabby's silhouette, and embroidered in gold thread. The *DC* logo in its centre bore a striking resemblance to the "DRINK DC COLA" sign hanging above the counter. They stopped in front of Karnage's booth. Karnage saw a gloved thumb rubbing the end of his night stick.

"Hi there," the taller of the two cops said.

Karnage tore off another chunk of zardburger, chewed slowly, and swallowed.

The fatter cop put a hand on his night stick. "Hey. My partner's talkin' to you."

Karnage picked up the pitcher and drank. He took large exaggerated swallows. He tilted his head back and drained the pitcher while he wrapped his fingers around the golf club nestled by his thigh. He placed the empty pitcher back on the table and wiped his mouth.

"Hey!" Bad cop smashed the pitcher off the table. "I'm talkin' to you!"

Good cop placed a hand on bad cop's shoulder. "Take it easy there, Harvey."

Karnage looked straight at bad cop's mirrored visor. "You best listen to Princess there, Harvey."

Bad cop shrugged good cop's hand off his shoulder. "You hear what he just called you?!"

"I did," Princess's tone remained neutral.

Harvey's face went red. "You gonna just stand there and take it?!"

"We're going to do this like the captain said."

"He's not *my* captain."

"He's *our* captain until brass says otherwise."

"Oh yeah? Well *fuck* brass!"

Karnage grinned to himself. *Maybe their good cop/bad cop routine is more than just an act.*

"Jesus, Harvey! Not now."

"Yeah, Harvey. Learn your place," Karnage said.

Harvey's face went purple. He pointed a gloved finger at Karnage. "You need to learn a thing or two about respect, old man."

"Care to give me a demonstration?" Karnage said.

Harvey grinned. "If you insist." He went for his night stick.

Karnage was quicker. His fist came up with the golf club and smashed Harvey across the face. The visor crumpled inward. The golf club shouted "Fat Shot" while the Sanity Patch crooned "Peachy Keen." Harvey grunted and staggered backwards, blood oozing from the crumpled visor. He dropped to the floor.

"Harvey!" Princess grabbed his taser and fired. Karnage slid under the table. The taser barbs slammed into the bench leather inches above his head. Karnage shoved himself out from under the table, slamming Princess in the shins. Princess fell. Karnage leaped atop him and smashed his helmet against the floor. The Sanity Patch crooned "Tangy Orange" as Karnage bodily hefted Princess up and launched him through the plate glass window. Princess's scream was drowned out by the sound of shattering glass.

The Sanity Patch buzzed again. "Warning. Sanity Level upgraded to Sharp Cheddar. Please refrain—"

"Shut up. I'm trying to hear something." Karnage strained his ears. There, just beyond the soothing tones of the Sanity Patch, Karnage could make out more high-pitched buzzing. This time mixed with sirens.

Karnage pulled Harvey's gun from its holster and vaulted through the shattered window. In the distance, he could see a flood of flickering red and white lights barrelling towards him on the highway.

"Shit!" Karnage jumped on the nearest hoverbike. It bobbed and swayed, nearly tipping over. Karnage struggled to keep his balance. A screen on the centre console flashed to life.

"Please place your palm on the scanner for biometric—"

"Shit-shit-*shit!*" Karnage punched the screen.

"Warning. Sanity level upgraded to—"

"*Shut up!*"

Karnage jumped off the bike and ran back into the diner. He grabbed Harvey's moaning body and threw it through the broken window. He upturned tables and chairs, propping them in the windows, bracing them against the doors.

"What the hell are you doing?"

Karnage turned around. Charlie stood in the kitchen doorway, thrusting the mop forward like a spear.

"Defensive perimeter." Karnage ripped a booth table from the floor. Tiles and sheared bolts flew in all directions. "Dunno how much good this formica shit will be against bullets, but at least it'll give me some cover. You keep any ordnance around here? Artillery? Heavy weapons?"

Upchuck looked at his mop, then back at Karnage. He shook his head.

"How about emergency rations? No? Guess it don't matter much. It's a restaurant, right? Gotta have at least some food supplies. Don't look so worried, bub. I been in tougher scrapes 'n this. I'll get us outta here alive."

"Alive?!"

"Now here's what we'll do. You go round the back—"

The mop made a loud clatter on the floor. Karnage turned to look. The doors to the kitchen were swinging violently on their hinges. Charlie was gone. Karnage shook his head. "Civilians."

He grabbed the mop and a chrome napkin dispenser from under

the counter. He jammed the dispenser onto the mop handle and lifted it above the counter. He rotated the finely polished surface until he had a clear view of the front window.

The cops had parked their hoverbikes and cruisers in a line across the lot. Cat ears peeked over the vehicles, angry black gun barrels held before them. A pair of cops had run forward and were dragging the limp bodies of Harvey and Princess behind the cruisers.

Karnage swivelled the dispenser, trying to gauge the number of cops. He stopped counting after ten. He couldn't handle more than that. Not alone. He pulled out Harvey's pistol. He didn't recognize the make. It was a revolver of some kind. He popped open the cylinder. The rounds looked like pill-shaped pink bubble gumballs. *What the hell kinda ammo is this?*

A shout came from outside: "Officers clear!"

A megaphone squawked: "Break out the Sudsy!"

Karnage heard the *beep-beep-beep* of a vehicle reversing. He raised the napkin dispenser to get a look. A giant gun turret rose into view. Something slick and oily dripped from the barrel.

"Chemical warfare! You bastards!" Karnage dove behind the counter and swept stacks of napkins out from the bottom shelf.

There was a shout from outside: "Sudsy in position!"

Karnage rolled into the bottom shelf and pressed his body into the corner.

The megaphone squawked: "Fire!"

There was a torrential whoosh, followed by an explosion of glass and tables. The liquid blast slammed into the counter. Karnage felt the cheap particleboard shudder under the impact. He prayed it would hold. Sudsy gurgled and rioted over everything, like white water rapids on steroids. Tables tumbled. Dishes shattered. Electrical circuits shorted out. Dollops of Sudsy splattered Karnage's back.

The torrent stopped. A steady *drip-drip-drip* filled the gaping silence. Karnage felt bits of Sudsy run down his straitjacket. Karnage rolled away from the corner to survey the damage. Sudsy flowed across the floor in great foamy blobs. He could hear the floor drains struggling to suck it all down.

Wet footsteps—like galoshes wading through mud—approached the diner. They stopped. A voice barked out, "Clear!" The footsteps started forward again. *They're comin' for me*, Karnage thought. *They think I'm done for and they're comin' for me! Well I ain't goin' down without a fight!*

Karnage slid out from under the counter and crouched on the—

—his feet slipped out from under him. Karnage fell hard on his ass. Sudsy soaked through his pants.

"Sonofabitch!" Karnage wiped his Sudsy covered hands on his straitjacket. His hands shot straight down his jacket, near frictionless. *What the hell kind of chemical shit did these bastards dump on me?!*

Karnage grabbed the counter and pulled—

His hands slipped off. Karnage flopped down on his back.

"What the GODDAMN HELL!"

The footsteps squished closer.

Karnage grabbed and yanked and pulled at anything within reach. He slipped off everything. The footsteps grew closer. Karnage braced his hands and feet against the walls. He slipped off, and spun into the middle of the room, like a turtle on its back.

"If I gotta make my last stand from here, then so be it." Karnage pulled the gun from his pants and—

—the gun popped out of his fingers. It shot across the Sudsy-drenched floor, ricocheted off a table leg, and disappeared from sight.

The doors burst open. A pair of Dabneycops marched in. The soles of their boots were covered in a pink goo that sucked and pulled at the floor with loud, wet, sloshing noises. The cops wore large tanks strapped to their backs. Hoses ran from the tanks to large, oversized nozzles in the cops's hands. The nozzles were caked in pink goo.

"Subject has been incapacitated," the first one said.

"Goober him."

Pink stringy goop slammed Karnage in the chest, propelled him across the room, and slammed him into the wall. The goober solidified instantly.

"You may think you got me," Karnage struggled against the goober, "But I ain't that easy to—"

They fired again. Long strings of goober licked up and down Karnage's body, enveloping him in a pink cocoon of darkness.

They got him.

CHAPTER THREE

"You know what's wrong with this world?" Charlie asked.

"What, Charlie?" Darla was on her knees, scrubbing Sudsy off the floor. Charlie was supposed to be scrubbing the walls. Instead he stood in the middle of the diner, gesturing wildly with his brush.

"A lack of respect for the working man, that's what! We were just getting by as it was, and now—well, just look at this place!" Charlie threw his arm out in a sweeping arc.

Soap splattered across Darla's clean floor. Darla moved to wipe it up. "I can see it just fine, Charlie."

They had cleared up as well as they could manage. What furniture and stock that remained was stacked neatly on the counter. The rest lay in a jumbled pile of broken wood and glass in the middle of the parking lot.

"I don't know what's worse," Charlie shook his head, "that lunatic throwing around my tables, or those damn pigs sprayin' chemical gunk all over the place trying to arrest him. I mean, he was just one man!"

"They did what they had to do."

"They could have done it a little more carefully! Hell, even I could have done better than that!"

"Really? I seem to recall somebody marching out there with a mop mumbling something about putting an end to this, then running back with his tail between his legs."

"And what exactly was I supposed to have done? He was *armed* then. He could have killed me, you know."

"Uh-huh."

"Did you hear what I said? I said he could have *killed* me!"

"You want to maybe put a little more effort into those walls?"

"Well, how do you like that. I stare death full in the face, live to tell the tale, and all you can think about is your damn—"

A noisy shriek came from the radio resting on the counter. Charlie jumped and stepped in a pool of Sudsy, nearly falling on his ass in the process. "Sonofabitch!" He half-slipped, half-stormed across the room and grabbed the radio. "Would you look at that? It ain't even on!" Charlie yanked the plug out of the wall. The radio squawked in protest, then went silent. "Guess we're gonna have to add this to the . . . well, what the hell's gotten in to you?"

Darla's face was white. She stared intently at the radio, then looked at Charlie. "Did that sound . . . squiggly to you?"

"Squiggly?!" Charlie curled his lip. "Oh hell. You're as crazy as that—"

The radio screeched again. The lights in the diner went out. A solid wall of pitch black slid over the sky, as the world descended into darkness. Flickering panels of light shot back and forth across the sky.

"Wow, would you look at that?" Charlie moved over to the window. "Looks like it's gonna rain something fierce!"

Darla went pale. Her voice was barely a whisper. "I don't think those are clouds. . . ."

"Well, what the hell else—"

Their world was consumed by an intense painful green.

MK#3: KARNAGE BEHIND BARS

CHAPTER ONE

Karnage's arms and legs were strapped to his chair. He was sitting at one end of a long table, dressed in an orange jumpsuit. His scowling reflection stared back at him from the two-way mirror in the far wall.

Could be worse, Karnage thought. *At least I don't got a catheter shoved up my pisshole.*

He watched in the mirror as the door behind him opened. A pair of hulking Dabneycops squeezed through the door. Tasers and stun sticks hung from their belts. They were followed by a tiny figure in a Dabneycop uniform, conspicuously lacking a matching helmet to cover his face. He was a thin, pallid man wearing thick glasses and a cowlick. The binder he carried was thicker than his rib cage. He shuffled across the room and sat in the empty chair. His two Dabneycop flunkies stood behind him. He pushed up the frames of his glasses, and cleared his throat. "Hello. I'm . . . ah, Dr. Huang."

Karnage let the silence hang in the air, hoping to unsettle Huang. It worked. "You a shrink?"

Huang's head jerked and bobbed like a trained seal. "Ha! I suppose that you could, ah . . . put it that way."

"I ain't talkin' to no shrink."

"That's rather, um, unfortunate as, ah . . . you're sort of stuck with me. Ha!"

"Ha," Karnage said.

Huang paled. He put his binder on the table and sat down.

"That my file?" Karnage said.

"It's, ah . . . your medical records. Which I suppose is your 'file.'"

"It say anything in there about how many shrinks I put in the hospital?"

Huang jerked back as if he'd been slapped. He stared at Karnage with wide, hurt eyes, then swallowed. He cleared his throat, and opened the binder. "So, ah . . . let's get this party started, shall we? Ha!"

"Ha," Karnage said.

Huang quickly looked away from Karnage and buried his face in his binder. "It says here you've spent a lot of time incarcer—ah . . . impris—ah . . . rather, I mean . . . you've, ah, spent quite a bit of time under psychiatric—yes! Psychiatric care. Ever since the W—" Huang stopped himself. His face went white.

Karnage felt the blood race to his ears. "Ever since what, Huang?"

The guards reached for their stun sticks. Huang swallowed hard. "Ah . . ."

Karnage strained at his bonds. "Ever since *what?!*"

Huang's eyes darted around the room. "Ever since—ah . . . hostilities! Hostilities!" Huang grabbed at the word like a drowning man going for a life preserver. "Ever since the hostilities ended. Ha! World peace and all . . ."

"World peace." Karnage resisted the urge to spit. "Don't talk to me about World Peace."

"You, ah . . . weren't happy about that?"

"Not like it did me any good."

"You would have preferred that the W—hostilities! Hostilities!" Huang repeated the word as if it were a talisman to ward off evil spirits. "You would have preferred that hostilities had continued?"

Karnage wrenched forward. "I would've preferred not being locked up like some kinda goddamn animal!"

"AH!" Huang jerked back. His pen flew out of his fingers and went flying across the room. He grinned sheepishly. "Ha! Yes! I can see why you'd feel that way." Huang pulled another pen from his pocket and clicked it open. "Ah! But, ah . . . you know it wasn't, ah . . . malicious. You were—rather, you are, ah . . . not exactly 'well.'"

"You saying I'm nuts?"

"I wouldn't put it quite like—"

"I'm not crazy!" Karnage barked.

Huang shrank back. "Well, ah . . . what about the, ah . . . hospital?"

"What about it?!"

"You don't think that, ah . . . blowing it up—"

"Is that what this is about?"

Huang looked at the two-way mirror as if trying to get guidance. He looked back at Karnage. "Well, ah . . . yes."

Karnage leaned in and growled. "Get this straight, Chuckles. I didn't blow up a goddamn thing."

"No?"

"NO!"

Huang squealed, then tried to laugh it off. "Ha! Is this where the—ah . . . 'aliens' come into play?"

Karnage grit his teeth. "You best lose that patronizing tone, Doc, before I tear it outta your throat and shove it up your—"

Karnage's neck buzzed. "Warning. Sanity Level upgraded to Citrus Blast. Please refrain from violent behaviour. Thank you."

"You should, ah . . . watch that temper, Major. We wouldn't want you to, ah . . ."

"Lose my head?"

"Ah. You've, ah . . . heard that one before? I should probably, ah . . . stick with my day job, then, eh? Ha!"

"Ha," Karnage said.

Huang shrank back behind his binder. He cleared his throat. "So, ah . . . is it your contention that these, ah, 'aliens' blew up the hospital?"

"It is my contention that you are a royal pain in the ass."

"Ah!"

"It is also my contention that aliens are gettin' ready to invade this here dirtball, and you kitty cops need to get the hell outta my way so I can find my troops and we can do our job!"

"So, ah, it is also your, ah . . . contention that your fellow inma— ah, patients are alive?"

Karnage leaned forward, his voice a low growl. "Lemme tell you something, Doc. I may not have all your fancy degrees or a big thick binder to hide behind, but I can tell you this: you do not declare your buddies dead until you got dog tags or body bags. And right now I got nothing. They are MIA. Missing In Action! You get me, Huang, or do I gotta draw you a goddamn diagram?!"

Huang jumped in his chair. "No, ah . . . thank you. I believe I, ah . . . get you." Huang took a moment to straighten his collar. He shuffled his papers. "Ah . . . if I may—er, rather, would you be willing to, ah . . . entertain an alternate theory?"

"Like what?"

Huang cleared his throat. "Well! Ah . . . perhaps . . . if you could just, ah . . . picture for one moment, ah . . ."

"SPIT IT OUT, HUANG!"

Huang jumped. "Ah! Well, ah . . . what if these 'aliens' as you call them weren't really, ah . . . aliens at all?"

"Well, what the hell else could they be?!"

"Ah! Ha-ha! Well, perhaps they are, ah . . . part of some sort of, ah . . . hallucination?"

Karnage leaned back. "So that's how it is, huh? Keep the old mushbrain talkin' and maybe we can eventually get him to come around to seeing things our way."

"Ah, does that mean that, ah . . . you won't, ah . . . consider—"

"You can take your goddamn theory and shove it up your ass!"

"Ah! I see." Huang shut the binder. "Captain Riggs will be very, ah . . . upset to hear about this."

Riggs! Karnage's mind reeled. His ears rang. That single word echoed in his head.

Riggs!

Karnage's hands balled into tight fists. "What do you know about Riggs?"

Huang nodded eagerly. "He, ah . . . served you with you during the—ah, during the hostilities. And he was most disappointed to—"

Karnage laughed. Huang cringed at the sound. Karnage glowered at Huang. "Nice try, Huang, but you boys gotta do better research. Sergeant Riggs bought it back in Kandahar. I don't know who this captain you're talkin' about is, but it ain't him."

Huang blinked. "But . . . but I assure you that—"

"You got wax in your ears? Riggs is dead! Don't think I don't see what's goin' on here. You're just pushin' my buttons, hopin' I'll crack!"

"But I assure you it's the same Riggs!" Huang said. "The very same sergeant who served with you during The War—AH!" Huang slapped his hand over his mouth.

The War!

Karnage's blood boiled. Bullets and flames and death rained down on his psyche.

The War!

Huang staggered up from his chair as the two Dabneycops pulled their stun sticks and charged forward.

The War!

Karnage pulled at his restraints. There was the heavy creak of metal fatigue. A wrist restraint snapped, and his right arm was free.

A stun stick came plunging down into Karnage's vision. Karnage's free hand whipped up and grabbed the wrist that was holding it. A quick twist snapped it. Somewhere outside of his vision a man screamed. A second stun stick came thrusting in after the first. Karnage adjusted his grip so he held both the broken wrist and the accompanying stun stick and swung it around to meet the second one barrelling towards him. The metal tines of both sticks struck naked flesh. Hot sizzling and the stench of ozone filled Karnage's nostrils. Two sets of screams filled his ears. Somewhere deep in his vocal chords, a guttural primal laugh flowed up and out and reverberated throughout the room.

The two Dabneycops fell to the floor. Huang was pressed against the two-way mirror, clutching the binder to his chest. Karnage grabbed his remaining restraints and ripped them open with his free hand.

"Don't talk to me about *The War!*"

Karnage tossed the table out of his way and charged Huang. Huang pressed himself against the two-way mirror, screaming. Karnage's fingers wrapped around Huang's throat. He slammed Huang's head against the mirror. The mirror sprouted a spiral of jagged spiderweb cracks starting from the back of Huang's head.

"You want to talk to me about The War?" Karnage hissed. "I'll tell you about—"

The door behind Karnage burst open. Boots stomped into the room. A familiar voice shouted, "Karnage!"

Karnage turned around. There, standing in front of a line of Dabneycops, was Riggs. His tall, lanky frame had filled out. His hair was grey and pulled back in a ponytail. Crow's feet had sprung up around the eyes. But there was no mistaking those eyes. It was him.

"Riggs?" Karnage stared at his former sergeant. His fist stayed closed around Huang's throat.

"Mercy," Huang weakly clawed at Karnage's tightened fist. "Please . . ."

A Dabneycop beside Riggs cocked his rifle. "Let the doctor go or we will be forced to open fire!"

"Negative!" Riggs pushed the Dabneycop's rifle down. "Nobody fires until I give the order! Do I make myself clear, Murtaugh?"

"That's not how Sydney would have us play it, sir."

"Sydney's not in charge here!"

"We found your dog tags. Half-melted, lost in that sea of rubble. How could you . . . ?" Karnage's fists clenched tighter around Huang's throat. Huang gasped in his grip. Karnage growled: "You ran. You got scared and you turned tail and ran! Riggs The Roach. Always comin' out okay! Always! Right up until the end. Right up until the goddamn end!"

"John—"

"We were counting on you to hold your position. When we came back, there was nothing there but a pile of smoking rubble. Nobody to meet us but Uncle Stanley. They came outta the hills like hornets, Riggs. Like a goddamn *swarm!* We thought for sure you were dead. The Roach had finally been crushed. We shed tears for you, you asshole. We shed goddamn tears!"

"I can explain—"

"You left us behind!" Karnage's fists tightened around Huang's neck.

"John, you're killing Huang!"

"You left us, Riggs. YOU LEFT US!" Karnage dropped Huang and lunged at Riggs.

Murtaugh levelled his weapon. "Open fire!"

"NO!"

Riggs's cry was drowned out by the *pop-pop-pop* of automatic weapons fire. The rounds slammed Karnage in the chest, throwing him into the cracked mirror. It shattered. Karnage fell through. He landed in a tumble of desks and screams on the other side.

The wounds in his chest went from hot to cold. Karnage looked down. Brightly glowing ping pong balls covered his chest. *Tranquilizers*, Karnage thought. The icy coolness spread from his chest to his limbs. He lost consciousness.

CHAPTER TWO

Karnage woke in a holding cell. Its thick metal bars were covered in barbed wire. Blue sparks danced and crackled from the wire to the bars. He stood up.

"Where the hell am I?"

A monitor on the wall behind him came to life. A *DC* logo splashed across the screen. Dabby Tabby bounced onto the screen and leaned against the logo. He was decked out in an orange prison jumpsuit. His ankle sported a ball and chain. A gentle, female voice wafted from the screen.

"Welcome to the Dabney Correctional Executive Class Hospitality Centre. We hope your stay with us is a pleasant one. Please enjoy these pastoral images and soothing mood music while you await trial and sentencing. And remember—at Dabney Correctional, we believe everyone is innocent until proven guilty. And it shows."

Treacly music blasted from the walls and ceiling. Karnage clamped his hands over his ears. The music vibrated through his body and threatened to shake the fillings from his teeth. It was unbearable. "Jesus Christ!"

The gentle female voice returned, now at a much higher decibel. "Rather than use offensive language to express yourself, try to articulate what you're feeling." Dabby Tabby unrolled a list of words on the screen. "Please feel free to use this vocabulary of handy alternatives to many common expletives."

"You want vocabulary? How's this? Shut up, you fucking fuckknuckle!"

"Rather than use offensive language to express yourself, try to—"

Karnage screamed in frustration and kicked the wall. His neck buzzed. "Warning. Sanity Level upgraded to Frothy Cream. Please refrain from violent—"

"Goddammit! What do I have to do to get you cheery bastards to shut the fuck up?!"

A voice shouted to him over the noise. "I can't help you with that voice in your neck, but I can get that music to stop for you."

"Who the hell said that?" Karnage whipped around. A grizzled old man in an orange jumpsuit sat in the cell across from his. A pair of reading glasses sat perched on his nose. He held a tattered paperback in his right hand. His left hand ended in a stump. He pointed to the monitor with his stump.

"Tell it you're hungry," he said. "It gives you a fork you can use to short the system."

Karnage did. A tray popped out of the wall. A bowl full of steamy grey pulp was bolted to the middle of the tray. A fork lay beside it. Karnage picked up the fork.

"It's attached to the tray with a cable."

"Don't worry about that," the old man said. "Just bend up the tines and jam it under the bowl. On the other side. You want it to get jammed up inside the wall when the tray retracts."

"How's that?"

"Perfect."

"What now?"

"Empty the bowl."

Karnage eyed the oily grey slop. "I ain't eatin' that shit."

"I don't blame you," the old man said. "It tastes worse than it looks. Like ground-up cardboard soaked in bacon grease. There's enough sedatives and hypnodrugs in there to kill an elephant. Scoop it out and dump it in the toilet. But don't spill any. The sensors in the floor call the cleaning staff when it's dirty."

Karnage scooped out the gooey grey mush with his hands, and dumped it into the toilet. It was so heavily laced with narcotics it made his skin tingle. Once the bowl was empty, the tray retracted. The fork's bent handle slid under the rim of the wall with a satisfying *thwock*. The tray seamlessly disappeared into the wall. The music kept playing."It didn't work!" Karnage said.

"Yes, it did," the old man said.

"Then why the fuck can I still hear music?!"

"Tell it you're hungry again," the old man said.

Karnage did. The edge of the tray appeared in the wall, then stuck. Somewhere inside the wall, gears ground. Engines whined. Karnage caught the faint scent of burning plastic. Something inside the wall snapped. The tray shot forward an inch, then sagged back, its bottom edge sticking out from the wall. The music stopped. The monitor flashed blue. Three red Dabby Tabby heads appeared on the screen.

"Error 503. Please wait for assistance."

"See? What did I tell you?" The old man grinned.

"Sounds like it called for assistance," Karnage said.

"Yeah. Tech support. Don't worry about it. It'll take them days to get here." The old man jerked his thumb toward his own blue monitor. "Mine's been like that for a week now and they still haven't fixed it."

"You mean nobody's noticed?"

"Oh, sure, they noticed. Nobody's done anything about it, yet, though. Other than charging me with cyber-terrorism."

"Cyber-terrorism?"

"Circumventing security measures. Defacing public property. All falls under the same law. Can't say I was bothered by it. It's what got me locked up in here in the first place."

"You some kind of terrorist?"

The old man snorted. "Yep. If you define terrorism as being too curious for my own good. All I wanted to know was how those biometric scanners worked. Is it my fault they're so easy to get around? All you have to do is pop the top off and twist the red and green wires together. Bingo! Instant access."

"That's it?"

"That's it."

"That doesn't exactly sound secure."

"Of course it isn't. But they're not going to go around fixing these things. There's too many of 'em! It's a lot cheaper to pass a law saying its illegal to even look at 'em funny. Justice, my ass."

"That's idiotic."

"That's the Dabney Corporation."

"Thanks for your help. You some kind of engineer or something?"

"Nope. Just a Lineman from the old C&E."

"Communications and Electronics Branch?"

"That's the one."

"You're a military man."

"Was. Corporal Russel J. Stumpton. Haven't been military in over twenty years."

"That how you lost the hand?"

Stumpton nodded wistfully, absently rubbing his stump. He shook it off. "But that was a long time ago. Now I'm just another veteran, like you."

"What do you mean 'like me'?"

"You're Major Karnage, aren't you?"

Karnage eyed him suspiciously. "How do you know my name?"

"Oh, come on, Major. Don't look at me like that. Of course I know who you are. They said your name enough times when they brought you in here. Besides, even if they didn't, I'd have figured it out for myself. Nobody's talked about anything but you for a while now."

"They been talkin' about me, have they?"

"It's all anyone's been able to talk about for days. 'Where is he? How do we get him? What do we do when we've got him? Do we even want to catch him?' They prepared that cell especially for you, you know. It's been quite a show."

"Sounds like you've been enjoying it."

"You're damn right I have. In case you haven't noticed, there's not a lot to do for fun around here. I take my amusement where I can get it. And just when I thought it couldn't get any better, that Riggs fella showed up and threw a monkey wrench into everything."

Karnage's pulse quickened at the mention of the name. "What do you know about Riggs? What can you tell me about him?"

"Not too much. Just what I've heard through the grapevine. Apparently he was brought in by the brass to take care of you personally."

Karnage scowled. "Oh he was, was he?"

"He's been talking up a storm about how easy you'll be for him to take down. Apparently you're nothing he can't handle."

Karnage cracked his knuckles. "I look forward to proving him wrong."

"You're going to have to get in line. Nobody here likes him much. Especially Sydney."

"Who's Sydney?"

"The former captain of this precinct. Sydney got pushed aside when they brought Riggs in. There aren't many people here pleased about that, least of all Sydney."

A door opened in the distance. Karnage looked down the hall. Riggs came striding into the room. He smiled at Karnage. "Good. I'm glad to see that you're—" Riggs's eyes darted to the screen behind Karnage's head. His features darkened and he turned to Stumpton. "Did you do this?"

Stumpton's eyes went wide. "How could I? I'm locked up."

"Disseminating information on circumventing systems security is a class five felony under the Dabney Intellectual Property Ordinance."

"You make one hell of a bureaucrat, Roach."

Riggs winced at his nickname. He turned to Karnage and smiled. "Nobody calls me that anymore, John."

"Oh yeah? Why not? Looks to me like it's still true. Things go to shit and you come out smellin' okay. Just like old times, isn't it, Roach? Oh, except for the part where you stabbed us in the back."

"I didn't stab anyone in the back, John."

"No. You just dropped your dog tags and ran."

"It's a lot more complicated than that, John."

"How complicated can it be, Roach? You're here. You're alive. You ran. End of story."

"I would have been killed!"

"You don't deserve life, Roach. And one day, I'm going to make that happen for you."

"Warning. Sanity Level upgraded to Lemon Breeze. Please refrain from violent behaviour."

"John, please." Riggs sighed. "Look, you've been through a lot. I understand that. And I'm sure you had your reasons for doing what you did."

"Doing what I did? What the hell are you—? Oh, I get it. You think I blew up the asylum."

"I didn't say that, John."

"You think I'm crazy."

"You're not crazy," Riggs said. "You just need help. There are some very angry people out there who want your head."

"There's a very angry fella in here who wants yours."

"These are some very powerful people, John. Some very powerful people. I'm doing everything I can to help. All you need to do is sign a few forms for me, and we can get you out of here."

"What kind of a slow-witted bohunk do you take me for?"

"I'm just trying to help you here, John."

"Fuck you and your help, Roach."

Riggs shrugged. "All right. If that's the way you feel about it. I'll stop in tomorrow. See how you're doing. Let me know if you change your mind."

Riggs turned and headed for the door. Karnage tried to glare him to death as he walked out. It didn't work. "I'm gonna kill that asshole."

Karnage's neck buzzed. "Warning Sanity Level upgraded to Daffodil. Please refrain from violent behaviour."

"What's that voice in the back of your neck about?" Stumpton said.

"It's nothin'." Karnage examined the cell door. "What are these bars made of?"

"E-nium," Stumpton said.

"E-nium? What the hell is E-nium?"

"It's a reconstituted alloy. Made from the shavings of scrap metal. They mash it up into a kind of polymer. Supposed to be stronger than titanium. It's one of those E-friendly products."

"What the hell is an E-friendly product?"

"It's one with a big 'E' sticker on it."

Karnage jerked a thumb at the monitor in his cell. "What about these computers? Can we use 'em to get out?"

Stumpton shook his head. "They're not tied to any of the main systems. Just the food and lavatory stuff."

"That food's got to come from somewhere, and that shit's got to go someplace else."

"I don't know about that."

"What do you mean?"

"Might be a closed-circuit system."

"You mean shit gets recycled into food?"

"Might be."

"What makes you say that?"

"Wait 'til you taste it."

"I don't plan to be here that long." Karnage ran his fingers along the corner of the tray jutting out from the wall. "What's behind these panels?"

"I don't know. I haven't been able to get behind them."

"Maybe I can." Karnage slipped his fingers into the gap between the tray and the wall. He pulled on the tray. He could feel the resistance of the bent fork pushing against the inside of the wall. Karnage pulled harder. He heard the creak of metal as the fork bent inside the wall. Something snapped, and the tray popped out. The mangled fork dangled from the cable, its head sheared off. Karnage looked up at the monitor. The red kitties of death were still on the screen. Karnage's neck buzzed. "Warning. Sanity Level upgraded to Citrus Blast. Please refrain from violent behaviour."

"Looks like the system has to be reset manually," Stumpton said.

"Looks like." Karnage picked up the fork and gave it a solid yank.

"You're wasting your time with that," Stumpton said. "That carbon nanotube stuff doesn't break."

"I don't expect it to." Karnage wrapped the fork's wire around his fist. He braced his foot against the wall and pulled hard.

Metal groaned. Something inside the wall snapped. The tray fell halfway out of the wall.

Karnage braced himself against the wall and gave another pull.

There was another screech of metal and the tray broke free. It landed with a heavy thud on the floor. The Sanity Patch buzzed.

"Warning. Sanity Level upgraded to Peachy Keen. Please refrain from violent behaviour."

Stumpton whistled. "What are you going to do with that?"

"I'm gonna pick the lock." Karnage unwrapped the cable from his hand and grabbed the fork by its handle. He stood in the middle of the cell and started swinging the tray around in a circle, like an athlete prepping for a hammer throw. After a few spins, he let the cable loose, and the tray slammed into the bars.

Sparks exploded. Electricity crackled and buzzed. The bars bent outwards.

Karnage's neck buzzed. "Warning. Sanity Level upgraded to Tangy Orange. Please refrain from—"

"How do you like that," Karnage said. "E-nium's stronger than titanium just like biometric scanners are tamper proof."

"How did you know?" Stumpton said.

"I didn't." Karnage kicked the tray clear of the sparking bars. "But if this stuff is so strong, then why go to all the trouble of electrifying it?"

Karnage swung the tray over his head again and lobbed it into the mangled bars. The Sanity Patch upgraded to Coral Essence. Karnage didn't pay much attention to it. He was more worried about the tray. The bars had bent so far in that the tray was wedged inside the bulge. Karnage gave the tray an experimental kick. It was stuck fast. "You don't suppose these trays are conductive, do you, Corporal?"

"I . . . I don't know. . . ."

"Best guess?"

"I'd guess not."

"Good enough for me." Karnage launched himself across the cell and slammed his shoulder into the tray. The bars twisted farther out. A corner of the tray pushed clear of the bars. The Sanity Patch chirruped again. "Warning. Sanity Level upgraded to Frosty Pink. Please—"

"Guess you're right," Karnage said. "I didn't get fried."

Karnage threw himself into the tray again. The entire rear of the tray pushed clear. "One more oughta do it."

"—upgraded to Strawberry Shortcake. Please refrain from violent behaviour."

Karnage froze. He looked at Stumpton.

"Come on, Major," Stumpton said, "one more shot and you're through!"

Karnage pointed at his neck. "Did that thing say what I think it said?"

"What?"

"Strawberry shortcake."

"Yeah, I guess so. What does that matter?"

"Shit." Karnage moved to punch the tray in frustration. He stopped himself mid-swing. "Shit-shit-*shit!*"

"What's wrong?"

"I can't do it," Karnage said.

"Sure you can! It's just gonna take one more hit! Hell, if you've done something to your shoulder, just give it a good solid kick. That's all it'll—"

"*I can't!*"

A door burst open in the distance. Boots marched down the hall. A pair of extra large Dabneycops emerged from the darkness. The beefier of the two looked from Karnage to Stumpton, then back to Karnage.

"Which one of you knuckleheads is Karnage?"

A high-pitched voice piped up from behind them. "It's the one who still has both his hands, you idiot!"

The beefy one looked at Karnage suspiciously. "You sure?"

"Of course I'm sure! Now get the hell out of my way before I make you sad tossers regret it!"

"Sorry, Sydney." The two brutes jumped to either side as if they'd been bit. Standing behind them was a third Dabneycop who barely came up to their waists. She removed her helmet, revealing spiky strawberry blonde hair and piercing blue eyes that stared cold and hard at Karnage.

"So," she said. "You're Karnage."

"So," Karnage said. "You're Sydney."

"I've heard a lot about you," she looked Karnage up and down. "Can't say you live up to the hype."

"Feeling's kinda mutual," Karnage said.

"Oh yeah?" Sydney smirked. "Expecting someone a bit more manly, were you?"

"Nah," Karnage said. "Just a little taller."

Sydney scowled. She poked at the tray jutting out of the cell. "Trying to escape, I see?"

"You noticed that, huh?"

"I've got a good eye." She pointed a finger at Karnage. "You cost me my command."

"You shoulda done more to hold on to it."

Sydney smiled. "You got a mouth on you."

"So I've been told."

"You got the goods to back it up?"

"You lookin' to find out?"

"I am." She motioned to the beefier of her two associates. "Tiny. Open the cage."

"But Riggs said—"

Tiny buckled. Karnage hadn't seen Sydney move, but her left pinky finger was now pressed against Tiny's knee. Tiny whimpered and gasped. Sydney never broke eye contact with Karnage.

"Sorry, Tiny. Didn't quite catch that. Try again?"

Tiny squeaked. Sydney poked a smidgeon harder. Tiny's eyes started watering. "I'm afraid you'll have to speak up, Tiny," she said. "Funny thing. Y'see, I thought I heard you mention the name 'Riggs' to me. You wouldn't do anything that stupid, would you, Tiny?"

Tiny shook his head.

"Good. Now be a good lad and open up the cage. Okay, Tiny?" Sydney curled her finger away from Tiny's knee. Tiny fell to the floor, gasping.

"Whenever you're ready, mate," Sydney said.

Tiny caught his breath. He stood up and wiped the tears from his eyes. Giving Sydney a wide berth, he placed his palm on the biometric scanner. It beeped, and the mangled cell door swung open. Sydney pulled a pistol on Karnage.

"This here's the real thing. None of that goober stuff. Spragmos Industries Max Atom-17. Explosive-tipped bullets. Any funny stuff, and I blow your head clean off. You get me?"

"Any funny stuff and my head blows clean off," Karnage said.

"Glad to hear we understand each other. Cuff him, Chuckles."

Chuckles did. Karnage didn't resist.

"Guess you're not so hard to handle after all," Chuckles said.

"Not under the right circumstances," Karnage said.

"You sucking up to me?" Sydney said.

"Nope."

"Good. I hate suck-ups. Isn't that right, Tiny?"

Tiny jumped and whimpered. He favoured his right leg.

"Right. What say we go for a little walkabout then?"

"You're in charge," Karnage said.

"That's right. I am." Sydney flicked a salute at Stumpton. "Cheers, mate."

Bewildered, Stumpton watched as they effortlessly led Karnage away.

CHAPTER THREE

They took Karnage down through a series of corridors and several flights of stairs. They stopped for a bit in a stairwell while Sydney grabbed a heavy duffel bag from a utility closet.

"What's in the bag?" Karnage said.

"Emergency supplies," Sydney said. "You know, just in case."

"In case of what?"

"In case you get out of line."

"The gun ain't enough?"

"Not if I still want you alive."

They led Karnage down several more flights of stairs. Karnage noted every twist and turn, committing it all to memory. He'd be able to find his way back blindfolded if need be. No matter what happened, no matter how things went down, he'd do his damnedest to make sure he got Stumpton out of there. He was one of his soldiers now. The only way he'd leave him was under pain of death.

And what about the others? Karnage twinged with a pang of guilt. Velasquez. Cookie. Koch. Heckler. They all needed him, too. He'd wasted too much time already. No telling what those aliens were doing to them.

Karnage had plenty of time to observe his captors as they led him into the bowels of the building. Tiny and Chuckles were fools. All brawn and no brains. Karnage suspected they'd made their careers putting on the tough guy act without ever having to play the part. They relied on their size to do all their work for them. It was probably why Sydney was able to exert such exacting control over them. Her existence defied their sense of logic. How could anything that small be that strong? When the time came, they'd be no threat to Karnage. They'd go down easy.

Sydney was another matter. Her movements were incredibly precise. Not a motion wasted. He'd have to be careful. If he hadn't been a single Sanity Level away from blowing his head off, he could have used Chuckles and Tiny as a diversion to get clear of Sydney. But for now he was helpless.

Karnage fumed. How long did it take him to downgrade a Sanity Level? He hadn't a clue. He cursed himself for not paying closer attention. *You're gettin' sloppy, you old fool. You can't keep going off half-cocked like this! Your troopers are counting on you. Cookie, Velasquez, Heckler, Koch. And now Stumpton, too. What the hell happened to your military discipline?*

"We're here."

The corridor they stood in was poorly lit. A single fluorescent bulb clung to a flickering half-life in the middle of the hall. At the far end, Karnage could make out a battered wooden door locked with a heavy padlock. Sydney fished a key from the duffel bag and unlocked the padlock. She opened the door, one hand on the doorknob and one hand holding her pistol level with Karnage. She motioned with her pistol.

"After you," she said.

"You're too kind." Karnage walked into the darkness, conscious of Sydney's pistol pointing at his mid-section.

The door closed behind Karnage with a loud thunk. The world went black for a second. There was the flick of a light switch, and an incandescent light bulb popped to life above Karnage's head. The sickly yellow glow reflected off the cracked cinder block walls and rusting furnace in the corner. The air was thick with the smell of dust and mould.

"Cozy," Karnage said.

"Used to be called the hospitality suite," Sydney dropped the duffel bag by the door and rolled up her sleeves. "Used to bring suspects down here when they needed a little extra encouragement to confess."

"Aggressive interrogation," Karnage said.

"You're familiar with the technique?"

"A little too familiar," Karnage said.

Sydney pulled off her boots. "You gonna give Tiny here any trouble when he uncuffs you?"

Karnage felt the weight of the Sanity Patch on his neck. "Won't lay a finger on him."

Sydney nodded. "You heard the man. Uncuff him."

Tiny didn't look convinced. "Are you sure, Sydney? I mean—"

Tiny froze. Sydney had placed a finger against his shoulder. She leaned in close to his ear. "Un. Cuff. Him."

She pulled her finger away. Tiny staggered backward, gasping. He shot Sydney a fearful glance, then approached Karnage warily, and uncuffed him.

Karnage rubbed his wrists. "You mind telling me what this is all about?"

Sydney pulled off her socks and wiggled and stretched her toes. "I worked hard to get this command. Fought tooth and nail. Had to fight twice as hard as any bloke half as good. Old boy's network. You know how it is. Even then, the best I got was this lousy outpost on the outskirts of civilization. Most of the men out here are rejects from elsewhere. Worst of the worst. The armpit of the force."

"Hey!" Tiny said.

"Nothing personal, Tiny. You know it's true."

Tiny hesitated, then nodded. "Yeah."

"But I did what I could," Sydney was stretching her calves. "Weeded out the cops on the take. Brought in much-needed discipline. Whipped this place into shape. We weren't top in the region, but we did all right."

Sydney pressed her leg against the wall, doing a vertical leg split. "Then Brass calls. Tells me some nutty combat vet is loose in my district. Dangerous stuff. A real menace to society. And I'm thinking, finally, here's my chance to show them what my boys can do. But Brass has got other ideas. They think this might be more than old Sydney can handle. So they bring in this guy Riggs. A real up-and-comer, they tell me. Real hot shot. Bees knees. 'He's got the inside scoop on this Karnage fella. You're gonna love him,' they tell me. 'Just wait until you meet him.'

"So old Riggs shows up. And he tells me he's been given my command. Temporarily, of course. Just until this whole Karnage affair is dealt with. So why don't I go sit back, grab a tea, and let the Real Men deal with things in the meantime. And he'll be sure to give me back my command when he's done with it. Honest. There's a good girl."

"Sounds harsh," Karnage said.

"I am, of course, paraphrasing."

"That still don't explain why I'm here."

Sydney sat down, braced her fingers against the floor, then lifted her body, balancing her weight on her fingertips. "It's like this: Brass claims you're more than old Sydney can handle." Sydney bounced on her fingers a couple of times. Once resettled, she was balancing on just her pinky fingers. "And I aim to prove them wrong."

"And you're gonna do that how?"

"By kicking your ass," Sydney said. "In a fair fight, of course."

"That doesn't sound too rational."

"Never said it was, mate." Sydney stood up and stretched her neck. She bounced on her toes. "You ready?"

Karnage felt the weight of the Sanity Patch against his neck. "I'd be up for this more in the morning."

"You trying to be funny?"

"I couldn't be more serious."

"Sorry, mate. We don't got all night. Just do your best. I'll go easy on you at first. Let you get warmed up."

"You're too kind."

"Thanks. Don't let that get around."

"Won't tell a soul."

"Appreciate it." Sydney shook her body out, then lowered into a crouch. She stuck out her pinkies like she was holding twin cups of tea, and rose to the tips of her toes. She nodded once. "Here we go."

And then she was on him.

Fingers and toes flew at Karnage with blinding speeds. Karnage dodged, bobbed, danced and weaved. Once he was too slow and a pinkie brushed his side. His vision exploded in black dots as pain shot through him. He gasped and struggled to stay upright enough to dodge a follow-up baby toe heading for his neck.

He'd never seen anyone move like this before. It was like a martial arts version of shiatsu. Sydney knew all the right pressure points to cause extreme pain in the body. It was brilliant. It was like ballet, except it didn't suck. Sydney's every move was graceful. The lines of her attack were beautiful. Karnage had never enjoyed fighting someone so much in his life.

That joy was tinged with worry. He'd never had to move so fast. He could barely keep up with her frenetic pace. It burned him up inside that he couldn't fight back. Not that he'd seen many opportunities to do so. Once or twice he thought he saw an opening, but they closed so fast it became obvious they were carefully laid traps. Had he made a move, he would have exposed himself for a crippling blow. Karnage had never seen Sydney's equal. She was an artist.

They moved back and forth across the room, swaying and bobbing and weaving in a violent dance of bear and doe, the doe attacking and the bear defending, clumsily dodging each finely thrust hoof and horn. Karnage scrambled to avoid a toe that seemed to sneak up on him from behind Sydney's back. He heard a yelp from behind as Tiny shouted, "Hey! Watch it! You almost hit me!"

"Stay out of my way and you won't get hurt!" Sydney barked.

"Easy for you to say. You guys are all over the place. Hey!"

Karnage saw Tiny scramble to one side. That gave Karnage an idea. He worked on dodging and ducking, moving in a slow arc towards Tiny. Sydney made it near impossible. Her every attack demanded specific precise counter-manoeuvres. But slowly, Karnage moved them back in Tiny's direction.

"Quit comin' towards me!" Tiny screamed.

"Quit getting in my way!" Sydney yelled back.

Karnage heard Tiny scrambling behind him again. He ducked between two fingers and a toe while sliding out his back leg for balance. He felt the knocking of a leg as Tiny stumbled into Karnage's foot. Tiny squealed as he fell. Another toe raced towards Karnage. Karnage grabbed a handful of Tiny and pulled him on top as a human shield. Karnage heard a crunch and a scream as Sydney's toe slammed into Tiny. Tiny went still.

"Sorry, mate." Sydney patted Tiny on the shoulder before tossing him off Karnage and relaunching her attack.

Karnage rolled across the floor. A series of fingers and toes slammed into the floor behind him.

Karnage heard the crackle of a stun stick in front of him. "I got a bead on him, Sydney."

"Stay outta this, Chuckles!"

"No worries. I got him." A boot stamped onto Karnage's back, stopping him mid-roll. There was the crackle of electricity by his ear and the smell of ozone. Just as quickly, it spun away as something crunched and Chuckles screamed.

Karnage looked up. Sydney was balanced on her pinkies atop Chuckles's twitching chest. "Sorry, Chuckles. Got to do this on my own," Sydney twisted on her pinkies. There was a sickening crunch and Chuckles went still. "You understand." She backflipped off Chuckles and stood before Karnage. She was shining with sweat. Karnage took the opportunity to catch his breath.

"You're better than I thought."

"I gotta say," Karnage panted. "I'm a little disappointed."

"How so?"

"Your aim sucks. You're good at hitting your own men. Not so good at hittin' me."

Sydney smirked. "So what say we stop playing around and get down to business?"

Sydney launched forward, fingers and toes flying at Karnage in every direction. Karnage threw himself to the floor. A finger grazed his back. His lungs seized and the breath shot out of him. All his limbs tingled. He struggled up as best he could, clutching his knees to his chest to catch his breath.

A toe nicked him in the ear. His left leg went numb. A finger tapped his elbow. Spots exploded in his vision. Shot after shot tapped and poked and prodded his skin. Pain exploded all over his body. He felt like he was being carpet bombed. His every instinct screamed at him to fight back. To kill!

He fought it. He wouldn't succumb. He wouldn't blow his head off by giving in to his rage. His troopers were counting on him. *Velasquez. Heckler. Cookie. Koch.* He recited his mantra, his reason for living. *Velasquez. Heckler. Cookie. Koch.* He struggled to his feet, avoiding some blows, wincing under others. *Take it, soldier! Do it! Your troopers need you! Velasquez! Heckler! Cookie! Koch!*

"Fight back, goddammit!" Sydney screamed.

Karnage spat blood. The animal in his head was screaming: *Do it, dammit! Look at her! She's tired! Angry! Her guard is down! Take the shot, soldier! TAKE THE SHOT!*

Karnage didn't. *Velasquez. Heckler. Cookie. Koch.* He slowly pulled himself to his feet. *Velasquez. Heckler. Cookie. Koch.* He spat another mouthful of blood. *Velasquez. Heckler. Cookie. Koch.*

"This is stupid!" Sydney shouted. "You're supposed to be better than this!"

"I am," Karnage said.

A toe threw Karnage across the room.

"Then take a shot at me!" Sydney yelled.

Karnage struggled to his feet. Blood was freely flowing from his forehead.

"I can't," he said.

"What's the matter? Don't you fight girls?"

"Oh hell, yeah. I'm an equal opportunity combatant."

"Then what's the problem?"

Karnage wiped the blood from his face. "Let's just say I'm waitin' for a sign."

Sydney leaped at Karnage, pinning his arms to the floor, straddling him with her tiptoes. "What kind of sign?"

Karnage's neck beeped. "Attention: Sanity Level downgraded to Frosty Pink. Thank you for refraining from violent behaviour."

"That." Karnage's legs flew up, grabbed a surprised Sydney by the neck, and slammed her into the floor. She was out cold.

Karnage's neck buzzed. "Warning. Sanity Level upgraded to Strawberry Shortcake. Please refrain—"

"Shut up." Karnage looked down at Sydney. "You gotta learn to control your temper there, Captain. No reason for you to lose your cool. Unless, of course, you object to mindlessly beatin' on a man. Which I think you do. So fair's fair, I guess. Your own moral code brought you down. Worse ways to lose."

He pulled the pistol from Sydney's belt, happy to finally have his hands on some serious hardware. He frowned. It felt far too light. He pulled the gun's clip.

"Goddammit." It was empty. Karnage tossed the gun away in disgust. Sydney had been bluffing him the whole time. "You got guts, Captain. I'll give you that." He tried hard to suppress a smile.

Karnage looked around the room. All three Dabneycops lay in varying stages of unconsciousness. The duffel bag lying by the furnace caught Karnage's eye. He opened it, revealing handcuffs, chains, ropes, and other means of restraint, including—

"Hot damn." Karnage held up the straitjacket. He smiled. "Looks like it's my size, too."

He slipped it on. The heavy canvas felt good against his skin. Like coming home. He cut down the sleeves with the bowie knife from Tiny's belt. The cuffs were cut much cleaner this time. It felt more like a uniform than ever. He was growing to like this.

He cuffed Tiny and Chuckles to the furnace, and gagged their mouths with the cut sleeves of the straitjacket. Sydney was another matter. Karnage wrapped her in chains, ropes, and every bit of restraining material in the bag. He stared at the unconscious form of the captain. From the neck down she was wrapped in a cocoon of rope and metal. But he still wasn't satisfied.

"Frankly, Captain, I think I'd have to encase you in concrete before I thought you were good and trussed up." Karnage eyed the empty duffel bag. "Matter of fact, I think I'd rather keep my eye on you. . . ."

Karnage slipped the mummified Sydney into the duffel bag. It was tight, but she just fit. Just as he was about to zip the bag over Sydney's face, he was hit with a pang of guilt. She deserved better than this, a combat fighter like her. Definitely didn't deserve to be trussed up like somebody's badly packed luggage. He gave her a quick salute. "I hope you understand this ain't personal, Captain."

He zipped up the bag and slung it over his shoulder.

CHAPTER FOUR

"I want this son of a bitch caught."

Riggs paced the front of the squad room. His reflection paced back and forth across the mirrored visors of the men's helmets.

"He's a trained killer and he's going to kill again."

A voice called out from the back: "This wouldn't have happened if Sydney were in charge."

A slight nodding of heads rippled out from the source. Riggs tried to pinpoint who it was, but all he saw was his own angry glare reflected back at him from the sea of mirrored visors. "Nobody's happy with how things have gone," Riggs said. "There are a lot of unanswered questions here. I've got three missing officers and two missing prisoners. Did they help the prisoners escape? Were they overpowered? Considering Captain Sydney's skill as a fighter, that's doubtful. What's her role in all this? We won't know how much she's involved until we find her."

An angry murmur coursed through the crowd. Riggs spoke over it. "But our focus here is Karnage. He must be contained at all costs. I want every available body on this manhunt. From disposal to dispatch. Deputize them. Terrorize them. Whatever it takes. If they got a pulse, they're in on the search. Nobody rests until Karnage is found. Do I make myself clear?"

A hand shot up in the back. "Shouldn't we leave a skeleton crew here, in case—"

Riggs exploded. "I will not have anybody sitting on their asses and playing pinochle while that bloodthirsty maniac is on the loose! When I say I want everybody after that sonofabitch, I mean *everybody!* Is that clear?!"

There was a begrudging murmur of assent from the officers.

"Good. Now get the hell out of here, and find me that bastard. Dismissed!"

The squadron filed out, some of them grumbling under their

breaths. Their Dabby Tabby helmets seemed to mock Riggs with their mirrored visor grins. A couple of constables glanced up at Riggs as they left. He was sure they were giving him the evil eye. He tried to record their badge numbers, but their arms were conveniently covering them.

As the last of the men left the squad room, Riggs sighed. It was supposed to have been easier than this. But everything had gone wrong since he had accepted this assignment. No one had warned him about Sydney. And then there was Karnage. He was crazier than anybody had thought.

Riggs walked back to his office, thinking of his former commanding officer running around the desert, shooting at anything that moved while shouting about aliens. *The poor bastard.* Riggs felt a twinge of guilt. Maybe he could have done more to help. Maybe . . .

As he reached the door to his office, Riggs heard voices coming from down the hall. He ground his teeth. Nobody should have been left in this part of the building. They should be out on patrol, or packing their sorry butts into a patrol cruiser.

Riggs marched around the corner. A short, slovenly constable hunkered over the door to the armoury while a second taller constable leaned against the wall looking on, his foot resting idly against a large duffel bag.

"Just what the hell are you two doing?" Riggs barked.

The short constable stumbled back, tripping over the duffel bag. He fell to the floor. After picking himself up, he brushed off his ill-fitting uniform. "Uh, I—we, that is, uh . . . ah . . ."

The taller constable stepped forward and saluted Riggs. "Constable Zuniga, Captain. Don't mind old Chucky, there. He always gets like this around Brass. Doesn't stop him from bein' the best mechanic in the motor pool. Ain't that right, Chucky?"

"I, er, uh . . ." Chucky looked from Zuniga to Riggs and back again.

"Why the *hell* aren't you two out on patrol?!"

Zuniga pointed to the bag. "Chucky here's got this hockey game tonight, and he wasn't sure if we'd have time to come back to pick up his gear, so we thought—"

"You *thought?!* Who the hell asked you to *think?* If I wanted thinkers, I'd be commanding a goddamn think tank! I do the thinking, you do the following. So when I say everybody goes out on patrol, I mean everybody! No exceptions! Are you listening to me, mister?!"

The only signs of emotion on Zuniga's face was Riggs's angry reflection scowling back at him. "Heard every word, Captain," Zuniga said. He jerked a thumb at the armoury. "But before we go, sir, you might be interested in knowing someone's been tampering with the lock. Sir."

Riggs took a close look at the door. There was nothing left of the biometric scanner but a gaping hole and a mass of wires. Riggs ran his fingers through the tangle of wires. He pulled out a red and green wire that had been carefully braided together. The hairs on the back of his neck stood on end. "Stumpton."

He rounded on Zuniga. "Is there anything gone? Anything missing?"

Zuniga shook his head. "Haven't had a chance to look, sir. We were about to, but then you ordered us to—"

"Well look, dammit! Look!" Riggs kicked open the door and barged in.

Tasers, goober guns, and goober grenades packed the shelves, ripe for the plucking, yet entirely unplucked. Riggs let out a sigh of relief. "Thank god. Nothing's missing."

"Not yet, anyway," Zuniga said.

Riggs turned around. He found himself staring down the barrel of a goober rifle.

"Just what in the—"

Zuniga fired. Riggs flew across the room. He slammed into a wall of shelves. Guns and ammo rained down around him as the pink expanse of goober swelled, pinning him to the shelf. His arms stuck fast to his sides. He kicked futilely, his feet a good foot off the floor. Riggs heard a beep from the back of Zuniga's neck.

"Warning. Sanity Level upgraded to Frosty Pink. Please refrain from violent behaviour."

Riggs's eyes went wide. "Karnage."

Karnage stood to his full height and removed his helmet. His voice dropped an octave. "You know, Roach, you'd think after serving with me for so long, you might be wise to some of my tricks." Karnage aimed the goober rifle at Riggs's head. "Or were you too busy saving your own skin all the time to notice?"

Riggs swallowed hard. He adopted a calm, forceful tone. "Now, John, don't—"

Karnage fired. Riggs's world filled with dark angry pink. Over the crackle of the fast hardening goober, Riggs could just make out the words, "That's Major to you."

MK#4: KAMP KARNAGE

CHAPTER ONE

With the entire force out looking for them, Karnage and Stumpton marched through the halls of the precinct with impunity, saluting the occasional security camera along the way.

"Where we going now, Major?" Stumpton asked.

"Camp Bailey," Karnage said. "You know the Godmaster Array?"

"I do," Stumpton said.

"Think you can operate it?"

"You're asking a communications guy if he can operate a communications array?"

"You ever worked it before?"

"No, but I'm sure I can figure it out."

"Good enough for me," Karnage said. "Consider yourself drafted, Stumpton."

"My friends call me Stumpy."

"Does that mean you are offering me your friendship?"

"That I am, sir." Stumpy put out his hand.

Karnage shook it. "Then I accept. Now let's find ourselves some wheels."

The only vehicle left in the parking garage was the captain's cruiser. Stumpy hotwired it and the two of them took off across the desert. To avoid roadblocks and patrols, Stumpy steered them out into the open desert, avoiding the roads altogether.

"With hoverballs you technically don't need roads at all," Stumpy explained, tapped the dash. "Just got to be a bit careful over the bigger bumps. Don't want to risk a flat tire."

"You can get a flat with these things?"

"Kinda. You hit something hard enough, it can crack one of your hoverballs. Or worse, shatter it."

"How do they work, anyway?"

"The hoverballs?" Stumpy shrugged. "Nobody knows."

"You ever crack one open before?"

"Oh yeah. Huge mistake. Nothing inside but nasty yellow gas. Stinks something awful."

Karnage pointed to the steering wheel. "Nice to see the cops get steering wheels."

"Good thing, too. Those DabneyNet hookups won't let you leave the road."

Karnage looked at the mangled twist of wires that had been the DabneyNet screen. "You sure they can't track us?"

"Not without that antenna we ripped off. I'm telling you, Major, we're safe. They'll never find us out here. Nobody even goes near the old army base anymore. Not even the Dabneycops."

"Why's that?"

Stumpy shrugged. "Nobody knows. But that makes our job easier. We can waltz in there and get that Godmaster Array up and running without worrying about any Dabneycops breathing down our necks."

"Yeah." Karnage wondered what else might be waiting for them there. "How long before we get there?"

"Should get there by nightfall. You just relax, Major. I got everything under control. Shit, you look like hell. When's the last time you slept?"

"Does being knocked unconscious count?"

"Nope."

"Then it's been a while."

"Maybe you should try and catch a few zeds while you can. Be all fresh and prepped for the mission ahead."

"What about you?"

"Are you kidding? I haven't felt this alive in years. I feel like I'm just finally waking up, and I'm loving every minute of it." Stumpy gave a holler and pumped his stump.

Karnage smiled. He settled back in his seat, and closed his eyes. It was good to be back out under the sun again. And this time with purpose. He had a plan. He even had a platoon. Sure, his platoon consisted of a solitary one-handed rifleman, but it was a start. Progress was being made. He'd save his troopers yet.

Cookie. Velasquez. Heckler. Koch. Just sit tight. I'm comin' for you. I'm comin' . . . . "

CHAPTER TWO

Riggs blew his nose again. The tissue still came away pink. His body ached from being pinned against the shelves for so long. It had been hours before they had finally found him—another couple of hours before he was finally goober-free and sitting back at his desk, blowing pink goober into a thousand and one tissues, dreading the moment when that phone would finally ring. All the promises he'd made. The reassurances he'd given. How was he going to explain all this?

There was a knock at the door.

"What is it?"

Murtaugh stuck his head into the office. "Someone from head office here to see you."

Riggs's heart dropped into his stomach. They had skipped the phone call and gone right for the face-to-face meeting. He smoothed the wrinkles out of his uniform. "Send him in."

A man in a chauffeur's outfit entered the office, his coat buttoned from knee to collar. The visor of his cap sparkled. His boots shone. He wore elegant black gloves that came up to his elbows. Giant inkblack driving goggles covered his eyes. His tightly pursed lips carried the barest hint of a smile, as if he was amused by some private joke that only he was privy to, and had absolutely no desire to share with anyone else. He looked like a military officer come to deliver Riggs to his court martial.

"Captain Riggs?" The chauffeur extended a gloved hand towards Riggs. "I'm Patrick, Mr. Dabney's representative."

Riggs took the outstretched hand. "You'll pardon me if I ask which Mr. Dabney you're here on behalf of?"

The curled lips parted slightly—the movement reminded Riggs of a straight razor slicing open the soft white belly of a corpse—and Riggs caught the barest glimpse of teeth.

"Of course," Patrick said. "There are so many of them running around that it's hard to keep track. I'm here on behalf of Mr. *Steve* Dabney. Doubtless you've heard of him?"

Riggs's heart dropped out of his stomach, through his lower intestine, then slithered down his leg onto the floor. He did his best imitation of a smile. "Of course," he said.

Patrick reached into his coat. "Mr. Dabney sends his regrets. He wanted to deliver this message to you in person, but business has called him away." Riggs half-expected to see Patrick pull a gun from his coat. Instead, he pulled out an interoffice envelope. He unwound the string holding it closed. "I realize this all may seem a bit . . . dramatic, but he didn't want to risk sending this through regular channels."

Riggs nodded, pretending he understood. Whether the hatchet was delivered in person or by special courier, that blade was still whistling for his neck. It didn't much matter how it was delivered.

Patrick flipped open the envelope and pulled out a tablet. He held it in front of his chest and flicked it on. Steve Dabney appeared on the screen. He wore his trademark blue turtleneck and corduroy pants. His close-cropped hair and wireframe glasses made him look much younger than he was. He flashed a smile so charming it could sweep the habit off a nun; it only half-worked on Riggs. He knew what the man behind the smile was capable of.

"Malcolm! I'm sorry to have to handle things like this, but I'm in the middle of some sensitive negotiations and I can't pull myself away." Steve glanced from side to side, then leaned in closer to the screen. "Look, let's cut right to the chase: you fucked up. I mean, you really screwed the pooch on this one. The board is screaming for your head."

Riggs braced himself. *Here it comes.*

"So I'm removing you from the Karnage assignment." Steve raised his hands towards the screen, palms up. "Now, look. Don't panic. Things look bad, I know. But I've been talking you up to our silent partners here. They're very interested in your extensive knowledge of the good major. They want to make you part of their team. A consultant of sorts—we're still ironing out the details. I can't get too specific, but I *can* say that this is a fast-growing organization with plenty of room for advancement.

"Now, I may have jumped the gun a bit here, but I went with my gut and accepted the contract for you. You're not going to let me down by saying no, are you? This is a once in a lifetime opportunity here. You'd be a fool to pass it up. You're not going to let me down, Malcolm, are you? You're taking this position, yes?" Steve nodded, answering the question for himself. "Good. It's settled, then. You can hitch a ride with Patrick here. He'll deliver you to our silent partners. Be well, Malcolm. See you."

The tablet blinked off. Riggs stared at the blank screen. He looked up at Patrick.

Patrick returned Riggs's gaze. "Not quite the reprimand you were expecting, sir?"

CHAPTER THREE

Karnage felt something nudge his shoulder. He pulled himself up from sleep and saw it was Stumpy's stump. "Wake up, Major. We're almost there."

Karnage rubbed the sleep from his eyes. "How much farther?"

"Not far," Stumpy tapped the dashboard screen. "According to those Globesat coordinates you gave me, it shouldn't be more than a few klicks."

Karnage stretched and looked out the window. The desert landscape was dotted with massive pits of black tar. Gnarled pink plants grew around the edges. Ropey tendrils of orange interwove themselves around the pink, snaking from one tar pit to the next.

"What the fuck is all this?" Karnage asked.

"That's pinkstink," Stumpy pointed to a clump of pink flowers as they passed. "Scrunch it in your fingers and it gives off an awful smell. The viney stuff is orange creeper. Grows like a weed. It gets in everything. Tear it down one day, and it grows back up the next. A real pain in the ass."

Karnage gazed out at the landscape. "This all used to be trees, Stumpy. Pine and cedar and shit. And now . . . now there ain't even stumps. It's all so different. So . . ." A chill ran down Karnage's spine. ". . . *alien*."

There was an ear splitting bang, and the car lurched forward.

Karnage braced himself against the dashboard. "What the hell'd we hit?!"

"I don't know!"

There was another bang, and the back of the car pitched upward. Stumpy pointed his stump behind them. "It's comin' from the trunk!"

"I think our passenger is finally awake," Karnage said.

The rear of the car lurched again and slammed into the ground hard. Yellow gas spewed from the driver's side.

"We got a flat!" Stumpy slammed on the brakes and pulled the cruiser over. The banging and lurching got worse.

They got out of the car and inspected the damage. A crack had formed in one of the hoverballs. Yellow smoke spewed from the crack. The car lurched again, and the ball slammed into the ground. Another crack appeared.

Stumpy shook his head. "If she keeps this up, we won't have a ball left to float on!"

"Can you fix it?"

Stumpy ran his fingers along the cracks. "I think so. Grab me a goober rifle."

Karnage fished a goober rifle out of the back seat. Stumpy took the rifle, and cracked it open.

"What are you doing?"

"Breakin' the seals. Kills the pressure from the nozzle. It gets messy, but it should work." Stumpy snapped the rifle back together. He pulled the trigger. Half-hearted spurts of goober oozed from the nozzle. Stumpy placed the nozzle against the hoverball and ran it down the crack, leaving a line of goober in its wake that swelled and filled the crack. The yellow smoke thinned out to a fine trickle. Stumpy tossed the goober rifle to the ground as it was slowly engulfed in the pink stuff oozing from its seams. He patted the hoverball.

"That should hold us for a while. Should be enough to get us to Camp Bailey, anyway, so long as our passenger doesn't screw things up."

The car lurched again.

"It doesn't sound like she's gonna be all that cooperative." Karnage fished another goober rifle out of the backseat. He turned to Stumpy. "Get behind the wheel. When I give you the signal, pop the trunk."

Stumpy eyed the rifle. "What are you going to do?"

Karnage switched off the rifle's safety. "I'm gonna reason with her."

Karnage stood in front of the trunk, goober rifle at the ready.

He signalled to Stumpy. Stumpy popped the trunk. The lid flew open and the duffel bag launched itself into the air. It crashed into Karnage, knocking him to the ground. Karnage rolled out from underneath it and scrambled to his feet. He pinned the gyrating bag with the butt of his rifle. The bag writhed under the rifle like an angry snake, trying to wiggle free. Karnage reached forward and unzipped the bag. Sydney's tousled head burst out. Her face was red. Her eyes shot daggers at Karnage. Her mouth was covered with a strip of duct tape. It flexed in and out as she let loose an angry tirade of muffled curses that would have made Velasquez proud. Karnage waited until she had exhausted her expansive vocabulary, then saluted. "Evening, Captain."

Sydney glared at Karnage, her eyes full of hate.

"I apologize for the bumpy ride," he said. "I'll admit this ain't exactly the sort of treatment suited to an officer of your calibre, but it's the best we could do under the circumstances. We should be far enough from the enemy that your gag won't be necessary. If I may, Captain?"

Sydney stared at Karnage with a cold, burning hate. Karnage took that for assent. He grabbed the corner of the duct tape, and ripped it off with a quick snap. Sydney's teeth grazed his knuckles as he pulled his hand clear. The clack of her teeth snapping shut echoed across the desert.

"Easy there, Captain. You nearly took my hand off."

"Sorry," Sydney said. "I won't miss next time."

Karnage nodded. "Good. Either do the job right the first time or don't do it at all. Sometimes you don't get a second chance."

Sydney scowled. "You know, taking me hostage was probably the stupidest thing you could possibly have done."

"Hostage? Oh, no. You ain't no hostage. Not by a long shot. You're a POW, with all the inherent rights and privileges therein. And as for me bein' stupid, from what I've seen you're probably the only Dabneycop with even half a chance of bringin' me in. So long as I keep you with me, you can't be plannin' any nasty surprises for me and Stumpy here. This way I know exactly where you are and what you're up to."

"Am I supposed to be impressed?"

"If you like."

"Well, I'm not. You'll find I'm very hard to hold onto."

Karnage smiled. "You're angry. I get that. Mad. Pissed off. Hopin' to cause me a lot o' trouble as soon as you're able."

"You got that right."

"And you understand o' course why I can't let that happen."

"And what do you plan on doing about it?"

"Well, I could just knock you cold with the butt o' my rifle here. But I thought I'd give you a choice first. See if you'd be willin' to keep your temper."

"I'm sorry, are you asking me to behave myself?"

"I am," Karnage said. "Only until we get to our destination. Then you can jump up and down and scream and holler, and raise any kind o' holy hell you like."

"And where are you going?"

"Camp Bailey."

Sydney furrowed her eyebrows. "Camp Bailey? Why the hell would you go there?"

"Stumpy and I are gonna fire up the Godmaster Array and stir up some shit. Ain't that right, Corporal?"

Stumpy saluted. "Sir, yes, sir!"

Sydney looked incredulously from one to the other. "You can't be serious. Do you have any idea what's waiting for you out there? No, of course not. If you did, you wouldn't even be thinking of trying something so damn stupid."

"Why? What's out there?"

"The Church of Spragmos."

Stumpy fell back against the car with a loud thud. "Sweet Christ, say it ain't so."

"It's so. It's beyond so. It couldn't be more so. It's the biggest so in the whole damn universe, that's how so it is."

Stumpy slid down the car. "Fuck me running . . ."

Karnage turned from one to the other. "Wait a minute. Hold on here. The Church of *what*?!"

"The Church of Spragmos," Sydney said.

"Spragmos . . . you mean like the *gun* manufacturer?!"

"That's right."

"What the fuck do they worship? Guns?"

"No," Sydney said.

"They worship . . . The Worm." Stumpy was clutching his arms to his sides.

"Okay, so they worship a worm."

"Not a worm," Sydney said. "*The* Worm."

"All right. *The* Worm. What the hell difference does it make?"

Sydney stared at Karnage. "You really don't know, do you?"

"No, I do not fucking know. I spent the last twenty years locked up in a goddamn insane asylum. There is a lot I do not know. Now quit starin' at me like I got monkeys growin' outta my ears and tell me just what is so goddamn frightening about this goddamn worm!"

"There's not much to tell," Sydney said. "Nobody knows where it came from. But it's real. And it's dangerous."

"How dangerous?" Karnage asked.

"Dangerous enough that we stopped sending troops out to the base because they weren't coming back."

"So you just let those bastards dig in and grow stronger, while you hole up in your office suckin' yer thumb, hopin' they go away?!"

"You think I didn't try?! I filed thirty different requests for counter-terrorism support! Those bastards left me twisting in the wind! You tell me what I was supposed to—"

A shuddering screech hurtled across the desert, a violent, jagged line of sound that cut through Karnage like a knife ripping through fabric. "What the fuck was that?"

"That," Sydney said, "was The Worm."

"Oh fuck me." Stumpy buried his head in his hands.

Sydney looked around. "We must be a hell of a lot closer than I thought."

Stumpy turned to Karnage, his face white. "Major, we got to get out of here. There's got to be another way. Another old army base.

Camp Casey is just another few hundred klicks away. We could make it. I know we can!"

"Listen to Stumpy, Major," Sydney said. "If the Spragmites find you out here—"

The sound tore through them again, raking up and down Karnage's spine like an electrified cheese grater. It was so jagged. So angry. So unlike anything he'd ever heard before. And yet, at the same time, it felt so familiar. Like something from a dream. Or a faded memory. A jagged black line etched in skin, slightly red around the edges from being pressed too hard.

And that's when it hit him: the noise wasn't jagged at all.

It was squiggly.

Karnage turned to Stumpy. "Camp Casey's no good to me. I need that Godmaster Array, worm or no worm. Cult or no cult. Camp Bailey is our only option, and that is where we're headed."

Sydney looked at Karnage, aghast. "Haven't you heard a word I've said?"

"Every one of 'em."

"And you're still going in there?"

"I am."

"You're crazy!"

"I been told that before."

"You'll die!"

"I been told that, too." Karnage looked at Stumpy. Stumpy sat there, leaning against the car, staring into the distance, rubbing the end of his stump. "You ain't gettin' cold feet on me, are you, Corporal?"

Stumpy looked fearfully into the distance, then down at his stump. He set his jaw, and rose to his feet. "No, sir. I've come this far, I'll go the rest of the way." He saluted.

Karnage returned the salute. "Good to hear, soldier." He turned to Sydney. "And what about you, Captain? You gonna behave or am I gonna have to knock you out?"

Sydney gaped at Karnage. "You don't think you're taking me with you?"

"I am," Karnage said. "I ain't about to leave an officer out here to die of exposure."

"So instead you'll get me killed on this fool's mission. Well, you can forget it. I won't—"

Karnage cracked the butt of his rifle across Sydney's head, knocking her out cold. "Suit yourself."

CHAPTER FOUR

Riggs lounged in the backseat of the limo. He leaned against the ravaged remains of the mini-bar as he drank his third martini. His silk shirt and matching pants were cool against his skin. He looked down at his *Tommy Dabney* shoes. They sparkled so brightly they practically winked at him. He leaned back into the plush leather of the seat and sighed. He was drowning in luxury and he was going to savour every second of it.

Riggs watched Patrick drive. Patrick hadn't acknowledged Riggs's existence since they had left the precinct. Riggs leaned forward and tapped on the glass divider. The divider sank down behind the seats, and Patrick's goggles appeared in the rear view mirror. "Is there a problem, sir?"

"No. No problem," Riggs said. "Just wanted to talk is all."

"I see."

Riggs pulled himself up and rested his head on the back of the front seat. "Let me ask you something, Patrick. Are you happy?"

Patrick considered this. "Happy, sir?"

"Yeah. Happy."

"Do you mean with life in general?"

"Huh." Riggs thought about that. Was that what he had meant? He snapped his fingers. "Yeah. In general. Like life. Family. Career. All that stuff."

Patrick stayed silent a long while, watching the road. Riggs started to wonder if he had somehow offended him. Finally, Patrick replied. "All things considered, I suppose you could say that."

Riggs slapped the back of the seat. "Exactly! That's the way it should be! Everybody's always bitchin' about how everything sucks. This sucks. That sucks. Everything used to be better. Fuck that—pardon my French, Patrick—but fuck that! Things are good. Things are great! Look at the two of us! Happier than a couple of clams in shit."

"Pigs.",

"Sorry?"

"I believe it's 'pigs in shit.' Clams don't require shit to be happy, sir. They just are."

"Oh. Oh yeah." Riggs looked at his half-empty martini glass. He wondered if it truly was only his third. "Well, you know what I mean."

"I do. And may I say, it's refreshing to meet such an optimist," Patrick said.

"Yeah. Me, too." Riggs leaned back in his seat, then leaned forward again. "It sounds pretty exciting though, doesn't it?"

"What does, sir?"

"This job. This new gig."

"I suppose."

"Malcolm Riggs: fast, free-wheeling consultant."

"That's one way of looking at it."

"Hot and cold running booze."

"They may prefer you not to drink on the job."

"And the babes, Patrick. The babes!"

Patrick smiled. "You might find it's not all it's cracked up to be, sir."

"Oh, let me dream, Patrick. Let me dream."

"Dream all you like, sir. I just wouldn't count my chickens before they hatch if I were you."

Riggs swished a mouthful of martini in his mouth, then swallowed. "Good point, Patrick. Good point. Wouldn't want to end up with a basket full of rotten eggs, right?"

Patrick nodded. "Or something other than chickens." Patrick pulled the car over to the side of the road, and shut off the engine. "Here we are, sir."

Riggs looked outside. Nothing but empty desert stretched out in all directions. "Where?"

"Your destination."

"But there's nothing here."

"No," Patrick said. "There isn't."

Riggs stared at Patrick blankly. "You're just going to leave me here?"

Patrick nodded. "That's what I've been asked to do, yes."

"But . . ."

"But what, sir?"

"There's nothing here!"

"I believe we covered that already."

"You . . . you can't just leave me out here!"

"I can."

"I'll die!"

"You won't."

"I will!"

Patrick let out an exasperated sigh. "Trust me, sir. If Mr. Dabney wanted you dead, I would have made that happen quite some time ago."

Riggs did a double take. "What? Wait a minute. What are you saying? Did you . . . did you just threaten me?"

Patrick checked his watch. "I'm sorry, sir, but I just don't have the time for this." Patrick leaned forward. His expression hardened into an ice sculpture of cold hate. "Exit the vehicle, Captain. *Now.*"

While Patrick hadn't raised his voice, something in its tone came out so hard and sharp that Riggs practically tripped over himself as he scrambled out of the car. Before he even realized what was happening, he was standing on the side of the road, watching the car speed off down the highway, leaving a cloud of choking dust in its wake.

Riggs was alone.

He could feel the sun beating down on him. He could feel his shirt already starting to stick to his sweaty back. He wiped his forehead. *This is just great,* he thought. *What a hell of a first impression I'm going to make.* He looked down and realized he still held the remnants of his martini in his hand. Just looking at it made his mouth go dry. Should he drink it now? Or save it for later? *Oh hell, what does it matter anyway?* Riggs threw his drink back.

Violent winds picked up around him, blowing sand into his

mouth. Riggs spat sand out of his teeth, and looked up. The sky had gone pitch black. Flickering panels of light ran up and down the sky.

Riggs dropped his glass.

A panel opened directly above him. A giant phallic object emerged from the hole, crackling with green energy. Riggs turned and ran.

"Major!" Riggs screamed. "MAJOR!"

Riggs's world filled with an intense painful green.

CHAPTER FIVE

The closer Karnage got to Camp Bailey, the more alien the landscape became. The tar pits became a thick, black marsh covered in a cross-hatch of orange and pink. The squiggly cries of The Worm became more frequent. With each cry of The Worm, Stumpy grew paler and shakier. The only thing that kept him going was Karnage's steady banter. So long as Karnage reminded Stumpy that he was at his side, he knew Stumpy would find the resolve to keep going. He hoped things would improve once they reached Camp Bailey.

But Camp Bailey was anything but reassuring to either of them.

They reached the base after dark. The stoic buildings looked like giant tombstones against the starry night sky. As their eyes adjusted to the gloom, details of the buildings emerged from the darkness. Orange creeper covered everything. The roads were covered with pink and brown scrub. Orange vines slithered across the road from one building to the next. The whole base looked infected. Bits of crumpled paper blew by on the wind. In the distance, they could see the faint orange glow of campfires. Stumpy's eyes locked on the fires. "Spragmites," he whispered.

"Good news." Karnage grabbed Stumpy's shoulder and gave him a shake. "The fires are on the west edge of the camp. The Godmaster Array is to the east. All we gotta do is stay quiet and lay low. Those Spragmites won't even know we're—"

The trunk exploded with an ear-splitting bang. The duffel bag flew out and twisted across the road.

"Sonofabitch!" Karnage exploded out of the car. He chased after the squirming bag and stamped a boot on it. He ripped open the zipper. Sydney's head flew out.

"You picked a hell of a time to wake up," Karnage hissed.

"Why?" Sydney said. "Because you haven't got us killed yet?"

A squiggly torrent of sound shot across them, shaking the windows in the cruiser.

Stumpy's head appeared out of the car, his eyes wide with fear. "Major?" He whispered.

Karnage jerked a thumb at the car. "Break out the supplies, Corporal. We're gearin' up."

Stumpy saluted and got out of the car.

"You're just going to get yourselves killed," Sydney said.

Karnage didn't answer. He walked to the car, and took the keys out of the ignition. He walked back to Sydney, and tossed them beside her.

"What's this?" Sydney asked.

"This is where we part company, Captain. From here on in, you're on your own." Karnage turned his back on her.

"That's it?" Sydney asked. "I'm free to go?"

"That's it," Karnage said. "Try and chase us down if you like. But somethin' tells me you're gonna want to steer clear o' this place."

"Aren't you going to at least untie me before you go?"

Karnage turned and smiled. "Give me a little credit here, Captain. You probably got yourself at least half untied already. I'd do you the honour of untying you myself, but I think it'd be better if me and Stumpy were well clear o' here when that happens. Somethin' tells me the blast radius is gonna be pretty big."

Sydney smirked. "Maybe you're not quite as crazy as they say you are."

A violent torrent of squiggly sound hurtled across the landscape.

Karnage's face darkened. "Don't be so sure." He saluted. "It's been an honour, Captain."

He walked back to Stumpy. Stumpy had arranged their equipment in rows on the ground. Karnage surveyed the collection of goober rifles and grenades laid out before them. All of it was non-lethal. He picked up a goober grenade. Dabby Tabby's grinning face had been etched into its surface. Karnage hefted it in his hand. *Not even a goddamn pistol.*

"Pack light, Corporal." Karnage clipped the grenade to his belt. "We've got to stay mobile. Get in, get out. We fix up the Godmaster Array, find out what those alien bastards are up to, then get the hell out. Is that clear?"

"Sir, yes, sir!"

"All right, let's move out."

CHAPTER SIX

They slipped through the front gates into the camp. Each of them had a row of goober grenades clipped to his belt and a goober rifle slung over his shoulder.

Karnage led Stumpy through the camp towards the massive crater that housed the Godmaster Array. As they approached, the strange desert foliage grew thicker and thicker. The entire outer surface of the crater was covered in orange creeper and pinkstink. As they climbed the surface of the crater, they crushed the vegetation. Brown juice squirted out that stank of gasoline and cigarettes. The smell reminded Karnage of the smoke from the hoverballs.

They pulled themselves onto the rough lip of the crater. Below them was the Godmaster Array. The mirrored dishes spiralled out from the centre of the crater in a pixelated whorl, reflecting the night sky.

"So far, so good." Karnage pointed across the crater to a row of squat buildings glowing in the moonlight. "Control station's over there."

Another squiggling torrent of sound slammed into them, threatening to blow them off the lip of the crater and into the dishes below. The faint sound of cheering echoed in the distance. Stumpy froze in his tracks, staring out at the campfires, eyes wide with fear. Karnage grabbed him by the shoulder and shook him. "Corporal? Corporal, look at me."

Stumpy tore his gaze away from the campfires and looked at Karnage. His face was so white it glowed as brightly as the Godmaster Array.

"Corporal, we are within a hair's breadth of our goal. Don't go AWOL on me now. Are you still with me, soldier?"

Stumpy blinked, and swallowed hard. He nodded. "Yes, sir."

"That's the spirit, soldier. Let's move out."

They skulked around the perimeter—laying low to avoid being

backlit by moonlight—and approached the command centre. The orange creeper grew thick on its walls. Karnage brushed it aside and saw the windows underneath were still intact. Karnage grinned. "Tempered bullet-proof glass. None of that consumer-grade stuff like down below."

Karnage felt along the wall until he found the door. Buried under a tangle of creeper was a rusted padlock that still held the door firmly shut. Karnage placed the butt of his rifle against the padlock and waited for another blast of squiggly noise. When the noise hit, Karnage broke off the lock with the butt of his rifle. The sound of the metal snapping and his Sanity Patch buzzing was drowned out by the squiggling and cheering. Karnage pushed open the door. He and Stumpy snuck in.

Their eyes took a moment to adjust to the deeper dark of the command centre. Papers were piled in crisp stacks on desks. Chairs were uniformly tucked in to workstations as if they were still on duty, patiently waiting for a command. Not a scrap of paper was out of place. Not a speck of dust anywhere.

Karnage grinned. "Whoever was the duty officer here ran a tight ship."

"Couldn't have been much tighter from the looks of things," Stumpy said. "You wouldn't guess this place was abandoned for twenty years."

"He was full-on military, right to the end." Karnage ran his fingers along the edge of a desk. *Wonder if they locked him up in a padded cell, too?*

Stumpy tried a switch. "No power," he said.

"Can't say I'm too surprised," Karnage said. "If I get you power, can you get this system up and running?"

Stumpy ran his fingers over one of the consoles. "Running? Hell, I can probably get it to do backflips."

"I'll settle for a good steady jog," Karnage replied. "I'll try the emergency generators. See if they got any juice left in 'em. The second you get power, you get this thing up and running. Don't wait for me. And Corporal?"

"Yes, sir?"

"Barricade this door when I leave. No matter what happens—no matter what you hear goin' on outside—you stay put. Do not open that door for anyone 'less they give you the password."

"What's the password, sir?"

"Mayhem."

Stumpy saluted. "Won't open it until I hear the password."

Karnage returned the salute. "Good luck, Corporal."

"You, too, sir."

Karnage slipped outside. He heard the scrape of desks being pushed up against the door as Stumpy barricaded himself in.

The Godmaster Array glowed brightly before him, returning diffused moonlight heavenward. Karnage unholstered his goober gun and stared fiercely at the orange fires burning brightly in the distance.

He hadn't had the heart to tell Stumpy the generators were deep in the Spragmite encampment.

MK#5: PRAY FOR KARNAGE

CHAPTER ONE

Karnage crawled over a gnarled orange hedge at the base of the crater. The hedge contained the remains of a once mighty electrified fence topped with razor wire. It had long ago lost its battle against the invading onslaught of creeper. Karnage hoped he would fare better against the Spragmites.

He found himself facing a sea of cookie-cutter townhouses buried in orange creeper. He was on the outskirts of Camp Bailey's housing district.

Karnage felt a momentary pang of yearning. He wanted to find his old barracks. To check out the dumpsters behind the Mess where he and his buddies used to hide from annoyed drill sergeants and furious MPs. The military had been a lark back then. Duty something to be shirked. Work to be skirted at all costs. That was before they had been shipped out. Before their first big foray into . . .

The War!

Fresh-faced recruits bein' shoved into that meat grinder of death. Black smoke chokin' your throat and burnin' your eyes. Voices screamin' all around you, prayin' to gods of every stripe, shape, and colour. Nothin' answerin' those prayers but the hot spray of bullets and explosive death. And when the smoke cleared, the field was thick with charred, twisted bodies. Nothing moved. Nothing moaned. Nothing left alive. Nothing but a single, snivelling recruit hiding under his buddies' corpses. A cowardly little bastard who hadn't had the guts to fire one single shot.

And then the bodies were pulled away, and that recruit found himself staring into the face of Uncle Stanley himself! An enemy officer—with uniform so crisp, you could cut yourself on the crease of his pants—staring down at him through sightless, unseeing driving glasses. Big black pits of shine that reflected nothing but the gore around him, and the frightened face of that chickenshit little private. The officer aimed his pistol at the private's face, and squeezed the trigger—

—and nothing happened! No roar. No searing flash followed by pain, coldness, and death. Nothing but the tiniest click. The officer looked at his pistol, then at the recruit. The officer's lips parted, exposing jagged yellow teeth and a voice like crushed gravel poured out: "Looks like today's your lucky day, kid."

And he turned and walked away! Left that chickenshit little recruit to wallow in the rot and the filth, huggin' his knees to his chest, gazing out at the churned mass of blackened, twisted corpses, vowin' it would never be like this again never again never again never again—

The hallucination shattered as Karnage's hands found a wall to slam his head into. His Sanity Patch buzzed.

"Warning. Sanity Level upgraded to Sandy Dreams. Please refrain from violent behaviour."

Karnage scowled. He had barely begun, and was already burning through Sanity Levels. He had to keep a better handle on things. Too much was at stake. Too many lives were at risk. *Cookie. Velasquez. Heckler. Koch. And now Stumpy, too.* They were all counting on him. He wouldn't let them down. Not this time.

Not ever again.

"You all right, buddy?"

Karnage looked up. Two men stood before him. The one who spoke was moving towards him. He wore a tuxedo jacket over a flower print dress. The other wore a shirt made of orange creeper with a pinkstink boutonniere. He held a thin slab of smooth plastic in his hands. Images flickered across its back, lighting the man's frightened, bulbous eyes. "Carlos!"

The one moving towards Karnage turned and looked at his companion. He pointed at the plastic slab. "Why are you shooting my feet?"

"Carlos, look at—"

Carlos pointed to his face. "Here, Simon. Shoot here. I can't use this if all you get is my ass."

"But—"

Carlos moved back to Simon and grabbed his hands. He lifted the tablet so it pointed at Karnage. There was a lens on its front in the shape of a D.

Carlos moved back beside Karnage. "Am I in the shot?"

"Yes, but—"

"Good. Now shut up." Carlos turned towards Karnage, but kept his face pointed at the camera. This meant he was only looking at Karnage with one eye. "Are you all right? You sounded like you needed help."

"Carlos!" Simon hissed.

Carlos kept his grinning face on Karnage. He hissed at Simon through his teeth. "What?"

Simon pointed at Karnage. "His clothes, Carlos. Look at his clothes!"

Carlos looked at the open jacket of Karnage's police uniform, the leather straps of his straitjacket just visible underneath. Before Carlos could register the string of goober grenades on his belt, Karnage struck out with his fist and caught Carlos across the jaw. Carlos staggered backwards and fell to the ground and stayed there. Karnage's neck buzzed.

"Warning. Sanity Patch upgraded to Lemon Breeze. Please refrain from violent behaviour."

Karnage turned his attention to Simon. Simon stood frozen in place, his eyes glued to the tablet's screen. The lens still pointed at Karnage, albeit shakily. Karnage walked towards Simon. Simon stared at the screen, his hands shaking more and more violently with Karnage's every step. Karnage pulled the tablet out of Simon's hands. Simon looked up into Karnage's face. His eyes rolled into the back of his head, and he fell to the ground.

Karnage dragged the two men into the nearest townhouse. He stripped Carlos of his clothes, stuffed the unconscious men into a closet, and barricaded the door. Karnage threw the police jacket aside. He pulled the dress over his head. It neatly covered his belt of goober grenades. He slipped on the tuxedo jacket. It just covered his goober rifle. He took another look at Simon's camera. The glossy plastic was covered in smudges and scratches. There was a Dabney

Corporation logo engraved into its side. He flipped it over, and was greeted with a shot of his feet. A tiny red dot flashed in the corner. He couldn't figure out how to turn it off. He tucked the tablet into his jacket, and headed into the Spragmite compound.

CHAPTER TWO

Creeper and pinkstink hung between lampposts like garlands. Hand-cranked lanterns hung from the creeper, their blue LED glow bobbed and swayed in the wind like drunken fireflies. Pink and orange topiary worms dotted the front yards of the derelict houses.

People stood around bonfires in the streets, talking and laughing. Some toasted skewered lizards and bits of squiggly root over the fires. Everyone was dressed in the same haphazard improvised fashion as Carlos and Simon. Many of them carried D tablets similar to Simon's. They were unabashedly recording any and all of the festivities. Seeing this, Karnage fished his D tablet out of his pocket, and used it to observe his surroundings. Occasionally someone would wave to him through the viewfinder, but beyond that, he was invisible.

A squiggly screech pierced the air. Everyone stopped what they were doing, except those with cameras. Their lenses searched back and forth, as if looking for the source of the noise. Karnage found himself doing the same.

A young boy came running down the street. "The Worm is coming! The Worm is coming!"

The hairs on Karnage's neck stood up. He turned his camera towards the end of the street.

Another screech poured across the compound. It was followed by a chorus of drums. Their deep, pulsing beat throbbed through the air. People thronged to the edges of the street, staring eagerly into the distance. Karnage joined the throng. People happily moved out of his way when they saw his camera. He joined the other shooters at the front of the pack.

Flickering lights and dancing shadows played across the street in the distance. An enormous shadow writhed into view, making giant squiggling patterns against the surrounding houses. Dancers twirling flaming batons moved in time with the drums and the wriggling shadows on the walls. Their writhing caused the flames to write in huge, angled squiggles. The shadows grew closer, and finally, the beast emerged from the darkness.

The Worm was the size of a bus, writhing and wriggling as it squiggled down the street. A single horn protruded from its head, wobbling erratically with each thrust. The light from the flames reflected off the body in long, fluid sparkles. It was as if the beast was covered in tinsel. And as it grew closer, Karnage realized that it was.

Dark shadows of human feet could be seen just under The Worm's body. A whorl of cardboard teeth spun inside the worm's open mouth as if on casters. Circling the beast was a man on a bicycle that looked like the bastard child of a tuba and slide whistle. A giant piston bolted to the rear tire ran into what looked like a bagpipe bag attached to the end of a giant tuba bell. The rider blew into a mouthpiece mounted above the handlebars. An oscillating squeal blasted out of the tuba bell: the same damn noise Karnage had heard earlier.

Karnage nearly spat in disgust. Is this what it was all about? No aliens? No worms? Just a giant parade float and a mutant slide whistle?

A jagged noise tore through the crowd that threatened to rip the pavement from the road. The worm dancers lost their balance. The slide whistle cycle went crashing to the ground. A hushed silence fell over the crowd. Even the crackle of the bonfires seemed to die down.

A voice from the crowd shouted, "Spragmos has come!"

The crowd broke out into a cheer. The dancers jumped back into their dance, more energized than before. The parade picked up its pace, and the crowd fell in behind and followed them. Karnage stayed with the throng. For better or worse, they were heading in the right direction: toward the emergency generators.

CHAPTER THREE

At the heart of Camp Bailey was the Weapons Testing Facility: an exact replica of the Godmaster Crater. This artificial canyon was the military's testing facility for the latest in Spragmos Industries's military-grade weapons, hardware, and explosives. It had led to the facility being known as the WTF or the What-The-Fuck, as in "What the fuck was *that?!*"

Orange creeper now grew from the top of the WTF. It had been neatly trimmed back to expose the mile-high SPRAGMOS lettering etched into the mountain's side. Giant bonfires illuminated the lettering from below. Karnage was overwhelmed by its primal majesty. If he hadn't known about the WTF's history, he would have sworn it was built to be a temple.

As they approached the WTF, people broke out into spontaneous song. To Karnage's ears, the lyrics sounded like gibberish, punctuated with repetitive chants of "The Worm is the word! The Worm is the word!" followed with more gibberish. It had all the annoying catchiness of an ad jingle. Karnage caught himself humming along at one point. He vowed in that moment to track down whoever wrote it and knock out every one of their teeth before breaking a number of specially selected bones in their body. He stopped himself from determining exactly how many and which ones before he set off his Sanity Patch.

The creeper on the buildings grew thicker as they approached. The buildings here looked like little more than giant hills of creeper and pinkstink. He felt like he was tracing the vegetation upriver to its source. Was it alien in nature? Or a military experiment gone wrong? He didn't know. The only thing he knew for sure was how much it stank. It smelled like a giant mountain of burning metal, plastic, and tar.

The creeper was trimmed back in a wide semi-circle around the entrance of the WTF. The giant bonfires framed its massive doors.

As the crowd approached, the doors opened, and the parade made its way inside.

Just beyond the bonfires, Karnage saw the emergency generator building. It was adorned with pinkstink garlands. A pair of sombre men stood outside the doors, wearing long dresses and leis made of pinkstink and creeper. They carried what looked like shepherd's hooks with stylized worms on the ends. Karnage pegged them for priests. A long line of Spragmites were lined up outside the building. As people made it to the front of the line, they would kneel before the priest. The priest would place a hand on their heads, mumble something, hand them a slip of paper, then let them into the generator building. After a few minutes, the person would emerge, and the next would be allowed in.

Karnage decided his best bet to get inside was to get in line and wait his turn. He took a place at the end of the line. The woman in front of him was reading a book. The front cover showed a blue-haired man wearing a bowler hat stroking his chin. The title read, "Awaken The Worm Within." The woman looked up from her book at Karnage, and smiled.

"Hello," she said.

Karnage gave her his best imitation of a smile. "Hello."

She cocked her head. "I haven't seen you here before."

"Funny. I was thinkin' the same about you."

She gave a sheepish grin. "True enough. I mostly come on Arbiter's Day. I find the line is just too long otherwise. I know we're supposed to come more often than that, but . . . well, you won't tell anyone, will you?"

Karnage winked. "Won't tell a soul."

"Thanks." The woman extended her hand. "I'm Reshmi."

"John," Karnage said. He shook her hand.

"How long have you been following The Worm?"

Karnage shrugged. "A while now. You?"

"Only a few months. But it's really opened my eyes to how things work, you know?" She held up the book. "I used to be so confused about things, but now . . ."

"It just all kinda falls into place, doesn't it?"

Reshmi beamed. "Yes! Exactly!"

They were now at the front of the line. Reshmi knelt in front of the priest. The priest placed a hand on her head. "Are you ready to awaken The Worm within, child?"

"I am, Presbyter."

The priest nodded, and handed her the slip of paper. "Go with Spragmos, child."

Reshmi winked at Karnage. "See you later."

Karnage gave her a nod and a smile. Reshmi disappeared inside. The priest gave a disapproving gaze to the swell in Karnage's crotch. Karnage adjusted the material to hide the bulge of the goober grenade on his belt.

"May The Worm be with you, Prez Bitter," Karnage said.

"And also with you," the priest said. He looked ready to say something else, but Reshmi reappeared.

"Fancy seeing you again so soon," Karnage said.

Reshmi smiled. "I was going to go check out the Finale." She gestured towards the WTF. "Would you like to join me?"

Karnage smiled. "I wouldn't miss it."

"Great!" Reshmi did her best to look unexcited, failing miserably. "I'll just be waiting out here, then."

The priest cleared his throat. Karnage took the hint and got on his knees, careful to keep his goober rifle from poking out from the top of his jacket. The priest placed his hand on Karnage's head. "Are you ready to awaken The Worm within, child?"

"I am, Prez Bitter."

The priest handed Karnage a slip of paper. "Go with Spragmos, child."

Karnage stood and winked at Reshmi. "I'll try not to be too long." Reshmi did her best not to beam, and Karnage did his best to ignore the priest's disapproving gaze as he slipped into the generator building, and shut the door.

CHAPTER FOUR

Dried pinkstink and creeper hung from the doorway and ceiling. Karnage pushed through, and found himself in the main generator room. Pinkstink and creeper were stuck to everything. A table sat in the middle of the room, lit with candles. An altar on the table cradled a toolbox wrapped in vines of creeper. A cup of pencils sat in front of the altar. The generators themselves were jampacked with bits of crumpled paper. Karnage pulled out one of the papers and uncrumpled it. A child-like scrawl had written, "Great Spragmos, help me to awaken The Worm within." He grabbed another one. "Guide me to the True Path." And another. "Show us The Light."

You want light? Karnage crumpled the papers into a ball. *I'll show you light.*

He tore off his tuxedo jacket and whipped off his dress. He blew out the candles and cleared the table with a sweep of his arm. He jammed the table under the doorknob. Ripping open the toolbox, he found some duct tape and coiled wire. He slapped a goober grenade against the door frame and taped it in place. He looped the wire around the doorknob and tied it to the grenade's pin. He made sure the wire was taut, then turned his attention to the generators.

Karnage plucked the paper from the turbines. He tried turning the turbine on each generator. They were all seized except one. It turned with much effort and loud groans of complaint.

There was a knock at the door. "Is everything all right in there, child?"

"Everything's fine, Prez Bitter." Karnage worked the turbine back and forth until it turned freely. "Just working out what I'm gonna say."

"Speak from the heart, child."

"Will do, Prez Bitter!" Karnage grabbed the gas can from the altar. It was still full. He poured it into the generator, hoping these Spragmites knew the value of a good fuel stabilizer. Karnage said a little prayer of his own—"You better work, you dirty monkeyfucker"—and yanked the starter cord.

The engine gave a surprised gasp, belched out a plume of smoke, and promptly died.

The doorknob turned and rattled. The priest called to Karnage through the door. "What's going on in there, child?"

"Just conferrin' with Spragmos." Karnage gave the starter cord another yank. "Work, you sonofabitch!" Another gasp, another belch, another plume of smoke, then once again, death.

The banging on the door grew more urgent and the priest's shouts grew louder. Karnage ignored them. He pulled again and again on the cord. The engine grew louder and noisier each time. The banging on the door shook the table, threatening to loosen it from under the doorknob. Karnage gave one final yank on the cord, and the generator roared to life.

The room quickly filled with generator exhaust. Something wasn't venting properly, but Karnage didn't care. Light poured in through the windows, piercing the smoke in thick prismatic shafts.

The table finally gave way, and the door burst open. A pair of priests stood agape in the room. "What in the name of Spragmos—AAH!" The goober grenade went off. Pink blossoms of goober engulfed the shrieking priests and filled the doorway.

Karnage caught a glimpse of a shepherd's hook outside the window. It reared back and smashed the glass. Karnage unholstered his goober rifle and fired, filling the frame with fast-hardening goober.

"Warning. Sanity Level upgraded to Citrus Blast. Please—"

Karnage turned to the last remaining window and threw himself through it. He landed in a circle of shattered glass and wood, his Sanity Patch buzzing.

"Sanity Level upgraded to Peachy Keen. Please—"

Karnage levelled the goober gun at the window and fired. The frame filled with goober, blocking the last entrance to the generators.

"Sanity Level upgraded to Tangy Orange. Please—"

"John!"

Karnage looked up. Reshmi was running towards him. "What's going—" Karnage levelled his rifle at Reshmi and fired. She flew back with a cry and disappeared in an expanding ball of goober. Karnage's neck buzzed.

"Sanity Level upgraded to Sharp Cheddar. Please refrain from violent behaviour."

Karnage cursed himself. He was burning through his Sanity Levels too quickly! He had to make each one of them count. *Keep the Spragmites busy. Lead 'em away from the generators. Buy Stumpy time!*

Karnage ran out from behind the building. The doors to the WTF were open. Spragmites were pouring out. They caught sight of Karnage, and charged towards him. Karnage turned in the other direction. Spragmites poured out from behind and within other buildings. It was as if the creeper was giving birth to a raging, angry mob. They snarled, growled, roared.

Karnage roared back. He lobbed a triad of goober grenades in a circle around him. Mountains of goober swelled up, hemming him in, but keeping the Spragmites at bay. All the while, his Sanity Patch rocketed up the Sanity Levels: Coral Essence, Frosty Pink, Strawberry Shortcake—

He was done.

Karnage dropped the rifle and braced himself as the first of the Spragmites swarmed over the peaks of goober and threw himself at Karnage. Karnage sidestepped out of the way, only to catch a second Spragmite in his arms. Karnage staggered back under the weight, and tripped over a fallen Spragmite behind him. More Spragmites piled on top of him as they continued to pour down over the mountains of goober. Karnage quickly disappeared under the pile as more and more cultists threw themselves on. The air was forced from his lungs as the pile grew heavier. The last of his oxygen burned out of his system. The world grew dark. *Get the job done, Stumpy! Get the job done!*

Karnage blacked out.

CHAPTER FIVE

Karnage woke in Camp Bailey's stockade. Shafts of yellow light poured in through the windows. He looked outside and saw floodlights illuminating the streets and buildings. Far in the distance, he could hear the angry muttering of the generator still cranking out the juice. Karnage smiled. *It's all up to you now, Stumpy.*

"Good. I see you're finally awake."

Karnage turned around. There in the cell beside his was a woman dressed in a Hawaiian shirt and fancy cocktail dress. Despite the ludicrous contrast between the shirt and the dress, somehow she made it work. Her brown eyes stayed fixed on the book in her lap. She spoke without looking at him.

"There's a D-pad in the wall just to your right that is watching our every move. They keep the sound turned off in here, but I suggest you show far less interest in me, lest they decide to move you and ruin your only chance of escape."

From the corner of his eye, Karnage saw the familiar shape of a D-shaped lens hanging from the wall. He lay back in his bed and looked out the window.

"You can take direction," she said. "Good. I take it we have you to thank for all this lovely electricity?"

"You might."

She sighed, and flipped a page in her book. "My dear Captain, you have, at most, an hour to live. If you want to have any chance of leaving this complex alive, then I suggest you be as straight with me as possible. You are the gentleman who fired up the generators, yes?"

"Yes."

"Good. I offer my congratulations to you, Captain. Melvern had always intended to start up those generators himself. It's a shame he never figured out how to get them to work. He must be very angry with you."

"Who's Melvern?"

She held up her book, revealing it to be another copy of *Awaken The Worm Within*. She discretely pointed to the blue-haired man on the cover. "He prefers to be referred to as the High Prophet. No doubt you've seen his pudgy face floating around the compound."

Loud squiggling screeches rattled the bars, followed by a woman's terrified scream in the distance. Karnage sat up in his bunk. "What was that?"

She didn't bother to look up. "That is the fate that awaits you unless you listen to me very carefully."

"Was that The Worm?"

"Yes."

Karnage sprang to the window. "I've got to get near that thing!"

"I'm beginning to see why you are wearing the remains of a straitjacket. Do you have a death wish, Captain? If not, then please sit down. You are drawing attention to yourself again."

Karnage sat down. "Why do you keep calling me 'Captain'?"

"Why wouldn't I call you 'Captain?' You're ex-military, aren't you?"

Karnage scowled. "What the hell makes you think I'm ex-military?"

The woman sighed. "There's that poker face again. Let's go over the facts, shall we? You successfully infiltrated this camp without detection. With very little effort, you were able to get the emergency generators up and running. You are obviously very familiar with the layout of this complex and the technology herein. Not to mention the havoc you caused before being captured. Suffice to say, Captain, you could not have announced your military credentials any louder if you had ridden into this compound on a white horse wearing full dress uniform while rattling your sabre. Does that satisfy your curiosity?"

"I suppose it does."

"Good. As you learn more about me, Captain, you will find that I am quite clever. It is only through the most embarrassing series of events that I have ended up in this prison. This is, however, quite fortunate for you, as I am the only person in this compound who can get you out of here alive."

"And why is that?"

"Up until a few months ago, I was the High Priestess of the Church of Spragmos. You, however, may call me Tristan."

"A pleasure to make your acquaintance."

"You're a terrible liar. I don't blame you, though. I wouldn't be pleased to make anyone's acquaintance in here, either."

"How are you going to help me escape?"

"I helped Melvern build this religion from the ground up. We used to rule it side-by-side until he got it into his deluded little head that I was planning to depose him and take control of it for myself."

"Were you?"

"Of course. And I cannot tell you how put out I am that he successfully outmanoeuvred me. If I believed in Fate, I would say she had a hand in this. Fortunately, I do not. Melvern merely got lucky. But now that you're here, his luck is about to change."

"Why? What's so special about me?"

"You, my good Captain, are about to become the Messiah."

CHAPTER SIX

Tristan read from her book. "'And he who has truly heard The Word shall step forward and show us The Light. The Guiding Light which will show us The True Path. The True Path to Awaken The Worm Within.' Et cetera. Ad nauseam. It goes on for quite a while, but I think you get the gist of things."

"What does that have to do with me?"

"Have a look outside, Captain. You have brought us The Light."

Karnage looked out at the floodlights shining in. "That is The Light?"

"Yes."

"You sure about that?"

"Of course I'm sure. I helped write this book, you know. Why else do we call the generator building The Temple of Light?"

"But why didn't anyone else figure it out? How come nobody else fixed it first?"

"My dear Captain, you give these people far too much credit. They're mindless simpletons, easily led around by their noses. Leave them to fend for themselves, and they'll wander aimlessly, like cows grazing in a field."

There was another squiggly screech, followed by a scream.

"We are running out of time," Tristan said. "You will be summoned soon. When you are brought before Melvern, announce that you are the Lightbringer at the earliest possible moment. Once you have been proclaimed the Lightbringer, you will declare me as your High Priestess."

"Won't Melvern object?"

"My dear Captain, Messiah trumps High Prophet every time. Melvern won't know what hit him. Just remember to go in there and give a good performance. This will be broadcast all across the compound. You don't have quite the right look for television. They prefer them younger, and much more charismatic, but it can't be helped. You do have a sort of sad quality about the eyes when you're not trying to look so angry. Try to play that up a bit. You're the underdog in this production. And everybody loves an underdog."

"Anything else?"

"Yes. No matter what happens, no matter what they say to you, you must remain calm. And stay on message. You are the Lightbringer. You have brought the Light. If you repeat it often enough, it becomes true. That is the magic of television. But only if you don't lose your temper. No one likes an angry monkey. Can you do that?"

"I'll try."

"That's all I can ask of you, then. They'll be coming for you soon. Good luck, Captain."

"It's Major," Karnage said.

Tristan let slip a small smile. "Is it now? Well then. Good luck, Major."

CHAPTER SEVEN

They took Karnage to the observation deck of the WTF. Panoramic windows offered a wide view of the pock-marked ground in the canyon below. Remnants of military vehicles lay strewn amidst hillocks of churned earth. A throne stood upon the dais in front of the central window. The room was filled with Spragmites holding D-pads pointed at Karnage. Karnage caught sight of a shock of blue hair off to one side. It was Melvern.

Melvern stood beside a Spragmite holding a microphone who was interviewing him intensely. His face was broadcast on all of the D-Pads hung around the room. He and the interviewer stood in front of a green screen. The monitors around the deck showed them standing in the middle of the testing grounds.

"High Prophet, it has been said that this is our strongest slate of competitors yet. Would you agree?" The interviewer thrust the microphone at Melvern.

Melvern wore a heavy layer of bronze foundation and thick black eyeliner. He looked like a trampy hobo in person, but on the screens behind him, he looked like a golden god. Melvern looked directly into the lens, his gaze sucking in the viewer on the multiple screens. "Miki, I've been judging this competition since its inception, and I can say without a doubt that this is the strongest, brightest, most talented slate of candidates we have ever seen. I will be very surprised if the Arbiter doesn't find someone who is Worthy this year."

"Do you have any favourites among this year's candidates?"

The High Prophet laughed. "Honestly, it doesn't matter what I think at this point. It's all up to the Arbiter now. As I said, these are all worthy candidates, and if one of them isn't picked I will truly be surprised." At this point, he took an exaggerated pause and then shrugged. "But stranger things have happened. The opinions of people like you and I no longer matter. It is now in the hands of The

Worm, and as you know . . ." He looked directly into the camera, his blue eyes sparkling against the black eyeliner. He gestured towards the screen with a single knuckle. ". . . The Worm is The Word."

Miki nodded solemnly. "Mama-oo-pow-pow. Truer words were never spoken. I know you have business to attend to, so thank you for taking the time to speak with us today, High Prophet."

"Thank you, Miki. It's been a pleasure. May The Worm be with you."

"And also with you, High Prophet. Back to you in the studio, Paco."

The view switched to a Spragmite standing by the throne that Karnage stood in front of. "Thanks, Miki. I'm here in the High Prophet's chamber where he is about to pronounce judgement on the heretic who was caught rampaging through the compound."

Paco read off a long litany of crimes Karnage stood accused of while the monitors cut to footage taken from Simon's D-Pad. Karnage watched as he took down Carlos with a single punch and walked towards the camera in slow motion. The footage ended with a distorted close up on Karnage's grimacing face. It dissolved to a live shot of Karnage's face looking at the monitor. The scrolling caption under his face read "HEATHEN BROUGHT TO JUSTICE – LIVE!" Karnage tried to heed Tristan's advice and did his best to look sad.

Melvern was climbing the dais while Paco provided commentary. "The High Prophet is just ascending to the throne now, Miki. We should be getting a judgement in the next couple of minutes."

The High Prophet stood before the cameras and raised his arms as if asking for silence. After waiting a beat, he turned with a flourish to Karnage.

"So," he said. "You are the heathen."

"So," Karnage said. "You're Melvern."

There were several gasps from the crowd. The captions on the monitors changed to read "HEATHEN BLASPHEMES - LIVE!" A priest wearing a headset ran forward. He pointed a pen at Karnage. "You will refer to His Holiness as the High Prophet!"

The High Prophet stepped down and placed a hand on the priest's shoulder. "Gently now, Homski. Do not let him suppress your Inner Worm. Remember The Word."

Homski sighed and took a deep breath. "I'm sorry, your Holiness. I will seek guidance from my Inner Worm."

"As I knew you would." The High Prophet smiled warmly at Homski, then gently pushed him out of the shot. He turned to the crowd. "This savage has managed to break the majority of our most sacred laws. And in an incredibly short time frame." The High Prophet turned to Karnage. "That's quite an accomplishment, friend."

"I take pride in my work," Karnage said.

The High Prophet smiled. "And a sense of humour to boot." He turned grandly towards the cameras. "The Worm has sent us a true test with this one."

"Buddy, you don't know the half of it," Karnage said.

The High Prophet half-turned towards Karnage, ensuring the cameras still got a good shot of his face as he raised an eyebrow. "Oh? Then please, do tell."

Here goes. Karnage cleared his throat. He tried to make sure the cameras got his good side. As it turned out, he didn't have one. He gave up and blurted out, "I am the Lightbringer."

The crowd descended into chaos, everyone shouting at once. Faces went white. Others turned to panic. The captions under Karnage's face changed to "HEATHEN: LIGHTBRINGER? - LIVE!" Karnage fought the urge to grin. Tristan was right. He couldn't have asked for a better response if he had come running into the room naked with guns blazing.

The only one unfazed by Karnage's announcement was the High Prophet. He smiled serenely, blinked slowly, and sighed. He turned to the confused congregation and raised his hands. The crowd fell silent.

"Friend," he reached out an arm toward Karnage, "that is quite the claim. On the face of it, that is indeed what the scriptures would suggest. The Lightbringer is supposed to bring the Light, and you have brought light."

"That's right," Karnage said. "I'm the Lightbringer."

"Yes," the High Prophet nodded. "Of a sort."

"Of a sort?" Homski said. "Could that mean there's another meaning?"

The High Prophet bowed his head and shook it. "I would not presume to interpret The Word of Spragmos."

Homski covered his mouth. "Of course not, Your Holiness. I wouldn't dream—"

The High Prophet raised his hand. "I know, Homski. I know."

"I brought light," Karnage said. "That makes me the Lightbringer." A low murmuring rippled through the crowd like a pebble splashing the surface of a pond.

"Yes, you keep saying that," the High Prophet said.

Karnage said it again: "I'm the Lightbringer." The crowd's murmuring increased. The ripples grew stronger. Karnage wondered how big of a splash he could make.

The High Prophet shot Karnage a dangerous look. "Just because you continue to say it, that does not necessarily make it true."

"I'm the Lightbringer," Karnage said.

"Is he the Lightbringer?" Homski asked.

"It's not my place to say," the High Prophet said.

"I'm the Lightbringer," Karnage said.

A fist shot up at the back. "All hail the Lightbringer!"

"See?" Karnage said. "Lightbringer."

The High Prophet raised his hand. "We shouldn't rush to hasty conclusions."

"What should we do, Your Holiness?" Homski asked.

The High Prophet's face was serene, a stalwart rocky crag on which the crowd's waves had crashed to no effect. He remained calm. Tranquil. Unperturbed by the storm raging around him. He smiled into the nearest lens. "Why, we should do nothing."

Homski blinked. "Nothing?"

The caption on the screen changed to "HIGH PROPHET: 'DO NOTHING' - LIVE!"

The High Prophet shrugged. "There is nothing for us to do. We are but servants of The Word, and The Word . . ." The High Prophet leaned into the nearest D-Pad. His face filled the screens. His blue eyes sparkled. ". . . is The Worm."

The crowd bowed their heads and chanted, "Mama-oo-pow-pow."

"But I'm the Lightbringer," Karnage said. No one paid him any attention. They were too caught up in their *Mama-oo-pow-pow*s.

The screens changed to a two-shot of Karnage and the High Prophet. The caption underneath read "THE WORM IS THE WORD - LIVE!" The High Prophet placed a hand on Karnage's shoulder. He raised his other hand towards the congregation. "It is no coincidence he was sent to us on Arbiter's Day, my friends. This is all part of Spragmos's plan. The Heathen's claim will be tested by The Arbiter Himself!"

The crowd gasped. The screen caption changed: "HEATHEN: WORTHY? - LIVE!"

"But I'm the Lightbringer," Karnage said.

The High Prophet put an arm around Karnage. "So you keep saying. But we are mere mortal men. It is not our place to make these decisions. No, The Worm will decide." The High Prophet gestured towards the audience. "For The Worm is The Word. Mama-oo-pow-pow!"

"Mama-oo-pow-pow!" The crowd shouted.

The High Prophet grabbed Karnage's hand and shook it. "Congratulations, friend. You are heading for the Finale. Take him to the Green Room!"

The crowd cheered wildly as the guards led Karnage away.

The Green Room was an old fallout shelter deep in the bowels of the WTF. As far as Karnage could tell, there was nothing green about it. The walls were a dingy grey and a single LED lantern barely clung to life in the middle of the ceiling. A bench lay along the wall on one end of the room. On the other wall, a large D-pad displayed a steel double-door leading onto the testing grounds.

A young man sat on the bench, watching the screen raptly. Another lay motionless in a pool of blood on the floor. The man on the bench glared at Karnage as he entered the room. He sneered.

Karnage nodded. "Howdy."

The man ignored him. He turned his gaze back to the screen. The steel doors opened, and a young woman emerged from the darkness.

Miki's voice poured from the screen. "And now here's Stephanie Blyskosz, readying for her meeting with The Worm."

The doors shut behind Stephanie with a loud boom. She jumped, then put on a brave face. She waved to the stands. The crowd cheered.

Paco's voice joined Miki's. "Stephanie was our highest scoring female contestant this year, as well as the highest scoring on record."

A giant shadow overtook her. She looked up. Her eyes went wide and she screamed. The video cut out as an angry, squiggly screech shook the entire complex. As the screech faded, the video signal came back. Stephanie was gone. Nothing but churned earth remained at the base of the doors. The crowd cheered wildly.

The young man snorted and shook his head in disgust. "Pathetic."

The screen changed to show Miki and Paco standing on the arena floor, wearing headsets and holding clipboards.

"I think she just set a new record," Miki looked at his clipboard, "for the shortest-lived contestant, lasting for a grand total of five point six seconds."

"I thought for sure she'd last longer than that," Paco said.

"As I think everybody did. But, as always, The Worm has the

Final Word."

"Mama-oo-pow-pow, Miki. Mama-oo-pow-pow." Paco turned to the camera. "We'll be back after this."

The screen changed to a shot of Melvern staring into the distance, as his voice-over extolled the virtues of a life dedicated to Spragmos. The young man finally looked away from the screen. He stood and faced Karnage. A Worm-shaped nametag stuck to his shirt proclaimed him to be Ajay. He looked Karnage up and down. "So, you think you're Worthy, do you?"

"I'm the Lightbringer," Karnage said.

"Yes," Ajay nodded at the screen. "I saw your little performance."

Karnage nodded at the body near Ajay's feet. "What happened to your friend there?"

Ajay barely glanced at the corpse. "He dared to question The Word. And Spragmos judged him accordingly."

"Spragmos killed him?"

"No," Ajay said. "I did."

"Does that make you Spragmos?"

Ajay smiled. "You mock me."

"I do," Karnage said.

Ajay shook his head. "I pity you. Your Worm lies in a deep slumber. I can sense it. One wonders if it will ever waken."

"And your Worm's awake, is it?"

"It is. Thanks to Andy." Ajay looked down at the corpse and smiled. "Spragmos had a role for him to play. He was sent here to test my faith. To try and fill my head with lies and doubt. But I have passed this test. Walked through the fire as Spragmos decreed and emerged reborn. My Worm is truly awake now. And Spragmos will judge me Worthy." He puffed out his chest. "For I am the real Lightbringer."

"No you're not," Karnage said.

"I am," Ajay said.

"I'm the Lightbringer," Karnage said.

"No! I am the Lightbringer!"

"Just cuz you say it's so don't make it true," Karnage said.

Ajay bared his teeth. He looked as if he were about to attack Karnage. Karnage hoped he would.

The door to the Green Room opened behind them. Homski stuck his head into the room. "Ajay? It is your time."

Ajay closed his eyes and let out a deep breath. He opened his eyes and smiled at Karnage. "You are not Worthy. Spragmos calls for me now. I go to become one with The Worm. And once He has judged me Worthy, it will be your turn to meet your fate."

Ajay turned and left. The door slammed shut behind him.

Karnage had barely sat down before the door opened again and Tristan sashayed into the room.

"Oh good, you're still here," she said.

Karnage sprang to his feet. "How the hell did you get in here?"

"Keep your voice down," Tristan hissed. "If I'm caught in here, it's the end for us both."

"As opposed to just me?"

"What ever are you talking about?"

"Do I look like a Messiah to you? Your plan didn't work. Melvern saw right through it!"

"On the contrary," Tristan said. "He played right into it."

Karnage scowled. "What do you mean he played right into it?"

Tristan looked at him and blinked. "You mean you didn't think I knew this would happen?"

"Of course I didn't think that! What the hell was I supposed to think?!"

"Admittedly, that was exactly what you were supposed to think. But once things didn't go as planned, I thought for sure you would have assumed that I was playing a deeper, more Machiavellian game here. Frankly, my good Major, I'm a little disappointed in you."

"Disappointed in me?! Goddammit, I thought you were bein' straight with me!"

"I was straight with you. I said that so long as you do as I tell you, you will make it out of this alive. You're still alive, aren't you? Have some faith, Major."

"Faith?! You set me up!"

"I did nothing of the sort."

"You could have warned me this was gonna happen."

"And risk compromising your performance? I think not."

"My performance?!"

"The camera doesn't lie, Major. I needed to ensure you were authentic. And what better way to ensure an authentic performance than if you are simply *being* authentic. That Melvern is a snake. If I had told you the entire plan, he would have sensed something was up right from the start, and you would have ended up as worm food."

"It sounds like they're gonna make worm food outta me anyway!"

"Ah, but the difference is context, my good Major. Before, you were just worm food. Now, you are worm food with upward mobility! You have now been declared Worthy. That makes you a serious contender for Melvern's job. All you have to do is defeat The Worm, and Melvern will have no choice but to accept you as the Lightbringer."

"And how the hell do I defeat The Worm?"

Tristan smiled. "My dear Major, have you never wondered why Melvern has not fed me to The Worm? He's afraid that I've discovered his secret. That I know how to defeat The Worm."

"And do you?"

"Of course I do. We wouldn't be here if I didn't. Honestly, Major, I had you pegged for a better strategist than this. Do try to keep up, please."

"Fine. How do I defeat The Worm?"

"Ah," Tristan smiled. "Killing The Worm is both simple and complex. You must break off its horn."

"That's it? That's all it takes?"

"Trust me. It's enough."

"What's the catch?"

"The Worm is big."

"Okay."

"I mean big."

"Okay."

"Really, really big."

"I get the picture."

"No," Tristan said. "You don't."

The screen above them changed to show Miki and Paco back in the arena. "Welcome back to Arbiter's Day, folks. We're coming to the end of the Finale, and have we ever saved the best for last."

"We just got word that Andy Rudyk passed peacefully while waiting in the Green Room."

"Apparently the mighty Spragmos was keen to ensure our Top Ten stayed a Top Ten, Paco."

"Papa-oo-mow-mow, Miki. Papa-oo-mow-mow."

The shot changed to show the arena. The doors opened, and Ajay emerged from the darkness.

"And now here's audience favourite, Ajay Joseph entering the ring."

The doors slammed shut behind him. He didn't even flinch.

"No one has ever scored as highly as Ajay did in the preliminaries, Miki."

He turned to the crowd and threw his fists into the air.

"Listen to those fans. The crowd really loves him."

A shadow loomed up over him. A squiggly screech pierced the monitor's speakers, and shook the arena right down to the Green Room. The monitor screeched out, and when it came back again, Ajay was gone: nothing but a greasy smear left to mark where he had been. The crowd let out a gasp, then a cheer.

The shot changed to Paco and Miki again. They were smiling gleefully.

"Looks like Spragmos begged to differ. What was the final time on that, Miki?"

"Three point seven seconds. That's a record all right, but not quite the record any of us expected."

"The Worm has had the Final Say, and that Final Say is nay."

"Mama-oo-pow-pow, Paco. Mama-oo-pow-pow."

"Looks like Ajay's now one with The Worm," Karnage said.

"No he isn't," Tristan said. "He's just dead. Try not to follow his lead."

"I'll do my best," Karnage said.

CHAPTER NINE

Homski and a pair of sentries led Karnage from the Green Room into a giant antechamber. A pair of massive metal doors stood before them. Karnage could feel a slight breeze coming through the crack. There was a toxic smell to the air reminiscent of creeper and pinkstink. Karnage wondered if it was the plants or The Worm. *Guess I'll find out soon enough.* He cracked his knuckles.

Homski studied Karnage from the corner of his eye. "Is it true you are the Lightbringer?"

"I am," Karnage said.

"The High Prophet thinks you are a fraud," Homski said.

"And what do you think?"

Homski furrowed his brow a moment, then shook his head. "It matters not what I think. Spragmos will show the way. The Worm is The Word."

"Mama-oo-pow-pow," Karnage said.

Homski shot him a look. A voice crackled over Homski's headset. Homski nodded and turned to Karnage. "You will enter the arena. There is a spot marked with an X. You will stand on it, and wait for the High Prophet to finish his speech. Only then will you be allowed to face the Arbiter."

"And if I don't?"

"Then once Spragmos is done with you, you will have to face the technical director."

Homski pulled a switch. The doors swung open. The orange light of the rising sun blinded Karnage. Once his eyes adjusted, he stepped through. The door slammed shut behind him.

A vast wasteland of pockmarked earth opened before him. The ground bore the scars of a thousand and one weapons tests: blast craters and blackened earth stretched out in all directions. Bits of old military hardware were strewn everywhere. Massive trails of freshly churned earth crisscrossed in all directions.

Mile-high concrete walls fenced him in on all sides. Lines of observation decks wound around the walls of the canyon like a giant corkscrew. Thousands of faces pressed against the glass. Tens of thousands of D-shaped lenses flashed and flickered in the morning sunshine.

A crude X had been scratched on the dirt in front of him. Karnage stood on it. The High Prophet's voice echoed out from every wall as it was broadcast from every D-pad in the compound.

"There are those who say the end of the world is upon us. That our time upon this scorched earth is fast coming to an end. And they are right. This world is dying. Listen closely, and you can hear it gasp its last shallow breaths.

"But all is not lost! For as the Scriptures say, this is not The End Time. This is the Time For A New Beginning!"

The crowd cheered. The High Prophet waited for the cheering to die down, then continued. "Spragmos has shown us The Way. Spragmos has given us The Word. And The Word . . . is The Worm!"

The crowd chanted: "Mama-oo-pow-pow! Mama-oo-pow-pow!"

"And The Worm will show us the way. And one day, we will all awaken The Worm within. But the question remains: is that day upon us? The Scripture speaks of the Lightbringer. He who will show us the Light and illuminate the True Path. And now, there is one among us who claims to be this bringer of Light. But is he indeed the one of which the Scripture speaks? I have heard you ask, 'Is this the Light Spragmos speaks of?'

"And I say to you: I am but a man. It is not my place—nor any mortal's—to interpret the meaning of the Scriptures. But there is also no need. For in the end, there is only The Word. And The Word . . . is The Worm!"

"Mama-oo-pow-pow! Mama-oo-pow-pow!"

"Now, let us pray."

There was a mass shuffling as thousands of heads bowed. Melvern's voice echoed across the canyon. "Mighty Spragmos, we ask you to help guide us through these troubled times. Send us Your Messenger and show us The Way. Mama-oo-pow-pow."

"Mama-oo-pow-pow," the crowd replied.

"Mama-oo-pow-pow!"

"Mama-oo-pow-pow!"

"Mama-oo-pow-pow!"

"Mama-oo-pow-pow!"

A blood-curdling screech tore across the arena—a thick, jagged line of sound that ripped through the canyon. It slammed Karnage in the chest so hard he stumbled back. The noise ricocheted off the walls and echoed back across the arena, slowly fading into silence. The air itself grew still. The entire world was gripped by a sudden, terrible fear. Karnage wanted to scream into the void to break its spell.

That's when he felt it.

It started as a slight tremor at his feet, like the dull vibration of an approaching train. The tremor grew stronger and became a deep rumble. The ground shook. The earth beneath his feet churned and boiled. Karnage leaped off the fast-rising earth. He tumbled over the teeming mass until he found firmer ground. He turned just in time to see the expanding mass explode. A skyscraper shot out of the ground with lightning speed, sloughing mammoth chunks of earth in all directions. A dark shadow overtook Karnage, travelled the length of the arena, and shot up the full length of the wall behind him. Karnage found himself enveloped in cold, merciless darkness, as if the thing had risen up and swallowed the sun. Karnage craned his neck up, squinting into the sky.

The Worm towered over Karnage like a freight train balanced on one end. Hair covered a body that gyrated and pulsed like a sea of quivering tentacles. Its face was nothing but a giant mouth framed with row upon row of shard-like teeth spiralling deep into its gullet.

And jutting from the tip of its head, just barely visible against the orange-tinted sky, was a single, stubby horn.

"Well, shit," Karnage said.

CHAPTER TEN

A ripple ran down The Worm's body, and it toppled towards Karnage. As it fell, its hairy tentacled worm carcass became a crumbling mass of steel and concrete, and a voice called out from behind him.

"Tower's comin' down!" It was Cookie.

"Run!" Velasquez shouted.

Karnage's men started running in all directions. Panic hit him hard. This was where it all went to shit. Where they lost everything. Not this time. He wouldn't let it happen again.

"No! This way! Follow my lead!" Karnage turned and ran away from the surging tower at a forty five degree angle. Blood pounded in his ears, drowning out the raging roil of concrete and metal as it hurtled closer and closer. His soldiers followed closely behind. He could feel their urge to turn and look, to see if they would make it.

"Don't look back, soldier!" Karnage shouted through the cacophony. "Don't look back! Keep running! Keep running, goddammit!" Things would be different this time. He could feel it. He'd save them. He'd save them all—

The Worm's mass smashed into the ground, just missing Karnage by inches. He was thrown across the arena and crashed into the remains of a crumpled old jeep, his wind knocked out. The last remnants of New Baghdad were swept away by the mammoth flood of stars pouring across his vision. The crackling explosions were replaced with the fevered chants of the Spragmites.

"Mama-oo-pow-pow! Mama-oo-pow-pow!"

Karnage hugged his knees to his chest, wheezing, trying to catch his breath as the last few stars in his eyes turned to fading embers. *Keep it together, soldier! Keep it together!* His ribs burned. He hoped he hadn't broken any of them.

Karnage gripped the jeep's rusted fender and pulled himself up. The fender ripped off, leaving an edge of gleaming sharp metal. Karnage hefted it like a machete, and turned to face The Worm.

MAJOR KARNAGE

The Worm was on the other side of the arena, just coming out of a turn. It barrelled back towards him like an angry bullet train, its teeth circling its open mouth like a carnivorous black hole.

Karnage vaulted out of the way just as The Worm bore down on him. He reached out and grabbed a handful of tentacles as it blurred past. Pain shot through his arm as he was wrenched off his feet. The tentacle-like hairs whipped and lashed at his arm, wrapping around his limbs. Their grip was weak enough that Karnage could break it. In fact, rather than impeding him, they gave him better purchase on The Worm's flank, allowing him to stick to its side like velcro.

The Worm twitched and writhed, trying to throw Karnage off. Karnage felt like a mouse riding an epileptic elephant. He'd had to free solo climb before, but never on an angry rock face that was hellbent on bucking him off.

The world suddenly spun and Karnage saw the ground hurtling towards him. Karnage dove off The Worm, just clearing its massive girth as it slammed its side into the ground. Karnage tumbled away as The Worm rolled and writhed on the ground like a dog trying to scratch its flea-ridden back. It flopped back onto its belly with frightening speed, and shot clear across the arena.

Karnage struggled to his feet. He watched as The Worm banked and turned; the hard-packed earth bucked and roiled in its wake. Wrecked military gear flew in all directions as The Worm ploughed through it, barrelling towards Karnage. *It's too fast*, Karnage thought. *It's too damn fast!*

Karnage hefted the torn fender in his fist. His ankle throbbed. Probably twisted. He couldn't run anymore. He stood his ground, rusted fender at the ready. The Spragmites screamed and hollered. Karnage stared deep into The Worm's serrated maw. The whorl of teeth grew larger and larger, taking up all of Karnage's vision.

A high-pitched whine—like the cry of an angry bumblebee—pierced through the cacophony. Karnage looked up. There was an explosion of concrete and sparks as a battered Dabney cruiser burst over the edge of the wall. It spiralled through the air, and slammed into The Worm's head.

The Worm let out a horrid screech and recoiled, tumbling over itself. The cruiser bounced across the arena and rolled to a stop. The Worm's body crashed atop the cruiser just as a tiny figure leaped clear of the wreckage. Karnage smiled.

It was Sydney.

She ran up to Karnage. "You all right?"

"I'll live." Karnage tried to walk towards The Worm, but the pain in his ankle was too much and he crashed to the ground.

Sydney helped him up. "Where are you going?"

Karnage shook his head. "I have to do this. Now. Help me. Please."

Sydney propped Karnage up as he half-limped, half-hopped towards the massive beast. The Worm rocked itself, moaning horribly. Karnage grabbed its side, and started climbing. The tentacles made a half-hearted attempt to stop him, but they barely had any strength left. Karnage quickly scaled The Worm's bulk and emerged onto its head.

The horn was the size of a small tree. The cruiser had mostly torn it from its base. It lolled from side to side as if in a drunken stupor. Yellow smoke spewed from the wound. It smelled like a cross between nicotine and car exhaust. Karnage wrapped his arms around the horn and pulled.

The Worm screeched. It suddenly found new energy as it bucked and writhed, trying to throw Karnage off. Karnage wrapped his arms and legs around the horn. His weight tore it further and further as The Worm writhed more and more frantically. Karnage's sweaty hands started to slip. His strength was leaving him. He dug his nails into the horn's scaly surface. He had to outlast The Worm. *Stay the course, soldier! Stay the course!*

There was a wrenching snap, and Karnage and the horn toppled down The Worm and slammed into the ground. The Worm convulsed, contorted, then went limp. Smoke spewed from its mouth.

Karnage felt an arm on his shoulder. It was Sydney. She twirled a set of handcuffs on her finger.

"What are those for?"

"You're under arrest."

"You gotta be fuckin' kiddin' me," Karnage said.

"Nope," Sydney said. "Not kidding. Not kidding at all."

Spragmites poured into the arena. They were fast approaching Karnage and Sydney. "Captain," Karnage said, "may I respectfully suggest that this ain't the best time for you to be slappin' a pair of cuffs on me."

Sydney eyed the approaching horde, and tucked away her handcuffs. "You mind telling me what's going on here?"

"It's kinda complicated," Karnage said.

"Try me."

"Me killin' the worm was supposed to get me outta here."

"Why don't you sound like it worked?"

"Somethin' tells me you might have screwed things up."

"What? That thing where I saved your life?" Sydney said. "Sorry about that. Won't happen again. Promise."

The Spragmites surrounded them. Some stared at The Worm in awe. Others stared at Karnage and Sydney. Some in reverence. Others in fury. Among them was the High Prophet. He pushed through the crowd. A phalanx of D-pads followed him. He pointed an accusing finger at Sydney. "Interloper! You dare interfere in the affairs of Spragmos?! You will pay for this outrage!"

"What is this outrage you speak of, High Prophet?" All eyes turned to see Tristan standing amongst the crowd. Those near her backed away in surprise and fear.

The High Prophet's eyes narrowed. "I should have known. They are in league with the Blasphemer!"

"I am in league with no one, High Prophet." Tristan turned to the crowd. "You all saw, as I. Just when it seemed certain The Worm would not find this man worthy, this woman burst through the heavens like a saviour, as if sent by Spragmos himself—"

"Lies!" shouted the High Prophet.

Tristan turned her wondering gaze to the High Prophet. Her tone remained even. "Why such hostility, High Prophet? Are you filled with uncertainty for the future now that the Prophecy has been fulfilled? Do you fear the change the Lightbringer signifies?

Do you fear the True Path?"

"I fear nothing. And he is not the Lightbringer!"

"No," Tristan said. "He is not. They both are."

The crowd gasped. The High Prophet sneered. "More lies! The Scripture only speaks of one Lightbringer, not two!"

"Your interpretation of the Scripture is meaningless, High Prophet." She turned to the crowd. "Spragmos has spoken. The Worm is The Word, and The Worm has chosen."

A few voices in the crowd called out "Mama-oo-pow-pow!"

The High Prophet waved frantically for silence. "No! My people, do not be fooled!" He pointed an accusing finger at Karnage and Sydney. "These two are blasphemers! Heretics come to destroy The Word and The Worm! Come to destroy Spragmos himself! Awaken The Worm within you, and you will see the truth as it has been revealed to me!"

"But The Worm is The Word," Tristan said. "There is no other truth to be revealed. There is no need to try to read further into what has occurred. The Worm has spoken. They are the Lightbringer."

"No!" The High Prophet shouted. "They cheated!"

"You can't cheat The Worm. And The Worm is The Word."

A larger chorus of voices picked up the chant: "Mama-oo-pow-pow!"

"Don't lecture me about The Word! I know more about the Scriptures than you could ever—"

An ear-splitting alarm cut through the air.

"What the hell is that?" Sydney shouted.

"Proximity alarm," Karnage said. "Somethin's invadin' our airspace."

Winds whipped up in the arena, throwing dust and debris everywhere. The Spragmites scattered in all directions. Karnage, Sydney, and the High Prophet stood in the midst of it all. Tristan had long disappeared.

"The coward!" the High Prophet cried. "She knew she lost, so she fled! Run, Tristan! Run! For when I find you, I won't make the mistake of sparing you again! Oh no!"

MAJOR KARNAGE

The sky suddenly went pitch black. Karnage looked up, squinting through the sand and wind. Flashing lights littered the sky, illuminating mammoth panels running the length of the horizon. Something had blocked out the sun. Something that looked like . . .

Unidentified Flying Objects of Death!

Karnage grinned.

"You see?!" The High Prophet pointed at the darkened sky, shrieking to be heard above the wind. "Spragmos has come! He will not stand for this outrage! He will smite you! He will smite you all!"

A panel on the ship slid open. Something large and phallic descended towards them. Spragmites ran in all directions as green energy crackled along the shaft, collecting on its bulbous end. Sydney grabbed Karnage's arm and screamed in his ear. "We have to get out of here!"

Karnage shook her off. He raised his arms towards the ship, and closed his eyes. "Come get me, you bastards."

Karnage's world filled with an intense painful green.

MK#6: ALIEN KARNAGE

CHAPTER ONE

Karnage woke lying face up on a hospital gurney. Soft white light enveloped him. He sat up. Medals jangled against his chest. He looked down. He was wearing a full-dress uniform. Karnage looked around. The world was empty: nothing but soft white light gently warming his skin. He lay back on the gurney, and closed his eyes.

So, Karnage thought, *this is death.*

"Major?"

Karnage opened his eyes. Cookie stood before him. He was wearing a hospital gown. His bald head was smooth and free of scars. Glowing green squiggles danced up and down his forearms.

"Major? Are you awake?" Cookie said.

"I dunno," Karnage said. "Am I dead?"

Cookie shook his head. "No, sir."

"You sure about that?"

Cookie smiled. "I'm sure."

"Well that's a relief." Karnage sat up. "What with all this white shit everywhere and me bein' decked out in full military dress and all, you could see why I might jump to that conclusion."

"Nobody's dead yet, Major."

"Nobody? You mean Velasquez? Heckler? Koch?"

Cookie nodded. "All still alive, sir."

"I knew it. I just knew they weren't . . ." Karnage dropped his shoulders and let out a sigh of relief. "Good. That's good." He looked up at Cookie. "I found 'em, Cookie. I found 'em! It was just like you said. Comin' in all squiggly and on an angle and shit. I don't know what they done to me. Last thing I remember they opened up some monkeyfucker of a death ray on my ass. Next thing I know I'm here, talkin' to you! And look at you." Karnage grabbed Cookie by his arms. The squiggles squirmed hotly under Karnage's grip. "You got no bandages on your head or nothin'. You've never looked better. Except those squiggles. Shit, they're writhin' and spreadin' and dancin' like . . . like some kinda . . . hell, I don't even know! What's it all mean, Cookie?"

"It means you still got a lot of work to do, Major. You found the aliens. Now you gotta find a way to stop 'em."

"But how, Cookie? How?"

Cookie tapped his temple. "You just gotta use your head."

"My head is fucked up," Karnage said. "I still see things, Cookie. Things from—" Karnage cut himself short before he could finish the thought.

"It's okay," Cookie said. "You can say it here. The War."

Karnage cringed, ready for the visions to explode in his head. But nothing happened. No fire. No chaos. No pain. Just peace. He nearly wept.

"You're not crazy, Major," Cookie said. "You got a good handle on things. Better than any of 'em would have thought. But you're not done yet. You still got a ways to go." The squiggles on Cookie's arms grew brighter and hotter. They twined around Karnage's fists, now so hot they burned his skin. He tried to pull away, but they wouldn't let go. They twined up his arms.

"What's happenin', Cookie?"

"It's time for you to go, Major."

"Go where?"

"You'll see." The squiggles grew brighter. They washed everything out into a fierce, pulsing green. The squiggles pulled Karnage's hands from Cookie's arms, and Karnage tumbled backwards, falling through the ever thickening tangle of squiggles. As he fell, Cookie's voice floated down to him through the distance:

"We're with you, Major. Every one of us. We're with you. . . ."

CHAPTER TWO

Karnage slowly drifted up into consciousness.

His entire body felt weightless. He waited for the dream-like feeling to dissipate.

It didn't.

The burning stench of pinkstink and hoverballs filled his nostrils. He opened his eyes. They were met with a stinging yellow mist. Karnage gasped and coughed, struggling to breathe the toxic air. He could barely see his hand in front of his face. He reached out. His fingers hit a smooth concave surface. He ran his hands across, feeling out how the surface arched and curved around him, enveloping him in a compact sphere. He felt like he was trapped inside a hoverball.

Karnage punched the walls of the sphere. His Sanity Patch buzzed "Frothy Cream" as the entire sphere rocked forward, tilting and listing. Karnage braced his hands and feet against the walls of the sphere, trying to right himself. The sphere stopped listing. Bracing with his other limbs, Karnage lifted a foot and kicked hard into the sphere. Cracks bloomed out under his boot and the sphere jerked down. His Sanity Patch crooned "Sandy Dreams." He lifted his leg, and kicked into the cracks. His foot smashed through. The yellow smoke poured out through the hole, and the sphere plummeted.

It crashed into a hard surface, shattering everywhere. Karnage coughed as thick plumes of yellow smoke puffed out of his lungs. It tasted worse than it smelled. He retched and gagged until nothing but spit came out. Throat raw and nostrils burning, he felt like he'd been breathing hot ash. He lay against the floor trying to catch his breath and draw in clean air, but the stench lingered. Finally, he pulled himself to his feet.

He stood in a gleaming metal chamber that was all angles. Thick translucent tubes wound across the walls, creating squiggling patterns. Green light flowed through the tubes with the occasional blip of white streaked through the green. The lights pulsed and flowed like blood pumping through veins. Karnage touched one of the squiggles. The white bursts spun around his fingers a moment, as if scanning them, then sped off. He felt the heat of each green pulse. *This is it,* he thought. *The belly of the beast.*

The path of the squiggles was interrupted by an arched doorway large enough to fit a commuter train. The door looked to be made of a spiral of roughly hewn blades. The squiggles cut a path around the door, collecting around a nodule of translucent spheres that throbbed and fluttered in time with the light passing through it. Support beams in the shape of talons flowed up the walls into the curved ceiling. Pearl-coloured spheres hovered above him, nestled together in the apex of the ceiling's curvature.

As light glowed fiercely around the door and collected in the nodule, the blades of the door spiralled open. Karnage pressed himself up against the wall. His heart beat in his chest. He was about to get his first glimpse of an alien.

Another pearl-coloured sphere floated into the room, and the door closed behind it. The sphere began to rise towards the ceiling. As it did so, a dark shape floated down against the side of the sphere. It was human. Karnage awkwardly made a grab at the sphere, pulling it back down so he could peer inside. The human shape touched the side of the sphere, and Karnage saw the face of the person inside.

It was Sydney. Her eyes were closed. Her knees were curled up to her chest, her arms gently wrapped around them. She looked like she was sleeping.

Karnage braced the sphere on the floor and banged on it with his fists. "Captain! Captain, can you hear me?!"

She didn't respond.

Karnage heard a *crack-hiss* behind him. He turned and saw a wooden matchstick floating before the door, its freshly struck flame flickering. Above the match and to its right floated an unlit cigar. The match rose up, and kissed the end of the cigar. The end glowed to life as unseen lungs inhaled. Grey curls of smoke blew out around the cigar, as an explosion of colours flowed and poured like liquid across an unfamiliar silhouette.

The colours settled and receded to reveal a seven-foot-tall insect with a squid for a head. The cigar sat nestled in a quivering fringe of small tentacles that covered its mouth. A pair of longer tentacles hung from the creature's temples like sidecurls. One of the side tentacles held the lit match, which shook it out. Its bony arms clutched a gnarled spear with a surface covered in squiggly carvings. Green energy pulsed along the grooves.

Karnage's body tingled. Here he was: finally face to face with an alien! It was more alien than Karnage could have imagined. Squigglier than he could possibly have imagined. He did his best to suppress a gleeful grin. "Well, ain't you one ugly lookin' squidbug,"

The squidbug turned an eye towards Karnage as it puffed on its cigar. Its pupil was a long squiggle smeared across a mottled eyeball. It took a drag on its cigar, plucked it out of its mouth with a side tentacle, and tossed it away. It flicked the wrists of its bony claws, and the spear glowed. Green energy crackled across its surface, collecting around the bulbous head. The squidbug's skin darkened to a deep crimson, and it thrust the spear forward. A sizzling ball of green shot out at Karnage.

Karnage side-stepped the blast. He could feel its electric charge pull at the hairs on his skin. The ball collided with the wall and disappeared, leaving a smoking black crater. Karnage dove forward and grabbed the shaft of the squidbug's spear. He slammed it up into the squidbug's mouth. It made a loud *clack* on impact. The squidbug lost its grip on the spear as it staggered back. Karnage's neck buzzed as the Sanity Patch upgraded to Daffodil.

The squidbug let out an indignant screech. It pressed itself against the wall. Its skin changed colour, pulsing and flowing through different shades and patterns until it had blended perfectly into the wall, disappearing from view.

Karnage charged with the spear as the squidbug vanished, hitting nothing but wall and nearly jarring the spear out of his hands. The Sanity Patch crooned "Citrus Blast" as he stumbled backward. Somewhere behind him he heard a squiggly screech that sounded far too much like laughter for his liking. He spun around and squinted his eyes, trying to catch any hint of the beast.

CRACK! A tentacle shot out and caught Karnage across the jaw. He lost his grip on the spear and it clattered to the ground.

"Son of a—"

CRACK! Another tentacle clocked him from the other side, knocking him away from the spear.

"—bitch!"

Karnage staggered back. He turned in the direction of the last hit.

CRACK! A third blow caught him in the back of the head. He stumbled forward, stars shooting across his vision.

"Monkey—"

CRACK! Another blow caught him across the face. Karnage grabbed the tentacle before it could recoil. He yanked it hard towards him, throwing a punch along its length.

"—FUCKER!"

His fist sank deep into soft flesh. There was a terrible squeal, and the squidbug appeared in a flash of cycling colours. It fell to the ground, lying limp on the floor as all the coloured drained out of its skin, leaving it an insipid grey. Karnage's neck buzzed.

"Warning. Sanity Level upgraded to Peachy Keen. Please refrain from violent behaviour."

Karnage grabbed the spear and used it to fish Sydney's sphere down from the ceiling. He braced it against the wall with his foot and stabbed it with the spear, cracking open the shell. He tore it apart with his hands as his Sanity Patch upgraded from Peachy Keen to Tangy Orange to Sharp Cheddar.

Sydney lay on the floor, coughing and gasping. Yellow smoke poured from her lungs. Karnage threw her over his shoulder and headed to the closed door. He tried pressing on the nodules beside it. The green lights seemed to ignore him. A sliver of white flowed down into the nodule, stopped, and circled around Karnage's hand. White slivers started flowing down into the nodule from the surrounding tubes, and it soon filled with white. The door spiralled open, and

Karnage stepped through it.

CHAPTER THREE

Karnage walked down the dimly lit corridor. Giant doors lined either side. Soft green pulses of light flowed through the squiggles along the walls. Karnage felt like he was walking through Cookie's forearms. The occasional line of white light would stop, bunch up into a hovering ball as he walked past it, then streak off again, lost in the green mass.

Karnage felt a strange tingle at the base of his neck. Suddenly he lost all feeling in his body and he fell to the ground. "Right, mate," Sydney said. "Now we do it my way."

"Captain, it's me," Karnage gasped. "Major Karnage."

"I know who you are," Sydney said. Karnage heard the familiar jangle of handcuffs.

"What the hell are you doing?!"

"Arresting you," Sydney replied, as she snapped the cuffs on Karnage's wrists.

"Goddammit, Captain, this is neither the time nor the place! Look around you! Do you have any idea where we are?"

Sydney looked around. "Dimly lit corridor. Probably somewhere underground."

"UNDERGROUND?!"

"We'll find our way out, though, no worries."

"Are you outta your mind?! We are deep inside an alien ship! Hurtling across space! Probably halfway across the damn galaxy by now!"

"Sounds like you're the one out of your mind." A finger touched Karnage's neck, and he could move again. Sydney pulled him to his feet. She thrust a pinky in his face. "No funny business or I cart you out of here like a sack of potatoes."

Sydney jerked Karnage forward. "For god's sake, Captain, how can you not believe me? Didn't you see that ship come hurtlin' outta the sky? How the hell do you think we got here?!"

She frowned in reply. "I can't remember, exactly. My head's still fuzzy. I remember the sky went dark, like a freak thunderstorm or something—"

"That was no thunderstorm! That was a goddamn unidentified flying object of DEATH! It opened up one monkeyfucker of a death ray on us, and here we are!"

"Sounds like it's not a very good death ray. Come on, keep moving. We need to find our way out of here."

"This is a hell of a way to treat your rescuer! They had you all trussed up in a big hoverball thing. I had to break you out. I saved you from bein' bottled up like . . . like a goddamn pickle in a mason jar!"

"A hoverball, huh? Then that proves it. We're not on an alien spacecraft."

"What?!"

"Come on, Major. Hoverballs? That's not exactly alien technology. This probably has something to do with the Dabney Corporation. Probably some top secret operation. We just need to find somebody in charge—"

"Captain, did you miss the part where I told you they had you locked up?!"

Sydney stopped walking, and looked at Karnage. "You really think we're on an alien spacecraft?"

"YES!"

Sydney looked around, and shook her head. "I'm not convinced."

"Open your eyes, Captain! What the hell more proof do you need?"

"Some aliens would be a nice start."

"Oh there are aliens, all right. I've seen 'em with my own eyes! They're giant squidbuggy things with squiddy heads atop of buggy bodies with eyes like . . . like . . ."

"Like squidbugs?"

"NO! Like squiggles! Squiggly like the walls! Squiggly like the worms! Squiggly like the squiggles on Cookie's arms! Goddammit, Captain, can't you see the connection? Its all fallin' into place. They got squiggly tentacles, too, and they shoot giant squiggly balls of electricity from their squiggly spears and . . . quit lookin' at me like that! They're here! I've seen 'em!"

"Where? Where are they? Where are these aliens?"

Karnage eyed every darkened corner suspiciously. "That's just it. They could be anywhere. All around us. Ready to attack at any moment. Now get these cuffs off of me before they launch their squiggly squidbug attack!"

"They could be anywhere?"

"That's right. Anywhere. Just lurking, waiting for the right moment to strike."

"Where?"

"Where what?"

"Where are they hiding? Why can't we see them?"

Karnage leaned in close and hissed. "That's cuz they're invisible."

"Invisible?"

"Yes!"

"And you've *seen* these invisible aliens?"

"YES!"

"Are you seeing any right now?"

"No! They're not actually invisible. It's more like camouflage— goddammit, Captain, get these handcuffs off of me!"

"So far, Major, you have said nothing to make me want to do that."

A squiggly squeal echoed in the distance. Sydney turned in its direction. "What the hell was that?"

"That," Karnage replied, "was a squidbug."

Sydney backed down the corridor. "It sounded like a worm."

"They all sound like that," Karnage said.

Sydney rounded on Karnage, her eyes narrowed to suspicious slits. "This is a military thing, isn't it? That worm was some kind of superweapon, wasn't it? Some mutated superweapon grown out of control—"

"Now who sounds ridiculous? Why can't you accept the simple fact that this is aliens?"

Sydney looked around. She shook her head. "That's just so crazy. I mean, this place doesn't look that alien."

Karnage did a doubletake. "What do you mean it doesn't look alien?! What the hell do you want it to look like?"

Sydney shrugged. "I don't know. Just more . . . alien."

They heard another squiggly scream, much closer this time.

Karnage rounded on Sydney. "Captain, with all due respect, *get these fuckin' cuffs offa me!*"

Sydney shook her head. "I'm not convinced. I have to see 'em for myself."

"So we're just gonna wait here until one of those squiggly bastards comes up and bites us in the ass! Jesus, Captain, what do I gotta do to prove it to you?"

As if on cue, a collection of white slivers of light shot through the walls and collected in a nodule by a door. The door spiralled open, and a squidbug that had been leaning on the door stumbled back and fell out. Other squidbugs sat inside, collected around an old car idling in the room. Bits of broken hoverball shell lay around it. The room was thick with grey smoke. A garden hose had been taped to the car's exhaust, and a squidbug was sucking on the end of it. His eyes were crossed and purple polka-dots covered his skin. He passed the hose to the next squidbug who eagerly sucked on the end and turned a kind of chartreuse shade of plaid.

The squidbug that lay at Karnage's and Sydney's feet groggily stood and shook its head. It looked at Karnage and Sydney with crossed eyes. It worked hard at uncrossing its eyes and focused on Karnage and Sydney. It blinked slowly as its skin changed colour from green paisley to blue ripples. Its eyes suddenly went wide and its skin flowed to solid purple then dark red. It raised its mouth tentacles, exposing a clawed beak, and screeched at Sydney.

Sydney whipped her pistol from her belt and fired a shot of goober in the squidbug's face. The alien's head disappeared in an expanding ball of goober as it staggered back into the room. It crashed into the car, kicking the garden hose out of the exhaust. The other squidbugs finally looked up from the hose at their struggling companion.

Gradually, they turned their attention to Karnage and Sydney and worked hard at uncrossing their eyes.

Karnage and Sydney backed away from the door.

"Is that enough empirical evidence for you, Captain?" Karnage said.

Sydney nodded. "That should just about do it."

The squidbugs slowly rose to their feet as their eyes focused on Karnage and Sydney.

"How many rounds you got left in that goober gun?" Karnage said.

"Not enough," Sydney said.

One of the squidbugs turned dark crimson. It reached down for a squiggly spear lying on the floor.

"Only one thing left do," Karnage said.

"What's that?"

"Run!"

They raced down the corridor, the squidbugs stumbling after them. The aliens levelled their energy spears at Karnage and Sydney, and fired balls of energy at them. The balls went ridiculously wide, slamming into the floor and ceiling far behind them. One of the squidbugs tripped on his spear and accidentally shot himself. He vaporized instantly.

"These guys are the worst shots I've ever seen!" Sydney said.

"Quit bitching!" Karnage stumbled and nearly fell. "You picked a helluva time to come around! You know that?"

"Now who's bitching?!"

"I am! And I got every right to! You know how hard it is to run in handcuffs?"

"How was I supposed to know there were aliens?"

"How about because I fuckin' well told you?"

"I make it a point never to trust anybody in handcuffs."

A crackling ball of green energy flew over their heads.

"Maybe you should rethink that policy!"

"I'll take it under advisement."

They rounded a corner, and came face to face with a sealed door.

"How do you open this thing?" Sydney said.

Karnage motioned with his head at the nodules beside the door. "It has something to do with this."

Sydney pressed it and punched it, but nothing happened. "How does it work?"

"I don't know. I just pushed it, and it worked."

"It's not working now."

"I can see that."

Energy blasts shot wildly down the corridor, some of them disturbingly close.

"Goddammit, we have to do something!"

Karnage kicked the nodule. "Open up, you stupid monkeyfucker!" White light burst out of the nodule and flowed into the floor. The Sanity Patch crooned "Coral Essence" as the floor spiralled open beneath them.

They fell into the bowels of the ship.

CHAPTER FOUR

Karnage plummeted through twisting pipes, slid through long chutes, and spiraled through giant drains, liquid flowing all around him. An occasional burst of white light shot down the tunnel in front of him, opening up new chutes while sealing off others, redirecting his course as he alternately slid and fell deeper into the squidbug ship.

The tunnel finally gave way to open air, and he fell through the pitch black and landed with a splash into liquid. It stung his eyes and tasted like toxic sludge. He tried to kick his way to the surface. The handcuffs holding his arms behind his back did nothing to help.

He wasn't sure if he was swimming up to the surface or down into the depths. He just kept kicking, hoping eventually he'd reach the top. He felt something grab his collar and pull him sideways. His head broke the surface and he gasped for air.

Karnage could feel Sydney pulling again as she swam towards a circle of white light shining in the distance. It illuminated a half-open grate in the wall, just above the water level. A particularly large wave slapped her full in the mouth.

She spat out a mouthful of foul liquid. "Christ, this stuff tastes awful!"

"Just keep swimming." Karnage did his best to kick and help propel them forward.

It was much farther away than it looked. The white ring slowly grew in size, from a man-sized hole to something that would accommodate a jumbo jet. Exhausted, Sydney pulled them through the grate onto its dry smooth surface. They lay there a moment, catching their breath. Finally, Sydney spoke. "There really are aliens, aren't there?"

"Not just aliens," Karnage said. "Squidbugs."

Sydney looked out at the giant vat of liquid. "What the hell do we do now?"

"First," Karnage twisted his back towards Sydney, "you can take off these handcuffs."

"Right," she said. "Sorry."

Karnage heard her fumble in her pockets. "Shit," she said.

"What?"

"I can't find the key. I must have dropped it." She ran her hands along the base of the tunnel, then looked with dread out at the liquid. She looked back at Karnage.

He ground his teeth. "This is great. No, this is beyond great. Fantastic! How the hell am I gonna defend myself against a squidbug attack?"

"Maybe you can kick 'em to death."

"Can't you just poke the cuffs with a toe or something and snap 'em off?"

Sydney shook her head. "It doesn't work like that."

"No," Karnage said. "Of course not."

"Come on." Sydney helped Karnage to his feet. "Maybe we can find something at the end of this tunnel."

Karnage looked down into the darkness. "Where does it go?"

"It goes that way. Come on."

They walked down the shaft for what felt like hours. Karnage rolled his shoulders and stretched his arms. They were starting to get sore. He tried glowering at Sydney's back to make himself feel better. It didn't help.

The tunnel slowly slanted upward. It ended at a bend that took it straight up a few feet before ending at a giant sealed grate. Nothing but darkness was visible beyond the grate.

A set of rungs led up to the grate. Sydney climbed up and tried to lift it. It didn't budge. She looked around the edges. "Maybe there's a nodule thing we can hit."

"I don't see one," Karnage commented.

"Keep looking."

"What's that?"

A flashing pinprick of white light shot across the grate. The edges of the grate glowed, and it lifted and slid open.

"Nice work," Karnage said.

"I didn't do anything."

"Worry about the who and the why later. Help me up."

Sydney helped Karnage up the rungs, and the two of them pulled themselves through the open grate. Karnage felt like a rat crawling out of a drain. Every movement echoed through the cavernous darkness. The only light in the room was the ring of white light around the grate. All that it illuminated was Karnage and Sydney and a soft circle of grey floor.

The ring of light pulled itself from the edges of the grate, and pooled into a puddle under their feet. It shot a squiggling luminescent tendril forward and formed a second puddle just a few feet ahead of them. A third tentacle shot out of the second pool, forming a third, and then a fourth formed out of the third. The pools propagated themselves off into the distance until they were barely visible at the edge of a black horizon, ghostly white lily pads in the dark, quivering and fidgeting.

"That looks like a path," Sydney said.

"I know," Karnage replied.

"Think we should follow it?"

Karnage shook his head. "Fuck no."

"Me neither."

The lily pad beneath their feet flickered for a moment, then winked out.

"Is that supposed to be a hint?" Sydney asked.

"If it was," Karnage said, "I'm not listening."

The next nearest lily pad winked out. Then the next and the next in a chain reaction of winks that looked like a long line of eyes closing in a Rockettes-style routine. Finally, only one tiny pinpoint of light flickered in the distance.

"I think they really want us to follow the path," Sydney said.

"Well, they can go fuck themselves." He looked up into the dark. "I'm not gonna be led around like a rat in a trap! You hear me?!"

The pinprick of light shot off angry squiggling lines in all directions, stretching from horizon to horizon. Then, impossibly, the lines turned sharply upward and shot up walls the height of cliffs. They disappeared behind dark rounded masses above them, and spanned out, soaking the walls in a grey luminous glow.

Karnage and Sydney stared up at the dark mounds high above. White light flashed and popped from bulbous mound to bulbous mound. Suddenly, the mounds twitched, and the entire ceiling slowly lowered towards them.

"Back through the grate!" Karnage shouted. But it was too late. The grate had slammed shut behind them.

They looked up and watched as the ceiling slowly moved down.

As the ceiling grew closer they saw it was composed of thousands of translucent spheres of varying sizes. Dark shapes bobbed within them. The spheres stopped lowering just inches above their heads. The sudden stop forced the dark shapes to float down against the bottom of their spheres. A human face appeared. It was a man with his knees hugged to his chest, sleeping peacefully. He bobbed back up and disappeared into the mists of the sphere.

"They're human," Karnage said.

"Not all of them." Sydney reached up and grabbed a sphere the size of a basketball. She pulled it down. Its curled dark shape bobbed down and up, a tail clearly drifting from its back. "This one's got a cat in it." Sydney let the ball go, and it pushed up into the mass, forcing the other spheres to make room. The spheres rippled and bobbed out.

There was a faint rumbling, and suddenly the spheres parted to make room for one the length of a bus. It pushed itself well down through the mass, forcing Karnage and Sydney to drop to the floor. The sphere slowed to a stop inches above their heads, and moved back up again. The enormous black shape within pushed at the curve of glass for an instant, before the sphere and its contents disappeared back up into the ocean of spheres. Karnage and Sydney looked at each other in shock.

"Was that . . . a whale?" Karnage said.

"I'll pretend I didn't see it if you will."

They tentatively stood. Karnage looked at the millions of spheres floating above them. "What do you think? Two of everything? Maybe more?"

Sydney shook her head. "What the hell is this?"

"Maybe it's their larder."

The spheres began to rise. The grey lights flickered out of them and moved back into the walls. The lights in the walls narrowed into tight lines and pulled back down into the floor where they collected in a pool of light under Karnage's and Sydney's feet. The room descended into darkness, but Karnage kept staring up, thinking of the millions of spheres hovering above him.

The puddle of light under their feet flowed forward, pulsing patiently just in front of them.

"I think it wants us to follow it again," Sydney said.

"Yeah." Karnage stared at the pulsing spot of light. It waited patiently as he tried to stop thinking about what loomed above him. He looked at Sydney.

"Well," he said, "so long as they're bein' polite."

CHAPTER FIVE

They followed the light across the floor for what felt like days. It stayed a half-step in front of them, rhythmically jumping ahead to prevent them from touching it with the tips of their feet. Karnage's feet were starting to hurt and his neck ached from looking down at the light when it finally stopped moving.

Once they were standing on it, the glowing pool shot a coil of light forward that instantly sped straight up a wall directly in front of them. The lights flared out into tiny filaments and outlined a door the size of a hangar bay. The filaments broke apart, and rained down into a large glowing ring around the door. The door spiralled open with a loud aching groan. The lights flowed back into the lily pad under their feet. The lily pad drifted through the doorway, and pulsed patiently on the other side.

Karnage and Sydney followed it into the room. Once they were through, the lily pad shot strands of light in all directions. They travelled twice as far as the first room, literally disappearing over the invisible horizon. They were barely visible as thread-like strands as they snaked their way up distant walls the height of mountains. The lines eventually disappear behind an ever so slightly mottled ceiling in the distance. Pinpricks of light flickered and danced across the ceiling like stars. They grew larger in size as they slowly descended, finally revealing themselves to be glowing spheres.

The spheres were immense. Each one was many times larger than the biggest ones they had seen in the other room, each one practically a mountain floating unto itself. The dark masses moved down, revealing incredible shapes: great pyramids of crumbling stone; mammoth pointed steeples of a giant cathedral; winding twisting walls that looked like finely carved chunks from the Great Wall of China. Each monument ended in a perfectly smooth scoop of earth that encased its foundations. It was almost too much to take in.

Sydney craned her neck. "It's like a giant museum."

"Yeah," Karnage scowled. "And we're the exhibits."

The spheres floated back up as the light drained from the walls. It shot back across the floor and coalesced into a tiny lily pad, bobbing and pulsing before their feet, urging them forward.

They followed into the darkness.

CHAPTER SIX

The light led them through another airplane-sized door into another room. This one wasn't pitch black. There were faint flickerings of green in the distance that highlighted floating orbs. The toxic smell was more pungent in the air, and the white light didn't launch boldly into the room. It cowered near their feet, before working up the courage to flicker and bob forward. It jumped erratically as it climbed the walls, as if trying to avoid the pulses of green light that occasionally ran through the room.

The light briefly flashed in one of the larger spheres, and the silhouette of the dark blob within was all too familiar to Karnage.

It was a giant horned worm.

"Jesus."

As the light flitted about, it illuminated other alien objects including myriad squidbugs.

"They're doing it to us, and they're doing it to themselves," Sydney gasped. "But why?"

Karnage twitched with energy. "Maybe this is it," he said. "Maybe this is what Cookie meant."

"What? What are you talking about?"

"Our chance," he turned to Sydney. "It's our chance to stop 'em. Look at 'em up there! All lyin' in them spheres. Sittin' ducks. Maybe this is where I can stop 'em. Before they wake up. Before they get out!"

"How?"

"I don't know. I've just gotta . . . I've just gotta use my head. Goddammit! What did Cookie mean?"

"What are you talking about? Who's Cookie?"

"We need a weapon," Karnage said. "Something big. Something massive. Something that'll nuke these squidbugs to kingdom come!"

"Maybe we can find something in one of these rooms," Sydney suggested. "They seem to have everything down here. Maybe we can find something from The War."

The War!

Karnage's eyes bugged out of his head. Explosions, bullets, and screams filled his ears.

The War!

He jerked his arms and his handcuffs broke with a loud snap. His mind clouded over with smoke and flames and death.

The War!

Karnage's fist shot out and grabbed Sydney by the throat. He lifted her off the ground, his fingers squeezing her neck as her gasping face disappeared behind the haze of battle.

"Don't . . . talk to me . . . about *THE WAR!*"

Sydney strained for breath as Karnage's tightening grip closed her windpipe. Stars danced before her eyes. "What are you . . . ?" she gasped, but Karnage choked her off. A voice in the back of his neck cheerfully informed her that he had hit Coral Essence.

"You want to talk to me about The War?!" Spittle flew from his mouth and his eyes blazed. "I'll tell you about—"

Sydney thrust a pinky forward and danced it across Karnage's arm. Joint by joint, she numbed Karnage into submission: a pinky *jeté* to his wrist, a thumb *glissade* to the elbow, followed by an index finger *piqué* into his neck. Karnage went down like a rag doll. He craned his head toward Sydney. His eyes blazed. Veins popped in his neck as he screamed at the top of his lungs.

"North Uzhorod! 8-8-4-2-1! Uncle Stanley had us on the run!"

The voice in the back of Karnage's neck hit Frosty Pink as his voice echoed through the cavernous room. The green glow above them became brighter. The bits of white retreated from the spheres, and the green chased after them. The lines of white shot down the walls with torrents of green streaking after them. The white light retreated beneath their feet, as if trying to hide itself. The green streaks fired through on all sides and obliterated the white completely. The floor went black, and the only light was the agitated green among the spheres, flickering across them like lightning. The green lights pulsed brighter, and the spheres started to lower. The dark shapes within moved in time with Karnage's cries.

"Blood and brains flew in all directions! Those monkeyfuckin' *skerks* used our own people for cover! Those merciless bastards!"

The voice at his neck hit Strawberry Shortcake.

"Major!" Sydney shouted. "You have to shut up!"

"Snipers to the right of us! Snipers to the left of us! Snipers all around us! DIE DIE DIE!"

"THAT'S IT!" Sydney performed a *grand jetée* into Karnage's ear lobe and he dropped unconscious, his head drooping against his chest. She heard something shatter above her and tiny bits of sphere showered the floor.

She swung Karnage's body over her shoulder in a fireman's carry. The broken handcuff bracelet around Karnage's wrist glinted in a quick flash of green. She ground her teeth. *Fucking E-nium.*

She turned to run back through the door. A lightning bolt of green flashed down the wall and hit the door. It spiralled shut instantly.

"NO!"

Something clattered to the ground behind her. She turned around. A squidbug was charging towards her, its skin flashing deep crimson. She drew her goober pistol and fired. The shot hit the squidbug in the chest, knocking it onto its back. Its limbs flailed futilely as the goober swelled, sticking it fast to the floor. Sydney heard another smash above her. She turned back to the door. It glowed with green light that flickered like flames around its frame. She found a small nodule of bulbs flashing green by the door. She hit them frantically with her fist. They flashed green, almost defiantly. Hearing a squiggling screech, she turned around and took down another charging squidbug with a ball of goober. More spheres burst above her. She turned back to the door nodules and gave them a hard kick.

"Goddammit! You picked a hell of a time to abandon us! You know that? You have to let me back through! You brought us all the way in here, now you're just going to let us die? You can't do this!"

A sliver of white light shot across the floor towards her. A flare of green shot out and shattered the white into nothing. Another squidbug dropped to the floor and charged, but was repelled by another ball of goober. Sydney checked her pistol. She only had five rounds left. She heard a giant crash, and a massive black shape crumpled to the floor.

It was a horned worm.

Sydney looked back up into the black.

"You have to get us out of here! *Help us!*"

An assault of tiny needle-like white lights rained down the walls on the glowing green door. The green lights lashed out in angry flaming tentacles, knocking away the light. The persistent rain of white whittled away at the green, knocking back its defences. The green and white roiled and boiled around the door until the white overtook the green just enough that the door slowly opened a few inches. As the glow slowly changed from dark green to paler and paler shades, the door spiralled open just enough for Sydney to push Karnage through the gap. She scrambled through after him before the door slammed shut behind her.

A tiny spot of white light appeared on the floor in front of her and lurched forward. She heaved Karnage back onto her shoulder and ran after it. A shot of green blasted across the floor and obliterated the white, leaving Sydney stranded in the darkness. Another sliver of white careened towards her from the distance. She started running toward it, but another blast of green obliterated it before she got there. Behind her, green lights were attacking the cracked door frame. The door's spiral panels shook and shuddered as they tried to open. The worm on the other side was beating against the door, the cracks on its surface growing larger and larger.

White light coiled down the wall. Sydney followed it as fast as she could, Karnage's limp bulk weighing her down. The light gathered around another door farther along, and it spiralled open. There was a loud crash behind her. Sydney turned around. Bits of door exploded into the room. An angry torrent of green light flowed up from the door and flared across the wall towards her.

She raced for the glowing white door ahead of her. She could practically feel the heat of the green light behind her as it collected and flared, making everything before her glow green. Her shadow on the floor grew longer and longer as the light flickered and flamed up. There was a loud smash and scattering of debris as a horned worm screeched behind her. Sydney didn't look. She stayed focused on the door. Licks of green light shot ahead of her and attacked the white ring. The fingers of white slapped back at the green. The green lashes swooped down and seemed to devour the white. The light around the door grew dimmer. Sydney dove through the door just as the green light consumed it, and the door's blades spiralled closed behind her.

Sydney dropped Karnage like a dead weight, panting. The room was dark. Angry tentacles of green light lashed at her feet. She desperately searched for any glimmer of white.

A dull grey sphere pulsed high above her in the middle of the room. As she ran towards it, the sphere slowly lowered down to the floor. It was larger than her, its innards oblong and mechanical. She saw a giant nozzle press against its side. She recognized it instantly, and grinned from ear to ear.

It was the barrel of a Sudsy tanker.

She pulled out her stun stick and smashed an opening in the sphere's surface. She crawled through, coughing in the thick yellow haze as she pulled Karnage through after her. Mist poured out of the sphere, and she could see the Sudsy tanker in detail. Sydney opened the tanker's hatch and dragged Karnage inside. She locked the hatch behind her.

"Lucky for you I got my start on the force in riot control." She strapped the unconscious Karnage into the co-pilot seat. "Might not be quite as good as, say, a plasma cannon, but it's a good start, right?" She lifted Karnage's inert face and gently slapped his cheek. "Now you just sit back and enjoy the ride, okay, mate?"

She strapped herself into her seat and flicked on the console. It hummed to life, the controls vibrating under her fingers. She was thrilled to see the tanker's Sudsy vats were full. She put the machine into gear and crashed it through the remnants of the sphere. She swung it around so it faced the glowing green door. The door spiralled open, revealing the angry sawtooth maw of the horned worm.

Sydney took a breath. "Right, here we go."

The worm shot forward, and Sydney hit the guns. Sudsy sprayed across the floor. She backed the tanker up out of the path of the worm. The worm tried to bank, but its bulk hit the Sudsy and it slid across the floor, missing the tanker completely. It spun wildly as it disappeared into the black, screeching horribly. Its screeches faded to nothing.

A flash of white light appeared on the floor, and shot across the cavernous room into the darkness. Sydney steered the Sudsy tanker towards it and followed at full speed.

She checked her rear monitors. A pair of worms chased after her. Squidbugs rode atop each worm, their clawed hands holding the horns. They were catching up quickly. Sydney sprayed Sudsy behind her across the floor. The worms moved to twist out of the way. One of them made it, but the other caught the tail end of the Sudsy. The sudden loss of traction on its rear end caused the worm to flip violently. The squidbugs were thrown from its back and crushed as the worm rolled across the floor.

The streaking white light in front of the tanker was obliterated by a sudden ferocious flash of green. Sydney kept going, hoping she was still moving in the right direction. She pushed the engines as hard as she could, their gauges quivering at maximum.

A squidbug riding on the worm behind her levelled its staff. A ball of energy collected on its end, and buzzed towards the tanker. Sydney yanked on the controls, trying to dodge the blow. There was a loud sizzle, and she smelled burning plastic as she felt her hair stand on end. Warning lights on the console flashed. She wasn't sure at first what had happened. The engines were still going strong. But then she noticed the Sudsy vats were emptying fast.

Oh no.

Sudsy was pouring out over the outside of the tanker. It coated the exterior monitors with a greasy smear. The tanker suddenly bucked and spun as the Sudsy hit one of the treads. It soon soaked the other and the tanker slid out of control. The monitors showed brief flashing blurs of the worm behind her also spinning wildly, squidbugs desperately clinging to its back. There was nothing left for Sydney to do but brace for impact.

The impact never came. She caught a white blur in her monitors and saw a grate on the floor open in front of the tanker. The tanker dropped through.

Sydney was jarred as the tanker collided with the wall of the chute. The tanker slid down the pipe toward a T-junction. White light collected in a ring around one of the openings and it slammed shut. The tanker bounced off its cover grate and slid down the other corridor.

Sydney shut her eyes. She felt like she was riding a tilt-a-whirl careening down a rocky mountainside. The tanker was being rocked and buffeted through the innards of the ship. She felt a huge lurch, and wasn't sure whether it was the tanker or the ship that tilted down.

She opened her eyes again. Where she expected the salvific white light, instead, she saw flashes of blue at the end of the black tunnel. These turned to blue and beige as the tanker flew out of the belly of the ship and plummeted towards the desert floor.

When Karnage came to, he was hanging upside down in a mangled cockpit. Sydney stood beside him on the ceiling, right side up.

"What happened?" Karnage asked.

"We escaped from the alien ship."

"How?"

Sydney frowned. "It's . . . kind of complicated."

"Try me."

"I think we had help."

"Why can't I move?" he asked, tentatively testing out his frozen muscles.

"That was me." Sydney rubbed her throat. "You sorta . . . tried to kill me back there."

"Oh." The memories of what happened came flooding back to him: his fist squeezing her trachea. The shocked, terrified look in her eyes. The explosions, the smoke, and the flames, and then . . .

Karnage looked away, ashamed. "I lost it, didn't I?"

"Yeah," Sydney answered. "You did."

"I'm . . . I'm not always right in the head."

"Apparently," she snorted. "So how are you feeling now?"

"A little better."

"Only a little?"

"A lot."

"Okay." Sydney gave him a suspicious look. "But the next time you try something like that, I might not go so easy on you." Sydney pressed a finger against Karnage's earlobe. He felt the warmth flow back into his tingling limbs. She unstrapped him from his seat, and helped him drop down to the ceiling. His legs felt like rubber.

"Where are we?"

Sydney jerked a thumb to the mangled hatch that hung open in the wall. "I think you should see for yourself."

They were resting in the bottom of a smooth crater. Just visible above the edges of the crater were the mile-high walls of the WTF.

"What the fuck?" Karnage said.

"My thoughts exactly," Sydney replied with a smirk.

"How did we end up exactly where we started?"

"Like I said before. I think we had help."

Karnage climbed out of the hatch and immediately set to work scaling the walls of the crater. "But who? Who would have helped us?" As he reached the top, he looked up into the sky, squinting into the blue. There was no sign of the aliens. It was as if they had never been there. Except for the smoking crater, and that lingering feeling. . . .

"We're with you, Major. Every one of us. We're with you. . . ."

He whipped around. "Cookie! It must have been!"

"Who's Cookie?"

"One of my troopers. Former Communications engineer. He was already interceptin' the alien communications before they struck. Maybe he finally cracked 'em! Maybe he hacked into the alien ship. Maybe that's what he meant when he said they were with us. Like the French resistance! Maybe—"

An invisible fist smashed into the back of Karnage's shoulder, spinning him back around. He heard the echo of the gunshot seconds later.

Karnage stumbled forward. Blood welled from his shoulder. He turned back to see Sydney charging up the crater's wall.

"No!" He barked. "Stay there! It's a sniper!"

"You're bleeding! I can't leave you out there!"

"Yes you can! I won't let that monkeyfucker take us both down. You stay where you are, Captain. Wait for your opportunity. Find a moment to strike!"

Sydney nodded, and disappeared behind the darkened hulk of the Sudsy tanker. Karnage suddenly felt light-headed and fell to his knees. Karnage looked at his shoulder. Blood welled from a jagged wound the size of a baseball. *Thank god. It went right through.* He clamped his hand over it, trying to stem the flow. Blood poured through his fingers. He squeezed harder, did his best to shut out the pain, and looked across the arena for signs of the sniper.

Walking across the torn landscape was a slim dark figure.

Karnage squinted, trying to make out the details through the desert haze. It was a man with a sharp military brace. Calm. Self-assured. Like he didn't have a care in the world. Karnage thought he could make out a uniform of some kind.

An Uncle Stanley uniform! His heart thudded in his chest and the blood spurted from his shoulder at a quicker pace. It was an enemy officer all right, emerging from his nightmares, coming to finish him off once and for all! Karnage watched his Angel of Death approach, preparing himself for the end.

But as the stranger approached, Karnage saw that it wasn't an Uncle Stanley officer at all. It was a man in a crisp black chauffeur's uniform.

Even though it only took a few minutes, it felt like hours before the chauffeur closed the gap between them. Karnage couldn't hear anything above the sound of his own breathing. He thought he heard some rustling behind him that might have been Sydney moving for cover, but it also might have just been the sound of his own blood spilling out his back. He felt relief again at the gaping wound in his shoulder. Thank god the bullet hadn't played pinball with his internal organs. He might live through this yet.

His vision was slowly whiting out—his blood pressure was dropping fast. The pain began to ease. It felt like it was being pulled from his body with the blood that was passing through his fingers.

The chauffeur stopped a few feet in front of him. His fingers twitched with energy. He knelt down in front of Karnage, his face practically beaming. "Hello, you," he said.

Karnage looked at the chauffeur's gun. "Spragmos X-75?"

"It is."

Karnage tried to focus on the Observation deck in the distance. "How far away were you when you took that shot?"

"Hundred and fifty metres, give or take."

Karnage tried to nod. Pain exploded through his neck. *Bad idea.* Blood spurted through his fingers. He clamped his hand tighter on the wound. "Sloppy," he said.

"Sorry?"

"I said sloppy." Karnage tried to sit up, realized that was a mistake, and dropped to his side. "Your aim was off. You should have been able to hit me square in the chest from that distance."

The chauffeur cocked his head, a bemused smile on his face. "That is just so you, isn't it? Look at you. Still putting on a brave face, even now, when there's no one here to see it. I'm not even sure it's an act, to be honest. Not with your reputation. You must have been quite the sight to behold on the battlefield."

"What do you know about any of that?"

"Oh, I know everything—absolutely everything—about you, Major. And may I say, it is an absolute pleasure to make your acquaintance."

"It is?"

"It is. Believe me, it is. I've been waiting my whole life for this moment."

"Who the hell are you?"

"My name is Patrick. That's really all you need to know for now. Perhaps we can catch up later. Oh, I sincerely wish it hadn't had to happen quite like this."

"Like what?"

"Me nicking you like that from afar. It was a potshot, really. Not very sporting at all."

"No," Karnage muttered. "It wasn't."

"I would have loved to have settled this in a fair fight. To see how good you really are. Still, orders are orders, and I must carry them out as directed."

"You're not supposed to kill me?"

Patrick looked at him with genuine affection. "Now why would anyone want to do a silly thing like that? Look at you. You're simply . . . brilliant." Patrick stood and started to remove his gloves. "I'm going to take a look at that wound, now. Don't want you bleeding out on me until I deliver you to my employer. You're not planning to give me any trouble, are you?"

"No," Karnage said.

"But I will," came another voice.

Patrick looked up, and a ball of goober struck him in the chest, knocking him to the ground and instantly swelling up to cover his arms and head.

"Took you long enough to do something," Karnage said.

"I had to wait until I had a clear shot." Sydney holstered her goober pistol.

"I thought he was gonna talk me to death."

"I kept waiting for him to kiss you and get it over with. He sounded like your biggest fan."

"He had a helluva way of showing it." Karnage winced as Sydney pressed on the wound.

"You're lucky," she said. "Looks like the bullet passed right through. Jesus, you're bleeding pretty badly."

"I know," Karnage said. "I think I'm in big trouble here, Captain."

"You'll be all right," Sydney said.

"Unless you're a trained field medic," Karnage said, "I'm in big trouble."

"You're not gonna die. I won't let you."

"It's all right, Captain." The last of Karnage's vision washed away. He had to force his lips to form the words: "Promise me one thing. Cookie. Velasquez. Heckler. Koch. Stumpy. Find 'em. Save 'em. Stop the squidbugs."

Sydney's voice came from far away. "You won't need me to do that, Major. You'll be able to do that yourself."

He tried to answer but his mouth wouldn't form the words.

Karnage strained his ears as Sydney's voice faded away. "Don't give up on me yet, Major. I think I know someone who can . . ."

He passed out.

MK7: LESSONS IN KARNAGE

CHAPTER ONE

Karnage dreamed of squiggly beasts and black-clad men with pistols for hands. The beasts lashed out with tentacles that sucked him down and wrapped him in their grip. The man in black stood behind the fray, at one moment wearing a chauffeur's outfit, the next a charcoal grey medal-laden Uncle Stanley uniform. Always smiling, always the teeth flashing, telling him it's his lucky day. Gloved fingers pointed at him, the end of the fingers open and hollow like a gun barrel. White hot muzzle flashes burst from the leather-clad digits. Squiggles shot out from the fingers, stabbing into his shoulder, poking and prodding, searching and burrowing, leaving a fiery trail of absolute agony in their wake.

The pain became more focused in his shoulder, and the squiggles finally pulled away, leaving him alone in the darkness.

Karnage opened his eyes. A silvery sphere floated above him. A giant lens sprouted from the ball, pointing down at his shoulder, as long metal tendrils quivered below the lens, poking at bandages. Karnage tried to scramble away, but he couldn't move anything below his neck.

"Get the fuck away from me, you squiggly bastard!"

The lens swivelled up and looked at Karnage. Its inner aperture quickly irised shut and open again, as if it were blinking. A mechanical voice crackled over a speaker. "Sydney, it seems your comrade is awake."

The sphere pulled up and away, and Sydney moved into Karnage's field of vision.

"Hello, Major," she said.

"Captain, what the fuck is going on here?! What the hell was that thing?! Where are we? Why the hell can't I move?!"

"You were shot," Sydney said. "You were in danger of bleeding to death. So I brought you here."

"Where the hell is here?!"

The sphere floated down again, and blinked its lens at Karnage. "Here is home."

Karnage craned his neck. He was lying in a rescue basket, a thin sheet draped over him, the basket suspended from a complex grid of scaffolding running across the arched ceiling. Floodlights dotted the scaffolding. Just visible beyond the lights were more hoverballs fixed with lenses and tentacles. They stared down at Karnage, the lenses zooming in and out, changing focus as the spheres hovered closer or farther away.

A pair of oval bay windows projected out from the wall, filtering sunlight through the grime-streaked glass. Various bits of medical equipment were pushed up against the walls.

"Home? Whose home? It sure as hell ain't mine! And you still haven't told me why the hell I can't move!"

"You can't move because you're a very uncooperative patient," Sydney replied. "I don't need you pulling your stitches out. Not after all of Uncle's hard work. As for whose home this is, it belongs to Uncle."

One of the spheres dropped down from above. It placed a tentacle on Sydney's shoulder. "Don't be so modest, dear. You know this home is just as much yours as it is mine. If only you would visit more often. And in less brutish company."

Karnage's eyes goggled. "That *thing* is your uncle?!"

The sphere blinked its lens at Karnage. "Of course not. What a preposterous supposition. What you are looking at is simply a drone. One of many, in case you haven't noticed. They are my eyes and ears in the compound. I am sequestered elsewhere."

"Why?"

"I have my . . . reasons."

"He's a close family friend," Sydney said. "And he is doing everything in his power to save your life."

Karnage looked down at his bandaged shoulder. "Why? What's wrong with my shoulder?"

The drone bobbed up and down. "Very little, actually. The bullet passed right through the shoulder, missing the scalpula and brachial plexus completely. You should be laid up for a few days at the most. No, your shoulder isn't the problem."

A second pair of drones floated down and pulled back the sheet covering Karnage's leg. A shining metal band wrapped around the middle of its shin.

"What the hell is that?" Karnage said.

The nearest drone flashed its lens at Karnage. His tentacles quivered with excitement. "That is all that stands between you and the unknown frontiers of science!"

"What the hell's he talking about? What the fuck is wrong with my leg?"

"Technically, nothing," the drone said. "Which is the source of your trouble."

"What do you mean? What the hell are you talking about!" Karnage barked.

"It's your ankle," Sydney said. "You twisted it in the arena. You could barely walk on it. Remember? And then on the ship, hours later—"

"It was fine." Karnage looked down at his foot. The hairs on the back of his neck stood on end. "What did those squidbugs do to me?"

Sydney turned to a drone hovering by her shoulder. "Show him."

The drone beside Karnage swivelled its lens at Sydney. It squealed: "Delighted!"

Three drones descended from the ceiling. Their lenses zoomed out, and projected light, each one projecting a different primary colour. The beams intersected, creating a holographic projection of a DNA double helix.

"Human DNA," the drone beside Karnage said. "The building blocks of all life on earth."

The double helix shifted to the right, and three strings of vibrating noodles affixed with shifting coloured beads squiggled in beside it. They tangled and untangled themselves randomly, twitching in agitation whenever they made contact. The coloured beads jumped from one strand to another when the strands touched.

The drone beside Sydney hovered closer to the projection. "Extraterrestrial DNA," it said. "The building blocks of the alien infestation. Unstable. Volatile. Infectious."

The twitching strands lashed out and grabbed the double helix, tearing it apart, wrapping itself into the debris. The beads flew loose from the strands and rocketed about the morass like a hurricane. It looked like a violent feeding frenzy.

"What happened? What is that? Is that what's happenin' inside o' me?!"

"As near as Uncle can tell," Sydney said, "the squidbugs fixed your ankle with an injection of their own genetic material. But it's doing something more than just repairing the damage. It's . . . rewriting your genetic code."

"Rewriting it into what?!"

"And that is where we stumble into the unknown!" The drone beside Karnage squealed. "It is rewriting your genetic structure, taking the best genes from your DNA and combining it with select genes from itself, synthesizing a new hybrid creature."

"What do you mean a hybrid creature? What the hell is it turnin' me into?!"

The drone clapped a set of tentacles together. "It's unpredictable! The infestation takes so many shapes. The possibilities are endless!"

"I wish you wouldn't sound so pleased about this, Uncle," Sydney said.

The drone beside her placed a tentacle on her shoulder. "I'm sorry, my dear. I just get so excited about new discoveries. Please. Forgive my enthusiasm, Major."

Karnage didn't care. He was staring at his foot. It didn't feel different. And yet, somewhere, deep inside of him, the squidbug DNA was attacking, changing him into something he didn't want. Suddenly the invasion had become personal. So much more personal than Karnage could ever have imagined. Rage boiled up inside him. He wouldn't let them get away with it. He wouldn't let them win. Not like this. Not now.

MAJOR KARNAGE

Karnage laid back and closed his eyes. "Cut it off," he said.

He heard the whirring of the lens on the drone beside him. "What?"

"I said cut it off! I'm not gonna just lie here and let those squidbugs turn me into something I'm not. I'm me. I'm Major Karnage. Any part of me that says otherwise can go to hell. So cut this fucking thing off. NOW!"

Sydney stared at Karnage in shock. "You can't be serious."

"What part of my little tirade made it sound like I was joking?"

"You won't be able to walk—"

"I'll strap a fucking chainsaw to my leg if I have to! I'm not lettin' those squidbug bastards get the upper hand!"

"Upper hand? Listen to what you're saying! It's like cutting off your nose to spite your face!"

"Who said anything about cuttin' off my nose?! It's my foot that's gettin' all up in my face! So cut that monkeyfucker off!"

"Ooh!" Another drone descended from the ceiling, squealing. It stopped above his leg. "So dramatic. So final! And so wholly unnecessary." The drone tapped the metal band on Karnage's leg. "The UVL blocker is containing the infection. It soaks it up, like a sponge, and should prevent further contamination until I discover a means of extraction."

"Extraction? You mean you could cure me?"

"Not at the moment, no, otherwise I would have. Extraction is not yet within my grasp. But I will find a cure, rest assured. Some sort of stem cell vaccine is my current favoured approach. While not exactly the most elegant of solutions, it just might do the job. I've taken the liberty of harvesting some of your unfused genetic material and cataloguing it in my database. You don't mind, of course. I thought it would be prudent in case some unforeseen complication causes the infection to spread."

Karnage's mind was reeling from the mental assault. "Wait. How do you know so much about the squidbugs?"

Sydney took a breath, as if she'd been dreading this. "He's been studying them," she said.

174

"Oh yes," the drone beside Karnage's head chirped. "Quite extensively, if I may be so bold."

"How extensively?" Karnage asked.

"Would you like me to show you?"

"Please," Karnage said. "Do."

The drone clapped its tendrils. "Excellent!" It turned to Sydney. "Please be a dear and let the good major up."

Sydney looked warily at Karnage. "I don't think that's such a good idea," she said.

"I do," Karnage said.

"As do I." The drone beside Sydney patted her on the arm. "You have been outvoted, my dear."

Sydney moved beside Karnage's bed and prepared to tap him on the neck. "I've always hated democracy," she said.

CHAPTER TWO

A drone led Karnage and Sydney out of the room and down a spiral staircase. They came out into the glare of sunlight, at the base of a water tower. The tower was in the shape of Dabby Tabby's head, the oval windows making up the cat's long-faded eyes. Streaks of rust ran down its face. The words WELCOME TO LAKE DABNEY were still visible across Dabby's forehead.

The water tower stood in the middle of an abandoned amusement park. Twists of sagging roller coaster stretched across the sky, threatening to give way and fall on their heads. The bright colours of the fairground had long faded to a dull grey. Splash pads stood empty and cracked. Bright red water slides had faded to sickly pink in the harsh sunlight. Tattered canopies on sagging shelters leaned against each other like drunkards so that the whole compound looked like a teetering house of cards that threatened to fall down if you looked at it funny.

"What kind of idiot builds a waterpark in the desert?" Karnage said.

"Waterpark?" Sydney said. "What is this waterpark you speak of?"

"The one we're standin' in," Karnage said.

"You must be mistaken," Sydney said. "There is no waterpark."

"What the hell are you talking about? We're standin' right in the middle of it!"

"Nope," Sydney said. "Must be your imagination. The Dabney Corporation never built a waterpark. Especially one that failed catastrophically. Not here. Not anywhere. If they did, people would know about it. And they don't. And that has nothing to do with the Dabney Corporation wiping their failures off the record books. Because the Dabney Corporation never makes a mistake. Never does anything wrong. Go ahead. Ask them. They'll set you straight."

"Okay, I get it. Thank you, Madame Sarcasm."

"Are you sure?" Sydney said. "I could go on."

"I'm sure you could."

"This way, if you please." The drone led them towards a cracked concrete building. A sagging fish-shaped sign read JOURNEY UNDER THE SEA. They entered the dark building, its cool concrete walls a relief from the harsh desert sun. The drone led them through a long grey tunnel, their only company the echo of their own footsteps. The tunnel walls changed from crumbling concrete to an arched corridor of scratched acrylic. Beyond the tunnel walls lay an entire alien world. Karnage recognized orange creeper hanging from a grey alien tree, its branches twitching like fingers. Giant purple ladybugs scuttled through the pinkstink undergrowth, hiding behind massive blue seed pods that swelled and exhaled plumes of yellow mist. Occasionally a drone appeared through the yellow gloom, repositioning a purple lady bug, or pruning a bit of creeper before disappearing back into the mist. They reminded Karnage of old women tending their gardens.

The drone stroked the glass with a tendril. Its lens zoomed in towards the enclosure. "Such fine specimens. It's taken me so long to develop this collection. To think it all started with just a few spore samples. They matched nothing in the records. They weren't even carbon-based life forms. They were sulphur-based. At least, in the beginning. Then they did something marvellous. Something I still can't quite explain. They became compatible with carbon-based life. You recall the Carpathian Flu epidemic?"

"No," Karnage said.

"I do," Sydney said. "It killed thousands. Took 'em years to come up with a vaccine."

"That wasn't a vaccine," the drone said. "It was a genetic modifier, designed to improve our compatibility with the spores. They were the cause of it, you know. Not the Carpathians."

"It's always easier to blame Carpathia," Karnage said.

The drone bobbed, as if nodding. "Better to blame Carpathia than admit the truth: they were taking the first steps to adapting us to the alien DNA."

"I thought you said the squidbugs were adapting to us?" Karnage said.

The drone nodded. "They were. And we, in turn, have been adapting to them."

Karnage gazed out into the misty alien landscape and scowled. "Evolution at work."

The drone's lens flickered, as if blinking in surprise. "Oh no. There is nothing natural about these selections." The drone turned towards the glass. "Look at these creatures. They have been adapted so perfectly to life on this planet. One establishes a foothold, subtly alters its environs, allowing the next in the chain to establish a foothold. Each successive creature becomes more and more complex, until . . ." The drone stared into the mist, adjusted its lens as if searching for something. "Now where *is* he?"

A soft shadow was just barely visible through the gloom, shambling slowly. The drone tapped the glass excitedly. "Here, Fido. Come here."

The shadow stopped, as if listening, then drew back, and disappeared into the mist.

It burst out of the fog, and slammed into the glass, scratching at it with its claws. It snarled and screeched, its skin flashing a deep crimson red.

It was a squidbug.

"This is my latest acquisition," the drone said cheerily. "I only picked him up about a week ago. I'm hoping that he completes my collection. Admittedly, this collection still requires the horned worms and winged leviathans, but they're simply far too large to keep in this enclosure. One must make sacrifices after all."

The squidbug snarled and scratched at the glass, pounding at it with its fists. The tentacles around its mouth splayed out, revealing a sharp beak. It turned to bite and snap at the glass, its twin tongues slithering out, smearing slime across the glass.

"I've never seen one so enraged," Sydney said.

"That's because it has been cut off," the drone said. "These creatures do not act of their own free will. There is a guiding force behind everything they do. They are analogous to workers and warriors in a giant ant colony. There is something—a queen of sorts—that guides the entire ecosystem. These creatures adapt and change to their environment almost instantly. They have been engineered by some sort of intelligence, and that intelligence continues to mold them as the infestation progresses."

"How?" Karnage said. "How do they do it?"

The drone shot out a hologram of a rotating three-dimensional graph of gyrating squiggles. As Karnage saw it from different angles, he was reminded of the squiggles on Cookie's arms.

"The alien infestation uses ultra-violent transmissions," the drone said.

"Don't you mean ultra-violet?" Sydney said.

The hologram disappeared and the drone turned its lens towards Sydney. "Absolutely not. I meant ultra-violent. Ultra-violent transmissions are unique to this invasion. They are actively assaulting the electromagnetic spectrum, intermittently obliterating and inserting themselves between the extreme ultra-violet and super ultra-violet wavelengths. Theoretically, this should be impossible. And in practice, it often is. Yet this unique band consistently and continuously shows up in my data, usually in erratic oscillations measured in yoctosecond bursts. Millions of orders come in on each burst. One for each and every creature in the invasion, right down to the smallest bacterium."

The drone hovered down to Karnage's shin and tapped on the metal band under his pants. "It is these very same transmissions which I am using to contain the genetic infection. The band gives off ultra-violent transmissions, ordering the exo-DNA to maintain itself in a holding pattern and await further instructions."

The drone hovered up and tapped on the acrylic ceiling. "I have similar shielding around the entire compound. I have reason to believe that these ultra-violent transmissions are two-way. This intelligence has been keeping tabs on every step of the invasion, right down to the mutation and division of individual cells."

It gazed longingly out into the mist. "I would love to see it up close. I find myself wondering what it would look like. We always speak of the human race as being made in God's image. I'd love to see the god that made all this."

Karnage pressed his hands against the glass. He felt more helpless than ever. How were they going to stop this? *If only we'd known about it sooner,* he thought. *If only—*

He turned to look at the drone. "How long have you known about this?"

"Decades," the drone said. "Not the full extent, of course. I didn't fully realize the implications until—GRAAK!"

The drone squawked as Karnage slammed it against the glass. His Sanity Patch buzzed. "Warning. Sanity Level upgraded to Peachy Keen. Please refrain—"

"Why didn't you tell anybody?! Why didn't you try and do something about it?!"

The drone's tendrils flickered and stabbed at Karnage's fist in agitation. Its voice stayed cheerful and bright. "I *have* been doing something," it said. "I've been studying it quite extensively—"

"You've been sittin' back and lettin' it get away with blue bloody murder!" Karnage slammed the drone against the wall again. His Sanity Patch crooned "Tangy Orange." "They practically got us swallowed up whole, and all you can do is sit here and *study* the fucking things?!"

Pain stabbed into Karnage's shoulder. His arm dropped, letting the drone go. The drone quickly flew up out of reach. Karnage saw Sydney's pinky on his shoulder. She shot him a warning look. "That's enough."

Karnage set his jaw. "What about you, Captain. Did you know about this?"

"No," she said. "He never told me."

"Why not?"

Sydney dropped her eyes. "He was trying to protect me."

"Protect you from what?"

"Perhaps you've glossed over the bit where I mentioned the genetic modifications handed out under the guise of vaccinations?"

the drone said. "Where do you suppose they came from?"

"The Dabney Corporation?" Karnage said.

"Precisely," the drone squealed with glee. "You're not quite as dumb as you look, Major." It was feeling braver now that it was out of Karnage's reach. "Until I could understand the full extent of the infestation, I did not want to endanger young Sydney. I am her guardian after all. Perhaps that was an error in judgement on my part, but what else could I have done?"

Karnage set his jaw. He shot the drone a dangerous look. "Plenty."

"I beg to disagree."

"Beg all you like. You still chickened out!"

"Let it go," Sydney said.

"No, I'm not going to let it go." Karnage turned towards the drone, and stabbed a finger at it. The drone drew itself up against the glass. "I want to meet that fucker face-to-face. Let him tell me man-to-man why he didn't have the guts to do something about this. No more of this hiding shit, Unk. You hear me?!"

"No," Sydney said. "You can't."

"Why? You afraid I'm gonna hit him?"

"Yes."

"You're goddamn right I will!" The Sanity Patch crooned "Sharp Cheddar" as Karnage rounded on the drone. "Come on, you coward! Show yourself!"

Sydney brandished her pinkies. "You'll have to go through me first."

Karnage cracked his knuckles. "Fine by me."

"No!" The drone dropped down between Sydney and Karnage. "No violence. Not on my account." It focused its lens on Karnage's face. "You wish to see me face-to-face?"

"I do."

The drone nodded. "Very well."

"Uncle, no!"

The drone turned to Sydney. "The major is right. I owe him an explanation. I owe it to the world. I have hidden away long enough." The drone drifted down the tunnel, calling, "This way, please."

MAJOR KARNAGE

Sydney glared at Karnage. "If you hurt him, I will kill you."
She turned and walked away.

CHAPTER THREE

The drone led them through the terrarium. The tunnel curved around and came back up into a concrete structure. The drone stopped right before the exit in front of a door marked EMPLOYEES ONLY. They passed through, and down a flight of stairs into a maintenance hall. Rust-streaked pipes lined the wall of the narrow corridor. A few aging fluorescents flickered inside their steel mesh cages above them, providing spotty lighting. The floor was cracked and stained. The concrete had crumbled away in places, showing rusted reinforcing rods.

The corridor came to an end in front of a dented metal door marked KILLER WHALE TANK. The drone opened the door, and soft blue light poured through the frame. They walked through.

The room was filled with a giant inverted dome made entirely of acrylic. The tank held a dark pulsing mass. Giant rusted pipes ran down the sides of the tank and into the floor. Pools of water lay on the floor. The room was filled with drones, adjusting valves and manning small digital consoles. Wires spread from the consoles into the tank.

"There I am, Major." A drone dropped down in front of him and pointed towards the tank. "Do with me what you will."

Karnage moved closer, squinting his eyes. The pulsing mass was composed of coils of grey flesh as thick as his forearm, looped endlessly together, packed tightly within the dome. As he drew closer, he saw a small shadow hanging from the base of the dome.

It was a body, curled in on itself, hanging from the dome by its head. A band of gleaming metal attached its head to the base of the dome. Its pale skin was translucent. The limbs were shrivelled, pulled up against the swollen torso. It wore a nothing but a thin sleeveless shroud, lines of purple, blue, and green visible on the skin.

As Karnage drew closer, he saw the band cut across the body's head just above the eyes. It was missing the top half of its skull.

Karnage looked up at the tangles of grey coils that filled the tank. It was as if they had spilled out of the head, and were now pulsing inside the giant tank. *That's his brain.*

Its face was drawn and tight, eyes closed, the pale lids tattooed with tiny purple capillaries. The face pinched tighter as the eyes struggled to open. The pink pupils drifted towards Karnage and tried to focus while its tiny lips curled slightly at the corners.

The drone beside Karnage turned to him. "Now do you understand?"

The smile dropped from the lips, replaced by a painful grimace. The eyes unfocused and the eyelids closed.

"No," Karnage said.

"Of course you don't," the drone said. "Nor would anyone else. It is too different. Too . . . alien. And so I stay hidden. Protected."

Karnage looked up at the pulsing mass of brain. "How . . . ?"

"Decompressive craniectomy and extensive transcranial magnetic stimulation. Does that help you understand at all?"

"Not really."

The drone nodded. "It would not. It is too foreign to you. Just as your ways are foreign to many. We are both very much alike. Outcasts. Incomprehensible to the outside world. Damaged in so many ways, and yet so very able in others. You owe your very life to my abilities. My research. My path. Perhaps your path will lead you to return that favour. Except . . ."

"What?" Karnage said.

"I accept my limitations, Major. And I have chosen to work within them." The drone poked at Karnage's bandaged shoulder. Blood was seeping through. "You would be wise to learn to do the same."

CHAPTER FOUR

Karnage watched as a drone restitched his shoulder. He was sitting on a stool in the water tower in front of the oval windows. He peered through the grime-covered glass at the broken water park below. Somewhere beyond the sagging roller coasters and broken water slides lay the squidbugs. He turned to Sydney. "I'm a mess."

"You just tore out a few stitches," Sydney said. "Uncle will have you stitched up again in no time."

Karnage shook his head. "It's more than that. We were there. Right there. Starin' them squidbugs square in the face. We could have ended it all right there. We could've . . ."

"You don't know what you could have done," Sydney said.

"I do," Karnage said, "and it was nothing. I had my chance, and I blew it. Goddammit, how the fuck am I supposed to fight anything without blowin' my head off?!"

"What do you mean?" Sydney said.

"He's referring to the explosive device implanted in the base of his skull," the drone said.

Sydney did a double take. "What?!"

Karnage looked at the drone. "How did you know about that?"

The drone's lens looked up at Karnage. "It's rather hard to miss, isn't it?" It tapped the LED screen of the patch. "Frankly, I'm surprised you haven't brought it up before."

"I try not to think about it too much," Karnage said.

"Yes, and as a result you've come precariously close to blowing your head off on a large number of occasions."

"How do you know that?!"

"It's all recorded here in the device's on-board computer. It was automatically scanned and downloaded when Sydney first brought you in. I must say, it is an amazing piece of technology. The gentleman who designed it is either a genius or a complete and utter madman."

"That sounds like Flaherty."

"Dr. Paul Flaherty? The neuroscientist?"

"You knew him?"

"I knew *of* him. He was involved in a number of horrifying scandals which left many of his patients either brain-dead or just plain dead. His theories were occasionally interesting, while his methods were . . . impractical, let's say. I'm shocked to see that he finally achieved some measure of success."

"Depends on your definition of success," Karnage said.

"The fact you are still alive should be considered success enough."

"Can you remove it?" Sydney said.

The drone zoomed its lens in on the device. "Any attempt to cut power to the device will cause it to detonate. Any attempt to improperly tamper with the device will also cause it to detonate."

"Sounds like I'm fucked," Karnage said.

"Not necessarily," the drone said. "There are other options available to us outside of the surgical. Alternative therapies. We could take a more holistic approach."

"What do you mean?"

"Instead of tampering with the device," the drone tapped Karnage's head, "we tamper with the subject."

Karnage swatted it away. "What the hell do you mean tamper with the subject?! I'm not gonna let anybody carve up my brain!"

"I assure you no carving would be required. All adjustments would be behavioural in nature, not surgical. The sensors respond to specific signals from the amygdala, hypothalamus, and to a lesser extent, the pituitary gland. It interprets these responses in order to determine the instinctual motivations of the subject. In effect, it is tied directly to your lizard brain. Remove the lizard brain from the equation, and the sensors will have nothing to respond to. No stimulus, no response. No earth-shattering kaboom."

"So how do I cut out my lizard brain?" Karnage asked.

The drone tapped a tentacle against Karnage's forehead. "By becoming attuned to your Eleventh Sense."

CHAPTER FIVE

"Of course we are all familiar with the five Primary Senses: Sight, Sound, Smell, Taste, and Touch. But beyond that, there are a further three Secondary Senses from which the body draws from.

"Intuition, the oft-cited and poorly understood Sixth Sense which unthinkingly pulls from the first five senses and manifests as a 'gut reaction.' In essence, this is your lizard brain.

"Logic, the Seventh Sense, is an understanding and application of the underlying mathematics and order of the universe as well as our place within it. The Seventh Sense is the level at which we first truly begin to experience consciousness.

"Emotion, the Eight Sense, is an awareness of one's own emotions and emotional states, as manifested by the five Primary Senses in conjunction with the Sixth and Seventh Senses.

"Above the Secondary Senses, we have the Tertiary Senses. Sensitivity, which relates to an awareness of others' emotional states and how our own emotions affect them, as well as the creatures around us. Acuity, the Tenth Sense, is the sharpening of the previous nine senses into finely honed points of—"

"This sounds like a lot of bullshit to me," Karnage said.

"Of course it does," the drone said. "That is because you haven't mastered them."

Karnage threw up his hands. "Okay, now I *know* you're full of shit." He walked towards the door.

"I have the mathematical proofs to support my theories," the drone called after him. "I can show them to you if you like."

Sydney caught up with Karnage. "Where are you going?"

"To get some fresh air." Karnage glowered at the drone. "It's startin' to smell in here."

Sydney blocked his way. "Major, wait."

"What?"

"I know it sounds crazy—"

"It doesn't just sound crazy." Karnage shouted at the drone. "It *is* crazy!"

"Any crazier than an alien invasion?"

Karnage looked at Sydney. He shrugged. "Maybe just a little."

"Look, I know how it sounds, but trust me. Uncle knows what he's talking about."

"He sure as hell doesn't sound like it."

"Remember when you asked me to trust you?"

"Yeah, and you didn't."

"That's right. I didn't. And it nearly got us killed. Don't make the same mistake I did. He knows what he's talking about." She flipped up a pinky finger. "Where do you think I learned how to fight?"

Karnage looked at the drone, then back at Sydney. "Him?"

Sydney nodded. "Yes, him. He has a strange way of looking at things, but it works. Trust me, okay?"

Karnage looked at Sydney's outstretched pinky. He nodded. "Okay."

"All right, Unk," Karnage said. "You got up to the Tenth Sense. What's number eleven?"

"The Eleventh Sense is the most vital of them all. It is the culmination of the other ten senses into a cohesive whole."

"I thought that was Acuity?"

"No," the drone said. "Acuity is the honing of the nine *individual* senses into separate focus. The Eleventh Sense channels those nine points of focus into a cohesive whole. I call it Spirituality."

"Spirituality? What, am I supposed to find religion now? Let me tell you somethin', Unk. The last religion I found tried to feed me to a giant fucking worm!"

The drone wagged a tendril. "Do not confuse religion with the spiritual. Religion is a strictly human construct, designed to oppress the senses. It is geared specifically towards engaging the lizard brain. Spirituality, on the other hand, is the strict application of the scientific method to empirical data collected from all ten senses. So, while it can technically be argued that the Eleventh Sense is nothing more than the carefully synthesized application of ten senses, there is an even stronger argument that the whole is indeed far greater than the sum of its parts."

Karnage shot Sydney a doubtful look. "Okay, so how do I master this Eleventh Sense?"

"Oh it takes years of training to fully master the Eleven Senses. Which is why we will be attempting no such thing. Instead, I will teach you the equivalent of a series of parlour tricks. You don't need to understand all facets of human physiology to learn how to defeat a so-called 'lie' detector. Nor will you need a degree in neuroscience to learn how to defeat the workings of the Sanity Patch."

"So what do I have to do?"

"You must learn to stop acting on instinct, and embrace your conscious self. No more gut reactions. No more split decisions. They could cost you your life. In a word, don't feel—think!"

Karnage balked. "You want me to *think*?"

"Is that a problem for you?"

"You're goddamn right it is! I spent my whole life in the military. You're taught not to think! Thinking gets you killed! It slows you down! You learn to rely on muscle memory. It keeps you alive. I can't just throw all that away!"

"Yes. Your lizard brain is very well trained. So well trained, in fact, that it will most assuredly kill you if you continue down this path. You must undrill what has been drilled. Do not succumb to your primal urges. Make rational choices. Not thinking is now what will get you killed. You must learn to engage your upper brain functions. Do not mindlessly react to the impulses of the lizard brain. Take a moment. Listen to what the lizard brain wants you to do. Then, process it through the limbic lobe. Reason out why it is necessary to do what the lizard brain desires. Then, *act*—with direction and purpose—comfortable in the knowledge that you are in fact making a rational choice."

"Okay, wait a minute. Hold on. Let me see if I get this," Karnage said. "If I feel like I need to punch somebody in the mouth, I need to stop, think up a good reason why I should punch them, and then just . . . go ahead and punch 'em in the mouth?"

"A crude way of putting it, but essentially, yes."

"Isn't that just doing the same thing?"

The drone pointed an excited tendril at Karnage. "That is the intrinsic subtlety of the Eleventh Sense, and is the essence of the parlour trick. So long as you can logically reason that there is no rational alternative, then your course of action is free and clear. The inevitability of the desired action is the crucial piece in this puzzle. The keystone, if you will. Break the rock—not because of an urge to commit violence, but because it is a rational necessity required for you to achieve your goal."

"It's like the difference between punching a wall in anger, and a boxer throwing a punch in the ring," Sydney said. "A good one, anyway."

"All right," Karnage rubbed his chin. "I think I get it. So what do I get to practise my punches on?"

Sydney stood facing Karnage in the central square of the park. She gave him the evil eye. "You want to make any snide remarks about me being your punching bag?"

Karnage shook his head. "Nope. Not a one."

The drone floated down between them. "Rest assured, no one will be punching anyone. Not yet, at any rate. We will start small. Major, please place your hand on Sydney's shoulder."

Karnage did.

"Now, step forward, keeping your elbow locked, and your hand firmly on her shoulder."

Karnage kept his arm locked as he took a step forward. Sydney took a step back to keep her balance. His Sanity Patch was silent.

The drone's lens flashed in the sun. "Excellent! Now again. Faster this time."

Karnage took a quick step forward. He pushed Sydney two steps back. His Sanity Patch stayed silent.

"Most excellent! Now, again. Faster."

Karnage's step became a lunge. Sydney stumbled back a few steps.

"Good," the drone said. "Now, this time, you will push with the same momentum. Only this time, you will use only your arm."

Karnage gave Sydney a hard shove. The Sanity Patch buzzed. "Warning. Sanity Level upgraded to Frothy Cream. Please refrain from violent behaviour."

The drone tsked. "Concentrate on your emotional state. Remember: you are not striking your opponent. It is but a firm push. Necessity requires you to move her, using nothing but your open palm."

"Wouldn't it be a lot easier if I just asked her politely to move?"

"Yes, but that would defeat the purpose of the exercise. Concentrate on the objective."

"The objective's kind of dumb," Karnage said. "I'm pushin' her pretty hard. I know it. She knows it. We all know it. It's pretty much a shove, and in my books, a shove is a precursor to violence."

"Mine, too," Sydney said.

The drone's lens zoomed in and out impatiently. "Which is why we are attempting to skip over that particular chapter in your internal book. That is the crux of the trick. Focus on your long-term goal. Why are you attempting this? Why is it important you can accomplish this? It goes far beyond the short-term goal of completing the exercise itself. What is it you hope to achieve, Major? Concentrate on that."

Karnage closed his eyes and tried to think long-term. *I need to kick some squidbug ass.* He opened his eyes and gave Sydney another shove.

The Sanity Patch buzzed again. "Warning. Sanity Level upgraded to Sandy Dreams. Please refrain from violent behaviour."

"You are not thinking long-term," the drone said.

Karnage rounded on the drone. "I am thinking long-term! The problem is my long-term goal is still pretty goddamn violent!"

"That is because you continue to let your lizard brain drive you. Think, Major. Engage your rational thought process. Why is violence necessary? What is driving you to be violent?"

Karnage took a breath and closed his eyes. He wanted to stop the alien menace. He'd never really thought about why. It was just what he did. He'd always looked for another fight. Always craved another battle. But why? Was he such a prisoner of his lizard brain that he didn't have a better reason? Why was stopping the invasion so important to him? Was it saving the world? No, what had the world ever done for him? *Think, soldier. Think! What do you care if the world burns? It sure as shit hasn't cared about you. Why do you care? What does it matter?*

And then it hit him.

Cookie. Velasquez. Heckler. Stumpy. Koch.

Karnage opened his eyes. He gave Sydney a hard shove. She staggered back.

The Sanity Patch stayed silent.

The drone squealed. "Most impressive, Major! Most impressive!"

"I'm a quick study," Karnage said.

"Says you," said Sydney, rubbing her shoulder. "When do I get to push back?"

"In due time, my dear. In due time. We must complete our undergraduate degree before we move to our master's thesis." The drone's lens flashed in the sun. "Let's resume our classes on the fairground, shall we?"

The fairground was full of abandoned carnival games, frayed canopies over splintering wooden booths. The counters were chipped and pitted. Rows of nails where cheap prizes used to hang lined the walls of the booths.

Karnage hefted the softball in his fist, his thumb sliding over its shiny leather. He squinted his eyes at the dusty pyramid of milk bottles and threw. The pyramid exploded in a sea of tumbling bottles. His Sanity Patch buzzed.

"Warning. Sanity Level upgraded to Peachy Keen. Please refrain from violent behaviour."

"As I said, you are not ready. Return to your practise."

Karnage scowled. Sydney tossed him the softball. "Just relax and try to enjoy yourself," she said.

"I feel like an idiot," Karnage tossed the ball back. "What am I, twelve?"

She returned the throw. "We're just building up a sense memory."

"Yes." The drone restacked the milk bottles on the platform. "The sense memory will aid you in channelling a calm, rational state from which you may draw the necessary motivation to perform this act of violence."

"We better hurry up and build it, cuz my arm is about to fall off here," Karnage said.

"Do you wish to try and make another attempt?"

"I do."

"Very well."

Karnage aimed the ball at the beakers, and threw. The bottles went flying and his Sanity Patch buzzed. "Warning. Sanity Level upgraded to Tangy Orange. Please refrain—"

"Sonofabitch!"

"Lashing out only fuels your lizard brain," the drone said.

"The lizard brain can go fuck itself."

"If you truly wish for the lizard brain to go and 'fuck itself,' then you must embrace your conscious self, and let go your instincts. Channel your sense memory. Focus on your long-term goal. Embrace the Eleventh Sense."

Karnage aimed the ball at the bottles. He closed his eyes. *Cookie. Velasquez. Heckler. Stumpy. Koch.*

Karnage opened his eyes and threw. The bottles exploded in all directions. The Sanity Patch stayed silent.

The drone squealed. "Excellent, Major. Most excellent!"

Karnage looked at the fallen bottles. "Take that, you fuckin' lizard."

Karnage stood before the WAK-A-KAT game. He hefted the giant mallet in his fists, and eyed the holes. Dabby Tabby's wide grinning face was just visible in the gloom of each hole. He looked up at the drone.

"Do it."

The drone pulled a switch. Carnival music started up. Lights around the machine flashed, and Dabby Tabby's grinning face popped out of one of the holes. Karnage smashed it with the mallet.

His neck buzzed. "Warning. Sanity Level upgraded to Sharp Cheddar. Please refrain from violent behaviour."

"Dammit!" Karnage stepped away from the machine like a frustrated batter stepping away from the plate, swinging his mallet.

"Perhaps that is enough for today," the drone said.

"No. I can do this." He rolled his shoulders and shook out his arms. "Start it up again."

The music cranked up and the lights flashed. Dabby Tabby popped up in the middle hole. *Cookie*. Karnage struck the head back down. The Sanity Patch stayed silent.

Dabby Tabby's head popped up in the corner. *Velasquez*. Karnage banged it back down. The Sanity Patch didn't complain.

Two Dabby heads popped up in the middle row. Karnage knocked them down in quick succession. *Heckler. Koch*. Another head was just starting to rise before the head of the mallet smashed it back down. *Stumpy*. The music's rhythm increased. Dabby heads popped up faster and faster as the lights increased their pace. Karnage knocked them all down, repeating his mantra with each mallet blow. *Cookie. Velasquez. Heckler. Koch. Stumpy. Cookie. Velasquez. Heckler. Koch. Stumpy*. There was no buzzing. No crooning voices. Nobody's head blew off.

The game reached a crescendo. A buzzer went off, and a blast of confetti shot from the top of the machine. "HIGH SCORE!" it screeched.

The drone squealed. "Excellent! Most excellent! I was not expecting you to make such quick progress. I do believe you have finally completed your undergraduate degree. You have come very far very quickly, but you still have a long way to go. You must now take this training to the next level, and move to a live opponent."

"Is this where I'm supposed to volunteer?" Sydney said.

"In a manner of speaking," the drone said. "I suggest you rest up tonight, Major. Think on what you have learned."

"Why stop now? I've come so far. I'm ready for more."

"Yes, but your Sanity Patch however is starting to become a little . . . overheated, shall we say?" The drone tapped on the flashing orange screen. "It would be best if it were to get a fresh start tomorrow. I have provided you with sleeping quarters in the water tower. I bid you adieu until the morn."

The drone flew up and off, heading for the concrete aquarium bunkers.

Karnage turned to Sydney. "I hope you don't snore."

CHAPTER TEN

Karnage lay in his cot, staring out the bay window. The sky was a pale midnight blue. Stars winked and twinkled over the broken skeletal silhouettes of the park. He wondered how many of those stars were hostile. He clenched his fists, then remembered what Cookie had told him. *I'm trying to do like you said, Cookie. I'm trying to use my head. I only hope I can get it under control before it's too late. Before . . .*

Sydney rustled in the next cot. She turned to look at him. "What's up?"

"What do you mean?" Karnage asked.

"You're breathing heavy," Sydney said. "Through your nose. Means you're pissed about something."

"It does?"

"Yeah. You never noticed that before?"

"No."

"Well, you do. So what's up?"

"Just thinkin' about the squidbugs," Karnage said. "Hope I can stop 'em before it's too late."

"You know how you're gonna do that yet?"

"No," Karnage said. "Figure I should work on gettin' my own head worked out first."

"You plan to do it all single-handed?" Sydney asked.

Karnage shrugged. "I dunno."

"There's kind of a lot of 'em."

"Yeah," Karnage said. "There is." He looked over at Sydney through the gloom. She was barely a lump in her cot. "You interested in givin' me a hand?"

"Hell, no," Sydney said. "Once you're better, I'm gonna arrest your ass."

"Still?"

She sat up, grinning. "Oh hell, yeah. I still got my career to think about, after all."

"So how do you think they'll react when you bring me into that precinct again?" Karnage said.

Sydney shrugged and lay back on her cot. "I don't know. Probably throw me a ticker tape parade. Give me a medal. You know, the usual."

"Uh huh. And what about all that stuff about you breakin' me outta my cell and tryin' to kick my ass? Think they'll just overlook all that?"

She stuck her hands behind her head. "Oh, for sure. I mean, it's nothing. I only helped you escape, is all. Not on purpose, of course. You know, it just kinda happened. I'm sure they'll understand."

"You don't think they might have a problem with that?"

"Nah."

"Well, what about that part where you tried to show up Riggs by proving you could beat the crap outta me?"

"Oh, well I'm sure once I explain to my superiors how big of an asshole Riggs is, all will be forgiven. It's not like they ever screwed me over before."

"Not once, huh?"

"Oh no. Not ever."

"This that sarcasm thing again?"

"Yep."

Karnage lay back in his cot, staring out at the stars. The black outline of a vulture soared past in the distance. "Lemme ask you somethin' Captain. You ever think of givin' up the whole law and order thing and embarkin' on a life o' crime?"

"Well, that depends. What kind of crime we talkin' about here?"

Karnage shrugged. "Probably big stuff. Security breaches. Vandalism. Terrorism. Stuff you'd do while fightin' squidbugs."

"And what do I get out of it?"

Karnage shrugged. "Probably nothing. Probably just get yourself arrested. Or killed. Maybe even turned into a giant mutant squidbuggy thing."

"You mean like you?"

"Yeah. Like me."

"You make it all sound so tempting."

"Well, there's the off-chance you might accidentally stop the squidbugs."

"And save the world?"

Karnage shrugged. "Maybe."

"What do you think the chances are of doing that?"

"Pretty bad."

"Yet you're gung ho for it anyway."

"I got a vested interest."

"What's that?"

Karnage grew serious. "Cookie. Velasquez. Heckler. Koch. Stumpy."

"Your troopers."

Karnage nodded.

"These troopers of yours," Sydney said. "They good people?"

"Yep," Karnage said. "The best."

"Worth dying for?"

"Ten times over."

Sydney nodded. "Let me think about it. Maybe sleep on it. Get back to you. Okay?"

Karnage nodded. "Okay."

"'Night, Major," Sydney said. "I hope you can kill something in the morning."

"Me, too," Karnage said.

CHAPTER ELEVEN

Karnage and Sydney stood across from each other in the carnival square in front of the fountain. Karnage stretched his hands. Sydney wiggled her toes. The drone hovered down between them.

"Working with a live opponent should be no different than the simulations. Channel your sense memories, Major. Engage the limbic lobe. Remember why you are doing this."

Karnage nodded. "I won't forget."

"Then let us begin," the drone hovered up and out of the way. "Start slowly, at first. Telegraph your strikes. Allow your body time to adjust to the idea that these movements are nonviolent."

Karnage did as the drone said. He threw his punch slowly, thinking about every movement, working to convince himself there was nothing violent about it. *Just makin' a fist. Just pullin' it back. Just twistin' my body forward while I'm extendin' my arm.* Sydney caught and easily deflected the punch. Karnage did it again. And again. Slowly, he picked up the pace. All the while, he repeated his mantra: *Cookie. Velasquez. Heckler. Stumpy. Koch. Cookie. Velasquez. Heckler. Stumpy. Koch.*

"Excellent, Major! Excellent!"

His punches were moving at a normal pace now. It was like a dance: Karnage was leading, throwing his punches, and Sydney would block and deflect. Like a violent tango where the music kept going faster and faster, picking up the pace. Karnage and Sydney picked up their pace with it. He couldn't help it: he was enjoying it.

Karnage let loose with a combo that almost took Sydney off guard. She smiled and nodded, showing appreciation for his work. They were perfectly matched in this mock combat. Karnage felt something stirring inside he hadn't felt in a long time—

"Warning. Sanity Level upgraded to Lemon Breeze. Please refrain from violent behaviour."

"Shit!"

The drone hovered down. "Don't be so disappointed. You were doing very well there, Major. Your progress has been absolutely remarkable. I foresee only another four to six weeks of training before—"

"Four to six weeks?! We don't have that kind of time! I thought you said this was gonna be quick and dirty!"

"This is quick and dirty, Major. To properly master the Eleven Senses would take years. It is as much of a shortcut as we are able to take. Now, retake your positions, and . . ." The drone suddenly twisted away, its lens frantically pushing in and out. "Wait. How is this possible? Why didn't—"

A shot rang out, and the drone exploded. Bits of sphere and lens fell to the ground. Karnage whipped around.

Patrick stood at the entrance to the water park. He held a smoking pistol in his hand. Karnage and Sydney dove into the fountain. Chunks of concrete flew from the rim as bullets whizzed overhead.

"How the hell did he find us?" Sydney said.

"I don't know." More chunks of concrete exploded from the rim. "Is it just me or is he a little more determined this time?" Karnage waited until he heard the empty clip fall to the ground before calling out over the fountain. "I thought you didn't want to kill me?"

"Sadly, my orders have changed." Patrick reloaded his pistol. "Please note I didn't shoot you first. After our last encounter, I just didn't think that would be very sporting of me."

"You mind telling me who wants me dead?" Karnage said.

"Sorry. Client confidentiality. You understand."

A drone flew overhead towards Patrick. "You've got a lot of nerve," it said, before a bullet caused it to explode into pieces.

Another drone quickly followed in its wake. "I simply can't abide violence." Another bullet. Another explosion.

A third drone flew by. "Not in my compound." It exploded.

A fourth quickly followed. "Not ever." It too exploded.

A fifth and a sixth flew by. "Games on the other hand—" the fifth said before blowing apart. "—I quite enjoy," the sixth finished, then shattered.

Another three drones flew past. "Would you like to play a game with me now?" one of them said, then promptly went boom.

"I call it Wak-A-Kat." Boom.

"You be the mallet, and I'll be the cats!" Boom.

"Would you like to play?"

"No." Patrick fired, and the drone shattered.

"Too bad," another drone said. "Wak-A-Kat!"

Patrick blasted it to bits.

"Excellent shot," another drone said as it flew into his face. "Wak-A-Kat!" Patrick fired, and it shattered. Another took its place.

"Wak-A-Kat!"

The air grew thick with drones. They swarmed around Patrick. He shot frantically as they closed in, crying, "Wak-A-Kat! Wak-A-Kat!" Bits of drone shrapnel flew off in all directions in time with the gunfire.

"Stop saying that!"

"Wak-A-Kat!"

A drone flew over the fountain. Its lens focused on Karnage and Sydney. "Sydney, my dear, I believe you have a weapon in the water tower?"

Sydney nodded. "My goober pistol. Yeah. It's not much—"

The drone exploded. Karnage and Sydney covered their heads against the bits of drone that fell onto them. Another drone quickly flew into its place. "Then I suggest you go now, before I run out of—" The drone exploded.

"Good enough for me," Karnage said. "Let's go!"

Karnage and Sydney crawled around to the back of the fountain. They leaped out. Patrick was covered in drones, firing wildly. The drones all crying, "Wak-a-kat! Wak-a-kat!" The two soldiers ran to the water tower and climbed the stairs.

Sydney rifled through the nest of blankets on her cot. "Where the hell is it?"

"Where did you leave it?"

"Right here!"

"Looking for this?" Karnage turned and saw Patrick step out

from behind some medical equipment. He held Sydney's gun belt in one hand and her goober pistol in the other. He fired, and Sydney flew back in an expanding ball of goober. It stuck her to the wall, covering her left hand and head. She kicked and struggled at the goober.

"There." Patrick tucked the goober pistol back into her gunbelt, and dropped it to the ground. "That should even things up a bit. No last-minute surprises this time, eh, Major?"

"How'd you get up here so fast?" Karnage said.

Patrick smiled. "I'm sure you'd love to know, wouldn't you? But a good magician never reveals his secrets. Though I must admit, a part of me would love to let you in on the secret. A shame I have to kill you now." He drew his pistol. "I'm dreadfully sorry it has come to this."

"So your orders have changed, then."

Patrick pulled his pistol. "Indeed they have. And may I say, I'm dreadfully sorry it has come to this."

Karnage looked around. There was nowhere he could hide. He was trapped. He already knew how good Patrick was. He couldn't dodge a bullet. Not at this range. *You've got to use your head, Major.*

Karnage shook his head disapprovingly. "And you call yourself a professional."

Patrick looked injured. "What do you mean?"

"You say you know everything about me, and you want a chance to really fight me. And yet, here you are, holding a gun."

"I told you, I'm a professional. It's my job."

Karnage sneered. "Sure. Go ahead." Karnage turned his back. "Make it quick."

"Oh, Major, please. I can't shoot you in the back. It's just not sporting."

"It's about as sporting as you shooting me in the front. Or did you forget about this?"

Karnage punched the wall. His Sanity Patch buzzed. "Warning. Sanity Level upgraded to Daffodil. Please refrain from violent behaviour."

Karnage turned back to Patrick. "You gettin' it yet? You want a chance to fight me. Well, here it is. Let me go down fighting. It'll be messy, but your boss won't care. I'll be dead. And you'll have had your chance to fight me. That's your life-long dream, isn't it? To fight the legendary Major Karnage? Here's your chance."

"And you can die like a true warrior." Patrick grinned broadly. "That's very tempting."

"I thought it might be," Karnage said.

Patrick bit his lip, considering his options. Finally, he smiled. "Oh, why not?" He put his gun away in his jacket. He approached Karnage cautiously, his arms hanging loosely at his sides, yet tense with energy.

Karnage raised his fists. All the while, he repeated his mantra in his head: *Cookie. Velasquez. Heckler. Stumpy. Koch. Cookie. Velasquez. Heckler. Stumpy. Koch.*

He hoped it would be enough.

They circled one another like lions. Karnage threw the first punch. His Sanity Patch buzzed "Citrus Blast." Karnage cursed himself. *Don't feel! THINK! Cookie. Velasquez. Heckler. Stumpy. Koch.*

Patrick easily ducked the punch and tried to strike Karnage in the gut. Karnage blocked the blow. The Sanity Patch crooned "Peachy Keen." *Focus, dammit! FOCUS! Cookie. Velasquez. Heckler. Stumpy. Koch.*

He tried to remember how it felt to trade blows with Sydney. *Just sparring among friends. Nobody's tryin' to kill each other here. Even though we are. But we're not. Fuck! How do I sort this out?*

Patrick's moves were long and fluid, his arms and legs like blades. Karnage blocked and dodged, all the while trying to get back into the right mindset. He tried to focus on why he needed to do this. He tried to focus on his long-term goals: *Cookie. Velasquez. Heckler. Stumpy. Koch. Cookie. Velasquez. Heckler. Stumpy. Koch.*

Patrick swept out with his leg and knocked Karnage off his feet. Karnage went down hard. He spun away from a foot coming for his head and leaped back to his feet. He shoved a table on casters at Patrick. Patrick tumbled out of the way, and the table smashed through one of the oval windows. Karnage's neck buzzed. "Warning. Sanity Level upgraded to Tangy Orange. Please refrain from violent behaviour."

He cursed silently. *Come on, mister, get it together! Cookie. Velasquez. Heckler. Stumpy. Koch.* He dodged another blow, trying to prepare himself. *They ain't just names. They're people. Your people. If you don't win this, they'll die! You can't let that happen. They're countin' on you. You're the only one they have left! Cookie! Velasquez! Heckler! Stumpy! Koch!*

Karnage saw an opportunity to strike Patrick's exposed throat. *Do what you have to do, soldier. Do what you have to do!* He took it, throwing a punch into Patrick's neck. Patrick gasped, and reeled back.

The Sanity Patch stayed silent.

Keep it up, mister. Keep it up! Cookie. Velasquez. Heckler. Stumpy. Koch.

Patrick sliced the air with a gloved fist. Karnage dodged and landed a punch to Patrick's stomach. Patrick doubled over. The Sanity Patch ignored the blow.

Cookie. Velasquez. Heckler. Stumpy. Koch. Cookie. Velasquez. Heckler. Stumpy. Koch.

Karnage ripped open the front of Patrick's jacket, exposing the pistol.

Cookie. Velasquez. Heckler. Stumpy. Koch. Cookie. Velasquez. Heckler. Stumpy. Koch.

He whipped the pistol out of its holster and kicked Patrick away. Patrick staggered back, dazed. He looked at Karnage in amazement. "You're not supposed to be able to do that."

Karnage levelled the gun at Patrick. "I wasn't sure I could."

Patrick smiled. "You are far more magnificent than I could have imagined." He looked at the pistol pointed at his chest, and smiled. "Are you that good? Can you do it? Can you get away with killing me without taking your own head off?"

"Only one way to find out," Karnage said.

"Please," Patrick said. "Do it."

Karnage fired.

The Sanity Patch buzzed. "Warning. Sanity Level upgraded to Sharp Cheddar. Please refrain from violent behaviour." And then it was silent.

Patrick staggered back, a shocked look on his face. He looked down at the small hole in his shirt. Blood poured from the wound, staining the fabric. He looked up at Karnage, and smiled. Blood poured from his mouth.

"Brilliant," he said, then fell back through the broken window.

CHAPTER TWELVE

Karnage grabbed a can of goober solvent from Sydney's belt, and sprayed down the goober holding her to the wall. It fizzled and bubbled and melted away. Sydney slid down the wall, wiping the remnants from her face. "You all right?"

Sydney pinched at her nose and sniffed. "I'm gonna blow pink snot for a few days, but other than that I'm fine. How about you?"

"I'm not dead."

"Sounds like you're doing pretty good, then. What happened to Patrick?"

Karnage jerked a thumb out the broken window. "He's dead."

Sydney blinked. "You killed him?"

"Yep."

"How?"

"With my fists," Karnage said. "And a gun."

"And the Sanity Patch didn't go off?"

Karnage shrugged. "It went off a little."

"But not enough to kill you."

Karnage grinned. "Nope."

Sydney looked out the window. "Where's his body?"

"What do you mean where? He should be right—" Karnage looked down at the square. There was a smear of blood at the base of the water tower, but otherwise the square was empty.

Patrick was gone.

"No," Karnage shook his head. "That's not possible. I got him square in the chest. Right in the heart. He couldn't have stood up and walked away from that!"

"Looks like he did," Sydney said.

Karnage heard a buzzing behind him. He started. He had a moment where he thought it was the Sanity Patch finally realizing he had indeed been violent these last twenty minutes, and was enacting retroactive retribution. But it wasn't.

A cell phone vibrated around on the floor behind them, its display flashing. Karnage picked it up. The name on the display read STEVE DABNEY. A picture of a strapping young man with close-cropped hair and glasses smiled out of the screen. A list of details ran down the screen, including "Employer: Dabney Corporation. Job Title: CEO." Karnage showed the name to Sydney. She whistled.

"Does that mean it is who it looks like it is?"

"It does," Sydney said. "You gonna answer it?"

"Be rude not to." Karnage answered it. Steve Dabney appeared on the screen, smiling broadly. "Patrick, how—"

The smile left his face. He blinked.

"You're not Patrick," he said.

"Nope," Karnage said.

Steve stared blankly at Karnage. Karnage stared back.

"I take it Patrick can't come to the phone right now?" Steve said.

"Nope," Karnage said.

"Can I expect him to ever come to the phone again?"

"I wouldn't bet on it," Karnage said.

"I see," Steve said. He looked at something offscreen, then back at Karnage. The congenial smile was back in place. "Well, I'm afraid I'm rather busy here, so . . . so long."

The screen went black.

"Be seeing you." Karnage said. He tossed the phone out the window.

CHAPTER THIRTEEN

The phone had shattered on impact. Its shrapnel lay splayed in a wide dispersal pattern around the bloody splotch on the cobblestones. Sydney pointed to a spotty trail of blood leading through the park's main gates. "See? He walked."

"Or he was carried," Karnage said.

"You think he had help?"

"There's no way he could have survived that."

"He could have been wearing a bulletproof vest," Sydney said.

Karnage shook his head. "I would have felt it when I was beating the crap out of him."

"Good to know you're so thorough about these things."

"I try."

They followed the blood trail out to the parking lot. Sydney pointed to a pair of swooping crescents carved into the gravel shoulder of the road.

"Skid marks," Sydney said. "You've got to be leaving in one hell of a hurry to make hoverballs do that."

Karnage squinted down the road. "Looks like he's long gone, then."

A drone flew down in front of Sydney. Its lens zoomed towards her. "Oh, thank Darwin! I am thrilled—nay, ecstatic to see that you are unharmed." The drone tentatively poked at Sydney's head with its tentacles. "You *are* unharmed, aren't you?"

Sydney swatted the drone away, rolling her eyes. "Yes, Uncle."

"Excellent! That is such a relief!"

"I'm good," Karnage said. "Thanks for asking."

The drone spun and flashed its lens at Karnage. "Indeed you are! Well, this is most surprising. Does this mean you were able to defeat the marksman?"

Karnage looked down the highway. "Mostly," he said.

"Wonderful! I am pleased to see that your 'crash course' in the

Eleven Senses has provided you with such stellar results. I must admit, I am completely flummoxed. It should not have been possible for that gentleman to have breached the perimeter. I am at a loss to explain why his presence went undetected."

"There's a lot about this guy that isn't possible," Karnage said.

"So it would seem. As a result of this puzzling bit of data, I am afraid I must now ask you to leave. I am instigating a security lockdown until I can pinpoint the faults in my system. It's nothing personal, I assure you. I simply must make my personal safety my highest priority. Despite a complete understanding behind the theory of all martial arts, I am compelled to admit I have no skill in their execution myself. You understand, I'm sure."

"Don't worry about it," Karnage said. "We were just leaving, anyway."

"Excellent! Well, I must see to my diagnostics. *Bon aventure!*" The drone sailed back into the compound.

"And just where are we going?" Sydney said.

"To talk to our buddy Steve, of course," Karnage said.

"Steve? As in Steve Dabney?"

"Yep."

"That's crazy."

"Why?"

"He's in Dabneyville."

"So?"

"You can't go to Dabneyville!"

"Why not?"

"Do you have any idea what Dabneyville's like? It's a fortress. Cameras everywhere. Dabneycops crawling all over the place. You'll never get in. And even if you did, he probably already figures that you're coming. He'll be expecting us."

"Good," Karnage said. "That'll give him time to get good and scared."

Sydney shook her head. "Steve Dabney's not afraid of anything."

"Maybe he should be."

"Maybe you should be."

"Does that mean you're not coming?"

Sydney stared off down the highway. She hung her head and sighed. "No. No, it doesn't. If I don't come with you, you'll just end up getting yourself killed. And where the hell will that leave us?"

"Squidbugged," Karnage said.

"Squidbugged?"

"Yeah." Karnage knocked on the metal band under his shin. "Squidbugged."

"You just love inventing new words, don't you?"

"Yep. I'm a regular wordicologist."

MK#8: KARNAGE GOES TO TOWN

CHAPTER ONE

Sydney and Karnage drove to Dabneyville in a black limousine. Sydney explained that she had "borrowed" it from Patrick after he had shot Karnage at Camp Bailey. The biometric scanner on the dashboard had been ripped off and the red and green wires had been twisted together.

"Tampering with security systems is a criminal offence under the Dabney Intellectual Property Ordinance," Karnage had reminded her.

"You want me to go and turn myself in?" she had said.

Karnage had told her not to bother.

They brought the only weapons they had: Sydney's goober pistol and stun stick, and Patrick's pistol that Karnage had "liberated" from its holster. The goober gun had three rounds left, and the pistol had seven. While not the kind of heavy artillery Karnage would have liked for taking on the Dabney Corporation, it would have to do.

They took off down the highway in the same direction as Patrick's skid marks, following him towards Dabneyville.

"Anything I need to know before we get to the city?" Karnage said.

"If we can help it, we're not going to be seen. But if we are, you're going to have to work hard to blend in. Look happy all the time. If you go around frowning and scowling at everything like that, Dabneycops will assume you're up to something."

"I am up to something."

"Yeah, but you gotta keep that info to yourself. You can't just go barging in, shooting at anything that moves."

"Don't worry," Karnage said. "I wasn't planning on doing that anyway."

"Good."

"I only got seven bullets."

"Just try to look happy, okay?"

Karnage bared his teeth. "How's this?"

"Hideous. Just keep your mouth covered."

The desert stretched out in a flat plain before them. Nothing marred the view but the occasional bit of debris on the gravel shoulder. Slowly, a cloud-covered mountain peak appeared on the horizon.

"There it is," Sydney said. "Mount Dabney."

The mountain slowly revealed itself. It sat alone on the flatlands. A gleaming white wall ran around the mountain's perimeter. Roof peaks and spires jutted up behind the walls, running up the mountain's sides in an erratic spiral. A needle-thin tower with a bulbous top dwarfed all the other buildings, its antenna peak just touching the clouds above it.

"Seems kind of weird. A single mountain sittin' out there all by itself," Karnage said.

"Used to be a whole range of mountains out here," Sydney said. "But they tore 'em all down. Used the aggregate to build Dabneyville."

Ahead of them, the road began to rise. Sydney pulled the car off the road and started driving on the plain.

"What are you doing?"

Sydney pointed to the road as it rose up from the desert floor, revealing giant pillars of pitted concrete underneath. "That's the GDE. Don't want to get caught up there."

"GDE?"

"Gail Dabney Expressway," Sydney said. "It's the only road in or out. They call it the Bridge to Nowhere, cuz no one in the city ever wants to leave, and no one outside of the city ever wants in. They all think they got it better than each other."

Karnage thought about the squidbugs. "Little do they know they're all screwed." He looked up at the road. "If that's the only road into town, then why aren't we on it?"

Sydney pointed to cameras mounted on lampposts above them.

"They monitor all traffic in and out of the city. Not that there's much of it."

"Wouldn't they have spotted us already?"

Sydney shook her head. "Cameras don't work this far out. Those are only for show. It's once you get closer to the city you have to worry."

She pulled the car under the GDE, and tucked it up on the inside of one of the pillars. "We walk the rest of the way," she said.

Karnage looked out towards Dabneyville. "Looks awful far to walk."

"We're almost inside the perimeter of aerial surveillance. If we don't ditch the car soon, they'll pick us up for sure."

They stayed under the shade of the road, picking their way through the rocks and debris. Garbage littered the underside of the road: broken electronics, tatters of clothing, crumpled potato chip bags and coffee cups, all emblazoned with the Dabney Corporation logo.

"Is there anything the Dabney Corporation doesn't make?" Karnage said.

"No," Sydney said. "They own everything. And everybody."

"And now they're handin' it all over to the squidbugs." Karnage touched Patrick's pistol in his pocket. *Only seven rounds.* He hoped he wouldn't blow his own head off when he used them.

They heard a high-pitched buzzing overhead. Sydney pressed Karnage against the pillar. He peered around the side. He saw a small circular shadow flowing across the desert floor. He looked up. A Dabneycop flew overhead. He had a pair of hoverballs strapped to his back. A pair of arching handles rose over the hoverballs into the pilot's hands. It sounded like a giant wasp. Karnage fought the urge to swat him with the pistol. They waited until he disappeared from sight.

"There's the welcoming committee," Sydney commented.

"Something tells me they won't be that welcoming," Karnage said.

"How very perceptive of you."

"How are we going to get in?"

Sydney pointed into the distance. "There's an unused maintenance hatch around the west side of the wall. We can make our way in through there."

"Don't they know about it?"

"When you're in the business of wilfully forgetting your failures, there's a lot of things you train yourself not to know about."

"So how come you know about it, then?"

"Because I make it a point to remember everything."

The sun was setting when they finally reached the gleaming white walls of the city. They waited under the bridge for night to fall, then Sydney led them out along the perimeter of the outer wall.

The walls were at least a kilometre high. Moisture had flaked the paint off along the bottom, revealing pitted grey concrete underneath. They heard the buzz of an air patrol above them and saw a spotlight fly across the desert. Karnage was reminded of the pools of light that had helped them on the squidbug ship. Except this particular light was anything but friendly. Karnage held his pistol tight in his fist. The light passed by, missing them completely, and disappeared around the curve of the wall.

Sydney pointed ahead of them. "There it is."

Karnage squinted in the gloom. He could just make out a faint dark patch on the wall. As they approached, he saw it was a rust-stained door. It was slightly ajar. Sydney tucked her hand behind it and pushed it open. The door's hinges groaned in complaint. Sydney looked into the darkness beyond, then turned to Karnage and winked.

"Open sesame," she said.

CHAPTER TWO

Karnage ducked his head to avoid hitting a pipe as they walked through the dank narrow corridor. "What is this? Some kinda sewer system?"

"No." Sydney kept her flashlight in front of her. "It's the old subway system. They shut it down decades ago."

Karnage eyed the narrow corridor. "Must have been one hell of a skinny subway."

"This is just a steam tunnel," Sydney said.

"Why do they call it a steam tunnel?"

Sydney pointed to a giant pipe running along the wall beside them. The words CAUTION: STEAM – HOT! were stencilled onto its surface.

"That explains that mystery," Karnage said.

"We'll hit the main system up ahead," Sydney said. "These tunnels run under almost every building in the city. You can get anywhere you want, so long as you know the right route to take. Problem is there are no maps. They purged everything when they shut it down. Most people don't even know these tunnels exist."

"How do you know about it, then?"

"I told you. I was stationed here. I made it a point to know about them."

"That mean the other Dabneycops know about them?"

"Not like I do," she said. "There are a few main routes they patrol, looking for fugitives and the like. But that's about it. They don't bother with the rest."

"But you did."

"As much as I could," Sydney said. "These tunnels go on for days. It'd take years to find them all."

"Sounds like a helluva big subway," Karnage said.

"It's a helluva big city. It's not just subway tunnels, though. There are maintenance corridors, steam tunnels ... it's crazy. If you're not careful, you could end up anywhere."

The corridor ended at a half-open door. They squeezed through, and found themselves on a subway platform. A row of rusted turnstiles divided the platform in half. On one side, wide stairs led straight up to a brick wall. On the other, the platform led off to a steep drop into darkness. The floor was covered in mosaic tiles of Dabby Tabby's grinning face. A torn poster on the wall showed Dabby Tabby wearing a train engineer's cap and sitting astride a long gleaming bullet-shaped subway train. RIDE THE BLUE ROCKET ran across the bottom of the poster in faded blue text.

They climbed off the edge of the platform down onto the tracks. The floor of the tunnel was covered in ankle-deep water. Karnage recognized the toxic smell of squidbug. The beam from the flashlight caught glimpses of orange creeper and pinkstink hanging on the walls. Bright red lily pads with yellow veins drifted past their legs.

"This stuff always down here?" Karnage asked.

"No," Sydney said. "This is new."

They heard muffled voices up ahead. Sydney quickly turned off her flashlight. Their eyes adjusted to the pitch black of the dark, and they saw a soft blue glow lighting the tunnel ahead.

"I thought you said these tunnels were deserted," Karnage whispered.

"They're probably just refugees."

As they approached the light, the voice grew clearer. ". . . and you, too, will learn to awaken The Worm within."

"Well, shit," Karnage said.

They rounded the corner and came into another station. The light came from a giant D-Pad that was propped against a turnstile. It showed Melvern standing before a clear blue sky looking off into the distance. A pair of Spragmite priests stood to either side of the monitor, nodding their heads solemnly.

A small group of people stood in front of the monitor. A man held a baby in his arms, a young boy clutched to his leg. An old woman sat in a wheelchair. An old man in a suit leaned against the handle of the chair, a hand on the woman's shoulder. A young man with spiky green hair stood off to one side watching morosely. A pair of teenage girls huddled together in the back, holding each other for support. They occasionally exchanged terrified looks. Strings of numbers were printed across the backs of the girls' shirts. Karnage pointed them out to Sydney. "What are those? Like serial numbers?"

"No," Sydney answered. "They're expiration dates."

"Expiration dates? For what?"

"For the clothes. Lets you know when they go out of style."

"That's ridiculous."

"I know," Sydney said. "Used to be they'd put it inside the clothes, so you'd know when to buy new ones. Then the fashion conscious started putting them on the outside, to declare to the world how trendsetting they were. Those poor girls. Look at those dates. They're at least six weeks old."

Karnage found the sorrowful look on Sydney's face a bit perplexing, but surprised himself by keeping his opinion on the matter to himself. "How are we gonna get by 'em?"

"Don't worry about it," Sydney said. "They're fugitives. They won't pay us any mind."

"Fugitives?" Karnage looked the crowd over again. They appeared completely harmless. "Fugitives from what?"

"Debt," Sydney said. "You can't make your payments, they ship you out to the labour camps. Most of these people wouldn't last five minutes outside the city, and they know it. So they hide here. Pray for salvation."

"And in come the Spragmites."

Sydney nodded. "That's right."

A searchlight flicked on at the top of the stairs, striking the group of refugees, before a group of Dabneycops bounded down the steps brandishing goober rifles.

"Everybody freeze!"

The green-haired youth leaped up and bolted. A Dabneycop raised his rifle and fired. Screams erupted from the crowd as the young man disappeared in a giant ball of pink goober. Nothing was visible but a small tuft of green hair.

One of the priests charged forward. "You dare interfere with the work of Spragmos?!" He gave a yelp as he disappeared in another ball of goober. The crowd had pulled itself into a tight circle, clutching each other and whimpering. One of the girls was crying.

The fattest of the Dabneycops waddled forward. He raised a megaphone to his lips. "All right, everybody settle down and nobody else will get goobered. Now there's no point in running. We've got all the exits covered. Everybody step forward in a line. Come on, let's go. You, too, grandpa. You'll do your part and pay your own way." He put down the megaphone and turned to the other Dabneycops. "Round 'em up."

The Dabneycops moved down among the crowd. The other priest shot the fat Dabneycop a glowering look. "You will pay for this outrage," he said.

"Tell it to the magistrate, Father."

"You will refer to me as Presbyter, heathen!"

"Stick a sock in it, Father, or I'll goober it shut."

"He's talking a big game," Sydney whispered, "but look how he's coverin' his badge number. Doesn't want the priest to figure out who he is."

"McClaine! We got everybody?"

"Just gotta unstick the kid, sarge." McClaine was spraying a can of solvent at the base of the goober ball with the shock of green hair. "We should do a full scour of the tunnel. Make sure the other platforms are clear."

The sergeant shook his head. "Forget it."

"But our orders say—"

The sergeant stuck a finger out at McClaine. "I know our orders, constable. And I am telling you that the lieutenant can go piss up a rope. I am marking this sector as clear and that is final. Powell! What the hell are you gawking at?"

"Behind you, sarge!" Powell pointed to a cigarette floating in mid-air, smoking itself behind the sergeant's head.

Karnage tightened his grip on his pistol. "We got a problem."

The sergeant turned just in time to see a squidbug appear around

MAJOR KARNAGE

the cigarette. "What the hell is that?!"

The squidbug took a long drag on its cigarette, and levelled its spear at the sergeant. The sergeant had just enough time to raise his rifle before he disappeared in a ball of crackling green light.

More squidbugs shimmered into existence around the platform, surrounding the Dabneycops and the fugitives. Shouts and screams filled the air as the refugees ran in all directions. Squidbugs and Dabneycops aimed their weapons at each other and started firing. The air was soon thick with green energy balls and pink goobers shooting across the platform.

"Let's get the hell out of here before we're spotted." Karnage and Sydney moved away from the chaos, retracing their steps down the corridor.

A pipe floated in the middle of the subway tunnel in front of them. A squidbug flowed into existence around it. It aimed its crackling energy spear at them. Sydney drew her goober pistol and fired. She caught the squidbug in the face, throwing it backwards. Its shot went wide, green energy vaporizing a large scoop out of the ceiling. Something groaned in the crater and bits of concrete and metal dropped around them.

"Quick! Through here!" Sydney led Karnage up a set of concrete steps. The groaning overhead turned to cracking, and increasingly bigger chunks of concrete fell from the ceiling. Sydney pulled on the door. "It's locked!" Karnage aimed his pistol up at the knob and shot it off. His Sanity Patch crooned "Frothy Cream" as they dove through the door. The ceiling gave a final creak and came crashing down behind them.

CHAPTER THREE

Karnage and Sydney lay coughing in a heap on the floor. The dust slowly settled around them.

"You all right?" Karnage asked.

Sydney nodded. "I think so."

They got up and looked at the doorway behind them which had disappeared, replaced with a twisted pile of metal and concrete.

"Guess we're not goin' back that way," Karnage said.

Sydney looked down the other end of the hatchway. Pipes ran along the walls. "Looks like a maintenance tunnel," she said. "Hopefully it comes out somewhere on the other end."

"Hopefully? You mean you don't know where this goes?"

"It should come around to another platform or tunnel."

"It should?"

"Yeah." She pointed at the mangled mess behind them. "So long as it doesn't end like that."

They followed the tunnel deep into the darkness. It ended at another maintenance hatch. They opened it, and found themselves in another subway tunnel. The air was thick with toxic yellow mist. Creeper hung from the ceiling in long draping strands. The floor of the tunnel was thick with pinkstink, and Karnage caught a glimpse of the back of a purple ladybug burrowing into the undergrowth.

Sydney brushed the creeper aside and read a set of numbers on the wall. "88-01," she said. "We're near the city's core. We're on the wrong side of it, though."

"What do you mean, wrong side?"

"The city's built around the mountain, so the core is spread around the base. It's going to take some time to get to the other side."

They felt the ground shake and rumble as if a subway train was approaching. They scrambled back through the maintenance hatch as a train of horned worms rumbled past, squiggling and screeching as they went.

They waited for the shaking and screeching to fade to nothing before peeking back out.

"What the hell is going on down here?" Sydney exclaimed.

"Only one way to find out." Karnage stepped out and looked down both ends of the tunnel. Light seemed to be coming from a junction near the north end. "What's down that way?"

"Nothing," Sydney said. "It's a dead end."

"Doesn't look so dead to me. There's light coming from down there."

"There shouldn't be. That would lead straight into the mountain. There's nowhere for the track to go."

"But it's goin' somewhere. Let's find out where."

They pressed themselves against the wall of the tunnel, following it towards the light. They kept an eye out for maintenance hatches in case another train of worms came down the tunnel.

The air grew thicker with yellow mist, stinging eyes and offending nostrils. Karnage heard Sydney cough and gasp behind him.

The tunnel ended at a thick canopy of creeper. Bright shafts of light poked through. Karnage and Sydney parted the creeper and walked through.

They were in a wide clearing. Sheer rock walls scaled up behind them. The ground was covered in pinkstink. Grey trees grew up from the underbrush, their bare branches laden with orange creeper. Giant pods expelling yellow mist covered the ground. Karnage felt like they had walked into Uncle's squidbug terrarium.

Sydney tugged at Karnage's arm. She was staring straight up. "Look," she whispered, eyes wide.

They were at the bottom of a chasm. Sheer rock walls rose up on all sides, hemming them in. Tunnel entrances laced with orange creeper ran around the perimeter. The mountain had been hollowed out, and they were standing inside it. High above them, just visible through the yellow mist, green lights flickered across a black, panelled mass.

GORD ZAJAC

It was the squidbug mothership.

CHAPTER FOUR

Karnage grinned. "Perfect."

"Perfect?" Sydney stared at him, her mouth agape. "I think this is a hell of a long way off from perfect! In fact, I don't think you can get any further away from perfect than this! We have to get the hell out of here."

"No," Karnage said firmly. "I'm not goin' anywhere."

"You can't take on all these aliens by yourself."

"I know that," Karnage said. "I'm talkin' about gatherin' intel. That's why we're here. To figure out what's goin' on. We wanted to know what the Dabney Corporation had to do with the squidbugs. Now it's lookin' like they've got quite a bit to do with 'em."

He led them away from the tunnel and behind a creeper-laden boulder. Karnage peered out from behind the boulder, observing the squidbug invasion in action.

A line of trucks emerged from a tunnel entrance beside them. Dabby Tabby was painted on the side, jumping out of a blue container. Karnage pointed them out to Sydney. "What are those?"

"Automated sanitation trucks," she said.

The trucks pulled up to a giant pile of debris in the middle of the clearing. They dumped their contents onto the pile and disappeared back into the tunnel. Squidbugs stood around the pile, sorting the debris into bins. One of the squidbugs picked up a plastic water bottle and covertly ate it. Another squidbug swatted the first, and pointed to the pile. The chastised squidbug bent down and resumed sorting.

A horned worm rumbled up to the pile. Its face was covered with a metal plate. A squidbug stood atop the worm, steering it by the horn. It lined the worm's metal faceplate up with the nearest bin. The bin latched itself onto the metal plate, as if pulled by magnets. The squidbug steered the worm around and carried the bin to a massive smoking pit where it dumped the contents of the bin into the pit. Flames shot up from the pit's depths.

"What the hell are they doing?" Sydney hissed.

"They're suckin' up our resources," Karnage said. "Suckin' the planet dry." He watched the recycling trucks motor back through the creeper, and clenched his fist. "And the Dabney Corporation's helpin' 'em do it."

"But why? What's in it for them?"

"Let's find old Stevie boy and ask him," Karnage said.

They heard a rustling behind them, turned, and saw a bright burning ember just visible through the trees. Green energy crackled along an invisible shaft as the air behind the trees started to shimmer.

"Run!"

Karnage and Sydney jumped clear just as an energy ball vaporized their boulder. Sydney rose up on one knee and fired a blast of goober, pinning the squidbug to the tree. Other squidbugs were racing towards them, their energy spears crackling.

"Let's go, Captain!"

Karnage ran towards the nearest tunnel opening. He ripped aside the creeper, surprising a squidbug in the middle of eating a D-Pad. Karnage punched it in what he hoped was its jaw. He didn't hit bone, but the squidbug squealed and went down. His neck buzzed, and the Sanity Patch hit Lemon Breeze. The air behind him sizzled as an energy ball flew by.

"Keep moving, Major!" Sydney shouted.

Karnage raced down the corridor with Sydney close behind. They pushed through creeper as energy balls crackled behind them. A deep, jagged line of sound tore through the tunnel, nearly knocking them off their feet. The earth shook. Without looking back, Karnage knew that somewhere behind the veil of creeper there was a worm hurtling towards them.

"Over here!" Sydney pointed to a set of concrete steps poking out of the creeper. She raced up the stairs and pushed the vines aside, revealing a metal door. She pulled on the knob, and the hinges squeaked in protest. It opened a fraction of an inch. Karnage stuck his fingers through the opening, and together they yanked the door open. A green ball burned a tunnel through the creeper behind them. They caught a glimpse of squiggly crimson head as they ran through the door.

It was a steam tunnel.

They ran blindly down the corridor. They could hear the clattering of squidbug claws on the concrete, and on the giant pipe running beside them. Karnage looked down at the pipe, and watched the stencilled words fly by on its surface as he ran. The words flew by in sync with the squidbug's clattering: *caution-steam-hot-caution-steam-hot-caution-steam-hot.*

Karnage looked at Sydney's back through the gloom getting smaller and smaller. She was pulling ahead. Karnage was starting to slow. His muscles burned; he wasn't as young as he used to be. He heard the squidbugs getting closer behind them, their claws clacking along the pipe: *caution-steam-hot-caution-steam-hot-caution-steam-hot.*

Sydney turned. "Come on, Major! You can do it!"

Karnage shook his head. His shoulder was starting to ache. He stopped and caught his breath. The clacking along the pipe grew louder: *caution-steam-hot-caution-steam-hot-caution-steam-hot.*

Sydney stopped running. "What are you stopping for? Come on, let's go!"

Karnage shook his head. "I can't." He drew his pistol.

"Don't be an idiot, Major," Sydney shouted. "You can't take them on by yourself!"

"I'm not." Karnage emptied the gun into the steam pipe, ripping open a wide gaping hole. Fountains of steam shot into the corridor, billowing towards him. Karnage turned and ran. His Sanity Patch buzzed incessantly as the steam burned the back of his neck. He heard loud squiggly cries of pain behind him. There was a faint whiff of steamed calamari in the air, and the rhythmic clacking on the pipe stopped.

CHAPTER FIVE

The steam tunnel joined with a narrow maintenance shaft that Karnage could barely fit in. Thick cables marked HIGH VOLTAGE hummed inches from his face. As they shuffled along, the Sanity Patch downgraded from Strawberry Shortcake all the way down to Citrus Blast. Karnage hadn't realized how close he had come to blowing his own head off. *So much for thinking.*

They finally came out into a dimly lit maintenance room. Karnage leaned against the wall and slid down. He looked at the empty pistol in his hands and tossed it away in disgust.

"What's up?" Sydney said.

Karnage stared at the discarded pistol lying on the floor. "It didn't work."

"What didn't work?"

"All of Uncle's training. At this rate I'm still gonna blow my head off before I make any headway."

"It didn't work because you weren't thinking," Sydney said. "You were reacting. And under the circumstances, I think that was the way to go."

Karnage ran his fingers through his hair. "I came this close to runnin' out of Sanity Levels. I almost . . ." He moved to throw a punch in the air and stopped himself.

Sydney crouched down beside him and gently took his clenched fist. She uncurled his fingers and clasped his palm in her hands. She looked into his eyes. "You haven't been doing this long enough for it to be automatic yet. Don't be so hard on yourself. Just try and focus on your long-term goals. It's like learning to ride a bike. You've been able to get up a few times now, but you're still gonna fall off now and again."

"If I fall off much more than that then I'm gonna lose my head."

"Then it's a good thing there's two of us down here, isn't it? Why don't you let me be the brawn for awhile, and you can play at being the brains. Okay?"

You've just gotta use your head. Karnage nodded. "Okay."

Sydney playfully slapped him on the cheek and stood up. "Right, now what say we figure out where we are?"

They opened the door of the maintenance room and found themselves in a wide hall. The marble floor gleamed. Extravagant chandeliers hung from the ceiling. A giant statue stood in the centre of the room of Galt Dabney holding the hand of Dabby Tabby. Great slabs of marble jutted from the walls, an engraved plaque stamped on each.

"What is this place?" Karnage said.

Sydney looked around, her eyes wide. "I'd heard the rumours, but I never thought . . ."

"What?" Karnage asked. "What is it?"

She turned her eyes back to Karnage. "It's The Vault."

"What's 'The Vault'?"

"The official Dabney archives." She eyed the slabs lining the walls. "And crypt."

They followed the length of the hall to a set of gleaming golden doors. Galt Dabney's face was etched into its surface. "This is it." Sydney stroked the door in awe. "His final resting place. I wonder . . ." She pulled on the door.

"What are you doing?" Karnage said.

"I have to know," she said. Her eyes gleamed. "I have to know if it's true."

She pulled the door open a crack and slipped inside. Her voice echoed from the other side. "They did it. I can't believe it. They actually did it!"

"What?" Karnage said. "What did they do?"

"Come in and see."

Karnage pushed through the door into the room. The walls were covered with shelves upon shelves of books. Circular stairways led up to long catwalks running the length of the room. Crystal chandeliers hung underneath the catwalks, casting the room in soft yellow light. The guard rails were decorated with Dabby Tabby faces constructed from wrought iron. Two arm chairs sat facing a giant screen set into a carved oak cabinet in the middle of the room. A polished glass case had been mounted on top of the cabinet.

Inside the case was the head of Galt Dabney.

"They did it," Sydney said. "They actually went and did it."

"Did what?" Karnage looked up at the head. "What did they do?"

The eyes of Galt Dabney opened, and the cataract-laden pupils drifted down at Karnage.

CHAPTER SIX

The screen below the head flickered to life, and a much healthier Galt Dabney appeared smiling on the screen.

"Hello, and welcome to the Dabney Family Archives. The geniuses at the Dabney Imagino Labs have worked their magic and given me the gift of everlasting life. Using the latest in cryopreservation technology, my mind and body will be specially preserved until such time that a cure can be found for whatever ails me. In the meantime, while I'm 'cooling my heels,' I will continue to lead the company with the help of this nifty little device here."

The camera pulled out to show Galt standing beside the very oak cabinet and screen that Karnage and Sydney were now watching.

"Using this device, I'll be able to answer any questions that you may have. Go ahead and ask me anything. I've created a library of pre-recorded answers that should cover the most commonly asked questions. Financial advice. Managerial tips. Old Dabney family recipes. Ask about my grandmother's recipe for spiced peach jam: that's a good one! And should you happen to ask a question I didn't fully anticipate, this machine has full access to the Dabney Family Archives. That includes security footage of board meetings, company minutes, old softball games, school plays, birthday parties . . . why just about anything you could imagine. So go ahead. Ask me anything, and I'll do my best to answer with true Galt style." Galt drew an imaginary pistol. "Bam, like that." He winked.

The screen went blank.

Karnage and Sydney looked at each other. "Is this for real?" Karnage asked.

The screen blinked back on. It showed Galt Dabney's face in a close-up. He laughed, his eyes crinkling at the corners. "Yes, yes. I assure you it's all very real. There is nothing I won't be able to answer. So go ahead. Ask me anything."

"Maybe we should ask about the peach jam," Sydney said.

"I got a better idea." Karnage cleared his throat. "What do you know about the squidbug invasion?"

The screen stayed blank for a second. Galt's cheery face appeared again. "Sorry, I didn't quite understand your question. Can you please clarify the word—" The screen switched to black and white security footage of Karnage and Sydney standing in front of the screen. They heard Karnage say, "squidbug," and the screen switched back to Galt's smiling face.

Sydney cleared her throat. "He means 'aliens.'"

"Okay, that's better. Thanks." The screen went blank again. Galt's face came back. He clapped his hands. "Well, that's a real cracker, isn't it? I'm afraid I didn't anticipate that question. But you haven't stumped me yet. Give me a few moments to pull from the archives, and I'll try to answer your question as best I can."

The screen went blank. It stayed dark for a long time. Karnage looked behind them, and saw the security camera blinking down at him. He wondered who was watching it. He wondered if the machine was just stalling them until security could arrive.

Karnage was about to tell Sydney to take up defensive positions when the screen blinked on and Galt smiled down at them again. He rubbed his hands together. "Okay! That was a real corker of a question. Sorry it took me so long. I've done my best to put together a little video compilation that should clear everything up for you. Feel free to ask any follow-up questions when the film is done. So have a seat, relax, and enjoy the show. And, here we go!"

CHAPTER SEVEN

Horns trumpeted loudly as the letters DiN shot across the screen. A lens flare blasted everything out, revealing a newscaster with a striking head of hair sitting at a desk beaming at the screen.

"Welcome back to the Dabney Information Network," she said. "I'm Angela Lee, and I'm here with Steve Dabney, Chief Operating Officer of the Dabney Corporation."

The shot changed to show Steve Dabney sitting at the other end of the desk with his hands clasped. He smiled warmly and nodded at the camera.

"Thanks for being with us here today, Steve," Angela said.

"Thanks for having me, Angela."

Angela picked up a sheet and read from it dramatically. "'To the moon, Alex.'"

Steve laughed.

Angela put down her sheet and smiled at Steve. "Now that's a quote from an interview you gave last year to our own Xander Farnsworth."

Steve nodded. "Yes, I remember that. I'm not sure how serious I was about that at the time."

"But it turns out you were serious, because here you are, months later, getting ready to launch the first manned flight to the moon."

"That's right, Angela. If all goes well with the launch tomorrow, I will be on my way to being the first man to step foot on the moon."

"Now there are those who would argue that this isn't the first time we've been to the moon. What would you have to say to them?"

Steve smiled bemusedly. "Well, you know, I've seen the footage they're referring to and . . ." He shrugged.

"And you're not convinced?"

"Look, I wasn't there. You weren't there. Nobody alive today was there. Our experts have looked at this video that supposedly 'proves' we landed on the moon, but their findings came back inconclusive.

So I'm not going to comment one way or another. But what I will say, Angela, is this: a *Dabney* has yet to step foot on the moon. And there's nothing a Dabney can't do if he sets his mind to it, and my mind, as you can tell, is pretty much set."

Angela giggled. "Yes it is. Now, I know you have to go soon, but if I could ask just one more question. . . ."

"Shoot."

"What does it feel like to be one of the richest men on the planet?"

Steve smiled. "I have to say, Angela, that it feels pretty good."

Angela giggled again. "Thanks so much for your time, Steve. And good luck with the launch tomorrow."

"Thank you, Angela." Steve winked. "It's been a pleasure."

CHAPTER EIGHT

The screen changed to show a jet with a smaller bulbous white ship attached to its underbelly. The smaller ship had a *Dabney-1* logo printed on its side. A voice crackled over a speaker. "We are in the bin and ready to go. Ten seconds."

The conjoined ships flew in silence. A sheet of blue clouds drifted by far below.

"Okay, here we go."

A spurt of blue flame shot out the back of the *Dabney-1*.

"There it is. You can see the flame. The flicker of flame. Good old Dabney blue."

The *Dabney-1* separated from the jet and shot forward.

The shot changed to a camera mounted on the *Dabney-1*'s tail, looking up past the cockpit toward the nose at the blue sky.

"Our DiN viewers are enjoying an impressive site here. That's your downlink camera on the *Dabney-1* as it prepares to punch through into geostationary orbit."

The world started spinning and the camera shook violently. Bursts of snow that reminded Karnage of squiggles shot across the video feed.

"Uh oh. Uh oh."

The footage evened out, the squiggles dissipated, and the nose of the ship sailed through the black, the curve of the earth glowing just below.

"Wow. Look at that."

The sun appeared from behind the earth, shining bright and hard against the black.

"He's made it. He's made it."

A thin line of black sliced across the sun's aura. It grew thicker and thicker, slowly blocking out the sun's glow. It kept growing until it blocked out the blue of the earth. A dark shadow slowly enveloped the body of the *Dabney-1*. Green panels of light flickered across the black. The screen flashed a violent green, then turned to snow.

"Hold on. This is not a scripted manoeuvre. Oh my god. Communications with Dabneyville have been cut off. We're waiting for confirmation that Steve is okay. That systems are normal. That—"

The screen went black.

The screen cut to black and white security footage of a boardroom. Galt Dabney paced at the end of the table, his face pinched and scowling. A line of executives sat on either side. Their eyes stayed fixed on Galt until he stopped in front of a young executive at the end.

"How long has he been gone for?" Galt asked.

The executive pulled out a tablet. "About two hours."

"What are the chances he's still alive?"

The executive shrugged. "They don't know, Galt."

"Dammit." Galt sat at the head of the table. He sighed. "I knew we should have kept this quiet until he returned. What does the press know so far?"

An executive with her hair up in a bun slid a tablet over to Galt. "That he went up, and there's been a communications problem, and that we expect to hear back from him soon."

Galt steepled his fingers in front of him. He nodded. "All right. All right. Maybe we can make something positive out of this. Come up with an angle. He gave his life saving the earth." He looked around at the other executives. "How does that sound? Too over the top?"

"It might be a little, sir," one of them said.

"Maybe if it was just a continent," another offered, "instead of the whole planet."

"Or a city," someone else said. "He was having trouble on re-entry. Heading for a populated area. Rather than kill innocent people, he sacrificed himself to save their lives."

Galt nodded. "That's good. That's very good. Consult with astrophysics. Make it plausible. Airtight. He had to 'tech' the 'tech' in order to 'tech' the 'tech.' Something like that. But good."

"We could have him save Dabneyville," someone offered.

Galt shook his head. "No no no. It could look self-serving, like he was saving his own. Make it a small, backwater village somewhere."

"What about Carpathia?"

Galt scowled. "No good. Too much baggage there. We need someplace else. Somewhere on the southern continent."

An executive rushed into the room. "They just got word, Galt. He's all right. They've re-established contact."

"Oh, thank god. Where is he?"

"He's on his way back to Earth."

"Back to Earth? Why?"

"He won't say. He says he needs to talk to you. Privately."

CHAPTER TEN

The security footage changed to a lush office similar in design to the vault Karnage and Sydney stood in. Oak panelling was slathered over everything. Galt Dabney sat behind the desk, holding his head in his hands. Steve sat opposite him in a plush leather armchair, his feet resting casually on a footstool.

"I can't believe it," Galt said. "I just can't believe it."

"It's true, Uncle Galt." Steve leaned forward and slid a tablet across the desk towards the old man. "Astrophysics confirms it."

Galt waved it away. "I saw the report."

"So you know there's nothing we can do. They have superior firepower. Superior technology. We simply don't stand a chance."

"There has to be something we can do. There has to be."

"There is," Steve said. "We can cooperate."

"Cooperate? We can't just let them waltz in and take over!"

"Nobody will be taking over anyone. It's just a friendly merger. We'll get full value on our shares, access to all of their latest medical and technological advances, and other special perks."

"My god." Galt dropped his head into his hands.

"I know it's a lot to take in, Uncle, but it's going to happen sooner or later. They're going to take over whether we like it or not. It's better for everyone this way. No violence. No war. No unnecessary bloodshed. In effect, we get to rule over the entire world."

Galt looked up in surprise. "I'm a businessman, Steven. Not a dictator."

"Is there really that much difference?"

"Yes. Yes, goddammit, there is. And until you realize that for yourself, you will never be fit to run this company."

"I never said I wanted to—"

"You don't have to say it, you little shit. I can see it in your eyes!"

"Uncle, calm down."

"Well, I won't have any part of it. Do you hear me? I won't let you do it! I'm a businessman, and that is that."

"I'm afraid it's not your decision to make," Steve said quietly. "The board has already voted. They've fully endorsed the plan."

"How dare you. How dare you go behind my back over this. We're not the government. We're a private corporation!"

"We do everything, Uncle. We already are the government."

Galt banged his fist. "Don't say such things! This is a business, not a goddamn bureaucracy!"

Steve shook his head, as Galt stabbed a finger at him angrily. "I will bury you over this, do you hear me?"

"You really have no idea how much is stacked up against you, Uncle."

"Don't you dare threaten me. I won't let you. I won't let you do any of this. It's not our place. It's just not our place."

"It doesn't matter, Uncle. The decision's been made."

Galt shook with rage. "But I don't want to rule the world!"

"Now, Uncle—"

Galt's face went red. "I don't want to rule the world!"

"Uncle, your heart—"

Galt slammed his fist into the table and shouted. "I don't want to rule the world! I—"

Galt's face went white and he clutched his shoulder.

Steve watched silently as his uncle slid out of his seat and disappeared behind his desk.

CHAPTER ELEVEN

The screen went black. Sydney was staring at the floor, her limbs quivering with nervous energy. "People need to see this. They need to know what's going on." She looked up at the screen. "Can you give me a copy of that footage you just showed us?"

A slim silver disc slid out the front of the cabinet. Sydney picked it up and looked at it curiously. "I hope I can find something that still plays this." She tucked the disc into her jacket. "Come on, Major. Let's go." She headed for the door.

Karnage didn't follow. He looked up into Galt's cataract-laden eyes. "Where can I find Steve Dabney?"

The screen flashed, showing a helicopter view of Dabneyville. It zoomed in on the needle-like tower and the forest beyond. "Come visit the pristine forests of the Dabney Preserve, accessible exclusively from the canopy bridge, located on the observation decks of the Dabney National Tower, the world's tallest freestanding—"

"Where's the Dabney National Tower?" Karnage said.

The screen cut to old footage of Galt Dabney wearing a construction hat. His hair and moustache were black. "The DN Tower will be located atop the corporate headquarters of the Dabney Corporation, home to the expansive Dabney Family Archives, and—"

"What's the quickest way to get to the Dabney National Tower from here?"

The screen cut to grainy security footage of an engineer talking to Galt Dabney. "The executive elevator will run clear up the length of the DN Tower right down to the main lobby."

"Make it run all the way down into the vaults." Galt poked the engineer in the ribs. "You never know when I'll have to make a quick getaway." The engineer nodded and smiled.

The screen went black, and a set of bookcases whirred open behind Karnage, revealing a brass elevator car. Karnage looked up at Galt's head. "Thanks. I'll try and hit Steve once for you."

The screen showed security footage from Galt's corner office. He was talking to another executive. "That Steven is a smart fellow, but he is also one dangerous sonofabitch."

"I'll keep that in mind." Karnage headed for the elevator.

Sydney was standing halfway through the door. "Major, what are you doing?!"

"You do what you gotta do, Captain," Karnage said. "I've still got some questions for ol' Steve Dabney."

"You can't face him alone. What about your Sanity Patch? You don't even have a weapon!"

The elevator doors shut with a soft bing.

CHAPTER TWELVE

Karnage calmly rode the elevator. He watched the numbers above the door change, slowly making their way upward. He shut his eyes, focused his mind, and concentrated on his long-term goal: *Cookie. Velasquez. Heckler. Stumpy. Koch. Cookie. Velasquez. Heckler. Stumpy. Koch.* Then he felt his body relaxing, and the Sanity Patch downgraded to Daffodil, as if voicing its approval. Karnage took a deep breath. He was as ready for this as he'd ever be.

The elevator binged, and the doors slid open, as a cool breeze wafted into the elevator. Karnage stepped out, and found himself on a wide circular deck overlooking the desert, the elevator housed in a cylindrical beam in the centre. An absolutely breathtaking view stretched out on all sides. The glass floor gave him a clear view of the microscopically small buildings below while a guard rail ran around the perimeter of the deck at waist height, punctuated only by thick steel beams with a thin netting draped between them. The netting wafted in the wind as the chilled air blew through it and over Karnage's skin. Karnage walked slowly along the deck, and the mountain came into view on the other side of the elevator shaft. Soon the mountain loomed high beside him, the lush green of the pine trees intermittently broken by steep shanks of grey rock: lifeless desert on one side, forested mountain on the other.

"Hello, you."

Karnage turned around. Standing on the deck behind him, in front of a metal door marked EMERGENCY EXIT, was Patrick, aiming a pistol at Karnage's chest. A manila enveloped was tucked under his arm.

"Don't move," he said. Patrick flipped open the envelope with his free hand, and pulled out a slim tablet. He let the envelope fall free. The wind picked it up, and it flew into the netting where it flapped uselessly, like a fly stuck in a spider's web. Patrick angled the tablet so it was propped against his chest; he held it along the bottom with one hand, while the other kept the gun barrel firmly pointed at Karnage's chest. He flicked the tablet on.

Steve Dabney appeared on the screen. He smiled.

"Hello, Major," he said. "I'm sorry to deprive you of your big moment, but I'm afraid my priorities lie elsewhere. I think it's sweet the way you keep trying to save the world. I know you don't like to think of yourself as a romantic, but the zeal you've put into this endeavour belies the truth. You're like a samurai who has lost his master: rōnin, if you like. Rudderless. Directionless. Looking for answers. Life must be very difficult for you in this new world. I pity you.

"But I have to give you credit. You have proven to be a very worthy opponent. I'm sorry we had to be adversaries. We really wanted to make you a key player in this organization. It's unfortunate we couldn't come to an understanding. You'll be pleased to know we've since found a more qualified candidate to take the position, so your services will no longer be required.

"I've authorized Patrick here to terminate you in whatever way he sees fit. Despite his previous setbacks, he's assured me that you won't escape this time. He's given me his word on that, and if you knew Patrick like I do, you'd understand how significant that promise is.

"Before you die, I want you to understand: I have saved the human race. Not just the human race, but all life on Earth. Our biosphere will be preserved forever in the Archive. Our past will never be forgotten. As for the future, I've just put the finishing touches on the ultimate merger. I've just given the go-ahead to put our plan into action, starting right here in Dabneyville. A Dabney always leads by example, and this will be my finest example yet.

"Whatever it is you hoped to stop, Major, you're too late."

He winked, and the screen went black.

CHAPTER THIRTEEN

Sydney came out of the tunnels in the basement of her old precinct. She slipped through the maintenance door and down the darkened hallway. She stopped in front of a door with a peeling piece of masking tape stuck to it. The words "Digital Forensics" had been scrawled across it with black marker. Sydney opened the door and slipped quietly inside.

The room was lit by a bank of monitors. A hunched figure sat in front of the screens, his fingers working to either side of him on a set of ergonomic keyboards. He was surrounded by shelves stuffed with electronics in various states of destruction. The figure turned his face up to one of the monitors, and Sydney smiled as she recognized the profile. "Hey there, Campbell."

The figure jumped. He turned and squinted through the dark at Sydney. His eyes went wide with shock. "Oh. Oh my god. Sydney? Is that really you?"

"It is."

"What are you doing here? You're a known fugitive now. You know that?"

"I know."

"I mean like top ten most wanted fugitive. Top two, even! Only one they want more than you is that Major Karnage guy. Hey, is it true that he seduced you so you'd help him escape?"

"What? Where the hell did you hear that?"

"Captain Riggs said—"

"Captain Riggs is a lying fuckmonkey," Sydney said.

Campbell suddenly started and looked around nervously. "Oh man, you know what? You really—I mean *really* shouldn't be here. You're a wanted criminal! I mean . . . I should arrest you. I mean—"

"Campbell, come on now. You haven't arrested so much as a doughnut as long as I've known you. Do you really want to start now?"

Campbell shook his head. "Not really."

"Good. Now listen, I need your help." Sydney fished the disc out of her pocket. "Can you play this?"

Campbell took the disc and flipped it over in his hands. "Wow—I mean, really. Wow! I haven't seen one of these in years. Where did you find this? This is like . . . I mean, it really *is* a collector's item. Does it work?"

"I sure as hell hope so. Do you have anything that can play it?"

"I might. I just might." Campbell jumped up and sifted through the hardware stacked on the shelves. Tangles of wires and screws fell to the floor. "The captain's always bitching at me, telling me I gotta throw all this stuff out. But I keep telling him, you never know when this stuff will come in handy. You just never know. And now I'm right—I mean, really, I'm right. If I wasn't holding on to the stuff, you'd never—"

There was a loud crash somewhere above them, followed by shouting. Campbell looked up. "What was that?" He looked at Sydney. "Does that have anything to do with you?"

Sydney grabbed Campbell's face in her hands. "Campbell, for once in your life, I need you to stay focused. You've got to find something to play that disc. Can you do that for me?"

Campbell nodded. "I can. What's on the disc?"

"Video clips. I need to get them on DiN."

"Where?"

"Everywhere. All the official channels. All the unofficial channels."

"There aren't any unofficial channels left."

"Just get it on all the channels you can."

Campbell took another look at the disc. "Why? What is it?"

"You'll understand when you see it," Sydney said. "It's kinda self-explanatory. I promise you, Campbell, you get this data up there, you will have saved the world."

He gave her a funny look. "Huh?"

There was another larger crash, and someone screamed. A muffled noise tore across the floor above them.

It was squiggly.

"What the hell was that?" Campbell said.

"Nothing good." Sydney stared hard at the ceiling. She heard feet scrambling, and something crackled. "Give me your goober pistol, Campbell. Now."

Campbell's hand dropped down to it. "Why?"

"Because I'm a better shot than you."

Campbell opened his mouth to argue, realized she was right, and shut up. He handed her his pistol. "Don't let the captain find out about this."

"He won't find out, I promise." Sydney headed for the door. "Just get that video on the DiN. Promise me you'll do that, C. No matter what."

"What do you mean no matter what? What's going on up there? This has something to do with you, doesn't it?"

"No. Well, yes. Sort of. Look, it's just too much to explain. You have to get that video up on the DiN. Before it's too late."

"Too late? What do you mean too late? Sydney, what the hell is going on?"

"Trust me, Campbell. Please! And stay here. Otherwise . . . just stay here. You'll be safe." She gave Campbell the thumbs up, and left.

Sydney shut the door firmly behind her. She took three steps back, and fired three rounds of goober at the frame, sealing it shut. *Get those clips up, C.*

There was more crackling and screaming from upstairs. Sydney ran down the hall and through the door into the stairwell. She walked cautiously up the stairs, her gun drawn.

The door to the main floor was gone, nothing but a smoking circle where it used to be. Dabneycops ran past the door. Pink volleys of goober shot across the doorway. Green energy balls flew in the other direction. A squidbug stopped in the doorway, levelled its energy spear, and fired. It looked down and spotted her, but Sydney fired first. Goober bloomed out from the squidbug's chest as it fell to the ground. More squidbugs appeared in the doorway, their energy spears glowing, and Sydney raced back down the stairs. She could hear the clacking of feet on the stairs above her as she raced through the door at the bottom of the stairs back into the basement. She slammed the door behind her, and fired three more rounds of goober into it. She heard the squidbugs pounding on the door behind her, squiggling in frustration. Then, they grew quiet. Sydney reloaded her pistol, waiting for the goobered door to disappear.

She heard a *crack-hiss* behind her, and she spun around. Leaning against the wall at the end of the hall was a squidbug lighting a cigarette. The door to the maintenance tunnel swung on its hinges. Sydney moved to raise her pistol. The squidbug didn't even turn to look at her. It simply lifted its spear with one hand, and shot a crackling ball of energy across the hall.

Sydney's world filled with an intense painful green.

CHAPTER FOURTEEN

"He's quite an eloquent man, wouldn't you say?" Patrick tossed the tablet like a frisbee. It slid across the glass floor and flipped over the side into the netting.

"I'd say he's full of shit," Karnage said.

Patrick smiled. "Of course you would. That's exactly the sort of thing you'd say, isn't it?"

"Of course it is. I just fucking well said it."

Patrick wagged a finger at Karnage. "You've been very naughty. You didn't tell me you could overcome your little 'handicap.' It was quite clever of you, really. You certainly showed me up with that trick, I'll grant you. Tell me, Major. What did you think of *my* little trick?"

"You mean that thing where I killed you and you didn't stay dead?"

Patrick nodded. "Quite something, isn't it? Wouldn't you like to know how it works?"

"I'd rather you just stayed dead."

Patrick languidly shook his head. "That's not true. You're curious. And why wouldn't you be? Imagine what you could do if you could cheat death?"

"There's some who'd say I've been doin' that all my life."

"Indeed. But time marches on, doesn't it? You're fighting a losing battle on that front, aren't you?"

"Isn't everybody?"

"Not me." Patrick studied Karnage a moment. "I could share my secret with you, if you like. But you'll have to earn it." Patrick walked over to the railing and leaned against it. "Would you like to play a game with me, Major?"

"No," Karnage said.

"I call it Wak-A-Patrick." Patrick leaned out and grabbed a handful of netting above the tablet. He ripped it from its frame. The tablet slipped out of the netting and twirled end over end into the depths below. "How many times can you kill me before I kill you?"

"What the hell kind of game is that?"

Patrick grinned broadly. "A fun one."

"Me and my fists versus you and your gun?"

"You have a point," Patrick said. "That's not exactly fair, now is it?" He tossed his gun through the hole in the netting, then turned back to Karnage. He gave a slight bow. *"Et commence!"*

As the two circled each other warily, Karnage repeated his mantra in his head: *Cookie, Velasquez, Heckler, Stumpy, Koch. Cookie, Velasquez, Heckler, Stumpy, Koch.*

Patrick quivered with anticipation, as if overeager for this rematch. Karnage opted to hold back to see what his opponent would do. Patrick's impatience got the better of him and he lunged. Karnage sidestepped, grabbed Patrick by the back of his coat, and threw him head first through the tear in the netting.

Patrick's foot tangled in the net. He hung upside down. His foot was slowly slipping from the tangles, but he made no attempt to right himself. He looked at Karnage and winked. His foot came loose, and he fell from the tower, quickly disappearing into the distance.

Karnage's Sanity Patch stayed silent. He reached behind his neck and knocked on its screen. *Like riding a bike.*

The elevator binged behind him. Karnage turned around. The doors slid open and Patrick strode out, twirling a long black cane.

"I must admit, that was rather foolish of me," he said. "I was a little overeager, but I think I've found my footing now." Patrick pulled the shaft off the cane, revealing a long thin blade. "Ready for round two?" He raised the sword and ran at Karnage, bringing the blade down in a sweeping blow.

Karnage grabbed Patrick's sword arm, locked the elbow, and grabbed the sword by its hilt. He jerked it upwards, ripping it out of Patrick's hand. He brought the blade around and ran Patrick through. His Sanity Patch buzzed. "Warning. Sanity Level upgraded to Citrus Blast. Please refrain from violent behaviour."

Karnage whispered in Patrick's ear. "Let's see you survive that, fucker."

Then he grabbed Patrick and threw him over the railing and through the hole in the net. He made a point to watch Patrick fall. The reflective glint of the sword rhythmically winked at Karnage as Patrick tumbled out of sight. He waited until the winking had completely disappeared, then headed for the elevator.

Karnage heard a high-pitched whine coming from outside. He turned around.

Patrick flew up and hovered in front of the open netting. He wore a Dabneycop-issued hoverball flightpack. "Excellent technique, Major. Tell me, are you just as talented at dodging bullets?" Patrick pulled a pistol from his jacket and started firing.

"Give me a fuckin' break!" Karnage dove out of the way as bullets whizzed past his head. He ran around the central cylinder, trying to put anything between him and the flying gunman.

Patrick swooped and bobbed wildly, steering with one hand as he navigated through the net. Bullets exploded across the wall behind Karnage. He saw the discarded cane sheath appear on the deck as he charged around the cylinder. He dove to the ground in a roll, grabbing the empty shaft with a free hand, and leaped back to his feet.

As Patrick passed the hole in the netting, Karnage whipped the cane sheath through it. It smashed into one of the hoverballs, cracking it open. Yellow smoke spewed from its side, and the flightpack jerked out of control. Patrick frantically worked the controls as the flightpack spiralled out of sight. Karnage watched as the contraption fell. It struck the side of the tower, and the hoverballs broke off in either direction. Patrick's body continued hurtling toward the ground, colliding with the tower as it fell.

Karnage leaned against the railing and took a moment to catch his breath. He walked back to the elevator. The doors and the console were riddled with bullets. He tried pressing the buttons, but nothing happened. "Shit." He ran to the Emergency Exit door and placed his hand on the knob to pull it open.

He heard the faint sounds of feet running up metal stairs coming from the other side, getting louder with each frenetic step.

Karnage snarled. "Oh you have got to be fucking kidding me!"

He pressed himself against the wall, and the door kicked open. Patrick burst through, brandishing a rocket launcher. Karnage kicked the rocket launcher out of his hands and punched him across the jaw. Patrick stumbled across the deck and fell to the floor.

Karnage snatched up the rocket launcher and set it on his shoulder. Patrick rose to his feet, brushing down his uniform. He looked at Karnage and smiled. "Brilliant. Is there anything you can't defend against?"

"No," Karnage said, and fired the rocket.

There was the slightest shout from Patrick as he was engulfed in an explosion. Smoke billowed out and filled the deck. Charred bits of what was probably Patrick flew out in all directions from the cloud. When the smoke finally cleared, there was nothing left of Patrick but a blackened, mangled hole in the floor.

"Congratulations, Major," a voice said behind him. "You win."

Karnage turned and saw Patrick level a machine gun at him. The inevitable spray of bullets hit Karnage square in the chest, knocking him backwards. Stumbling, he fell through the hole in the floor.

Karnage tumbled through the sky, the bullet wounds hot across his chest. Suddenly, they went cold. Karnage looked down. Tranquilizer balls dotted his shirt. *What the . . .*

The tranquilizers knocked him out before he could finish the thought.

MK#9: DOUBLE THE KARNAGE, DOUBLE THE FUN!

CHAPTER ONE

The world spun in Karnage's head, twirling violently, like he was circling down into a drain without end. Then, without warning, the spinning stopped. The world dipped, and Karnage felt himself propelled upward. He felt like he was flying, pushing through damp clouds, bursting out into cold blue sky, flying higher and higher until he was floating in ice cold black.

Bright pinpricks of consciousness pierced the black. They swelled in size. Features became visible in the soft circles of light. Black glasses and mouths like belly slits that curved up slightly at the corners. The faint outline of chauffeur's caps resolved themselves in the gloom. They were all Patrick. Every one of them. They smiled and leered and stared down at him. The faces swirled around him as they talked amongst themselves.

"He's ugly."

"Much uglier than I would have thought."

"Are you sure it's him?"

"It's him."

"Amazing."

"Astounding."

"How many times has he killed us?"

"A hundred?"

"A thousand."

"Really?"

"No, nothing like that. You're exaggerating."

"He could, though."

"You're being silly."

"I've seen him in combat. He's brilliant."

"Simply brilliant."

Karnage tried to focus his mind, to wake him himself up from this dream. The faces swirled tightly together, merging from thousands into hundreds.

"He's trying to focus."

"Can he see us?"

"He can see us."

"Look at his eyes."

"So cold."

"So calculating."

"So brilliant."

Karnage tried to shake the vision away, but it wouldn't go. The hundred Patricks merged again, down to tens, then to three.

"Who caught him?"

"I did."

"Good work."

"Thank you."

"Bravo."

"Thank you both."

Karnage's eyes slowly came into focus, the three Patricks stubbornly staying apart. They were sharp and clear as day in front of him. And that's when he realized it.

There were three of them.

The three Patricks stood in a line in front of Karnage. He was sitting in a wheelchair. Thick ropes tied him to the chair by his wrists and ankles. A single set of fluorescent tubes hung from a fixture overhead. The walls and ceiling were a dull metallic grey. He was inside a cargo container.

The three Patricks looked down at Karnage. Their faces beamed.

"Congratulations, Major," the first one said.

"You've won the game," the second one said.

"You've earned the prize," the third one said.

"Would you like to see it?" the second one said.

The first one moved aside. "It would like to see you."

Behind him was an old man sitting in an electric wheelchair. He hit the joystick on the armrest with a gnarled hand, and wheeled forward. The other Patricks stepped back in deference to the old man. He wore an old Uncle Stanley uniform that hung loosely from his frame. Medals clanked and gleamed against his chest. Four stars were affixed to each of his epaulets. A pair of plastic sunglasses covered half his face. He reached up with shaking hands and pulled them off, revealing thick lenses affixed to thin wire frames. They magnified his pale eyes, showing white dots of cataract in the pupils.

"Hello, you," he said.

"Who the fuck are you?" Karnage said.

The old man smiled. "I was rather hoping introductions wouldn't be necessary. That perhaps you would have recognized me without me having to—well, that was all a long time ago, wasn't it? We were the greatest of enemies then. Oh, what a pair we made. But memories fade with time. Perhaps the name Patrick Mayhew will ring a bell?"

Karnage started. It did ring a bell. It rang a bell so loud and clear in Karnage's skull it felt like there was an alarm klaxon blasting from one temple to the other. Karnage looked at the three Patricks and back at the old man. Finally, he twigged to the similarities. He recognized the faces. All of them. All four of them. Karnage's heart thumped in his chest.

"General Patrick Mayhew," he said. "Otherwise known as . . . General Mayhem."

The old man shook his head. "I so wish you wouldn't call me that. I never cared for that nickname."

"Seemed a pretty accurate description to me," Karnage growled. "What with all the people you killed. The trail of destruction you left behind."

Mayhem smiled. "I was good at my job, wasn't I? You were no slouch yourself, Major. I lost count of the number of times you laid waste to my best plans. The number of missions that had to be scrapped because of a stubborn little *carpy* known as Major Karnage. Oh, how you vexed me at first. I wanted nothing more than to see your head on a pike. But after your ingenious escape from New Baghdad, I found myself taking a shine to you. I surprised myself with that. There you were, my most despised enemy, the very embodiment of everything I hated most about the *carpies*, and yet, I just couldn't help myself. You were so . . . brilliant.

"Your escapades amused me greatly. Your constant promotions and demotions—the demotions I loved most of all. You weren't just a pain in my posterior. Your own superiors despised you as well. And yet, they couldn't get rid of you. You were just too valuable to them, weren't you? By my calculations, you should have earned the rank of Field Marshal five times over in your career. But that never mattered to you, did it? You didn't care about your career. You cared only for the battle ahead, and for the men that served under you. If the *carpies* hadn't been in such desperate straits, I'm sure they would have had you shot a hundred times over—and what a horrible waste that would have been.

"Whenever I was in the field, I always secretly hoped you'd try attacking us. How I longed to see you—to meet you face-to-face. To see for myself the infamous Major Karnage on the battlefield. I was sure it would be brilliant. But we never got that moment, did we? We were never allowed to share that spotlight. They brought an end to it all, didn't they? Stopped the music, turned up the lights, and told us all to go home. But they didn't really let us go home, did they, Major?

"Once the Nagasaki Treaties were signed and World Peace fell upon the Earth, I knew it was only a matter of time before they turned their backs on us. I could feel it in the air. It was palpable. So I slipped away—went into hiding before they could make me disappear. And I was right: they did make it all disappear."

"Every battleship," the first Patrick said.

"Every missile," said the second.

"Every tank, pistol, and soldier," the third one said.

"Gone," the second one said.

"Right down to the last bullet," added the first.

"It didn't take them long to realize that they had acted rashly," Mayhem went on. "That they still had a need for us. But they couldn't admit that they were wrong. They had a reputation to uphold."

"They were the saviours of the human race," the first Patrick said.

"World Peace," said the second.

"And all that," said the third.

"And yet," Mayhem continued, "there were still insurgents to eliminate. Rebellions to be quelled. Assassinations to be carried out. And who better to fulfil those needs than good old General Mayhem? I found I was able to contract out my services and expertise on a freelance basis—discreetly, of course. They had no idea who I really was."

"They didn't want to know," the first Patrick said.

"They preferred not to ask," said the second.

"And we preferred not to tell them," said the third.

"If they had ever known my true identity," Mayhem explained, "they would have locked me away for sure. Just as they did you. We're terribly inconvenient for them, aren't we, Major? A reminder of how savage the human race can become—and how noble that savagery can be. It's easy to point to violence and blame it for all the world's ills. But in hands like ours, violence isn't simply a mindless force of destruction. It is performance art. Wouldn't you agree?"

"No," Karnage said.

"Your lips say no," the first Patrick said.

"But your eyes say yes," said the second.

"You understand my meaning precisely," said the third.

Mayhem smiled impishly. "And that is what makes you so brilliant."

"What do you want, Mayhem?"

"I wish for you to share in my glory, Major," Mayhem said. "To offer you an opportunity."

"An opportunity of a lifetime," the first Patrick said.

"A partnership," the second one said.

"A partnership like no other," said the third.

Mayhem gestured towards the three Patricks. "I appreciate the tact you've shown in not asking about my 'comrades.' They are the keystone to the structure of my entire organization. Right before the blight of World Peace fell upon the earth, my top scientists were hard at work on a militarized variation of cloning technology."

"Human bio-engineering." Karnage looked over the three smiling Patricks. "That's a direct violation of military ordinance number 778A5-3."

Mayhem waved him off. "Yes, yes, of course it is. But you of all people should understand the need to occasionally bend the rules in the name of the greater good."

"That doesn't mean experimentin' on your own men," Karnage barked.

"Of course not," Mayhem said. "And I did nothing of the sort. I was the sole test subject. And as you can see, the results were astounding. We learned to accelerate the growth rate. Discovered how to implant memories, emotions . . ."

"Experiences," the first Patrick said.

"All of human consciousness," said the second.

"The very soul," said the third.

Mayhem motioned to his clones. "What you see standing before you are not merely carbon copies of myself. They *are* me."

"We are me," the first one said.

"So very me," the second said.

"Delightfully me," said the third.

"Why do they keep repeating you like that?" Karnage said.

"They can't help it," Mayhem said. The clones nodded.

"We can't," the first one said.

"It's instinct," said the second.

"Completely involuntary," said the third.

"The consciousness transfer creates a permanent link between the clones and the host," Mayhem said. "In essence, we share one mind."

"One mind," said the first.

"And many bodies," said the second.

"So very many bodies," said the third.

"So if I were to get up and kick one of you in the nuts," Karnage said, "you'd all double over in pain?"

"It's not quite like that, Major," Mayhem said. "While we are cognizant of the others' thoughts and experiences, we are still individuals. We are more an interconnected network of minds and experiences. A hive mind, if you like. While each of us is a thinking individual, we are connected to a greater whole. And that whole is so much greater than any individual part."

Like the squidbugs, Karnage thought. "Why are you telling me all this, Mayhem? What the hell does all this have to do with me?"

Mayhem clapped his hands together in delight. "Why, everything, Major!"

"Everything," said the first.

"Everything," said the second.

"Everything," said the third.

"I am dying," Mayhem said. "Once I die, my reign will come to an end. My clones will live on, of course. They will live out their natural lifespan, and eventually die out as well. And my empire will die with them."

"Why not just clone the clones?" Karnage said.

Mayhem shook his head. "I have tried, but . . . errors pop up in the process."

The clones shook their heads in unison.

"Artifacts," said the first.

"Mutations," said the second.

"It's not pretty," said the third.

Mayhem's eyes sparkled. "But that is where you come in, Major. I wish for you to become my successor. To take up the mantle, and take this organization boldly into the next century."

Karnage's eyes goggled. "Are you kidding me?"

Mayhem shook his head. "Oh no, Major."

"We're very serious," said the first.

"Quite serious," said the second.

"Couldn't be more serious if we tried," said the third.

"But what about the invasion? The squidbugs?"

Mayhem waved him off. "The players may change, but the game always stays the same. There will always be a need for our services." Mayhem tapped a finger against his lips. "We will change your name, of course. Perhaps introduce you to our clients as a new partner. Call you John, perhaps."

"What do you think?" said the first.

"Too on the nose?" said the second.

"We could come up with a more clever *nom d'espionage*, if you like," said the third.

"So you're just gonna clone me and take me out and pretend I'm somebody else, and you don't think anybody out there is gonna recognize me?!"

"Of course they would—if we sent *you*. But we wouldn't be sending you out on assignments." Mayhem motioned to the cargo container door. The Patricks opened it, and a silhouetted figure stood on the threshold. "We would be sending him."

Karnage stared at the figure. It was Karnage, thirty years younger. He had dark black hair where Karnage's was grey. Smooth supple skin where Karnage's was scarred and wrinkled. He was Karnage in his prime.

Karnage's clone walked into the cargo container, squinting into the darkness. He looked as bewildered as Karnage felt. He wore a chauffeur outfit like the Patricks. Karnage recognized the wary look in his eyes, the stillness in his body, the deceptive looseness in his limbs. He could sense the clone's nervous energy.

Karnage's stomach dropped. He could sense more than the clone's energy in the room: he could sense *him*. As soon as the container doors had opened, it had felt like someone had cracked open a tiny door in his mind. Thoughts and emotions were flowing down through it. The presence of this clone was slowly cutting into Karnage's brain like a knife through a roast. He could feel the presence of the clone's thoughts inside his own. It made him want to throw up. The clone felt the same. They looked at each other, both horrified to realize they were sharing the same feelings of surprise and confusion.

They both turned to Mayhem. "What gives you—"

"—the right?!"

The two Karnages looked at each other in shock.

"Stop that," Karnage said.

"Stop that." The clone said barely a half-second behind.

"I said stop it!"

"I said stop it!"

They both rounded on Mayhem.

"You're mad!" Karnage strained at his bonds.

"You're fucking *mad!*" The clone Karnage tried to charge at Mayhem. The Patricks grabbed him, holding him back.

Mayhem nodded eagerly, looking from the younger Karnage to the older. "It's a mad world we're living in, isn't it, Major? Where great men like us are forced down into the sewers of society, while the vermin scuttle up into gleaming corner offices and heap riches and accolades upon themselves. This is your chance to grab a piece of that for yourself. We'll show these fools what real power is. I'll even give you top billing."

"Karnage & Mayhem," said the first.

"Has a nice ring to it, don't you think?" said the second.

"Like an old vaudeville routine," said the third.

"Karnage & Mayhem: One Night Only," the second one shouted.

"Held over due to popular demand," cried the first.

"We can't exactly hang that on a sign out front," Mayhem said, "but it can be our own private little joke. Karnage & Mayhem: together at last! Oh, how we'll laugh. We'll laugh at those bastards' expense." Mayhem grew more intense. "We'll laugh and we'll laugh . . ." Mayhem's face contorted with rage. "We'll laugh until their blood is running in the streets!"

Mayhem fell into a coughing fit. He grasped for the oxygen mask on his chest and placed it over his mouth, sucking greedily. The Patricks picked up on his mania.

"In the streets!" the first cried.

"All of them!" the second shouted.

"They'll pay!" cried the third.

Mayhem stopped coughing, and beamed. "I'll leave you two to get better acquainted," he said.

"Give you time to get to know yourself," said the first.

"To discuss your options," said the second.

"Who knows?" the third one said. "You just might start to see yourself in a new light."

Mayhem spun his wheelchair around and left. Once he had passed safely through the door, the three Patricks let go of the Karnage clone and pushed him into the room. Karnage felt his clone's rage at this treatment. The Patricks filed out the door. The last of them turned back a moment. "Please, feel free to take your time," he said.

There was a loud metal clank as he shut and locked the door.

CHAPTER TWO

The two Karnages eyed each other suspiciously.

"So," the old one said, "you're me."

"And you're me," the young one said. "Apparently."

The old one could feel the young one's scepticism. "You don't believe them."

"Would you?" The young one leaned against the container wall. "Shit, one second I'm fallin' through space thinkin' I'm gonna die. The next I'm wakin' up in some kinda goddamn lab full of these Patrick monkeyfuckers, all gushin' and gawkin' and sayin', 'Hello, you.' Christ, it's enough to make a man sick. And then they're makin' me look in a mirror and . . . well, shit, look at me. I'm fuckin' young again. All handsome and clean shaven and got all my hair and none of its grey—and I'm wonderin' what these crazy monkeyfuckers have done to me, and they're tryin' to tell me that I'm some kinda goddamn clone! And then I hear this voice in my head sayin' that these Patricks are all General Mayhem, and suddenly I can see the resemblance and I figure for sure I must be dreamin', but the Patricks keep tellin' me I'm not, and then they start pushin' me across the lab sayin' 'This way, this way' and they stick me in here and . . ." The young one looked down at the old one.

"And here I am," the old one said.

"And here you are." The young one ripped off the chauffeur's cap and loosened his collar. "I feel like a goddamn monkey in this thing." He eyed the old one's straitjacket enviously.

They stared at each other, wondering what the other was thinking, trying to ignore the presence in their head that they knew was the other's thoughts. They could feel each other's suspicions: the distrust. It made it that much harder to voice them. Why articulate what doesn't have to be said? They were thinking separately and yet the same. They could almost see themselves through each other's eyes, a kind of double vision that made them both a little nauseous.

They tried to block it out.

"What's your assessment of General Mayhem?" the old one said, pretending he didn't already know the answer.

"Batshit insane," the young one said, pretending that the old one didn't already know.

"You know what we have to do," the old one said.

The young one nodded. "We have to get out of here."

"We have to save our troops," the old one said.

"Cookie."

"Velasquez."

"Heckler."

"Stumpy."

"Koch."

"Sydney." They were both surprised at how their hearts had jumped slightly at the mention of her name. They looked at each other.

"We have to get back to Dabneyville," the young one said.

"We have to stop the squidbugs," the old one said.

They grew quiet. The sounds of their joined thoughts filled the silence. Dark things spiralled and swirled in their consciousness. Things that couldn't be spoken, otherwise they wouldn't be able to help anyone. Not even themselves.

The old one spoke. "You know we can't live like this."

The young one nodded. "It's too much."

"One of us has to die," the old one said.

They looked at each other, then spoke at the same time: "It should be me."

"Oh come off it, Major," the young one said. "You're the original. I'm just a copy. You should be the one to live."

"That's a load of horse shit and you know it. You're just as much me as I am. Maybe even more so: you're me in my prime. I'm me on my deathbed. Old and worn out like a broken-down race horse. You're a goddamn thoroughbred. Not an ache in your body. Don't act like I don't know, cuz you know I fucking well know—and I wish I didn't know, but too bad, because I do!"

The young one scowled. He balled up his fists. "It ain't right."

"None of it's right," the old one said. "We shouldn't both be here. We didn't ask for this. But here we are. We gotta assess the situation, and the situation is clear. You got the youth, the vitality, the experience . . ." The old one couldn't bring himself to finish his thought.

The young one looked up, and finished it for him. ". . . and I got no Sanity Patch."

The old one nodded. "That's right. You don't."

The young one stood up. He smoothed down the front of his uniform, and nodded.

"You do us proud out there," the old one said.

The young one saluted his older self. "You sure as hell bet I will."

"Good. We got that settled. Now how do we get you out of here?" The old one said.

The young one jerked his thumb at the door. "Looks like the lab is in some kind of hangar. All kinds of tubes and tanks and cloning shit everywhere."

The old one saw the picture the young one was bringing up in his mind.

"And hardware," the old one said.

The young one nodded. "Military hardware."

"Buncha hoverball flightpacks along one wall."

"Right by that open skylight."

"You thinking what I'm thinking?"

"Now there's a stupid question."

"It may be stupid, but I'll be fucked if we don't try and have a conversation like real people, and not like . . ."

The young one looked towards the door. "Not like them."

"I'll distract Mayhem," the old one said.

"Really piss him off," the young one said.

"To get the attention of all of 'em," the old one said.

"I'll get to the flightpacks."

"Head for the skylight."

"Get the hell outta here."

"Get to Dabneyville."

"Defeat the squidbugs."

"Find my troops."

"Find Sydney."

"Do you know how you're going to do it yet?" the old one said.

"Which part?"

"All of it."

"No," the young one said, "but I'll figure it out."

The old one looked over the young one. "Yeah, you will."

The young one reached down and shook the old one's hand. The touch was electric. They pulled away from each other, and nodded.

"Good luck, Major," the old one said. He wanted to salute.

The young one saluted for him.

"Good luck, Major," he said.

Karnage looked back at his older self, and nodded. "All right. Here we go." He banged on the door, and it opened.

Twenty Patricks stood in the middle of the room behind General Mayhem.

Karnage jerked a thumb at his old self. "He wants a word with you," he said.

Karnage stepped out of the way as Mayhem wheeled forward. The Patricks followed close behind. Karnage stepped back, allowing them to pass. He shuffled towards the wall. None of the Patricks were watching him. They were all fixated on the old Karnage.

"So?" General Mayhem said. "Have you considered my offer?"

"I have," the old Karnage said. "And you can shove it up your ass."

Karnage saw Mayhem's neck stiffen; his voice remained neutral. "Can I?"

"You sure as hell can," the old Karnage grinned, baring yellow teeth. "What did you think, General? That I'd want to kiss and make up after all those people you killed? That I'd find it in my heart to forgive the Butcher of Bereznyi? The Terror of Tatvan? The Siberian Slayer?"

The flightpacks were mounted on a raised platform just beyond the cloning tanks. Karnage inched towards them, keeping his eye on the Patricks. One of them clenched a gloved fist.

"You're a monster," old Karnage said. "You can try and hide all you like behind your shiny medals and little pretty stars. But that don't change the fact you're a cold-blooded killer. I did what I had to do because it had to be done. You? You did it all because you got off on it. You're no hero, Mayhem. You're a goddamn sociopath."

Karnage inched himself up to the platform, and unstrapped a flightpack from the wall. He watched the back of Mayhem's head shake slowly. "You Carpathians are all alike, aren't you?"

Handsome and dashing, Karnage thought.

"Dashing and handsome?" old Karnage said.

"No," Mayhem's voice slowly turned into a low growl. "Naive, short-sighted, and incredibly out of your depth, you ungrateful little carpy."

The Patricks moved in tighter around Karnage; their anger was palpable.

Old Karnage smiled, nodding. "There he is. That's the General Mayhem I know."

Mayhem jabbed a shaking finger at old Karnage. "You know nothing about me! Just lies and half-truths and propaganda fed to you by your superiors! Nothing about my struggles. Nothing of what I've been up against. You—"

The base of the flightpack scraped along the floor. One of the Patricks turned, and caught a glimpse of Karnage out of the corner of his eye.

"Stop him!" Mayhem shouted.

The Patricks turned and raced towards Karnage. Karnage tried to strap into the flightpack, but a Patrick tackled him to the ground. Karnage's world became a frenzied maze of gloved hands and angry gritted teeth shouting, "Stop him! Stop him! Stop him!"

Karnage lay on the ground, his face pressed into the floor. A sea of shiny black boots stretched out before him. Between them all, he could just catch his older self's face. *Sorry, old man,* Karnage thought.

It's okay, kid, the old Karnage thought. *You did your best.*

Mayhem looked at Karnage, then back at the old Karnage. "So that was the plan, was it? You keep me busy while your partner goes for help?"

Karnage felt lips near his ear. "A nice try, Major."

Another Patrick from somewhere in the crowd spoke: "But I'm better than you."

Mayhem smiled. He toyed with the joystick on his wheelchair. "Still, I shouldn't be too surprised. Admittedly, I was expecting a lot from a *carpy* like you. I had such high hopes, Major. I had hoped . . . ah, but it doesn't matter now, does it? There's nothing going on behind those defiant eyes of yours, is there? Just empty, primal rage.

You're a vacant meatbag. Good for spare parts, but nothing else."

The hair on Karnage's neck stood on end. *What does he mean spare parts?*

"What do you mean spare parts?" the old Karnage said.

"Your mind may be unwilling, but your body is quite strong. While not quite as effective as providing a new host, we can use your genetic material to repair artifacts in the clones."

"Like a patching material," said a Patrick.

"Or spackle," said another.

"The technique isn't perfect," Mayhem said, "but it should bring the error rate down to tolerable levels. Just think, Major. Instead of a partnership, it will be a hostile takeover."

"Quite hostile," said a Patrick.

"Very hostile," said another.

"Your strength combined with my mind. Mayhem & Karnage. Has a nice ring to it, doesn't it?"

"Much better than Karnage & Mayhem," said a Patrick.

"Much much better," said another.

"But first," Mayhem said, "we must dispose of the old material."

Karnage heard a bullet click into a chamber above his head.

"No!" The old Karnage struggled against his bonds. "Let him go, Mayhem! Or I'll—"

"Or you'll what, Major?" Mayhem leered. "There's nothing you can do. Look at you."

"Struggling," said a Patrick.

"Helpless," said another.

"You're done for, Major," Mayhem said. "Finally beaten. There's nothing you can do to change that now."

The old Karnage glowered at Mayhem. "You wanna bet?"

"I suppose you have an emergency backup plan, then?"

"I do," the old Karnage said.

Karnage looked up, as the realization of what the old Karnage was about to do sank in. His heart thudded in his chest. *No, Major! Don't do it!*

Sorry, kid, the old Karnage thought, *it's our only choice.*

"And whatever would that be?" Mayhem said.

"Just two words," the old Karnage said. He locked eyes with Karnage. "The War."

The War!

Karnage's mind filled with violent images. Fire-tinged hate billowed up from his belly, like napalm pouring out of guts.

The War!

He burst out of the pile of Patricks. Screams and chauffeur hats flew in all directions. He let out a cry of primal rage as he remembered . . .

The War!

He charged across the hangar towards old Karnage, who was struggling in the wheelchair against those same visions. Patricks leaped out at Karnage. They tried to grab him, to throw him down. Karnage's fists flew, clearing a path through the mob. He broke noses and snapped wrists with barely a thought. Screams of indignation and howls of pain poured out all around him.

He jumped up onto the wheelchair. The momentum of his landing threw the wheelchair backwards through the cargo container until it slammed into the wall. The blow knocked the metal door shut behind them. Something clanged against it, and shouting and banging from the other side confirmed that it was stuck.

Karnage ripped the restraints off of the old Karnage, whipped him out of the chair, and threw him against the wall.

"Don't talk to me about *The War!*"

The old Karnage's eyes were shut. His teeth gritted. Karnage felt him straining against the violent hallucinations running through their shared mind. Old Karnage's Sanity Levels rocketed upwards. The old man's mind reached out to his through the chaos and the flames: *Cookie, Velasquez, Heckler, Stumpy, Koch, Sydney. Cookie, Velasquez, Heckler, Stumpy, Koch, Sydney. Come on, kid. Concentrate. We can stop this. Think, kid. Think! Cookie, Velasquez, Heckler, Stumpy, Koch, Sydney. Cookie, Velasquez, Heckler, Stumpy, Koch, Sydney. Come on. We can do this.*

Karnage tried to focus on the chant. *Cookie, Velasquez, Heckler,*

Stumpy, Koch, Sydney. Cookie, Velasquez, Heckler, Stumpy, Koch, Sydney. He could feel it pushing through the noise and the fear. *Cookie, Velasquez, Heckler, Stumpy, Koch, Sydney. Cookie, Velasquez, Heckler, Stumpy, Koch, Sydney.*

That's it, kid. We're doing it. We're doing it!

The visions slowly pulled themselves apart, replaced with the faces of each of his missing comrades. *Cookie, Velasquez, Heckler, Stumpy, Koch, Sydney. Cookie, Velasquez, Heckler, Stumpy, Koch, Sydney.*

The last of the visions spilled away, and Karnage let go of his grip on the old man's neck. The old man's Sanity Patch went silent. They looked at each other and smiled. *We did it.*

The container door banged open behind them. A Patrick appeared in the doorway, holding a gun. "No!" Mayhem screamed. Another Patrick knocked the gun down. "We need the meatbag," he hissed.

"Follow my lead!" The old Karnage grabbed the wheelchair and charged forward, ramming through the crowd of Patricks like a battering ram. Patricks flew in all directions, some diving out of the way, others knocked away by the onslaught of the chair. Karnage followed close behind in its wake.

"Get to the flightpacks," the old Karnage barked.

Karnage headed for the platform while the old Karnage ran with the chair towards the cloning tanks.

"Protect the tanks!" Mayhem screamed.

The Patricks raced after the old man, but he slammed the wheelchair into the base of a tank, knocking it down. It smashed against the floor, spilling its underdeveloped contents across the concrete.

Karnage jumped onto the platform and grabbed a flightpack. He turned and saw the old man go down in a sea of Patricks. *Go on, kid. Get outta here!*

Karnage nodded and strapped himself into the flightpack. He hit the hoverball activators, and they hummed to life. He rocketed up towards the open skylight above.

Pain exploded out of Karnage's shoulders. The hoverball bucked and spun out of control, and he crashed back down to the platform.

He writhed in agony on the platform, the flightpack pinning him to the ground. He felt like he'd been hit by twin shotgun barrels. He could hardly breathe. The pain grew worse, coursing out of his shoulder blades in hot waves. It felt like he was being torn apart. He caught something squiggly from the corner of his vision. He looked over his shoulder.

A pair of tentacles hovered in the air above him.

He followed their squiggling length down, and was horrified to find them attached to his back, squeezing out between his shoulders and the flightpack.

He caught the eye of the old Karnage, who was pinned to the floor under a mob of Patricks. They all stared in horror at Karnage. Mayhem slowly backed his wheelchair away until he hit the far wall.

Karnage locked eyes with his older self, and the realization of what was happening hit them both at the same time. He wasn't just missing the Sanity Patch on his neck.

There was no band around his leg.

"Monkeyfucking squidbugs!" Karnage screamed. He writhed on the ground in agony. Squiggles danced across his vision as the alien DNA took over his body.

CHAPTER FOUR

Karnage watched in horror as his younger self writhed in agony beneath the flightpack. A second set of arms shot out from the kid's armpits. The straps of the flightpack snapped off as his body doubled in size. The shoulder tentacles grabbed the mangled flightpack and tossed it through a cloning tank. The Patricks scrambled off of Karnage and backed away.

The young Karnage slowly rose to his feet. He was at least eight feet tall. His shoulder tentacles waved violently above him. He opened his eyes. His pupils had become long drawn-out squiggles. His skin pulsed and flowed with colour like a squidbug. He looked down at his four hands and the tentacles flowing from his back. His clothes lay in tatters over his body. He locked his squiggly eyes on Karnage. He pointed with one of his four arms at the flightpacks. He opened his mouth to speak, straining to untangle his twin tongues into a single coherent syllable:

"Go!"

Karnage nodded and ran for the flightpacks. The mutant Karnage charged past him, his skin turning red as he let out a squiggly scream.

The mutant Karnage swatted the charging Patricks aside like flies. His open palms made loud scrunching noises when they collided with the bodies of the Patricks. Tentacles grabbed a pair of Patricks by their necks and whipped them back across the hangar. There was a loud smash, and Mayhem screamed something about the tanks, but Karnage couldn't make out exactly what over the mutant's angry, defiant roar.

Karnage pulled a flightpack from the wall. Gunfire whizzed past his head. He looped his arms through the straps. A Patrick tried to pull him out, but a tentacle appeared out of nowhere and grabbed the Patrick by his ankle and whipped him away. There was a painful scream and something exploded.

Karnage hit the activators and rocketed up through the skylight.

He came out above a small abandoned airport nestled at the base of a low ridge. He looked down at the hangar below and caught one last glimpse of the young Karnage through the skylight. He was looming over Mayhem, his tentacles quivering fiercely above him. Mayhem lay in the corner, his wheelchair knocked over, surrounded by the broken bodies of the Patricks. He shakily held a pistol up towards the young Karnage's chest, then smoke billowed out of the skylight, and they disappeared from view.

Give him hell, kid, Karnage thought. *Give him hell.*

MK#10: ALIEN KARNAGE

CHAPTER ONE

Karnage cleared the ridge and the flaming airport disappeared behind him. Nothing was visible but a column of smoke growing smaller in the distance as he sped away. *There's your funeral pyre, kid. Rest in peace.* Karnage closed his eyes and took a moment to mourn his wasted youth.

There was a loud bang, and the flightpack bucked violently, spinning out of control. Karnage's eyes flashed open to see a giant ball of pink goober growing out the side of one of his hoverballs. The ground was quickly hurtling up towards him.

The controls fought him as Karnage struggled to pull the flightpack out of its tailspin. He couldn't keep it flying for much longer. He aimed for a soft field of pinkstink nestled in a dry riverbed surrounded by dunes of shifting sand, and brought the flightpack down as gently as he could.

He bounced twice before finally skidding to a shuddering halt in the middle of the field. The flightpack listed over and fell on its side, taking Karnage with it. He fumbled with the straps, but the goober had swelled over the buckle. He touched the hardened pink ball, close to his head. Someone had taken a potshot at him. But who?

A loud squiggly screech ripped across the field. The ground shook under Karnage's feet as a horned worm lumbered over a sand dune and down toward the riverbed.

Karnage yanked and pulled on the straps, trying to rip himself free. A ball of goober shot out from the worm's back, and hit Karnage in the side, sticking him and the flightpack to the ground as it swelled. He was held fast.

The worm crawled across the field toward him. Karnage spotted a pair of tiny figures on the worm's back, standing to either side of the horn. They were human.

The worm stopped a few feet away. Karnage could see deep into the worm's mouth. Curls of yellow mist hugged the worm's serrated pallet.

A third figure moved forward, stopping at the tip of the worm's head. Karnage made out the outline of a rifle in its hands. A glint of sunlight reflected off of a scope as the rifle pointed towards him. A familiar voice called down to him.

"Don't move, pal. Not unless you want a face full of goober."

"Stumpy?" Karnage shouted. "Is that you?"

The figure lowered its rifle. "Major?" He motioned behind him, and a rope ladder rolled down the worm's flank. The figure disappeared from the head, and reappeared climbing down the ladder.

It was Stumpy all right. He wore a loud Hawaiian shirt with charcoal grey dress pants tucked into combat boots. The goober rifle was strapped to his stump. It had been heavily modified with an extra-long barrel made from some kind of iron pipe. The scope looked like it had been pieced together from a pair of binoculars.

Stumpy walked over to Karnage and looked down at him with a huge grin. "It's you," he said. "It's really you."

Karnage motioned with his head to Stumpy's rifle. "You shoot me outta the sky with that thing?"

Stumpy looked at his rifle, and his face went red. "Aw, gee, Major. I didn't know it was you. I thought—well, if I had known, I wouldn't have . . . I mean . . ."

Karnage smiled. "That was some shot, Corporal. Shame that kind of marksmanship got wasted in the C&E. You'd have made one hell of a sharpshooter."

Stumpy grinned. "It's good to see you again, Major."

"You, too," Karnage said. "You got some solvent to get me outta this thing?"

Stumpy turned to the figures on the worm and shouted. "Get me some solvent!"

"Is it him?" a voice shouted back excitedly. "Is it the Lightbringer?"

"Yes," Stumpy shouted.

"The Lightbringer! The Lightbringer has returned!" The worm riders jumped up and down excitedly, then disappeared from view as they ran down its flank.

"Lightbringer?" Karnage said. He eyed Stumpy's clothes suspiciously. "What the hell, Stumpy? Have you hooked up with them Spragmites?"

Stumpy watched the figures coming down the ladder. He leaned in to Karnage. "I'll tell you about it, later, Major. On the way back to the compound."

"Compound? What compound? What the fuck is going on!?"

Stumpy looked up at the figures running towards them. He waved and smiled at them, and spoke out of the side of his mouth at Karnage. "I'll tell you later, Major. Trust me, it's all right. I'm workin' with Tristan. She explained it all to me. I'm on her side."

"And who's side is she on?" Karnage said.

Stumpy gave Karnage a startled look. His mouth opened to say something, but the bounding figures of the two Spragmites coming within earshot forced his mouth shut again. They stopped before Karnage, eyes wide and blazing, and dropped to their knees to bow. "Ma-ma-oo-pow-pow," they chanted.

CHAPTER TWO

They freed Karnage from the goober, and the Spragmites led Karnage and Stumpy back up the rope ladder onto the worm, all the while chanting, "Ma-ma-oo-pow-pow."

A pair of tents had been erected on the worm's back, tied to the worm's hairs. Stumpy led Karnage into one of the tents while the Spragmites lowered a rope to bring up his flightpack.

The worm's body ebbed and flowed beneath Karnage's feet. Stumpy walked across the worm effortlessly, his legs adjusting to every roll. "You get used to it after a while," he said. "You just need to get your worm legs." He sat in an armchair beside a coffee table, and motioned for Karnage to take the chair on the other side. The table was covered in bits of technology. It rolled back and forth on the table as the worm's body moved beneath it. A lip running around the edge of the table prevented any of it from falling off.

"This is too weird." Karnage sat down. "Last time I was on one of these things, it was trying to kill me. Hell, every time I've seen a worm it's tried to kill me. And yet here we are, riding on the back of one like it's a goddamn elephant. How'd you figure it out?"

Stumpy grinned. "That was me. Once Tristan explained how things went down in the WTF, it got me to thinking. Seemed kind of stupid to have a horn on your head that'll kill you if it breaks off. Unless it was bred that way on purpose." Stumpy grew excited and leaned forward. "The horn's like a steering column. Lean on it to urge the worm forward, pull back to get it to slow down, push left and right to get it to turn. And if the worm's getting a little too ornery for your liking, you just give it a good hard yank and it snaps off, and the worm dies. Like a kill switch, or a self-destruct. Works like a charm."

"You're one resourceful trooper, Stumpy."

Stumpy shrugged. "I just like to know how things work, that's all."

The ground shifted and the worm's undulations became more pronounced.

"Feels like we're on our way. Shouldn't take us too long to get back to the compound. You should see how fast these babies can go. It's something else. I haven't had the guts to let one go full out. I don't know if I could hold on! But one day, maybe. One day . . ."

"How did you end up with the Spragmites?" Karnage said.

"Well, I did like you said," Stumpy said. "I got the array up and running, and, well, frankly, Major, I don't know what that array picked up, but the controls started goin' crazy! Lots of weird squiggling all over the monitors and—well, I don't even know what it was. But I just kept those dials hummin' and that array going, like you said. And then there was this blast of green light, and it all went quiet. All of it. Not a peep. Nothin'. Dials were up, and the array was still hummin', but whatever had been sendin' those signals was gone. I couldn't find 'em again."

Karnage nodded. "Probably ultra-violent transmissions."

Stumpy gave Karnage a funny look. "Ultra-what?"

"Never mind," Karnage said. "Go on."

"Well, anyway, I stayed holed up in there, and kept listenin' for anything goin' on, and the next thing I know I hear this knockin' on the door! And I go and I peek out the window, see? And there's this woman standin' there! And not just any woman. She was beautiful! I've seen some lookers in my time, but this one . . . so graceful and elegant. Anyway, she sees me lookin' out at her, so I duck back inside. And she starts talkin' to me through the door. Askin' me to let her in. And I tell her I can't, cuz I gave my word and . . ." Stumpy frowned, puzzled.

"And what?"

Stumpy shook his head. "Well, I don't know. I mean, she just kept talkin' to me, see, and I kept listenin', and she said she knew you! And the more we talked, the more it seemed like she knew all about you—like I mean everything! Like stuff you wouldn't be able to guess, right? So I ask her if you told her the password, and she said you did, but she got so scared that she forgot it—and she's tellin' me all about the Spragmites and how she got roped into bein' part of it all by this Melvern fella—he sounds like one right mean sonofabitch, let me tell you. And so she tells me how you gave her the strength to go on. How you helped her to stand up and fight back and together the two of you knocked that Melvern bastard from his pedestal, and brought him to his knees. But then that ship appeared in the sky, and you told her to get away and find me, and so she ran and then there was the green flash, and when she got up there was nothing left of you but a giant smokin' crater in the ground.

"She was sure you were dead, but I kept remembering what you'd said about your troopers, and I figured whatever had happened to them had happened to you. And if you had reason to believe they were all right, then I figured you were probably all right, too. I just had to find you!

"And then you know what she did? She turned you into like a messiah for her people. The Lightbringer, she called it. And then she put me in charge of tryin' to find you! And that's what I've been doin' ever since. I been workin' with this group—they call themselves the Illuminati. They say it's got something to do with light, but it just sounds like a load of horseshit to me—and we've been lookin' for you. We were gettin' reports of demons and the apocalypse from some of our contacts in Dabneyville, then one of our members sends us D-Pad footage of somebody in a hoverpack carryin' you out of the city. I hacked into the globesat network and traced the flight path, and . . . well, here we are."

"That's one hell of a story," Karnage said.

"It's been a hell of a ride," Stumpy smiled. "But it's all workin' out, isn't it? I actually found you. Tristan didn't think I would. I could tell. She was tryin' to let me down easy, I suppose. But boy is she gonna be surprised when we come walkin' back into the compound. I can't wait to see the look on her face!"

"Yeah," Karnage said uncomfortably, "that should be a sight to see."

They stopped in a low canyon filled with horned worms. The worms were tied down with guy wires attached to their horns. Long lines of tents had been set up on their backs. It looked like a squidbug trailer park. The largest of the worms sat in the middle of the compound. The tent on its back was essentially a mansion. Room upon room of heavy tapestry with peaked roofs and flags waving from the peaks. Karnage guessed it was Tristan's.

It was. Stumpy led Karnage towards it, beaming. Spragmites wielding D-Pads stood on all sides, quietly recording this moment. The occasional whisper of "Lightbringer" came up from the crowd.

They approached Tristan's worm. A pair of Spragmite priests stood guard at the base of the rope ladder. They bowed deeply to Karnage, and stepped out of the way. Stumpy climbed the ladder, and Karnage followed. D-Pads followed their path as they climbed, glinting in the evening sun.

As they reached the top, a line of Spragmite priests emerged from the tent. They lined up to either side of the tent's entrance. They wore extravagant headdresses in the shape of worm horns. Homski emerged from the tent in a long flowing robe and an even more extravagant headdress. A tiny white filament microphone stuck out from behind his ear. He walked to the end of the long line of priests, and unfurled a scroll. He began speaking; his voice echoed from unseen speakers across the compound.

"Presenting her Holiness, the High Priestess of Spragmos."

The crowd broke out into chants of "ma-ma-oo-pow-pow" as the flaps of the tent pulled back. Tristan sashayed out of the tent, her long flowing robes resplendent with jewels. Her headdress looked like a three-headed horn covered in white diamonds. A tiny white filament microphone was also visible above her ear. She glided past her priests, smiling warmly at Karnage. She leaned forward and embraced him. As she did so, she discreetly covered her microphone with her fingers and whispered in Karnage's ear. "Keep quiet," she whispered, "and follow my lead." She pulled back and turned to the crowd, smiling warmly.

"Humble servants of Spragmos," her voice echoed across the compound. "Our prayers have been answered. Behold, the return of the Lightbringer. Ma-ma-oo-pow-pow."

"Ma-ma-oo-pow-pow," the crowd cried.

Tristan turned to Karnage. "Come, Lightbringer. There is much to discuss."

Tristan guided Karnage back to the tent. Stumpy moved to follow. Homski rushed forward, blocking Stumpy's way. "No," he said. "Only the holiest of Spragmites are allowed to enter the Temple!"

"He's with me," Karnage said.

Homski jumped as if he'd been shocked. He looked up at Karnage with wide, terrified eyes, then looked to Tristan for guidance.

She nodded sweetly. "Let him pass, Homski."

"Of course, Your Holiness. Of course." He bowed his head and stepped out of the way. The priests looked on in confusion as Karnage and Stumpy followed Tristan into the tent.

CHAPTER FOUR

They walked through a long tapestry-laden hallway and into an antechamber, where a pair of handsome menservants took Tristan's headdress and outer robes, revealing a much more comfortable-looking dress underneath. Tristan smiled at them and waved for Karnage and Stumpy to follow her.

She led them into a massive library: bookshelves stood bolted to tent poles, gently bobbing and swaying on the back of the worm; thin wire mesh held the books in place; a table and chairs slowly rose and fell like boats moored to a dock. Tristan sat at the head of the table, and motioned for Karnage and Stumpy to sit farther down.

Once seated, Tristan dropped her austere look and gave Karnage a bemused smile. "Well, Major, you have surprised me once again. I can't say I expected to find you at all, let alone alive." She turned to Stumpy. "Russell, you are much more resourceful than I would have ever thought. I'm not sure whether to commend you or strangle you."

Stumpy started and blinked. "What?"

"You understand the predicament you have put me in, don't you? With the Major found, my authority has now been undermined. My orders and edicts will be open to questioning. What happened to poor Homski out there is but the tip of the iceberg.

She turned to Karnage. "So, my dear Major, what ever am I to do with you? You were supposed to be the Impossible Dream which my people were free to dream for as long as I wished to rule. Which, for all intents and purposes meant forever. Alas, you have crushed my dreams by bringing theirs to fruition. This really is quite the monkey wrench you have thrown into the works. I commend you for continuing to live up to your moniker."

"I do my best," Karnage said.

"What do you mean what do we do with him?" Stumpy said. "I thought you wanted to find him! I thought . . ."

Karnage put a hand on Stumpy's shoulder. "It's okay, Stumpy. Tristan wants people to think what she wants them to think when she wants them to think it, and then only until she thinks they should be thinking something else. Ain't that right?"

"A rather circuitous way of putting it, but yes." Tristan placed her chin in her palm and squinted at Karnage. "So, Major, how shall we proceed? Shall I have you declared a false messiah, and toss you to the worms?"

Stumpy jumped from his seat. "What? You can't do that!"

Tristan gazed up at Stumpy. "Of course I can, silly. I'm the High Priestess. I can do anything."

"I thought you said Messiah trumps High Priestess every time," Karnage said.

"That was High Prophet. And yes, Messiah trumps High Prophet every time. High Priestess, on the other hand, is another matter entirely. Currently, it would be quite easy for me to have you declared a fake. A demonic forgery sent to confuse and destroy us. The people are already running around scared thanks to all these reports of 'demons' in Dabneyville. A little fear is a good thing, but at the rate they're going, they are going to start turning on each other soon. You wouldn't happen to be able to shed any light on these demon sightings, would you, Major?"

"I would," Karnage said. "And I also might have a solution to your problem that doesn't involve me bein' fed to a bunch of worms."

"Really, Major?" Tristan's eyes sparkled. "Do tell."

CHAPTER FIVE

Karnage explained about the squidbugs and as much of their plans to take over the world as he knew. He included a few juicy tidbits about the human/alien hybrids, but without getting into his encounter with General Mayhem. He never wanted to relate that encounter to anyone if he could help it. Tristan listened intently through it all. Stumpy's eyes nearly fell out of his head five times, each revelation outdoing the last.

"They're gonna terraform the earth, and claim it for themselves," Karnage concluded. "And what with this 'merger' the Dabney Corporation's worked out, they're gonna turn the human race into half-human, half-squidbuggy things . . . humbugs."

Tristan arched an eyebrow. "Humbugs?"

Karnage nodded. "Yeah. Humbugs."

Tristan looked at Stumpy. Stumpy shrugged. "Beats callin' 'em half-human half-squidbuggy things."

"All right. Humbugs, then." Tristan turned back to Karnage. "Well, Major, this is all very interesting and tragic, but I don't see how it affects me and my current predicament."

"If the squidbugs win, then you're not gonna have any people left to lead. Just a bunch of squiggly humbugs, all servin' a different master."

"That would be this 'Queen' you mentioned."

"That it would."

"And what do you propose we do about this, then?"

"I propose we go on a Crusade."

"A Crusade?"

Karnage nodded. "You're wonderin' what your followers are gonna do now that I'm back? Why not have me lead them into a Holy Battle against the ultimate evil. They're already thinkin' the squidbugs are demons. We just gotta play that up."

"Interesting. And where would you send my people on this Crusade?"

"Dabneyville," Karnage said. "I got to get back there before that squidbug mothership leaves. I got to get inside and stop 'em."

"And how do you propose to do that?"

"I've got some ideas," Karnage looked over at Stumpy. "But I'm gonna need your help, Corporal."

Stumpy gave a start. "Me?"

Karnage nodded. "I need your expertise. You done a hell of a job out here figurin' out how to domesticate the worms. I could use some of that know-how to maybe domesticate a few other things."

"And what happens if you're not able to defeat the invasion, Major? What then?"

"You need to look on the bright side, your Holiness," Karnage said. "If I'm dead, then I'm out of your hair, and you'll never see me again. But that won't matter anyway, cuz the squidbugs will come and turn you and all your followers into humbugs worshippin' their queen. But if I win, then you get to hold on to your little kingdom here. And I promise you'll never see me again."

"Really? You can promise me that?"

"I can," Karnage said.

"I hope so, Major," Tristan looked at Karnage through half-lidded eyes. "Otherwise, I will be quite put out."

CHAPTER SIX

Tristan pulled a tourist map of Dabneyville from her shelves. They splayed it out in front of them. Illustrations of Dabby Tabby enjoying the splendours of Dabneyville littered the map.

"We'll break the worms up into battalions." Karnage pointed down at the figure of Dabby Tabby rocketing down the Gail Dabney Expressway. "First worm battalion will charge the main gate. Once they're through, the other battalions will follow fast behind. Overrun the place with a shock attack."

Stumpy looked up at Karnage in surprise. "A banzai attack?"

Karnage nodded. "It's the best we can do. We're dealing with conscripts here. These people ain't soldiers. We can't expect a lot from 'em."

"But it'll be a slaughter," Stumpy said.

Karnage shook his head. "Only if the enemy's got lethal weapons. Dabneycops are all armed with goober and Sudsy."

"And what about the squidbugs?"

"They've got their energy spears, but I think they use the same technology as the beams from the ship. Those don't kill. They just," Karnage waved his fingers in the air, "transport stuff."

Tristan arched an eyebrow and mimicked Karnage's finger waving. "Transport stuff?"

"Anyone who gets tagged by the squidbugs will just end up inside the ship," he said. "They might end up pickled, but they'll be alive. Casualties should be minimal."

"And where will you be through all of this?" Tristan said.

Karnage pointed to a depiction of Dabby Tabby leaning out from the Dabney National Tower. "While you got 'em good and distracted, me and Stumpy will come in from the north. We'll use my flightpack." Karnage turned to Stumpy. "You'll ride piggyback. Be our sharpshooter in case we encounter any trouble in the air. We'll fly up the side of Mount Dabney and make our way into the squidbug mothership."

Tristan tsked. "It's certainly not the most elegant of plans."

"It ain't pretty," Karnage said. "But it should work."

"I hope it does, Major," Tristan said.

"So do I."

"I got a question," Stumpy said. "How you gonna get the Spragmites keen on fightin'? You've always preached to them about love and peace and harmony."

Tristan patted Stumpy's stump. "You just leave that to me."

CHAPTER SEVEN

Karnage and Stumpy stayed sequestered in her private quarters at Tristan's insistence. She payed lip service to the idea of Karnage's personal safety, but they all knew it was about limiting his potential to undermine her authority. They sat in her personal library and watched the D-Pad Homski had provided them.

The screen showcased a stage that had been erected in front of Tristan's worm, framing a large swath of its massive bulk. Richly coloured fabric draped the sides, deep pinks and oranges that complemented the worm's body perfectly. Torches glowed warmly along the base of the stage. The hairs on the worm's flank had been given some kind of glitter treatment, and they shimmered and shone in the flicker of the torchlight.

Tristan strode out onto the stage. The long flowing robes were gone. She wore a sharp black suit, with a three-quarter-length coat. She carried a riding crop under her arm, its handle encrusted with glittering jewels. Her hair was swept up and pulled back into a tightly coiffed bun. The sharp stilettos on her feet stabbed at the stage floor with military precision. There was no fanfare or introduction to announce her arrival. Nothing but the soft crackle of flames, and the clicking of her stiletto heels, amplified and echoing throughout the compound.

The D-Pads shot her from a low angle, giving her a commanding presence. The flickering flames highlighted her sharp features. She stared out with a grim, solemn countenance at the crowd. Karnage saw the telltale white line of the microphone by her temple.

She looked out at her followers, studying them carefully. They hushed into absolute silence. Tristan nodded slightly to herself, then began her speech.

"Last night, I was granted a personal audience with the Lightbringer." She spoke in a deep, even tone. Karnage heard her voice echoing through the walls of the tent. "The Illuminated One has informed me of a dire threat to our people. A threat to the very might of Spragmos himself.

"Doubtless you have all heard the rumours: a plague of demons has erupted from that cesspool of depravity that is called Dabneyville. And I stand here before you today to inform you that these rumours . . . are true. The Lightbringer himself has grappled with these demons! And he has come here, at this time, to lead us in the ultimate battle of Good versus Evil!

"These demons conspire to destroy your Inner Worm. They wish to rip Spragmos from your hearts, and leave you empty—barren— with no Inner Worm to guide you. They will stop at nothing to destroy us. So we must act first, and destroy them! In the name of The Worm!" Tristan thrust her fist into the air. "Ma-ma-oo-pow-pow!"

The crowd answered her cry. "Ma-ma-oo-pow-pow!"

"I know that you have been taught that violence is against the teachings of Spragmos, and some of you have failed to understand the nuance in these teachings." Tristan paused, and looked out at the crowd, as if daring someone to speak. "In times of danger, when the Way of The Worm is under threat, battle is the most glorious endeavour in which a Spragmite may partake. It cleanses the mind, and awakens The Worm within. It is a test of your devotion. I know that you all pride yourselves on being the devoted servants of Spragmos."

Tristan leaned down towards the camera, the torchlight flickering magnificently across her face. "And you ARE devout! You ARE loyal! You are Spragmites: the Beloved Children of Spragmos! Ma-ma-oo-pow-pow!"

"Ma-ma-oo-pow-pow!"

Tristan paced across the stage, her heels rhythmically clacking in time with her words. "All of this talk against violence stems from fear. Now this is normal. This is natural. When you first enter battle, you will feel fear. But a true Spragmite will never let fear overpower their devotion."

She leaned in close, speaking softly. "For fear is the Worm-killer.

Fear is the doubt that sedates the Inner Worm. Confront your fear. Set your Inner Worm upon it, and you will feel it disappear. For in truth, there is no fear. There is only The Worm. And The Worm . . . is The Word! Ma-ma-oo-pow-pow!"

"Ma-ma-oo-pow-pow!"

Tristan continued. "As you head into battle, remember that the enemy, too, will be frightened—more frightened, in fact, than any of you could ever be. For they are not Spragmites! They do not have Spragmos on their side. Their Inner Worms lie in slumber. They have not heard The Word."

"Ma-ma-oo-pow-pow!"

"Ma-ma-oo-pow-pow!"

Tristan beamed out at the crowd. "Oh, I will be proud to lead you into battle. So proud to fight alongside you all. In the name of Spragmos! Ma-ma-oo-pow-pow!"

"Ma-ma-oo-pow-pow!"

Tristan strode purposely off the stage while the crowd cheered. They broke into spontaneous chants of "Ma-ma-oo-pow-pow."

The crowd was still chanting when Tristan appeared through the curtains. She smiled at Karnage. "So? How did I do?"

"You'd have made one hell of a military commander," Karnage said.

"Yes," Tristan said. "Yes, I would. I have done my part, Major. Now it is time for you and Russell to do yours."

Karnage nodded. "We'll move into position. Once we see the first of the worms hit the main gates, we'll head in." He turned to Stumpy. "Let's go, Corporal."

Stumpy saluted. "Yes, sir."

"Good luck, Major," Tristan said. "And please don't take this the wrong way, but I sincerely hope I never see you again."

"The feeling's mutual," Karnage said.

"They're on the move." Stumpy had his eye on the scope of his rifle. He stood up. They were on a ridge overlooking Dabneyville in the distance. Karnage saw the needle-like line of the Dabney National tower against the thick lush green of Mount Dabney. The clouds covering the squidbug mothership were white and fluffy.

"Let's go, Corporal." Karnage climbed into the front of the flightpack. Stumpy strapped himself into his makeshift harness on the back. He was seated higher than Karnage, his feet dangling above the ground. Karnage hit the activators and the flightpack rose into the air.

They flew high above the desert, slowly approaching Mount Dabney. Karnage saw the undulating bodies of the train of worms as they raced down the Gail Dabney Expressway. The train hit the gates, and burst through without even slowing down.

"Good old E-nium!" Stumpy shouted.

The line of worms disappeared behind the city walls. They caught sight of them again when they were closer to the city. The worms were moving slowly now, inching their way through the streets. Some of the Spragmites had dismounted. They were looking around, confused. Karnage could see why. There was no resistance. The streets were empty. There was no one for them to fight. Karnage's heart jumped, and he looked up at the clouds. *If they ain't there . . . what am I gonna do?*

Karnage caught a small dot of movement. A sewer grate popped open, and somebody crawled out.

No, Karnage thought. *Not somebody. Some* thing.

The creature had four arms and tentacles undulating from its back like Karnage's clone.

Karnage pointed it out to Stumpy. "Humbug," he shouted.

It carried something in its hands. Karnage couldn't tell if it was a goober rifle or an energy spear. One of the Spragmites rounded the corner and stopped when he saw the humbug. He turned back to his comrades, then motioned towards the humbug. The humbug levelled its weapon and fired a green energy ball. The Spragmite disappeared. More creatures poured up out of the sewer and charged the Spragmites head on. The humbugs charged through the streets, firing pink and green balls at the Spragmites. They were quickly decimated.

The second wave of worms came barrelling through the wall and ploughed through the humbugs, spilling them in all directions. Spragmites jumped down from the worms and grabbed stray weapons. A Spragmite grabbed an energy spear and accidentally shot himself, disappearing instantly. Another grabbed a goober rifle and fired, winging a humbug in an arm. The Spragmites and humbugs became a quivering, roiling mob of arms and tentacles, accentuated by the occasional green and pink flash.

"Major! Look out!" Stumpy pointed towards the mountain.

Karnage looked and saw a pair of Dabneycops flying towards them in flightpacks. As they approached, Karnage saw they had four arms sticking out from their uniforms, and a mess of mouth tentacles fringed the base of their visors. Their extra arms held goober rifles. They fired at Karnage and Stumpy.

"Squidcops!" Karnage shouted. He dipped down, out of the path of the goober. "Return fire!" he barked.

Stumpy aimed and fired, hitting a squidcop in the leg. It spun out of control and struck its partner. There was an explosion of yellow smoke and the two squidcops plummeted towards the ground.

"Here come some more!"

Another pair were flying up from the town. Karnage increased his altitude, heading for the cloud. *Almost there. Almost there.*

Stumpy strafed the incoming squidcops with goober. One of the squidcops took a blast to the face. The flightpack flipped end over end as the ball of goober expanded over the flightpack's controls. It tumbled back down to the town below. The other squidcop levelled a goober pistol at Karnage and fired. Karnage tried to duck, but it struck the back of his hoverball. He spiralled out of control and the flightpack started spinning towards the mountain. "Stumpy! Solvent!" he yelled.

"On it!" Stumpy pulled out the can of solvent. He reached over the edge of the balls and sprayed down the goober. It pulled off and liquified into a long stream of pink. Karnage restabilized, and just missed hitting the trees. A spray of pine needles stung his legs. Another couple of squidcops joined the first in the chase as Karnage banked up into the cloud.

"Major, look out!"

The mothership instantly appeared through the mist. Karnage pulled back and yanked the emergency brake. A parachute shot out of the back of the flightpack, slowing them down, but not enough. The flightpack clipped the top edge of the ship, and something sheared off. "Rear stabilizer's gone!" Stumpy shouted.

"Abandon balls!" Karnage and Stumpy unstrapped themselves and tumbled down onto the mothership, rolling across its surface. Karnage came to a stop facing up, and saw a pair of squidcops fly by above them in pursuit of their damaged flightpack that cavorted and frolicked until it disappeared into the mist. The squidcops followed, and the buzzing of their flightpacks slowly faded away. He turned and saw Stumpy struggling to his feet nearby.

Karnage looked down. He was standing on the squidbug mothership. Panels flickered with green light. An occasional sliver of white light cut a squiggling path along the surface.

Karnage sniffed the air. It stank of squidbug. He looked at Stumpy. "Looks like we made it, Corporal," Karnage said.

Stumpy looked around with wide, terrified eyes. "How do we get in?"

Karnage spotted a thin streak of white light flickering towards them. He dropped his foot on it as it was about to speed by. The light curled back and started spinning around Karnage's foot. Another sliver of white cut a zig-zag pattern across the surface of the mothership. It headed right for Karnage, and joined the first in orbiting his foot.

More and more lines of white joined the others under Karnage's foot, until it had formed a bright quivering puddle of white. Stumpy watched in awe as the puddle spilled forward, urging them to follow it. The light rippled and ebbed across the rough surface of the ship. It flowed around panels, occasionally darted back to avoid a random burst of green, and finally pooled in a ring around a large hatch. The ring glowed brightly, then winked out. The hatch spiralled open.

Karnage turned to the disbelieving Stumpy and grinned.

"Open sesame," he said.

MK#0: ZERO HOUR!

CHAPTER ONE

Karnage and Stumpy landed in a narrow tunnel. Long squiggly tubes of light ran along the walls, floor, and ceiling. The tubes were layered on top of each other, length-wise along the floor. Pulses of green light flowed through the tunnels at a frenetic pace, pulsing and strobing in a violent electric light show. The occasional line of white randomly twirled and flowed through the tubes, as it moved around and under the green.

Above them, the white ring of light around the hatch pulled away from its opening, and sprayed out, disappearing into the vast tubes of green. The hatch spiralled shut above them.

Stumpy shielded his eyes against the bright flashes of green. "Where are we?"

"I dunno," Karnage said. "This doesn't look like any part of the ship I've seen before."

"I feel like I'm stuck inside a fibre optic cable or something."

"Maybe that's what this is," Karnage surmised. "Like a giant fibre optic cable. Or a steam tunnel—or crawl space o' some kind."

"Seems kinda large to be a steam tunnel," Stumpy said.

"Trust me, this is cramped by squidbug standards." Karnage pointed to the squiggling green lights shooting all around them. "What do you make of all these lights?"

Stumpy studied the tubes as the lights shot through them. "Well, if I were to guess, I'd say it's some kind of communications system. There's something in the way that they pulsate. Like a sort of pattern to 'em, see?"

Karnage shook his head. "I ain't no C&E guy." A thin white streak shot through the green. Karnage pointed to it. "And what about the white lights? What about them?"

Stumpy studied them as they passed through. He shook his

head. "I don't know. I don't think they're the same. They don't fit the pattern."

"Don't fit the pattern how?"

"There's just something about them. The green ones are a lot more focused. Direct. They're going somewhere and they make no bones about it. But the white ones . . ." Stumpy pointed to one that was circling nearby. It shot off, heading back in the direction it had come from. "They're all over the place. Like they're trying to appear random."

"They're *trying* to appear random?"

"Yeah. Yeah, I think they are. Like a pirate broadcast. Like somebody's hackin' the system."

Karnage grew excited. "Can you track where the white ones are comin' from, Corporal? Trace 'em back to their source?"

"I don't know." Stumpy looked at Karnage with a glint in his eye. "But I can sure as hell try."

CHAPTER TWO

Stumpy followed the lights through the tunnel, with Karnage close behind, his goober rifle at the ready, keeping an eye out for squidbugs.

Stumpy traced them through the pipes, sometimes doubling back as they changed direction. At one point, the white lights stopped completely. The pair paused to wait for any further sign of them, slowly growing more anxious by the minute. Just when Karnage thought they would have to double back and try to pick up the trail, a white light shot straight past them, then diverted into a tunnel opening overhead. Stumpy cursed something fierce as they tried to find somewhere they could climb up after it, but the walls of the tunnel were too smooth. Karnage finally resorted to firing goober balls up the wall of the tunnel in order to give them something to hold onto.

As they delved deeper, the green lights grew less frequent while the white became more prevalent, the tint of the tunnels slowly changing to a soft grey. The toxic stink of squidbugs became less intense, the air cooler on Karnage's skin. It wasn't exactly fresh, but it stung his nostrils less.

Eventually, they arrived at a section of tunnel where there was no green light at all: just a single lone pulse of white rhythmically oscillating through the walls like a heartbeat. They traced it until they came to a hatchway where the white light was glowing in the surrounding tubes.

Karnage looked out through the hatchway into a main corridor. A single squiggling pipe ran along the wall and around the massive doors. Nothing glowed or squiggled in the hallway, save for the lone pulse of white coursing its way through the wall. It was deathly quiet.

Karnage looked back at Stumpy. "I'll go first. You see any squidbugs try to ambush me, you—"

Sparks flew around the hatchway as the corridor echoed with loud machine gun fire. Karnage and Stumpy threw themselves against the wall of the tunnel.

The gunfire abated, and Karnage heard the faint sound of spent shells tinkling against the floor. A voice called out to them from the darkness.

"You best come out of there, you fuckknuckling fuckmonkeys, or I will blow your donkeyfucking faces off!"

Karnage grinned so broadly that it hurt. He looked at Stumpy.

"What the hell are you smiling about?" Stumpy said.

"I know that voice." Karnage shouted out through the hatchway: "Captain Daisy Velasquez! You will stand down and cease fire! That is an order! You hear me?"

There was a long pause, and the voice called from the darkness: "Major? Is that you?"

"You're goddamn well right it's me," Karnage barked. "Now stand down and cease fire!"

Karnage heard the gun reload with a loud chunk. "Prove it," she said. "Show yourself, and maybe I'll think about not firing."

"What kind of backwater bohunk do you take me for, Vel? I know you. You'll shoot first and apologize for it later!"

"You stay hidden, I'll shoot you. You come out and I don't think you look like the Major, I'll still shoot you."

"What the hell kinda choice is that?"

"It's the only one you get. You got 'til I count to ten. Better make up your mind quick, cuz I count fast."

Stumpy looked at Karnage. "You trust her?"

"I trust her to shoot anything that moves," Karnage said. "Still, we don't have much choice. How do I look?"

"What do you mean?"

"Do I look like me?"

Stumpy shrugged. "I guess."

Karnage nodded. "Good." He called out to Velasquez. "All right, I'm coming out!"

Karnage stepped through the hatch. He was surprised and

pleased that he wasn't instantly hit with a hot spray of bullets. *She must be mellowing in her old age.*

Velasquez emerged from the darkness, holding a gun larger than she was. The muzzle was pointed directly at Karnage's chest. She slowly lowered it as her jaw dropped.

"Well, suck my dick 'til my hips cave in," she said.

"You don't have a dick, Captain," Karnage smiled.

"Neither do you." Velasquez returned the grin. "But that hasn't slowed you down none."

Karnage closed the gap between them and they shook hands.

"Major," she said.

"Good to see you again, Captain." Karnage turned back to the hatch. "Stumpy!"

Stumpy tentatively stuck his head out.

"Front and centre," Karnage barked.

Stumpy climbed out of the hatch and joined the two of them in the middle of the hallway.

"Captain," Karnage said, "this here is Corporal Stumpton, my latest conscript."

Velasquez shook Stumpy's hand. "Welcome aboard, Corporal."

"Call me Stumpy."

Velasquez nodded, and turned to Karnage. "We're glad you were able to find us, Major."

"Us?" Karnage's eyes lit up. "You mean . . ."

Two more figures emerged from the darkness. Karnage's eyes sparkled.

"Heckler," he said. "Koch."

Koch was leading Heckler from the darkness, an arm propping him up. Heckler's body tensed as he oppressed the occasional snigger.

"Heck," Karnage said. "You're not laughin' no more."

"He even talks some now," Koch replied.

Karnage turned to Heckler. "Is that true?"

Heckler whispered in Koch's ear. "He said he's doing better, but he's not one hundred per cent yet. And he's sorry. For all the laughing. Says he couldn't help it."

"You got nothing to apologize for, Sergeant," Karnage said, "with what you been through. I'm just glad to know you're gettin' better."

"He says you should thank Cookie for that," Koch stated after a moment's whispering. "It's all his doing."

Karnage grew excited. "Cookie? He's here?" He craned his neck, hoping to see the corporal emerge from the dark. "Where is he? Why isn't he here?"

Koch and Vel shared an uncomfortable look.

"It's . . . complicated," Vel said.

"What do you mean it's complicated?"

"He's not the same," Koch replied.

"Not the same how?" Karnage grew alarmed. "What the hell's happened to him?"

Heckler leaned in and whispered in Koch's ear. "He says we should just show him, Vel."

"All right." Velasquez leaned her gun against her shoulder. "Follow me."

CHAPTER THREE

Velasquez led Karnage and the others through the darkened corridor, the occasional white throb of light illuminating their way. The squiggly pipe on the wall grew wider the deeper they travelled down the corridor. Soon, the pulse of white squiggling down the tube was as thick around as a beach ball. They followed the tube into a round chamber where the tube coursed up into the middle of the ceiling and descended straight down, ending in an open sarcophagus held by three gnarled talons pouring up from the floor. Inside the sarcophagus, Karnage saw a familiar face.

"Cookie." Karnage walked up beside the sarcophagus. The tube ran down into Cookie's head, fading from translucence to the opaque flesh colour of Cookie's skin. White light throbbed out of Cookie's head like a heartbeat.

Karnage looked at Cookie in horror. "What the hell did they do to him?"

"They've made him part of the system," Velasquez said. "Like a fucking computer chip. He's supposed to be watching over some kind of subsystem. He told me what it was once. I can't remember what. Probably stuck working the shitters. Poor bastard."

Karnage could see inside Cookie's skull through the tube. His head looked hollow. Karnage turned to Stumpy. "You ever seen anything like this before?"

Stumpy just shook his head, his eyes fixed on Cookie's mangled body.

"They tried to destroy his mind," Velasquez said, "but he's still in there. He's still Cookie. Go on, Major. Talk to him."

Karnage stood over the sarcophagus. "Cookie?"

There was no reaction. Karnage tried again.

"Cookie? Are you awake?"

Cookie half-opened his eyes. His voice was barely a whisper. "Oh. Hey, Major. You made it. I wasn't sure—"

A crackling oscillation of green energy tore down through the pipe, coursing into Cookie's head. He convulsed in pain, his fists clenched.

"What's happening?" Karnage barked. "What's going on?"

Velasquez's eyes were hard and cold—like she'd seen this too many times before. "They keep doing that to him," she said. "That green light is fucking killing him."

The green light dissipated, and Cookie relaxed. He lifted his wrist from his lap and slowly crooked a finger at Karnage. "Sit down next to me, so I don't have to talk so loud."

Karnage knelt beside the sarcophagus. Cookie motioned him closer. Karnage leaned in until his ear was almost pressed to Cookie's lips.

Cookie let out a gentle sigh of relief. "That's better." His voice was nothing but breath. "What's on your mind, Major?"

"I came back to stop the squidbugs," Karnage said.

"That a fact?" Cookie whispered.

Karnage nodded. "It is."

Cookie stayed quiet a long time. He took a deep breath. "Do you know how you're going to do it yet?"

"I've got some ideas," Karnage said, "but I was hoping you could help me work out the kinks."

"Let's hear what you've got."

"I been told the squidbugs are like an insect colony. Or a hive," Karnage said. "That they take their orders from a central queen. And that queen is runnin' everything. How's that sound so far, Cookie?"

"Not bad," Cookie whispered. "Keep going."

Karnage went on. "The way I figure it, the squidbugs are nothin' without this queen. Just a buncha mindless squiggly beasts. We kill the queen, and their command structure goes down. The whole organization descends into chaos.

"The only problem is, I don't know how to do it. Where's the queen? What does she look like? How do I kill her? I'm hopin' you can help me with that."

"I'll try, Major," Cookie said. "I'll try."

He closed his eyes again. Karnage waited patiently, hoping Cookie was just mustering his strength.

"The queen," Cookie said, "isn't a queen. It's . . ."

"What is it, Cookie? What is it?"

"It's nothing."

"Nothing? What do you mean 'nothing'? It's gotta be somethin', Cookie. Everything's somethin'."

"Not this thing. It has . . . no body. No shape . . . no physical form. It's pure intelligence . . . nothin' else. Just a collection of energy . . . holdin' itself together through sheer . . . willpower . . . pure thought . . . pure energy . . .

"It controls everything . . . knows everything." Cookie gave a weak smile. "At least, it thinks it does . . . I been jammin' the signal when I can. It's not easy, but . . . I been tryin' to do my part. Not always well, but . . . I tried. I really tried." Cookie's face fell. "I'm sorry, Major."

"You got nothin' to apologize for, soldier. You done good." Karnage placed a reassuring hand on Cookie's shoulder. "How do I kill this thing, Cookie? Tell me how to destroy it."

"You can't," Cookie said. "You can't destroy . . . energy, but you can disperse it . . . convert it to other forms . . ."

"Disperse it?" Karnage said. "You mean like with an explosion?"

"An explosion might do it," Cookie said. "If it's big enough."

"How big?"

"Spragmos LV75 rocket . . . should do it," Cookie said.

"You wouldn't happen to have one of those lying around, would you?"

Cookie smiled. "Vel?"

Velasquez jerked a thumb to a darkened alcove. "Got everything you'll need over here."

Karnage looked down at Cookie. "You been plannin' this a while, haven't you?"

"I'm tryin', Major . . . tryin' to do everything I can. It's so hard. It's so . . ." Cookie closed his eyes. He opened them again in a few minutes. "You need to go, Major . . . need to hurry. The Intelligence

. . . it's dormant right now . . . lying in hibernation . . . inside the Nucleus . . . until a host can be prepared."

"If it's lyin' dormant, then what's runnin' the invasion?"

"The Intelligence," Cookie said. "It's so smart it can do it in its sleep . . . doesn't take any effort . . . like breathing. When it wakes . . . that's why you have to hurry, Major . . . have to stop it before it finds a host . . ."

"What's the host you keep talkin' about?"

"It takes a new body whenever it arrives at a new world . . . always something local . . . easier to adjust . . . more adapted to our atmosphere . . ."

Another oscillation of green stabbed down into Cookie's head. Cookie's mouth opened in a silent scream. Karnage shouted up at the tube. "Quit fryin' his brain, you squiggly bastards!"

The green dissipated, and Cookie lay silently frowning, his pupils fluttering back and forth beneath his shut eyelids. Finally, his eyes creaked open, and he licked his chapped lips. ". . . it adapts everything . . . takes bits and pieces of it all . . . creates something new . . . something that'll accept both lifeforms . . . a middle ground . . ."

"A merger," Karnage said with a scowl.

Cookie smiled. "Yeah . . . the squidbugs . . . they can't survive outside for long . . . that's why they smoke . . . acts like a filter . . . keeps our clean air out . . . for now . . . until they change . . . until they merge it all . . . until they merge us . . . until they merge themselves . . ."

"Why change themselves? Why not just change us to match them?"

"The Intelligence doesn't care . . . does what it needs to do to keep going . . . to survive . . . the squidbugs . . . everything . . . they all change from world to world . . . Intelligence adjusts their forms . . . to make them ideal . . . incorporates whatever it finds . . . fits it all in . . . like me . . . like you . . . it wanted you, Major, for its host . . . it picked you . . . most suitable . . . right genetics . . . that's why they wanted you for so long . . . why they hunted you . . . they were gonna change you . . . give you to the squidbugs . . . make you suitable for the Intelligence . . . but I stopped 'em, Major . . . I played a little . . . shell game . . . I made 'em think you weren't right . . . weren't suitable . . . I gave 'em someone else. . . ." Cookie's face fell. "I'm sorry, Major . . . I'm so sorry . . . if I had known, I wouldn't have . . . how could I know?"

"What Cookie? What didn't you know?"

"You'd been captured . . . they were going to . . . I had to misdirect them . . . there was no time . . . I made a choice . . . I didn't know who she was, Major . . . if I'd known that you . . . that she . . . I didn't know who she was . . ."

Karnage's heart jumped. "Sydney. It's Sydney, isn't it?"

"I'm so sorry, Major . . . I didn't know. . . ."

"Where is she, Cookie? Where is she?!"

"They're preparing her," Cookie said, "for the Intelligence . . . you have to destroy it, Major . . . before it takes its new host. . . ."

Cookie shut his eyes, wincing as a powerful blast of white shot up from his head and into the pipe. It careened through the walls, and collected around a sealed hatch. The hatch spiralled open, and the light flowed into it. The light flew down the tunnel, illuminating it with a dull grey as it went.

"That will take you to the Intelligence . . . but you have to go, Major . . . you have to go now . . . it knows I'm here. It's trying to . . . stop me. I'll hold it off long as I can . . . no one can go with you, Major . . . not Vel . . . not anyone . . . the Intelligence can jump from host to host . . . that's why you have to kill it now . . . before it wakes . . . it knows you're coming . . . it will try to stop you . . . be prepared, Major . . . it knows everything about you . . . about us . . . it will try to . . . you have to go, Major . . . you have to . . ."

Cookie shut his eyes. He didn't speak again.

CHAPTER FOUR

Karnage stood over Cookie's limp form, hoping for more.

It never came.

Karnage felt Cookie's neck. He still had a heartbeat.

Karnage rounded on Stumpy, pointing at Cookie. "Help him. Figure out what's wrong with him. How to stop him from bein' . . . how to stop that green energy from hurtin' him."

"Me?" Stumpy stared down at Cookie's empty skull. "I'm no medic, Major. I don't know the first thing about this. It's way beyond anything—"

Karnage grabbed Stumpy and shook him. "You have to try, Stumpy. You have to try!"

"Major." Velasquez pushed herself between Karnage and Stumpy, forcing Karnage to let him go. "There's nothing you can do."

Karnage returned Velasquez's gaze. "There has to be something. I came so far, and Cookie was there for me, every step of the way. Without him, we wouldn't be here. Without him, we'd all be— goddammit, Vel, there has to be something we can do!"

"There is," Velasquez said. "You can do what he asked you to do."

"I can't leave him like this," Karnage said. "Not now."

"You have to. Or we're all done for. Including Sydney."

Karnage looked down at Cookie. His fingers tightened into balled fists. He felt like he was being torn apart. "He stuck by me. Trusted me to help him. It's my fault. My fault he's here. If I hadn't opened my goddamn mouth. If I hadn't lost my head. . . ."

"You're doing like you always do, Major—the best you can. Just like Cookie. He knew that. He gave me something to give to you, just in case. Said I'd knew the time would be right, and I think that time is now." Velasquez put something cold and metallic in Karnage's hand.

It was a dog tag. Karnage read the inscription.

Cpl. Charles "Cookie" Blunderbuss
C&E – CPN FORCES

Karnage clenched his fist tight. He could feel the metal digging into his hands. "He may have given up on himself, but I ain't givin' up on him. Not yet." He handed the tag back to Velasquez. "Here. He'll be needin' that." He turned to Stumpy. "You do what you can. You're not a miracle worker, but you're pretty damn close, Corporal. Try and figure how this contraption works. Just do your best. That's all I ask."

Stumpy saluted. "I'll give it my all, sir."

Velasquez shook her head. "You never give up."

"Not on my troops," Karnage said. "Not ever. Show me this gear you got for me, Captain."

Velasquez led Karnage over to the alcove. She handed him a rocket launcher. "Spragmos Industries RPG-OX9."

Karnage looked it over. "This is space combat gear."

"You'll be going into the centre of the ship," Velasquez said. "The atmosphere's completely toxic there. No real oxygen to speak of. Only way to get rocket fuel to burn is if it comes with its own oxy. You've only got two rounds, so make 'em count." Velasquez handed him a pile of folded clothes and a helmet. "There's a suit to go with it. Rumour has it you're human and need to breathe just like the rest of us."

Karnage took the suit. "How much oxy I got in this?"

"Not a lot," Velasquez said. "Couple hours. Maybe more, if you only breathe through your nostrils. So try to stay good and pissed off."

"You know, I finally get that joke now, Captain."

"Good for you, Major. You're cleverer than I thought. That only took you, what, twenty years?"

"Twenty five," Karnage said. "But who's counting?"

Velasquez helped Karnage into his space suit. She attached the helmet to the metal neck ring with a loud *hiss-chunk*.

"Follow the white lights," Velasquez said. "They'll take you to the centre of the ship. Find the Nucleus, and destroy it."

"What's it look like?" Karnage slung the rocket launcher over his shoulder.

"Like a damn bowling ball," Velasquez said. "Small grey sphere, glowing green and sending out pulses. You'll know it when you see it."

Karnage nodded. He slung his goober rifle over his other shoulder.

Velasquez pointed to it. "If you think you need more firepower, I got stronger stuff than that. Stuff that actually fires bullets."

Karnage shook his head. "No point. Killin' stuff just pisses off ol' Mabel here." He tapped the Sanity Patch through his suit.

Velasquez nodded. "Good luck in there, Major."

"Do me a favour, Vel."

"Sir?"

Karnage pointed to the hatch. "You see anything come outta there that don't look like me, you shoot it. Twice."

"Only twice?" Velasquez looked disappointed.

CHAPTER FIVE

Karnage stepped through the hatch, and found himself in another fibre optic tunnel. Tiny spirals of white light spun along the walls, and he began to follow them as they shot forward a few feet, spun in place, then danced back before repeating the pattern again. It was hard to keep them in sight. He had to twist his entire torso in order to turn his head, otherwise he found himself staring at the inside of his helmet.

Karnage found the suit disconcerting, like he was walking through the world in a dream; his only real companion was his own steady breathing.

He repeated his mantra in his head, reciting a name for each step forward he took: *Cookie, Velasquez, Heckler, Stumpy, Koch, Sydney. Cookie, Velasquez, Heckler, Stumpy, Koch, Sydney. Cookie, Velasquez, Heckler, Stumpy, Koch, Sydney.*

The tunnel flashed as the occasional burst of green shot through the pipes. Curls of yellow mist hung in the air above him.

He came around a curve in the tunnel, and saw a figure draped in shadow sitting on the floor, a gnarled energy spear resting on its shoulder. Its torso was curled forward, head bent down. It cocked an ear towards Karnage and nodded approvingly to itself. "Oh! Hello, John."

Karnage froze in his tracks. He recognized that voice.

"Flaherty."

The doctor looked up. A burst of green highlighted his face, giving Karnage a quick glimpse of squiggly pupils. "It's good to see you again."

Karnage pulled his goober rifle off his shoulder as Flaherty shakily rose to his feet, leaning heavily against his spear with one hand. His other arm ended in a stump. An extra set of arms emerged from Flaherty's armpits, and they gestured towards Karnage. "I must apologize for not believing you. 'Unidentified Flying Objects of

Death.'" Flaherty chuckled. "Who would have thought it was true?"

Karnage held the goober rifle in front of him. "I did," he said.

Flaherty nodded, staring at the floor. "You did, John. You did. And you were right, weren't you? You were right about so many things." He looked up at Karnage with his squiggly eyes. "And yet, you were wrong. As you can see, there's been no death. I'm still here. They haven't killed me. In fact, they've rewarded me."

A pair of tentacles unfurled from Flaherty's back. "They've made me so much better than before. It's a reward, you see. For all of my hard work.

"You know, John, on some level, you were right about me. I didn't know about the invasion. But they were talking to me. In their own way. Much as they were talking to Charles, but differently. They . . . encouraged me. Helped me with my work. Provided me with insights. But I'm afraid I didn't get it all right. Not all of it. Not you.

"I'm afraid I must apologize, John. For the Patch. It's not what they intended. I was misinterpreting." Flaherty's skin filled with colour, changing from white to yellow to orange to red and back again. "I didn't quite get it right, you see. It was . . . an error in judgement on my part. A misunderstanding. There was so much I did right. But you . . . you I have done wrong.

"Please understand. I'm not a violent man." Flaherty pointed the spear at Karnage. Green energy crackled from the end. "I must rectify that mistake, you see. Undo what has been done. This is absolutely not personal. I hold you no ill will at all. It's just that I mustn't let this mar my perfect record. The mistake must be removed, John. Do you see? Do you understand? The mistake must be removed."

Karnage threw himself against the wall of the tunnel as the crackling energy ball shot past him. Karnage aimed his goober rifle at Flaherty and fired. The pink globule took Flaherty full in the face. It knocked him back against the tunnel wall, covering his upper body. The tips of his tentacles quivered violently at the top of the expanding ball. His energy spear clattered lifelessly to the ground.

Karnage picked up the spear and squeezed past the mound of quivering goober.

GORD ZAJAC

"See you around, Doc."

CHAPTER SIX

The air grew heavy with yellow mist as the tunnel opened up into a large chamber thick with squiggling tubes. A number of branching tunnels ran off on all sides, each spilling their mass of tangled pipes into the chamber. The pipes hung down from the tunnels above like twisting jungle vines. Karnage felt like he was walking through a giant junction box.

Green light flowed and coursed through the pipes in all directions. The white lights danced into the chamber, and dipped and dove into the maze of pipes. Karnage picked his way through, trying to keep pace. The flickering white lights flitted like fairies through an otherworldly forest burning bright with angry green flame.

Karnage felt the floor beneath his feet rumble. He twisted his body around, and barely caught sight of something large and black barrelling towards him through the edge of his helmet visor. Karnage jumped out of the way as the mass hurtled past, smashing through tangles of pipes before colliding with the wall. There was a sickening crunch followed by a far too human scream.

The mass rolled over. It looked like a giant maggot with human limbs sticking out from its body. The remains of a face were just visible on its snout. Karnage recognized the features.

"Riggs?"

The maggoty creature struggled up, turning to face Karnage. "I'm surprised you still recognize me, Major. There's not a lot of me left to remember." It's face scrunched up into a grimace as it let out a series of rhythmic noises that Karnage thought might be an attempt at laughter.

"How do you like it?" Riggs rasped. "My big promotion. They told me I was moving up in the organization. That they wanted my brain. And they got it. Oh god help me, they got it. My great reward for all my loyal years of service."

Riggs's face contorted. His nose flattened out, pushing his eye sockets out to either side of his head. He let out a strangled scream as his lips split. Jagged teeth poked through the gaps.

"You were right, Major," Riggs wheezed. "I should have died that day in Kandahar. Should have gone down giving my life for my buddies."

"Yeah," Karnage said. "You should have."

"It would have been better than this. This isn't living. This is hell!" Riggs rolled towards Karnage, gasping. "Please, Major. Put an end to this. Finish the job I didn't have the guts to do back in Kandahar. Please. I can't live like this anymore. I just can't."

Karnage pulled his rocket launcher off his shoulder. He looked down at the rocket glimmering in its tube, the spare one tucked against its side. Riggs moaned in agony, rocking back and forth against the wall.

Karnage shook his head. "Sorry, Riggs. You're not worth it."

Riggs started. "What?"

"I can't afford it. I've only got so many Sanity Levels. I'm gonna need 'em all for the battle to come." Karnage's eye caught a streak of white light dancing near the corner of his helmet. It darted down a mist-shrouded tunnel. He moved to follow it.

Riggs twisted his body, screaming. "You can't leave me here like this!"

"I have to."

"How can you do this to me?!"

"I didn't do anything to you, Roach," Karnage said. "You did it all to yourself."

Riggs snarled. "You're enjoying this, aren't you? Watching me suffer? Enjoying my pain?!"

Karnage turned back to Riggs. His face was fixed into a snarl. His body rippled and undulated like an angry worm. Karnage slowly shook his head. "You know, Roach, there was a time that I wouldn't have hesitated to pull that trigger. I'd have told myself I was doin' the right thing—that I was takin' the high road. Bein' the hero. But that would be bullshit. The truth is I want nothing more than to spray your guts all across the goddamn universe." Karnage tapped the side of his helmet. "But that'd be givin' in to the lizard brain. Lettin' my primal urges run the show. I'm thinkin' big picture now. Got to put that primal shit aside and get that lizard brain to take a powder. Got to remember my long-term goals. My reasons for bein' here. And they sure as hell don't involve you."

Karnage turned and walked down the tunnel. He heard Roach raging behind him, his voice becoming more and more squiggly by the second. "I'll get you for this, Major. You hear me?! *I'll get you for this!*"

The tunnel became brighter as more green energy flowed through the pipes. The white wisps grew timid, darting furtively away from the massive torrents of green. The slower pace suited Karnage just fine. The pipes had thickened and twisted, becoming so gnarled and ungainly that he had to crawl over them.

At last, the tunnel ended in a giant door. White threads of light slowly spun themselves into the outer rim, and the door spiralled open.

Karnage stepped through and found himself in an oval chamber. The pipes formed a thick strand that tapered into a single tendril in the centre of the room. The tendril coiled up and wrapped itself around a dull grey sphere the size of a bowling ball.

That must be it, Karnage thought. *The Nucleus.*

He lined the sphere up in the sights of the rocket launcher. The auto-targeting grid locked onto it with a flashing red cross-hair.

He heard a familiar voice behind him.

"Can I help you with something?"

Karnage turned around. Sydney stood behind him. Her pupils were pulled out into long squiggly Ws. She grinned. "Oh, I'm sorry. Were you looking for me?"

Karnage stared at Sydney, his mind a mix of emotions. The Intelligence stared back at Karnage through Sydney's squiggly eyes. He could feel its cold, piercing gaze. *I'm sorry, Cookie,* he thought. *I didn't make it in time.*

Karnage stared hard into Sydney's eyes, trying to look past the squiggles, hoping to catch a glimpse of her still inside. "Captain?" he said. "Can you hear me?"

The Intelligence made Sydney laugh. "Of course she can hear you. She is me. And I am her. We are the same." The Intelligence forced Sydney to look at the rocket launcher. "What's that?"

Sydney launched into a cartwheel, and flew past Karnage. A set of toes flew out and viciously jammed into his wrists. His hands went numb, and the rocket launcher fell from his grasp. Deft fingers whipped it up, and Sydney tumbled back in front of Karnage. She held the rocket launcher in her hands. "Oh, I know what this is. It's an RPG-OX9, isn't it?" The Intelligence slung the launcher over Sydney's shoulder. "Space combat gear, right? Like the suit. Great for zero oxygen environments. Too bad you don't need it in here. The air's quite breathable. At least for now. Please, Major. Take your helmet off. Stay awhile."

Sydney flipped up and over Karnage. Karnage heard a loud click-hiss, and his helmet twisted off. It flew across the floor, and rolled to a stop beneath the Nucleus. The toxic smell of the alien infestation assaulted his nostrils.

"There, that's better." The Intelligence made Sydney pace around Karnage, casually rotating the rocket launcher in her hands. "So what were you planning to do with this, hmm? Set off some fireworks? Get in some target practice? Oh wait, I know." The Intelligence had Sydney pull the rocket out of the launch tube and toss the tube aside. "You were going to destroy me with this, weren't you?" The Intelligence tapped the tip of the warhead with Sydney's fingers. "You thought you were going to just waltz in here, and blow me to smithereens." It casually dropped the rocket from Sydney's fingers where it clattered to the floor. Sydney's eyes swivelled up to Karnage, staring at him mockingly. "Did you really think it would be that easy? That I wouldn't know of your presence the moment you entered those hatchways?"

Karnage shrugged. "It was worth a shot."

The Intelligence forced Sydney's face into a derisive scorn. "Do you know how many explosions I've had to endure over the years? Too many to count. And many far more powerful than this. Frankly, I'm a little insulted. I thought the great Major Karnage would be able to hatch a far more clever plan than this."

"Sorry to disappoint. I'll try to do better next time."

The Intelligence cocked Sydney's head, staring at him like a cat looking down at a cornered mouse. "Do you know what I am, Major?"

"You're the Intelligence," Karnage said, "behind the invasion."

The Intelligence shook Sydney's head. "Is that what you think I am? Really? The Intelligence behind the invasion? You know so little, Major. Even less than I had imagined. Take a close look at me, Major. What do you see?"

"Something short, blonde, and squiggly."

"Take a closer look, Major." The Intelligence stepped forward, the light around it twitched with excitement. "I am energy. I am infinite. I am God."

"Which god?"

"All of them! Take your pick. Search through their teachings, and you'll find me at the core of it all. Your feeble little minds have been picking up on my ultra-violent transmissions for a long time now. Oh, you've tried to make sense of them, but you've failed. You've all failed so miserably! It's embarrassing! How can you live with yourselves? You've all been subconsciously anticipating my arrival for so long, and yet none of you—not one—was able to even remotely understand what was going to happen. I've never seen such levels of ignorance in any species anywhere in the universe!

"It's sad, Major. Truly sad. If you'd only known what gifts I would bring. The knowledge that I would share."

"Maybe you should have asked first," Karnage said. "See if we even wanted any of it."

The Intelligence forced Sydney's features into a scowl. "Excuse me? I never ask for anything. I see what I want, and I take it."

"Why do you want our world? What's so special about it?"

The Intelligence made Sydney shrug. "Nothing. My world was dying, and I needed a new one. So I came here. That's all."

"But why here? Why not somewhere else?"

"Why not here? It was available, so I took it."

"But it wasn't available! We were already here! This is our world!"

The Intelligence drew Sydney's lips up in a smirk. "Your world? Really? You think just because you happened to be here when I arrived that it somehow makes you the legitimate owners? I chose this world long before your kind could even think of rising up out of the primordial ooze. Just because it took a few million years to get to this planet, that doesn't grant you the right to claim it in the meantime. The fact you were stupid enough to evolve here isn't my problem. You're like a bunch of fleas jumping up and down on a dog's back, proclaiming, 'Hey, this dog is ours! We were here first! No one can take it from us!' And while you're all jumping up and down and talking about what great owners you are and what a great dog this is, the real owner is just above you, getting ready to slap on a new flea collar. This planet isn't 'yours.' Jump up and down all you like. You've no rightful claim. You're squatters. Nothing more. And I will dispose of you as I wish."

"If you think so little of us, then why are you savin' everything? Preserving it in all the spheres?"

The Intelligence shrugged. "It's my hobby. Some collect insects. Others collect butterflies. I collect biospheres."

"Why?"

"Why not? I enjoy seeing how the universe works. How each species has learned to adapt and survive. It also helps me to understand how best to adapt a planet to suit my needs.

"This world wasn't perfectly suited to my needs in the beginning. No planet ever is, so don't bother to start whining to me about finding another planet that's a better fit. I've heard it all before and I'm sick of answering that question. This planet had to be carefully transformed. Its atmosphere altered. Global temperatures raised. Thankfully, your beloved Dabney Corporation was very eager to help me in my efforts."

"They're no friend of mine," Karnage spat.

"So I've heard. You've been quite a thorn in their side. Practically the bane of their existence. Do you know how stupid you've been, Major? I'm not talking slightly stupid here. I mean bone-headed, drool-running-down-the-chin level of stupid. Nobody was ever out to hurt you, you know. They were never trying to harm you. They were acting as my agents. You were to be the vessel from which I would rule. My intellect would have been yours, as yours would have been mine. Our minds would have become one. It is the ultimate gift the universe can bestow upon anyone, and you threw it away. 'Thanks but no thanks, fellas. I'd rather just run around yelling at things while I pretend that I'm saving the world.' It has been embarrassing to watch, Major. Beyond embarrassing. To think, I was supposed to be bonded to you. I get nauseated at the very thought.

"Fortunately, I was able to find something a little more to my liking. Do you like it?" The Intelligence forced Sydney to arch her back and place an arm suggestively on her hip. "It's a bit of a tighter fit than I would have liked, but I'm sure it will stretch a bit with wear. Like an old shoe."

Karnage lunged forward, his teeth bared. "Leave her the fuck alone, you squidbug freak!"

"Ah yes. Squidbug. What a completely inappropriate name for my followers. Still, it does do a good job of degrading them, doesn't it? 'They're not intelligent creatures. They're nothing like us. They're *squidbugs*.' It always helps to dehumanize your enemy, doesn't it?

"Tell me, Major, how will it make you feel once I 'dehumanize' the entire human race? What then? Will you attack them as quickly as you've attacked my people? Would you gleefully destroy your own kind in some ill-conceived desire for racial purity? There's a part of me that's curious to know the answer. And it's that part that has brought you here."

The Intelligence forced Sydney to step back and spread her arms wide. "Here you are: faced with your own kind. One who holds a certain amount of affection for you. But she's no longer your kind anymore. She's a squidbug now. One of us. The Enemy. She may not look much like it now, but give me some more time. I'll make her beautiful. Like Flaherty. Or maybe more like Captain Riggs. Oh, I love that look in your eye. You really want to do something about it, don't you? Tell me, Major: do you have it in you? Would you kill her? I'm thinking no. You couldn't bring yourself to kill Flaherty or Riggs. And if ever there were two men on this planet who you would want dead, it would be those two. So what about Sydney, Major? What about someone you truly care about? Will you have an easier time killing her? Let's find out, shall we?"

The Intelligence stuck out Sydney's pinky fingers and raised her up on her toes. "I've been dying to put her martial arts skills to the test. Her knowledge of human anatomy is surprisingly extensive. I look forward to absorbing this 'Uncle' character. He should prove to be an interesting conquest. But first . . ."

Green energy shot from the tips of Sydney's hair. It ran up the walls and around the myriad hatchways lining the walls. The hatches sealed over with a translucent grey film. The floor shuddered, and the tunnels beyond the hatches whisked away in a blur of motion, replaced with misty grey, then brilliant blue sky.

Karnage felt himself thrown to the ground by powerful G-forces. Sydney stood above him, completely unaffected. The sky outside quickly faded from blue to dark purple, then finally worked into a rich, deep black. Tiny points of white dotted the sky. A curve of blue earth emerged through the hatchways, rapidly shrinking until it was just another tiny dot of light in a sea of sparkling black.

The Intelligence looked out the window approvingly. "There you are, Major. We are finally alone. No one around for millions of kilometres. It's just the two of us now. *Mano a mano,* as they say." The Intelligence raised Sydney up onto her tiptoes. "I look forward to thrusting you harshly into that good night."

At the Intelligence's insistence, Sydney leaped forward.

Karnage recognized the familiar attack pattern of fingers and toes flying at him from all directions. He tried to dodge, tried to defend himself, but the spacesuit slowed him down.

He felt a touch to the small of his back, and his legs buckled. A second touch to his shoulder shot pain up and down his spine, temporarily paralyzing him as he fell hard to the ground. He quickly rolled onto his back, his entire body screaming in agony. The Intelligence as Sydney sprang up onto his body, and perched on her pinky toes on his chest. Karnage could barely gasp and wheeze as she stood over him, her squiggly eyes glinting.

"Well, that wasn't exactly fair, now was it, Major? Those touches should have killed you. And yet, you live. Your spacesuit turned out to be of use to you after all. Oh well. Live and learn. I'll be sure to apply a bit firmer pressure this time. Say goodbye, Major."

Karnage looked up into those squiggly eyes. He was overwhelmed by their malevolence, their sheer self-assured arrogance.

"You've got to use your head, Major."

Karnage took in what breath he could, and he laughed. It was barely a wheezy chuckle, but he laughed. The Intelligence cocked Sydney's head to one side. "You find this all funny, do you? I'll be interested to see how much you laugh with my next blow. It should be quite excruciating. A real scream."

Karnage shook his head. "Go ahead. Do your worst, cuz the joke's gonna be on you. You're so cocksure. So goddamn full of yourself. So sure of your own infallibility. Oh, go ahead and kill me and make sure I'm in agony. Make it last a long, long time. Cuz I want to savour this moment, you little fuckmonkey.

"You never found a better choice than me. You were duped. Bamboozled. Cookie figured out a way to use your own damn arrogance against you. I get it now. Oh, I get how he did it. And it's a thing o' beauty. The kind of thing only somebody like Cookie would see.

"You think you're better than me. Thought you could do better than some crazy old man locked up in an insane asylum. I think I damn well offended your sensibilities. Hell, you probably hung your head in shame when you saw I was the best the Earth had to offer. You couldn't stand it, could you? And old Cookie, all he had to do was whisper that sweet poison in your ear: 'Here's someone better. Here's someone a little more to your likin'.' And you fell for it. Hook, line, and sinker. What a dupe. Oh, what a dupe.

"So go ahead. Kill me. Destroy your perfect host. Considerin' all the time and effort you put into finding little old insignificant me, I'm thinkin' you need the host to be perfect. Otherwise, why go with me? Why not a Dabney? I bet they were linin' up to volunteer. No. You need me for some reason. I don't get what, but you do. But it don't matter, does it? Cuz you're gonna kill me anyway."

"You lie," the Intelligence said. "You're trying to save your life."

Karnage shook his head. "Nope. Wrong again. It ain't me I'm

tryin' to save. It's Sydney. Let her go. She ain't a good match. She's a tight fit, remember? You're not gonna wear her in. You're just gonna wear her out. And what happens then? Shit, I'd love to see that. Love to see you with egg on your face. You'll probably spew some bullshit to cover your ass, but that won't matter. Cuz I know—I know right now. So you torture me all you like, cuz I'm gonna laugh my ass off the whole time. I'm gonna laugh my way right to hell."

The Intelligence looked suspiciously at Karnage from behind Sydney's eyes. Karnage went on: "You got ways of checkin' this, don't you? I'm sure someone as high and mighty as you must have some way of sniffin' out a primitive old mind like Cookie's. Go on. Give it a shot. See for yourself if I'm wrong."

The Intelligence made Sydney scowl. Green energy blasts shot out of her hair and up through the pipes. The pipes all glowed, flowing back and forth, coursing with activity, becoming more and more frenetic until a single little line of white streaked up out of the green. It shot through the green and back into Sydney's hair. The Intelligence made Sydney scream in fury.

"See? You're not so shit hot after all, are you? Just another blowhard, tryin' to act like you're all god this and infinite that. But you're nothin'. Cuz I'm right here, and you ain't inside of me.

"So come on, buddy. Let's go. You and me: brain to brain. *Cerebro a cerebro*. Quit hidin' inside her, and let me see what you're really made of."

The Intelligence filled Sydney's face with hate, and then her eyes rolled into the back of her head before she dropped to the ground.

A railroad spike slammed into Karnage's brain, splitting it in half. His vision clouded over as a strange voice inside his head reverberated strongly in his ears.

Ah, you were so right, Major. This is much more comfortable.

A jagged streak of squiggles tore across Karnage's eyes. His head throbbed. He felt the Intelligence stab needles through his brain, pulling apart his mind from the inside. The walls of his consciousness were caving in. His vision was a jumble of vibrating squiggles. Only a tiny corner of his eyes were his own. He struggled up on all fours. His body refused to work properly as it tried to process orders from two separate consciousnesses. He tried to crawl around the room, barely aware of what his own body was actually doing. Pain coursed through his head, ricocheting from one lobe to the other.

The squiggles populated and multiplied, filling every corner of his mind. He recognized each for what it was: a million and one communications to every part of the ship—to every part of the invasion. Even from this far out in space, the Intelligence continued to calmly give out its orders. He caught glimpses of Velasquez and Koch firing round after round into an oncoming horde of squidbugs that poured out of the hatchways. He saw the floating bodies of Darla and Upchuck in their spheres as the alien DNA slowly went to work beneath their skin, experimenting with new shapes and forms. Faint strands of white were also visible through the morass of squiggles. He reached out to them, and they gave him strength. Karnage wasn't sure if it was Cookie, or just his own mind trying to remind him of what he had to do.

Karnage was drowning in the Intelligence's thoughts. He felt like he was swimming in the ocean in the middle of a hurricane, trying to navigate a never-ending barrage of roiling tidal waves. Karnage twisted his head, trying to see what he could of the oval chamber— the cerebral cortex of the invasion. He knew how all of the pieces worked. How the Nucleus provided more than just a safe haven from attack, but was also a gateway to other dimensions. Other realities. It was an anomaly unto itself, created long before the Intelligence first gained awareness as it had slipped from its own dimension into this one.

And then there were the memories of all the times before, on other worlds, where again and again beings of impossible varieties had tried to stop the Intelligence and its invasion. It had been dispersed by thousands of explosions over the years. Some with the power of a hydrogen bomb. Some with the power of a hand grenade. But the result was always the same: it coalesced, willed itself back into shape, and resumed its attack. Sometimes it took years to pull itself back together. Sometimes millenia. But it always came back. And it always won.

But there was something else that was clear as well: it always hurt. It hurt like hell to be dissipated by an explosion. And it would do anything to avoid that pain. It had bluffed Karnage, banking on his affection for Sydney not to fire that rocket. And it had worked.

But it couldn't hide behind that bluster now. Karnage knew everything it knew. But if he didn't figure out something fast, soon he wouldn't know anything else. He was losing his mind to the Intelligence. He could feel his memories slipping away. He tried to hold on to what Cookie had told him:

"You just gotta use your head."

But Karnage was losing his head. He was losing it fast. His mind was being sucked into the Intelligence, becoming an indistinguishable collection of squiggly synapses within its vast consciousness. He thought of what Sydney's Uncle had told him:

"I have learned to work within my limitations. You should learn to do the same."

But he was becoming more limited by the second as the squiggles ripped layer after layer of his psyche away.

Karnage did what he could to hold on. Pulled together the bits of himself that he could. The white strands pushed through the squiggles and fed into his mind, reciting his mantra to him: *Cookie Velasquez Heckler Koch Stumpy Sydney.* He joined its chorus, repeating it more forcefully than ever: *Cookie Velasquez Heckler Koch Stumpy Sydney. Cookie Velasquez Heckler Koch Stumpy Sydney.*

The Intelligence laughed at his feeble efforts, and rubbed out each name as the squiggles flayed them from his mind and incorporated them into the Intelligence's psyche.

Cookie Velasquez Heckler Koch Sydney

Cookie Velasquez Heckler Sydney

Cookie Velasquez Sydney

Cookie Sydney

Sydney

Sydney

Sydney

He didn't know why, but his mind wouldn't give her up. Perhaps it was because she was still there where he could see her. Perhaps it was something else. Perhaps it was those persistent white strands. The squiggles poured in closer, and some of the white strands disappeared. But the few that remained kept pumping thoughts into him. They repeated her name louder and louder in his head: *Sydney Sydney Sydney!*

Karnage caught the tip of the energy spear in his vision. And suddenly he knew everything about it. He knew how it worked. It wasn't a weapon at all. It was a teleportation device. Any target shot with it would be taken to central processing on the main ship where it would be analyzed, filed, sorted, and then put into storage before being pulled out whenever the Intelligence saw fit to do so. Karnage grabbed hold of the spear and flicked it on—it was so easy to do now. How was it that he had never figured it out before? He aimed a crackling ball of energy at Sydney and fired. She disappeared, leaving a smoking crater behind. Karnage knew she would be safe in central processing. At least for a while. Until the Intelligence was done with him. Until he could figure out what to do. Until he could figure out if he could do anything.

The white strands pumped more thoughts into his emptying mind: *Good work, old man. We're not beat yet. Remember what Cookie told you. It's already in you. You just have to—*

Karnage felt his vocal cords vibrate with laughter. The Intelligence forced him to speak words. "My, my, Major. You are surprisingly resilient. I haven't had this much trouble absorbing a mind in quite a while. But I grow tired of this game and, really, there are just so many more interesting things for me to be doing, so . . ."

Karnage's vision clouded over completely, his world filling with frenetic squiggles. The last of his consciousness was being stripped away; only a single strand of white remained. It grew taut as the squiggles moved in, trying to rip apart his last connection. But it held fast, vibrating like a plucked guitar string. It pumped as many thoughts into his mind as it could.

. . . come on old man don't let that monkeyfucker win don't make all our sacrifices useless remember how we took out General Mayhem it's your only chance now old man remember what Cookie said remember what Uncle said come on old man come on . . .

The strand snapped, curling up into the core of Karnage's psyche, hiding within the last chunk of himself that still remained. A tiny vault, firmly held shut, stuck away in the darkest corner of his mind. The remains of the strand leaked out, but without the glue that held them together, they cluttered together into a collage of random thoughts with little meaning.

. . . I have learned to work within my limitations you just gotta use your head you should learn to do the same I have learned to work within my limitations you just gotta use your head you should learn to do the same . . .

The squiggles found the vault—little more than a safe deposit box—and Karnage felt fingers pulling at its seams, trying to force it to give up its secrets. It leaked the rest of the strand fragments, like radiation from a leaky nuclear reactor.

. . . I have learned to work within my limitations you just gotta use your head you should learn to do the same I have learned to work within my limitations you just gotta use your head you should learn to do the same . . .

The squiggles tore deeper and harder at the safe deposit box, slipping into the cracks, trying to pull it open. It leaked wisps of feelings and emotions, so powerful and terrifying that Karnage could almost remember them. But it wasn't him that was remembering: it was his lizard brain. The primal beast inside that lay dormant, that only emerged when it could break free. There was something that would let it go, but Karnage couldn't remember what it was. He tried to concentrate on the words leaking from the box, tried to decipher their meaning:

. . . I have learned to work within my limitations you just gotta use your head you should learn to do the same you just gotta use your head . . .

And then it hit him.

. . . you just gotta use your head . . .

Karnage stopped fighting. The squiggles tore apart the last of his mental blocks, ripping open the black box, releasing the lizard brain, and revealing Karnage's locked away memories of . . .

THE WAR!

Bullets and brains and smoke and death poured out into the squiggles, overwhelming them. The squiggles pushed back, twitching in fury, trying to sift through the chaos, put it all back in the box, but they were thrown into disarray again and again, as the vestiges of Karnage's lizard brain overwhelmed them with its primal rage—and with them, the Intelligence.

What's going on? It cried. *What's happening?*

You're supposed to be smart, Karnage thought. *You figure it out.*

Somewhere through the noise, Karnage could feel his Sanity Levels rocketing upwards, faster than they had ever gone before, each level upgrade truncating the next. He could feel the Intelligence's panic—its dread as the levels rose higher and higher.

You know what happens when I hit Tricycle Red, Karnage thought.

It won't affect me! The Intelligence screeched. *You'll just kill yourself! I'll still live! I'll still live!*

Sure you will, Karnage thought. *But it will hurt like hell, won't it?*

It doesn't matter! It cried. *I will return! I always return! Your death will be meaningless.*

Yeah, but I'll give you one hell of a bloody nose in the process, won't I?

You won't do it to yourself! You can't! The Intelligence started to panic. *You won't let yourself die like this! You're a fighter! A warrior! It's not your way. YOU CAN'T!*

Karnage heard his Sanity Patch hit Strawberry Shortcake. He grabbed control of his face and forced his mouth into a manic grin.

MAJOR KARNAGE

"Wanna bet, monkeyfucker?"

NO!

Karnage's head burst, and everything went black.

Karnage's vision cleared, and he found himself kneeling on the floor, panting for breath. The squiggles had disappeared. The presence in his head was gone.

He looked over at the Nucleus resting on its lone tendril. It throbbed with green energy. The Intelligence had returned to it. But something was wrong. He could hear it screaming in his head. *"THE WARRR! THE WARRR!"*

Karnage winced, ready for his lizard brain to launch into fury.

But it didn't.

He could still remember The War, but the rage he had long associated with those memories was gone. It was as if it had been ripped from his brain when the Intelligence had pulled out of his mind.

"THE WARRR! THE WARRR!"

Karnage could still remember being the Intelligence. He knew that his lizard brain wouldn't preoccupy the Intelligence for long. It would be like a cold, or a chill. Eventually the squiggles would figure out how to route around the damage, and the Intelligence would return stronger than before.

He had to act fast.

Karnage tugged the glowing Nucleus from its holder, the Intelligence still screaming in his head.

"THE WARRR! THE WARRR!"

He grabbed the discarded rocket. He picked up his goober gun and aimed it at the floor. He fired.

"THE WARRR! THE WARRR!"

He dipped the tip of the rocket into the expanding ball of goober and pulled out a gooey glob. He slapped the Nucleus into the goober before it solidified.

"THE WARRR! THE WARRR!"

With a final crackle, the goober hardened, gluing the Nucleus to the tip of the rocket. Karnage reloaded the rocket into the launcher. He locked the helmet back onto his suit, then slung both the goober rifle and rocket launcher firmly over each shoulder.

"THE WARRR! THE WARRR!"

He grabbed the energy spear, and with the last of the Intelligence's memories, fired it at one of the translucent hatches. The energy ball vaporized the grey translucent film.

Then the vortex of space sucked him out of the ship.

Karnage spun through the black. He let go of the spear, and pulled the goober rifle from his shoulder. He pointed the rifle in the opposite direction of his spin, and fired several rounds. He slowed down to a gentle twirl. He dropped the goober rifle, and pulled the rocket launcher off his other shoulder. He brought the sight up to his visor.

He waited until his slow spin put the flashing red cross-hair over the glowing orb of the sun, then fired.

He flew backward as the rocket shot forward, carrying the frenetically glowing Nucleus towards the sun. Some vestige of the Intelligence's psyche reminded him about gravity wells and fusion and only being able to convert energy rather than destroying it. But at this point, so much of the Intelligence was gone from his psyche that it all just sounded like bullshit to him.

Karnage aimed a middle finger in the direction of the disappearing rocket.

"Burn in hell, monkeyfucker," he said.

CHAPTER TEN

Karnage drifted through the pitch black of space. Tiny stars glittered in the distance.

He closed his eyes.

Whatever happened from here on in, he couldn't give a shit. To hell with the Sanity Patch. To hell with the Dabney Corporation, the Nagasaki Treaties, and the whole goddamn planet.

He'd saved his friends.

Victory was finally his.

There was nothing left to do but drift through space until he was dead.

And that was all right by Major Karnage.

EPILOGUE

A voice crackled across the intercom. "Major? Are you awake?"

Karnage opened his eyes. The infinite black stared down at him, blinking with a thousand pin-sized eyes of light. One of the lights grew bigger. It winked at him. "Cookie? Is that you?"

"It is, Major."

The light in the distance grew bigger. "Am I dead?"

"Not as far as I can tell," Cookie said.

"Where are you?"

"Same place I was before. Except now I'm in space, coming for you."

The glittering light grew brighter, and slowly resolved into multiple smaller lights. Karnage could make out the faint outline of a massive saucer-shaped ship. He watched it grow larger as it approached.

"I thought I was gonna die out here," Karnage said. "I figured it was inevitable."

"Nothing's really inevitable."

"I guess." The lights grew closer. Karnage took a deep breath, then let it out. "Cookie?"

"Yes, Major?"

"I think we won."

"I think you're right," Cookie said.

The ship's dark outline grew larger, overtaking Karnage's vision. The only stars he could see now were the artificial ones flickering and pulsing across the ship. They were all white.

"What the hell am I gonna do with myself now?" Karnage said.

The lights coalesced together into a single spot of light. It flooded Karnage's vision, bathing him in soft white.

"You'll think of something," Cookie said. "You always do."

ACKNOWLEDGEMENTS

Special thanks to Sandra and Brett. I would never have found the courage to commit this story to paper without them.

Thanks also to Maxwell Atoms for Spragmos Industries, hoverballs, shark fin hair, and teaching me everything I could ever want to know about trepanation.

ABOUT THE AUTHOR

GORD ZAJAC

Most of Gord's previous writing experience has been in television, but please don't hold that against him. He has written for *The Grim Adventures of Billy and Mandy* and *Evil Con Carne*. He is the prolific author of one short story, one half of a novella, and this book. He lives in Halton Hills with his wife, Alicia Land.

www.gordzajac.com